COUNTERSTRIKE

Sean Flannery

WILLIAM MORROW AND COMPANY, INC.
NEW YORK

Fiction
Fla

Library of Congress Cataloging-in-Publication Data

Flannery, Sean.
   Counterstrike / Sean Flannery.
     p.   cm.
   ISBN 0-688-08777-9
   1. Gorbachev, Mikhail Sergeevich, 1931–   —Fiction. I. Title.
  PS3556.L37C65 1990
  813′.54—dc20

90-5589
CIP

Printed in the United States of America

First Edition

1 2 3 4 5 6 7 8 9 10

This novel is for Laurie

WASHINGTON POST SERVICE
THE INTERNATIONAL HERALD TRIBUNE
FRIDAY, MARCH 31, 1989
front page

Kremlin Ends Conscription of Students
Troop cutbacks are cited after election losses by senior military officers

By Michael Dobbs
Washington Post Service

MOSCOW—The Soviet armed forces announced Thursday the abolition of the student draft.

Soviet officials said that the decision to exempt students from military conscription had been made possible by a cutback of 500,000 men in the size of the armed forces. It appeared to mark the first tentative step toward reshaping the Soviet Union's huge conscript army into a volunteer, professional force.

The announcement suggested that the Soviet leader Mikhail S. Gorbachev is succeeding in his drive to extend perestroika, or restructuring, to the military. Until just a few months ago senior military figures strongly opposed the abolition of the student draft on the ground that it could undermine Soviet defense capability.

The declining political influence of the Soviet armed forces was underscored by the poor showing of the top military in the elections Sunday for a revamped Soviet legislature.

Detailed results show that at least four generals and two admirals were defeated in the first multicandidate elections for a Soviet parliament in seven decades. . . .

PROLOGUE

He moved through the night silently like a cat, wary yet with self-assurance. In the distance to the northeast the horizon glowed from the city lights of Moscow, but here was mostly darkness beneath a heavily overcast sky. He was KGB from the Armed Forces Directorate, though these past months he had masqueraded as a guard here at the Orlovo Missile Defense Base. He had left his post and had made his way across the base, carefully giving a wide berth to the dozens of guard posts and checkpoints that honeycombed the high-security launch fields. So far he had been lucky; he had run into no one and so had not had to kill. But he was prepared to do so if need be. It was for the *Rodina*, Mother Russia, and Lieutenant Vitali Ivanovich Kobysh was willing and capable of doing whatever needed to be done this night to protect her.

Administration was housed in a two-story poured-concrete building a couple of kilometers from the main gate at the edge of a broad birch woods. To the west, away from the Moscow–Smolensk Highway, was the main silo field in which were housed the Galosh antiballistic missiles, which protected Moscow from incoming missiles as they crossed the Soviet border a thousand or more kilometers away, and the Gazelle system, which was designed to shoot down enemy missiles that had managed to penetrate Moscow's outer defense ring. Here and there a single light shielded from view by surveillance satellites or high-flying spy planes pierced the darkness. For the most part there was little indication from the outside that this was a major segment of the Moscow Defense District.

The duty officer's Zil-6 jeep was parked at the rear of the sprawling building, and Kobysh checked to make certain a lock had not been placed on the ignition. He didn't know how much time he was going to have to get out of here. But he wanted to cover his back. This was not going to be a suicide mission.

He walked around to the front of the building, where he hesitated in the shadows for just a moment. A half dozen Chaika limousines had been pulled up beneath the broad overhang, their drivers gathered in the glass-fronted guard post, talking and drinking what appeared to be tea but was probably vodka. Crossing the broad driveway, Kobysh angled directly to the main entrance. No one noticed him until he was just inside the glass doors. The security guard looked up.

"What are you doing here?"

"Major Yelistrov sent me. Comms are out with silo six."

The guard's hand strayed to the telephone. "I'll just call him then."

Kobysh shrugged. "Suit yourself. But he's pissed off, and he wants me back as soon as I get this mess straightened out." He nodded toward the dark corridor. "With all the brass here he doesn't want any fuck-ups tonight."

The guard nodded after a moment. "Go ahead then, but be quick about it. If they catch you wandering around away from your post, they're going to ask some tough questions."

"Nothing compared with the questions they'll be asking if we don't get that communications link fixed."

Kobysh turned and hurried down the corridor to the communications center in the first basement, eighty meters above the main command post hollowed out of the bedrock.

At the steel security door he hesitated before he rang the buzzer, long enough to pull out his 6.35 millimeter Tula-Korovin automatic pistol and screw the silencer on its barrel. He hid the gun behind his right leg.

Lieutenant Aleksandr Lavrishchev appeared at the tiny observation port. "What do you want, Vitali?"

"One of our comms links is down. Yelistrov sent me in to check it out."

"That *pizda* [cunt]," the comms duty officer swore crudely. "Tonight of all nights he wants to make waves. Just a second."

Kobysh stepped back, his thumb finding and switching the safety catch on his pistol to the off position. The heavy steel door swung open, and he stepped inside, the odors of unwashed bodies mingling with electronic smells immediately assailing his nostrils. Besides Lavrishchev, there were three communications officers on duty, each of them manning a console. None of them except the duty officer was armed. There was no need for it, although there were weapons in the center.

Lavrishchev had turned to close the door when Kobysh shot him in the back of the head just above the left ear.

"Fuck your mother," one of the operators swore in shock.

Kobysh turned on his heel and shot the man in the side of the head, driving him against his console. The two other men had no real idea what was happening. They were technicians, not soldiers, and were not combat-trained. They simply could not believe what they were seeing with their own eyes, nor were they able to react except in the most sluggish of fashions.

Kobysh shot both of them, putting two rounds into the first man's back and a single round into the neck of the last man, destroying his windpipe and carotid artery. He fell sideways off his chair, his fingers tearing at his throat as he thrashed around. Kobysh walked across to him and put a round into the back of his head at point-blank range. The man was suddenly still, blood everywhere.

After easing the hammer down, he ejected the nearly spent clip and slammed another into the butt of the pistol, then went to the first console, where he lifted the body away from the panel, careful to get no blood on his uniform.

Shoving the chair aside, Kobysh hurriedly flipped a series of switches, connecting his position with the building's internal monitoring equipment. Technically this was a KGB position. Officers from the Armed Forces Directorate were placed at every echelon of the Soviet military down to company level. They wore normal military uniforms, but they reported through their own chain of command directly to the Lubyanka Center in Moscow. The system had broken down, and the reports the center had been getting were either watered down to uselessness or missing altogether. The GRU (military intelligence service) had the upper hand here. Or had had until now.

Something is going on out there, Lieutenant, that is making us nervous. You will be our eyes and ears. Do not fail us.

Patiently Kobysh switched the master monitor control from room to room, most of which were quiet at this hour of the night. There was no place on base secure from monitoring through this center, one of the reasons the GRU had kicked out the KGB officer.

He got the first indications of the meeting he was searching for from the fiber optics microphones in the base commander's outer office. It sounded as if someone's voice were raised in argument, but at a distance.

Donning a pair of headphones, Kobysh turned up the volume. Still the voices were muffled, indistinct.

He switched the monitor control to the CO's office itself, but the voices disappeared. Quickly he switched back to the anteroom, where he heard them again, and then switched to the conference room next door. Instantly the reception became crystal clear. He had them!

He reached over and switched on the tape recorder and then, turning to face the door, leaned back against the console to listen with growing disbelief to what was unfolding upstairs.

"You are absolutely sure he is capable of it?"

"So far as we can determine. But men of his ilk . . . assassins . . . do not advertise their credentials."

"I understand that."

"Then understand this. If we are in agreement here, a messenger will be sent to him."

"I thought he had already been contacted, Riza Petrovich."

Kobysh's eyes narrowed. He had not recognized the first voice, but the other one was General Riza Petrovich Truchin, the chief of staff of the Nuclear Forces. Old school. One of the originals. One of Stalin's fair-haired boys.

"Yes, but only in the most vague terms, General. . . ."

"How vague?"

"Let him finish, Viktor."

"Thank you. The operational code, as we agreed, is counterstrike. He understands the significance and the difficulties."

"Which is why I am suggesting Geneva. We don't want him here."

"But he is demanding further information."

"Naturally . . ."

"Our names, Comrade General."

Kobysh glanced at the tape recorder to make certain it was functioning properly. He had one name; he needed the others. And he needed the name of the assassin and his intended victim. It was nearly impossible to believe. But at the mention of Geneva he knew who they were talking about.

He began to sweat. He would not be able to stay here much longer. He would be discovered sooner or later. Yet he could not leave now that he had learned this much.

GRU Major Ivan Borisov slammed the telephone down after the tenth ring. Fuck your mother, but he had just stepped across the corridor to take a pee and had not seen the red light on his board until he came back. Someone in the comms center downstairs was monitoring the conference room, contrary to strict orders, and now there was no answer on the phone.

He turned and rushed back out into the corridor. The two enlisted men on duty at the elevator jumped up when they heard him racing down the hall.

"Get down to the comms center and secure the door," he shouted.

"Sir?" one of the guards asked, confused.

"Now! If anyone comes out, arrest them. If they resist, shoot them."

The guards were scrambling aboard the elevator when Borisov burst into the base commander's outer office adjacent to the conference room. Sergeant Sergei Anastratov, the CO's bodyguard, stood facing the door, his Graz Buyra automatic pistol cocked.

"We have to stop the meeting, Sergei," Borisov blurted. "Now."

Anastratov didn't move.

"We've got to get them out of there."

"*Yeb vas* [Fuck you]." Anastratov swore, holding the big pistol on Borisov.

"He's in danger, you stupid bastard! The commander is in danger."

For a long beat Anastratov stood rooted to his spot. But then he straightened up, spun lightly on his heel, and pulled open the door to the conference room.

"What is it, Sergei?" Captain General Anatoli Zuyev said from within.

Borisov was right behind the big bodyguard, and before the man could speak, he shoved him aside. All seven of the officers around the table reared back in alarm.

Desperately he put his hands over his ears, then over his mouth and finally pointed up toward the ceiling.

Anastratov turned back. He grabbed a handful of the major's tunic and jammed the barrel of the automatic against his temple.

"No, Sergei," General Zuyev barked sharply.

There was something wrong. It was the telephone call he had not answered. They knew upstairs.

Kobysh ripped the earphones off his head and tossed them down, then hit the rewind switch on the tape recorder.

There wasn't much tape, and it was rewound in a couple of seconds. Kobysh popped the cassette out of its slot, pocketed it, and, picking up his gear, rushed across to the door. He looked out the peephole, but the corridor was deserted. There was still a chance that he could get out of here. He had not gathered enough evidence, but what he had would be convincing if he could get it to the center.

He hauled open the heavy steel door, stepped out into the corridor, and headed to the stairs in a dead run.

If he could reach the Zil-6 parked in back before the alarm spread, he would have a chance to get clear of the base. It would take the GRU a little while to blow the comms center door and find out that no one was left alive inside.

His luck held. The elevator indicator dinged, and the doors started to open just as he got to the stairway. He sprinted silently out of sight.

He held up for just a second at the top. He could hear nothing from below, and just edging around the corner of the stairwell, he could see the front door guard behind his counter, his back turned this way.

Kobysh stepped into the corridor and, moving swiftly on the balls of his feet, made it to the rear door, which he eased open. He stepped outside.

The Zil-6 was still in its parking spot. In a few quick strides Kobysh reached it and climbed in behind the wheel. The engine started easily. He backed out of the parking place, switched on the headlights, and headed at a normal rate of speed toward the main gates.

The communications radio was tuned to the tactical frequency which was used for normal base security operations. At the moment there was nothing but routine traffic between the various guard posts. He switched the receiver to the scan mode, which would pick up every broadcast from any of a dozen base frequencies. The moment the alarm was sounded he would know about it.

The road plunged darkly into the birch woods and dipped toward the river. On this side was the gate, and a few kilometers on the other side was the highway that eventually turned into Leninski Prospekt within the Moscow city limits inside the outer ring road.

Kobysh picked up his gun from beside him on the seat, switched the safety to the off position, cocked the hammer, and laid it on his lap. He felt in his pocket for the tape. It was still there. This had to get back to the center at all costs. General Truchin was at the meeting, and he was one of the most important men in the Soviet Union. Who else had been there? What other old-guard generals had gathered here to plot? It made his blood run cold.

We are a nation of laws, Vasili Ivanovich. In everything you do for the state, remember that, and remember that as much as you do for the state, he will do even more for you.

The words were practically written in stone at the KGB's School One outside of Moscow. After all, Kobysh thought, we were not like those CIA cowboys. At least not now we weren't.

He came around a long sweeping curve, and the main gate hidden beneath camouflage netting stood in the middle of the road, striped barriers down on both sides, a dim light shining from inside the guardhouse. Kobysh slowed down and came to a halt as one of the guards, his AK-47 unslung, came out. Still there was nothing on the radio.

The man came to attention and saluted when he saw Kobysh's rank.

"Open the gate," Kobysh said.

"Sorry, sir, but the gates stay closed until further notice."

There was no use asking on whose orders. Kobysh looked beyond the guard. There was another one at the window in the gatehouse. He was watching them, but he wasn't holding a weapon. Kobysh picked up his pistol and fired one shot, hitting the gate guard in the forehead, driving him backward off his feet.

Slamming the Zil-6 in gear, Kobysh floored the accelerator pedal, crashed through the striped barrier, and accelerated clumsily down the road.

He had gone barely twenty meters when the second gate guard opened fire, and Kobysh ducked down in his seat, the incoming rounds blowing out his windshield before he was finally around another curve and was grinding across the river bridge out of range.

The alarm would be sounded now, but he had overcome the first two hurdles. All he had to do was stay alive long enough to reach the Lubyanka. Once there he would be safe. The GRU would not be able to touch him.

"Blow it," Major Borisov ordered, ducking back into the protection of the stairwell. The young sergeant nodded and twisted the handle on the detonator. The plastique explosive charge that had been placed on the hinges of the comms center door blew with a heavy roar, almost as if an earthquake had hit the building. A second later thick dust billowed up from the lower corridor.

Borisov's GRU troops stormed down the stairwell, leapfrogging two by two, and ducked inside the comms center, their weapons sweeping left to right.

"Clear," the team leader shouted, coming back to the doorway moments later.

Borisov stepped over the debris, into the center. His left eyebrow rose slightly when he spotted the four downed men. No shots had been fired by his people; the intruder had done this. Borisov's jaw tightened.

"We must have just missed him, Major," his sergeant was

saying when Anastratov came racing down the corridor from the stairs.

Borisov spun on his heel.

"He has just broken out from the main gate," the big sergeant shouted. "He's driving a Zil-six."

"Call for a chopper," Borisov ordered, joining him at the door.

"I've got one on the way."

The two of them rushed back upstairs and down the corridor to the front entrance.

"Who is it? Did they get a look at him?"

"No name," Anastratov shouted over his shoulder as he ran. "Just that he was a lieutenant. One of ours."

"I think I know who it is," Borisov said as they reached the door. The helicopter, a Hind 28, was incoming from the helipad to the west, its landing lights bright in the pitch-black sky.

"Who?" Anastratov demanded. "General Zuyev wants him. He must not escape, Major. He cannot."

"He won't," Borisov said. "Because I know where he's going and we can beat him to it."

"Are you certain, Major?" The sergeant had to shout now over the noise of the chopper just overhead.

"Yes," Borisov said quietly. "Oh, yes."

It had been hours since the first helicopter had headed to the northeast, toward the city. From where he sat in the protection of a copse of trees on a slight hill, Kobysh could see across the plain to the spires and skyscrapers of downtown Moscow still at least twenty kilometers away. He thought the eastern horizon might just be beginning to lighten, but the more he stared at it, the less certain he became.

The radio had been alive with traffic for a long time, but it had settled down finally as the search moved toward the southwest. Apparently no one believed he would be heading into Moscow. Everyone thought he had run for the open country or perhaps for the Finnish border.

He had a fleeting thought which made him smile for just the moment. They believed their intruder had been CIA. All they needed now was for Spy Smasher to show up. He would know what to do.

But there was no Spy Smasher, hero of the Soviet peoples. This was real life. And real people, and not necessarily the guilty ones, got killed.

It was the first helicopter that worried him the most. He had watched it rise from the base and speed directly for the city. It had not been making a sweep. Whoever had been aboard had not been looking for the Zil-6. Whatever their mission was in the city it had not brought them back. He had carefully watched the sky as he drove. No, that chopper had not returned.

He looked at his watch. It was coming up on 0500. Soon it would be light. Soon the morning traffic in the city would be starting up. He could see the highway a few kilometers below him to the north. Nothing had come along for the past two hours, but now a big canvas-covered truck came lumbering in from the southwest. Produce from the *Kolkhoz* (collective farms) for the ravenous maw of the city. It was not an army truck.

There were a pair of binoculars in the Zil. He raised them to his eyes and carefully scanned the countryside and the sky toward the southwest. There was no other traffic, although he thought he might be seeing a pair of helicopters low to the horizon a long ways off; but then he wasn't sure, and he couldn't pick them out again.

Back at the Zil he tossed the glasses down and turned up the volume on the communications radio. Again there was little more than routine traffic, although there was an occasional reference to the search now well off to the west.

It wasn't right. Something was wrong. It had been too easy for him to escape. By now he would have thought the fields and skies around the base would be filled with searchers. They had guessed that he'd monitored the meeting between General Truchin and the others; they should have pulled out all the stops to find him.

But they had not. Why?

After climbing behind the wheel, Kobysh started the engine and, once again checking to make certain that nothing moved on the highway below or in the sky, pulled out of the woods and drove carefully down the narrow dirt track.

Once he was actually within the city they would not try anything. They wouldn't dare. Not in broad daylight in front of civilian witnesses. Yet there was something nagging at the back of his head, something he knew he was forgetting, something he should be considering. But the thought eluded him.

The Zil bumped up over a ditch onto the main highway, and he accelerated roughly through the gears, the big knobby tires beginning to whine as his speed mounted.

He had been recruited in his senior year at Moscow State University, where he had been studying electronic engineering. At first he'd thought he was being asked to work for the Technical Services Directorate, which in many ways was much like the Americans' National Security Agency. It was the section of the KGB that came up with the cryptographic equipment, the hidden transmitters, the electronic surveillance systems, the spy satellites. But his trainers had other ideas.

"You are every Russian boy, Vasili Ivanovich," his adviser, Captain Alekseyev, had counseled him. "We would like you to look for traitors for us. Within the Soviet Union."

If he kept up with his studies they'd promised that he might be used from time to time as a consulting engineer on projects. It hadn't happened yet, though he was still hopeful.

"Just be yourself. It is all we ask from you. That and, unswerving love for the *Rodina*."

It had been eight years since he'd graduated from School One and had been assigned to the Armed Forces Directorate. In the meantime, he had become something of an expert at killing people. At killing Russians.

He had to squint against the blast of wind through the blown-out windshield. It was very cold despite the fact it was nearly early summer.

His mother never talked about his work, and his father was frightened of him. He had seen it in the old man's eyes on the morning he'd found him with his KGB identification booklet. Before that they had thought he was training to work at the Baikonur Cosmodrome in Kazakhstan. It was a disappointment to him as well as to them.

He crossed beneath the outer ring highway, traffic definitely beginning to pick up. Trucks were parked along the road, the drivers leaning against the tailgates, ten-liter gas cans beside them. It was private enterprise. Moscow had plenty of cars, but not enough gas stations.

He passed the Academy of Sciences Hotel, Gork'iy Park across a sward along the river, then turned north at Oktyabr'skaya Square, following Dimitrova Street to the river, where he crossed on the busy Kamenny Bridge.

Streetlights were out now, and only the occasional car or truck ran with its headlights on.

Following the river along the south ramparts of the Kremlin, he turned up the hill at the massive Rossiya Hotel and, passing the towering domes of St. Basil's Cathedral, crossed Red Square in front of GUM, the big department store.

As he drove, he watched his rearview mirror for any sign that he was being followed. But no one was back there. Nor was there any sign of pursuing helicopters, and two blocks from KGB Headquarters at the Lubyanka he breathed his first sigh of relief.

It was still too early for the day shift to show up at the center, but there would be a lot of officers having breakfast across the street. There would be plenty of witnesses.

He pulled over to the curb at the edge of Dzerzhinsky Square and studied the approach to the complex of buildings. Traffic, both pedestrian and vehicular, was normal. Nothing seemed wrong or out of place. Yet something continued to nag at the back of his head, something he was forgetting.

Shutting off the Zil's engine, he pocketed his gun and got out. No one was paying him the slightest attention.

He started forward, his hand on the butt of the pistol. No one was going to stop him now that he had come this close. No one.

For a few moments he debated going into one of the restaurants across the street and waiting with his fellow officers until it was time to go to work. But he decided against it. Once inside the walls of the Lubyanka he would be safe. He kept that one thought sharp in his mind.

Across from one of the pedestrian entrances he checked traffic both ways and then started across the street. From here he could actually see the windows of his office on the second floor, and his step lightened.

He had to hold up to let a big canvas-covered army truck pass. He was exposed here in the broad square, but he was nearly home free. What he was bringing them would cause heads to roll. Even though he'd heard the conference with his own ears he could hardly believe it. But he had the proof.

At the last second the truck swerved sharply at him. He started to fall back, finally remembering what had been nagging at the back of his head all the way into the city.

The cassette tape recording of the general's meeting. His proof. He should not have carried it with him. He should have left it someplace secure so that if he were captured or killed, at least the tape would survive.

Now it was too late.

He made no sound as the truck struck him full on, nor was there any particular pain. Only a tremendous shove and he was off his feet, hurtling through the air.

His right shoulder struck the pavement, and then his head smashed into the concrete and he skidded on his knees and elbows toward the curb, finally coming to rest in a heap on his face over a storm sewer grate.

Someone was shouting something from across the street, and he thought he might be able to hear the truck lumbering past him.

The tape. The single thought crystallized in his head. His right arm was broken in a dozen places, but his left seemed to be usable. He managed to reach into his coat pocket and pull out the cassette tape.

People were running toward him—he could hear their footfalls on the pavement—and a darkness began to come up over his eyes, almost as if it were a dense black smoke rising from the storm sewer.

He brought the tape up to his face, looked at it, and then let it drop through the grate.

He saw it falling for just a split second, but he was dead before it hit the bottom.

PART ONE

No one in the crowd noticed the plainly dressed man who had worked his way to the front and was watching the militiamen who were standing guard over the body. A young KGB captain in uniform seemed to be in charge, though nothing was being done at the moment. They all seemed to be waiting for someone; the captain kept looking across the street at the mute facade of the Lubyanka.

The man gently pushed past a pair of old babushkas, stepped down off the curb, and walked over to where an orange ribbon was stretched between two street barriers. He was trying to step over it when one of the militiamen turned around.

"See here, get back now."

The man stopped, a slightly apologetic grin on his pleasant

face. He looked as if he didn't want to cause any trouble but merely wanted to get where he was going.

He was of medium height for a Russian, well under six feet, and he had the typical thickness of torso and slightly square jaw with thick black hair. But his eyes were different. They held an expression of worldly intelligence and a patience with his knowledge of people's failings. Physically he seemed to be in his late thirties or perhaps early forties, but his attitude suggested a much greater age.

He pulled out his Militia identification booklet, opened it, and attached it to the lapel pocket of his brown and green tweed jacket. The booklet identified him as Militia Chief Investigator Nikolai Fedorovich Ganin. The Militia was the Soviets' civilian police, equivalent to a combination of the American county sheriffs and local police forces.

"I was on my way to work," he said.

The younger militiaman stiffened to attention, and he saluted. "I'm sorry, Comrade Chief Investigator, I did not recognize you."

"What have you got here this morning, an accident?"

"He was hit by a truck."

"But the KGB is interested, I see."

"Yes, sir."

"Odd. What are your orders?"

"I didn't get a chance to call headquarters when ... they showed up. We were told to secure the scene and to stand by."

"Those are good orders," the chief investigator said.

The KGB captain had spotted Ganin and came over. "This is a secure area. Be on your way now."

Ganin touched his identification booklet. "I was just passing. Anything I can do to help the State Committee for Security?"

"No. Everything here is under control. If I might just have use of your people for a few minutes longer. My colonel should be here momentarily."

Ganin looked beyond the captain at the body lying facedown on the storm sewer grate. "Was he a spy or just a plain army lieutenant?"

"I don't know."

"I see. Then the KGB is helping us with routine traffic accidents? Has anyone gotten the registration number of the truck or sent out a bulletin to look for it?"

"That's not my responsibility," the captain said.

"Then I'll take it," Ganin replied, his grin broadening. He turned back to the militiaman. "I want you to telephone headquarters; have them send out a forensics van and a pathologist."

"Yes, sir," the militiaman snapped.

"Then I want the crowd questioned. Someone must have seen something."

"Sir."

"You are working for me now. No one else. Do you understand?"

"Yes, sir."

Ganin turned and without a word to the captain went over to the body. He bent down and touched his fingertips to the neck just beneath the left ear, but there was no pulse. The young man was definitely dead. With care he reached inside the uniform tunic and pulled out the young man's wallet.

"Step away from there," the KGB captain said from behind him.

Ganin looked over his shoulder. The captain was holding a pistol on him. It was extraordinary. Here in broad daylight in front of a crowd of people.

"Do you mean to shoot me?"

"Get away from the body."

Ganin turned back to look at the young lieutenant. He had died in great pain; his face was twisted in a grimace. Always at the point of death victims were struck with the sense that their time was being cut short, that there was so much left undone. With one so young it must have been worse. Before Ganin got up, he noticed that the left tunic pocket was unbuttoned, the flap up, as if the kid had taken something out of his pocket just before he died. Or as if someone had taken something out of that pocket.

Ganin stood up and faced the captain, who held out his left hand.

"The wallet."

"I don't think so. And if I might make a suggestion, lower your pistol before someone gets hurt."

It was Ganin's manner and the way he made the suggestion that caused the captain to look to his left and then behind him. All four of the militiamen had drawn their service pistols, cocked the hammers, and dropped into the shooter's crouch, their weapons trained on the KGB officer, who blanched.

"Put your gun away, Captain," someone said from across the street.

The captain turned that way. "But I—"

"Now, Captain. That is an order." A very tall, very husky man with thick Georgian eyebrows, dressed in a KGB colonel's uniform, strode imperiously across the street. His tunic was unbuttoned, and his shirt collar was undone. It looked as if he had just gotten up from the breakfast table.

The captain stepped back, lowered his pistol, and then holstered it. Ganin nodded toward his militiamen, who stood down.

"Good morning, Comrade Colonel," he said genially.

The colonel glanced down at the body. "What has happened here?"

"It appears to have been an accident. Apparently this young lieutenant was struck down by a truck. Is he one of your men, Colonel?"

The officer looked sharply at Ganin. "Of course not. Are you trying to make a joke here? That's an army uniform."

Ganin opened the dead man's wallet and studied the army identification card. "Kobysh," he said, looking up. "An unusual name, wouldn't you say?"

"It sounds Jewish to me," the colonel said with a sneer. "Do you suppose the Army is making lieutenants out of Jews these days?"

"Maybe not such an odd name."

The colonel looked sharply at him again. "Who did you say you are?"

"Nikolai Ganin, Comrade Colonel."

"Well, Chief Investigator Ganin, I suggest you get on with it," the colonel said. He turned and started away, motioning for the captain to follow.

Ganin called after them. "Of course, if we find any evidence that a crime against the state has been committed, we will call the KGB."

"Do that," the colonel said over his shoulder without looking back.

Ganin watched them until they had disappeared inside the Lubyanka, and then he glanced again at the ID card and finally back at his militiamen.

"Well, we have work to do," he told them. "Don't you think we should get started?"

* * *

A plainclothes militia investigator named Yurii Sepelev showed up just ahead of the forensics van and pathologist. He was a short, swarthy man who chain-smoked cheap Prima cigarettes. The forefinger and middle finger of his right hand were permanently stained by nicotine.

"Since when do we go after hit-and-runs?" he asked, climbing out of his Moskvich just beyond the orange barrier. "Especially army officers?"

"It's on the radio already?" Ganin asked.

"Naturally. Yernin has called twice. Do you suppose he wants to give you a promotion?"

Ganin had to laugh. "Why not? We've been making him look good recently. Now it's his turn to scratch our backs."

Sepelev glanced across the street toward the Lubyanka and lowered his voice. "The KGB has called asking about you, too."

Ganin looked at his old friend. "Oh? What'd they want, Yurochka?"

"I don't know. Probably wanted to find out if you paid your taxes this month." Sepelev shook his head. "Fuck your mother, Nikki, what are we doing here?"

They had walked across to where Kobysh's body still lay in a heap.

"Was he one of theirs?" Sepelev asked. "Poor bastard. Was he trying to make it back when someone killed him? Or was it just an accident?"

"I don't know, but they seemed interested. One of them even pulled a gun on me to get this." Ganin handed him Kobysh's wallet.

Sepelev looked through it. "Army. Could have been Directorate Three, a little *puffta* spying on the service."

Ganin nodded. He had had the same thought. "He brought something with him . . . or at least I think he did. And whoever killed him may have gotten it."

"Then why'd those bastards deny him?" Sepelev asked, nodding toward the impassive Lubyanka.

"I don't know that either . . . yet. But it makes for some interesting speculation."

Sepelev looked up. "We don't have to take this."

Ganin smiled. "What, and miss one of life's little pleasures?"

* * *

It was nearly four o'clock before Ganin drove to the Moscow town prosecutor's office south of the river on Novokuznetskaya Street. He came to attention in front of the desk and saluted.

General Arkadi Yernin was a pinch-faced, narrow little man of sixty-two who wore sharply tailored uniforms and had spent two years studying postgraduate law at Harvard University in the United States.

In Moscow a chief militia investigator actually worked for two bosses. The first, through normal military ranks, was the commissioner of the militia, General Filip Kislitsin. The second, much more important chain of command was through the Moscow town prosecutor's office, headed by Yernin.

Ganin had heard that it was much the same in the United States with a federal cop having to answer not only to his own section head all the way up the line to the director of the FBI but to the Justice Department as well, starting with the district attorneys and working all the way up to the attorney general himself.

He supposed he was one of the very few Russians who had no desire whatsoever to go to America. He had enough problems here.

"What progress with the case, Nikki?" Yernin asked, his voice oddly high-pitched for a man.

"Which case is that? Just now my men are very busy. It's the coming summer." It was true that incidents of violent crime rose dramatically during the months of June, July, and August. During the rest of the year the average Russian was too busy keeping warm to make war on his fellow citizens.

"The hit-and-run on Dzerzhinsky. Your investigation seems to have created some interest. Can you tell me why that is?"

"The KGB seemed concerned. I wondered why, but so far they've told me nothing."

Yernin's forehead wrinkled. "They are interested because it occurred in front of their headquarters building. It is embarrassing to them, having something like that happen under their noses. But it is just a simple hit-and-run, isn't it?"

"I don't believe so. There may be other indications. For instance, Lieutenant Kobysh was armed with a pistol which he had fired within six hours of his death."

"A firing range exercise?"

"Midnight or later? I don't think so."

"Possible?"

Ganin inclined his head, conceding that it was possible. "We found his jeep at the end of the square; his fingerprints are all over it. It comes from the Orlovo Missile Defense Base, but they tell us that it was stolen two days ago."

"All that in a morning and an afternoon," Yernin said. "I commend your department."

Ganin hesitated for just a moment. "Pardon me, but I think Lieutenant Kobysh was working for the Armed Forces Directorate, and I think he was killed trying to reach headquarters."

"An accident?"

"He was murdered, Chief Prosecutor. And I would like to know by whom and why his own people have denied him."

"Curious questions," Yernin said softly.

"Yes, sir. There is no telling where they might lead."

"Keep me advised."

2

A cold, driving rain hammered against windows, bounced off car roofs, and blew in great sheets before the strong winds that funneled down Madison Avenue. Sometimes late spring in New York was worse than the dead of winter. A deep overcast would often cover the sky in a leaden gray, day after day. And when the rains came, and they came often, it was cold and miserable.

Yet it was the most exciting city on earth. Everything happened here. Or if it didn't happen here, there were New Yorkers who would be able to provide the blow-by-blow description, the analysis of what should have been or of what could have been, and finally a postpartum lecture on why such a thing would have worked better here in the first place. The very best and the very worst lived and worked in New York.

World News This Week magazine occupied three floors of a forty-story building on Madison Avenue between thirty-ninth and fortieth streets. With bureaus in Washington and Los Angeles as well as twenty-seven foreign capitals it was the third-largest weekly behind *Time* and *Newsweek* and was growing fast. Last year two of its writers won a Pulitzer Prize, and there was an air of expectation around the editorial boardroom as everyone waited for the next big story to break. "Make it happen" was its motto for the nineties.

Mary Frances Dean, the "World Seen and Heard" section editor, didn't notice that it had begun raining in earnest as she stood hunched over a table next to a window in the magazine's research library. She was a good-looking woman in her middle thirties, with medium-length dark hair, a thin, angular face, what she called her ski-jump nose, and wide, startlingly green eyes. She was slightly built, almost bony in some respects, yet she had an air not of fragility but perhaps of wiry strength. At that moment she was comparing four differing points of view of a series of events leading up to what was being called the Geneva Accord: one by *The New York Times*, one by the *Times* of London, a third by the leading French newspaper *Le Figaro*, and the last by an English version of the Soviet party newspaper *Pravda*.

Her job was to prepare background reports to be used by the reporters in the field and for sidebars and other fillers when stories broke.

The Soviet Union and the United States had agreed to remove all troops and nuclear missiles from Europe by 1995. The Warsaw Pact was on the verge of being completely dismantled, and NATO seemed to be in a shambles at the highest command levels. Yet no one concerned with the continued security of Europe was particularly happy about the treaty, even on the heels of the democratization of most of the Eastern bloc.

It was believed in some circles, and rightly so in Mary Frances's estimation, that the two superpowers were deciding between themselves on an agreement to control a revanchist Germany. If and when hostilities were to begin again, they would be confined to German soil, a containment that would not be possible with nuclear weapons on the scene.

It was Mikhail Gorbachev's plan, one that the American President had wholeheartedly endorsed. Over the past months of the summit conferences in Geneva, the details had been worked out. Next week the treaty would be signed.

Two things had become clear in Mary Frances's reading. The first was that Gorbachev's *perestroika* and *glasnost,* while making a big impression in Europe, were failing miserably at home because of severe economic problems. He needed the treaty to bolster his position. And the second was that not a single military commander on either side of what had once been the iron curtain, had anything positive to say about the treaty. Such dissension really didn't matter in this country. But in the Soviet Union Gorbachev had been working to defuse the military's power over the government ever since the elections of 1989.

She decided that a comparison of the two systems of government and military, now versus the early eighties, before Gorbachev took over, not only would make interesting reading but would put at least one aspect of the Geneva Accord in perspective.

"A picture of the dedicated employee," someone said behind her, bringing her up out of her thoughts.

She turned as Bob Liskey, the foreign reports editor, came down one of the aisles through the stacks. He was a gray-haired, pince-nezed man in his mid-fifties. A product of the University of Missouri's School of Journalism, he had cut his teeth on daily newspapers, then the wire services and finally the newsmagazines. He and Mary Frances got along very well. But then, as he explained it, he was an Anglophile, and Mary Frances had been born in England and still had the accent to prove it.

"You've seen it with your own eyes," she said, smiling. "Now I demand a raise."

"You might just get your chance. Weaver wants to see you."

"When?"

"Now. He sent me to look for you. I'll ride up with you."

"What does he want?" she asked, falling in with him as they made their way back to the front desk. Lawrence Weaver was the managing editor and as distant as they came.

"I'll let him tell you."

"Robert," she said threateningly.

Liskey had to laugh. "You're getting your break. He's sending you to Geneva to do backgrounds and color."

She grabbed his arm and pulled him around so that they were facing each other. She wanted to look into his eyes to make sure he wasn't kidding. They joked a lot back and forth. She felt almost daughterly with him, though she'd never told him that. It would have hurt him. At thirty-six she was young enough, but she didn't think he wanted to be reminded that he was that old.

"No shit?"

"Crude, but correct. He's seen some of your work, and he says he likes it. Thinks you've got insight, whatever the hell that is, despite the fact you're only a female."

"Pig," she said, not unkindly, though there was a measure of resentment. In New York as everywhere, there were women in newsrooms and broadcast studios, but for the most part they were either secondary editors or simply pretty faces on the small screen. Even in this day and age no one took a woman journalist seriously, Barbara Walters notwithstanding. She wasn't a feminist, but sometimes it didn't seem fair.

"Don't shoot the messenger, kid. Especially when he brings you good news."

"You're right, you lovely man," she said, hugging him.

They stopped at the front desk long enough for Mary Frances to tell the research clerk who'd been helping her that she was finished.

"Find what you needed, Mary?" the young woman asked. She had her master's in political science and journalism, but she was stuck here and would probably never go any farther. She wore thick glasses, and her complexion needed help.

"Pretty much, but I'm afraid I left a mess."

"I'll take care of it."

"Thanks."

She and Liskey took the elevator up two floors, crossed the broad carpeted corridor, and entered through the main reception area, past the telephone operator and down the main corridor.

A number of editors and writers in their offices looked up and nodded or smiled. It seemed as if everyone on the staff knew what was going on.

Weaver's office was in front, overlooking busy Madison Avenue. He was studying the upcoming week's layouts. He looked up and waved them in, rising half out of his chair.

"Ms. Dean," he said politely.

"Good morning, Mr. Weaver."

Weaver glanced from her to Liskey, and a faint smile played around his narrow mouth. He was dressed correctly, as usual, in a three-piece pin-striped suit. "I see that Bob has already given you the news."

"Yes, sir, I wormed it out of him."

"Well, I think you'll do a fine job for us. I've been watching your recent contributions, and I think you've come along nicely."

For a woman, Mary Frances said to herself, and a split second later regretted her bitchiness.

"Bob will fill you in on exactly what the magazine wants. You'll be working with JD and, of course, his bureau people. But they're not going to have much time to talk you through your assignment. You're going to have to do a lot of catching up on the run."

Mary Frances was nodding. "When do I leave?"

"First thing in the morning. Gives you five days to poke around, get your feet wet, so to speak. I'll be expecting your first submissions on the third day before the actual summit and, of course, briefs before then."

"You want background and color?"

"That's right. Bob will get you pointed in the right direction."

"But, sir, I didn't know that the wives were coming to this summit." She was pushing it, she knew; she could see Liskey wince out of the corner of her eye, but she had to know.

"That's not what we want at all if that's what you're thinking. You're to do background pieces on Gorbachev himself and, of course, on President Bush. We're featuring your stories in this week's issue. I'm hoping that they'll spot your stuff and agree to an interview."

Mary Frances felt a secret little thrill. Look at me now, daddy, she wanted to shout.

"Gorbachev hasn't been willing to talk to any of our people yet. I'm hoping that you as a . . . good-looking woman will have a better chance over there."

Christ, she swore to herself. This time she could see that Liskey was grinning.

"I'm confident that you'll be able to handle it," Weaver was saying.

"I'll do my best."

"I'm sure you will."

3

G anin sat in his office finishing his preliminary report to
Yernin. It was eight. Everyone had gone home by now.
He had spent the last few hours looking through the various lab reports and statements from witnesses. Open and shut except for the fact that Kobysh almost certainly worked for the KGB, and it was denying him.

The door opened, and Sepelev came in. He had been drinking, his face was flushed, and there was a light sheen of sweat on his forehead. He'd brought a bottle of vodka with him.

"Thought you could use some company, Comrade Chief Investigator," he said. He was expansive but not drunk.

"Don't you have a home, Yurochka?"

"Shit. My wife doesn't love me at all, and yours loves you too much. Yet here we are. That's true socialism for you."

Ganin held out his half-empty tea glass, and Sepelev poured him a good measure of vodka, then perched on the edge of his own desk, took a pull from the bottle, and lit a cigarette.

"Did you have some supper?"

Sepelev shook his head. He took another pull from the bottle. "His name is Valeri Petrovich Markelov, your colonel." He pulled out a crumpled fascimile copy of the police artist sketch Ganin had had made. "Head of Department Twelve in the Armed Forces Directorate. We were right about that much." Sepelev leaned forward. "Guess what Department Twelve is all about?"

"It watches the Moscow Military District."

Sepelev sat back and laughed. "*Yeb vas*, the jeep. It was from Orlovo. And it was an army truck that hit the poor bastard. Moscow Military District. You knew all along."

"I was just guessing. How'd you come up with Markelov's name?"

"Oh, you know, I have friends, too," Sepelev said, shrugging.

It was a dangerous game he was playing. The Militia, like police anywhere in the world, depended in a large measure for its success on informants. When it involved the KGB, Sepelev had a number of friends who would talk to him. Even the State Committee for Security wasn't above the law, he liked to say. He had applied out of technical school to the KGB. It had turned him down. He hadn't passed the mental acuity tests or something. He'd never forgiven it. Every time he had a chance to stick it to the Komitet, he did.

"Still leaves us with the question of what the fuck he was doing there," Sepelev said.

"Obviously trying to make it back to the Lubyanka."

"From Orlovo."

"But someone didn't want him to make it."

"Someone from the army," Sepelev said. They were playing their game of one-on-one, in which they bounced ideas off each other. "Perhaps someone from the GRU. Maybe it was a grudge fight."

"They fuck each other for that; they don't go so far as murder."

"Not in broad daylight. Leastways. So we're back to the Army. They knew he was a KGB *puffta*."

"They would have sent him back. But he was trying to make

it into the center of his own. Remember his pistol. He fired a number of shots."

"A shoot-out at the base. Maybe you were right after all, Nikki. Maybe the little lieutenant was carrying something with him. Some evidence. But it's too late now."

"Why too late?" Ganin asked. "The truck didn't stop, and it was one of our boys who reached the body first. No one could have taken anything out of that pocket."

"Fuck your mother, if he had something with him, it must be out there on the street somewhere. There was nothing in his pockets."

Ganin stood up and reached for his coat. "I think I'll take a little ride. Want to come along?"

"Wouldn't miss it."

Moscow was at nearly 56 degrees north latitude; darkness came very late in the spring and summer. The evening twilight had a curiously flat quality to it when Ganin parked his Volga station wagon in front of the Ministry of Higher and Special Education around the corner from the Lubyanka. He went the rest of the way on foot. He carried a flashlight and the tire iron from his car.

Traffic was fairly heavy, and there were a lot of people out and about. It was a Thursday. They were getting ready for the weekend, when everyone in Moscow, it seemed, got drunk.

Ganin stopped about ten meters from the spot where Kobysh's body had been thrown by the truck. The place was partially outlined in yellow chalk. Someone had washed away the blood.

Although the Army and the KGB were denying the young man, Ganin was reasonably certain that he had been spying for the Komitet at Orlovo. Last night or sometime early in the morning he had apparently been found out and had engaged in a gun battle in which he had not been wounded. The only marks on his body, massive injuries at that, were those from the truck.

The notion that he had brought something here or had at least tried to get something back to the Lubyanka was thin, based only on the observation that one of his uniform pockets had been unbuttoned and on the fact that a KGB captain had pulled out a gun on a militia chief investigator in an attempt to keep him away from the body.

He looked across the street. The Lubyanka Center, which housed the prison and most of the KGB's departments except for Directorate One, the clandestine service, which was housed outside the city on the circumferential highway in the new building fashioned after the CIA's headquarters in Langley, was quiet. A few lights shone from some of the windows, but for the most part the building looked deserted, though in actual fact it was not.

Ganin withdrew the flashlight from his pocket, stepped off the curb, switched it on, and peered down through the grate into the storm sewer.

He spotted the cassette tape at once, floating in a pool of dirty water.

Using the blade edge of his tire iron, he levered the storm grate out of its bed and then pulled it the rest of the way off with his hands. The collection box was barely five feet deep, so he was able to lower himself inside with no difficulty, although the water, which was ice cold, came up over the tops of his shoes.

"Shit," he swore. He bent down, picked up the tape, pocketed it, and pulled himself back up to the street.

It had taken him barely a minute to retrieve the tape. No one on the street paid him much attention, and when he had the grate back in place, he turned and headed back to his car.

In a way he was disappointed. He thought that the KGB might be watching him and someone would be coming across the street the moment they saw him fiddling with the storm sewer. But they had not. So far as he could tell, they had posted no watchers in the square, though he certainly could have been under surveillance from the center.

It still made no sense to him why they hadn't taken over this investigation. But then perhaps the tape would clear up the mystery.

Reaching his car, he was about to call out when two men roughly dressed in workmen's coveralls came up from the basement steps of the ministry building in a dead run, pistols drawn. Ganin had no time pull out his own gun.

"Turn around, place your hands on top of the car, and spread your legs," one of them said. They both seemed calm. They were professionals. They would make no mistakes. For that much, at least, Ganin was thankful.

"What is this then, a robbery?" he asked.

"Turn around."

"I don't think so."

It was dark here, and at the moment there was no traffic. The one who had spoken stepped forward, raising his pistol. He had started to say something when Sepelev stepped out of the darkness of a doorway across from the car, his pistol held in both hands out at arm's length.

"*Stoi*, Militia!" he shouted in a voice loud enough to wake the dead.

The two men flinched, but their weapons did not waver from Ganin.

"Put your guns down, you cunts," Sepelev shouted, advancing a few paces.

"I would do as he says, comrades," Ganin warned them. "He is very excitable sometimes. Nervous, if you know what I mean."

"You may kill one of us, but not before the other kills the chief investigator."

Sepelev laughed. "Then you will have died trying to steal vodka money, whereas he will have died for his country. So I ask you, who will be the hero?"

The man nearest Ganin stepped back and quickly switched his aim to Sepelev. "We will leave now. There is no need for bloodshed here."

The other one, whose aim never wavered from Ganin, stepped back and to the left, away from his partner, making it more difficult for Sepelev to hit them both if a fire fight erupted. They definitely were professionals. Somehow Ganin got the impression that they were not KGB, however. Army? He wondered.

"It is a tie this time," Ganin said good-naturedly. "Go."

The first one stepped back a pace, and then the other one stepped back. In that fashion they slowly leapfrogged backward. They turned finally and ran down the street.

"Fuck," Sepelev swore, and he started after them.

"No," Ganin shouted. Sepelev turned back. He was clearly frustrated. "Not this time, Yurii. Besides, I think I know where they are going. They certainly knew who I was."

"**F**uck your mother, they were KGB," Sepelev swore, tossing his cap down on the desk and facing Ganin. "Why didn't we go after them?"

"They were probably GRU," Ganin said. He took the cassette tape out of his pocket. "And I didn't want to risk losing this. I think Lieutenant Kobysh might have dropped it. I fished it out of the storm sewer."

"Fingerprints?"

"It was in the water. In any event I think what it contains will tell us whether or not Kobysh dropped it and why he was killed."

Sepelev unlocked the file cabinet and got two Japanese-made cassette recorders and a blank tape. They were the only things that seemed to work in the building, so they had to be kept constantly under lock and key. Even in the office of a chief investigator, however, they were not safe. Already this year they had lost three of the machines. Somehow Ganin could not find any anger for such enterprising thieves.

"We'd better make a copy of it," Sepelev said. "Those bastards know your name."

"Good idea," Ganin said. He loaded the one tape recorder while Sepelev inserted the blank tape into the other. They switched them on and Ganin pushed his machine next to Sepelev's.

"You are absolutely sure he is capable of it?"

"So far as we can determine. But men of his ilk . . . assassins . . . do not advertise their credentials."

Ganin looked up at Sepelev. What the hell had they gotten themselves into here?

"I understand that."

"Then understand this. If we are in agreement here, a messenger will be sent to him."

"I thought he had already been contacted, Riza Petrovich."

Ganin quickly jotted the given name and patronymic on a pad of paper. The tape continued.

"Yes, but only in the most vague of terms, General. . . ."

"How vague?."

"Let him finish, Viktor."

Ganin wrote "GENERAL" on his pad, and then "VIKTOR." What was going on?

" Thank you. The operational code, as we agreed, is counterstrike. He understands the significance and the difficulties."

"Which is why I am suggesting Geneva. We don't want him here."

"He wants more information."

"Naturally . . ."

"Our names, Comrade General."

"Never."

Ganin sat forward. Sepelev was staring at the tape machines as if they were nuclear bombs about ready to explode. His eyes were wide and shining, a thin sheet of sweat glistened on his forehead, and a stray strand of hair dangled across his forehead like a comma.

"He's not a stupid man, General. He couldn't be and have lasted this long. We must give him something. Call it insurance."

"Suicide."

Ganin listened to what sounded like murmurings, and per-haps the shuffling of papers, and a match being lit. He could almost visualize the scene. The old men—they sounded old on the tape—plotting something, an assassination apparently, in Geneva, and suddenly they were embarrassed.

"We'll give him my name."

Ganin could hear the authority in the man's voice as well as a hint of desperation.

"Is that wise, Comrade General? You are the most important man here—"

Ganin could hear a commotion somewhere off in the distance. It sounded as if two men were arguing. Suddenly he could hear a door opening.

"What is it, Sergei?"

There was a slight nasal twang to the man's voice, unusual for a Russian. Ganin decided that he knew the voice. He had heard it somewhere, but he could not place it. Not yet.

Someone came in the room; he could hear the footfalls. A second later there seemed to be a shuffling, and then the last voice, the one with authority, spoke again.

"No, Sergei."

The tape ended.

The entire floor was deserted. Everyone had gone home long ago. Nevertheless, Sepelev got up and locked the door as Ganin rewound the tape. When he came back, he stood staring across the room at the dark windows. Night had finally fallen.

"This time I want you to sit down at the typewriter and make a transcript," Ganin said.

"This is something for the Army."

"I don't think so. The KGB wouldn't be interested if the GRU was simply planning on killing one of its own people. It's a civilian."

"But what do they have against the Swiss?" Sepelev asked.

For some reason Ganin was reminded of an old peasant proverb—The Russian is clever, but it comes slowly—all the way from the back of his head. We are a nation of dullards, he told himself, despite the fact that we have sent men and machines into space and fielded more world-ranking chess masters than any other nation. But we are plotters. A Russian loves nothing more than a deep, dark secret.

"Not the Swiss, Yurochka," Ganin said. "Think. Who else will be in Geneva in the next few days?"

Ganin could see the effort on his old friend's face. But then the detective had it, and he actually blanched; the color left his face. "The summit," he said softly. "Party General Secretary Gorbachev."

"Yes, and the American President."

"Nikki, this is something for the KGB, then. I say we turn this over to them immediately. Tonight. The lieutenant was spying on the Army, and now this has to be given to the right people."

"You're forgetting the murder here in Moscow. That is our jurisdiction. And you're also forgetting that the KGB has denied its own man. Why do you suppose that is?"

"I don't know. But let's get rid of it."

"I don't think so, Yurochka. Not just yet. First I will speak with Yernin."

"He will tell you to turn the case over to them."

Ganin smiled. "Then we will, but at that point it will be within official channels. In that way we will not be ignored."

Chief Prosecutor Yernin had a small but expensively furnished apartment on Gorkogo Street a few blocks from the Museum of the Revolution. A Tchaikovsky symphony was playing in the background when he came to the door, a drink in his hand.

"Nikki," Yernin said softly, his displeasure obvious. He looked beyond Ganin into the corridor. "What brings you here at this hour of the night?"

"I've uncovered some new evidence that you must see, Comrade Chief—"

"In which case is this?"

"The murder of the young KGB officer who'd been posing as an army lieutenant."

"Run down by the truck in front of the Lubyanka."

"He'd been carrying a tape recording with him, which he tossed down into the storm sewer before he died. There is a plot to kill President Gorbachev. In Geneva."

A faint smile played across Yernin's thin lips. "I see," he said. "And this evidence, you have brought it with you here?"

Ganin started to reach into his pocket for the thick envelope, but Yernin stayed his hand.

"Not here, not tonight," he said. "Bring it to me in my office in the morning."

"There isn't time—" Ganin tried to protest, but Yernin cut him off again.

"Let it not be said later that we were a part of some counterplot, meeting in private at all hours of the night. Besides, he does not leave for Geneva for several days yet. We have time."

Ganin didn't understand. He was missing something.

"Trust me, Nikki, in this. I think I know what I am doing. We will save his life, but we will also save our own."

"This should be turned over to the KGB now, tonight."

"No."

Ganin started to insist but then held back. He nodded. "As you wish, Chief Prosecutor."

Yernin reached out and patted him on the arm. "I will see you in the morning, in *official* surroundings, where we will make sure that the evidence you have means what you think it does. This we shall do together, you and I."

The Ganins' apartment was on the north side of Moscow in a place called Mar'ina Roshcha, a few blocks from the Savelovsky Railroad Station. They had a huge book-filled living room, a private kitchen and dining room, a large bathroom with a window that looked down into a courtyard, and two bedrooms, one of which was for the child they'd never had. The apartment as well as most of the furnishings had come from Ganin's wife's uncle as a wedding present seven years ago. No one in her family allowed him to forget that he couldn't have afforded such a place on his investigator's salary.

It was well after midnight when he parked his car half on the sidewalk in front of his building and let himself in. His apartment was dark, and he went upstairs quietly. He took off his shoes at the top and slipped into the bathroom, closing the door before he switched on the light.

He didn't want a confrontation tonight, especially not tonight. Lately Antonia had been carping about the hours he was putting in. "You are wearing yourself out," she said. "And for what, can you tell me at least this much?"

The suicide rate in Moscow was the highest among poets and artists, followed very closely by militia officers. He had made the mistake once of telling her that.

"What good will you be to anyone if you put a gun to your head or tie a rope around your neck and jump out a window?" she asked. If nothing else, she had a vivid imagination.

Ganin ran the bathwater as he took off his clothes, making certain he still had the envelope with the tape cassette and Sepelev's transcript. He had not wanted to trust it to the office safe. He stepped into the tub, steam already filling the bathroom. He lay back, letting the heat soak into his bones.

Perhaps he had jumped to the wrong conclusions—conclusions he had not yet voiced to Yernin—that the KGB was involved somehow in a plot to kill Gorbachev. It was possible that the KGB had no knowledge of it. Lieutenant Kobysh may have simply been one of its Directorate Three people on ordinary assignment to the military at Orlovo. Somehow he had gotten hold of the tape —perhaps he had run his own surveillance operation—and been discovered by the GRU, which had chased him all the way back to Moscow and killed him.

At this point the KGB would feel it was being faced with nothing more than another interservice fight. Such squabbles had been going on since 1920, when the military intelligence branch was formed.

He did not believe, however, that he was wrong about the intent. Someone was planning to hire an assassin to kill President Gorbachev. In Geneva. Under the code name COUNTER-STRIKE. Somehow he would have to be warned.

The door opened a few minutes later, and he opened his eyes as his wife came in. She was naked, her large breasts and broad Russian hips swaying provocatively as she came across to him and sat on the edge of the tub. She had brought him a glass of the good brandy he liked and a lit cigarette. It was a Marlboro, the cigarette of choice in Moscow for anyone who could afford it. She put it in his mouth and handed him the drink.

"How do you feel, Nikki?" she asked softly, her fingers at the back of his neck.

"Tired, but better now. I'm sorry I was so late."

"You work much too hard, my darling," she said. There was an edge to her voice.

"There was a murder."

"You have people to help. You are not the only investigator in Moscow."

He turned away. She reached down and turned his head back, then leaned over and kissed him, her tongue darting into his mouth. When they parted, she was flushed.

"Now hurry with your bath. I want you to make love to me."

Donald Moran knew that the messenger would be returning, and he knew that when the man did, he would accept
the assignment if the people had agreed to his terms in
Moscow.

At five feet eleven, 180 pounds, he was a compact olive-com-
plected man with dark hair who, when no one was watching,
tended to move on the balls of his feet, much like a cat, certain
of his movements, apparently indifferent to his surroundings, yet
aware of everything going on around him. His eyes were a violent,
almost bottomless blue. They were his only feature that belied a
possibly highborn Spanish background.

He was an exceedingly charming man who was intimately familiar with people on five continents and that many island groups,
yet whose background was totally unknown. In the words of a

woman he knew in Paris, the wife of a general in the French Air Force: "Tony is an exotic, perilous man. Frankly I don't know when he is at his best . . . or most dangerous: naked in bed beside you or dressed in a tuxedo across the baccarat table. But I do know that in either position you are bound to lose. *C'est ça*."

He had served in the U.S. Air Force intelligence service in the late sixties and early seventies, in the CIA until 1980, and for five years in the Mossad, where he had learned how to kill and where he had been truly and well blooded. He had enlisted in each service under a different name and background, his carefully constructed personas holding up even to the close scrutiny of the service vetting officers. His Donald Moran identity was no less false than his others, but it had served his purposes so far.

He had no friends, in the real sense of the word, nor did he need any. But he could be anything to anyone: a charming, gracious lover to a Continental woman, a sport to a Gulf Stream fisherman, an astute businessman to his Wall Street brokers, and a deadly, efficient assassin who had never failed his clients.

This time was different, though, he mused, propping himself up on one elbow and looking out his bedroom window down at the azure Caribbean Sea. The messenger had already come here to the island once about three weeks ago. That visit had been barely acceptable; there were other, safer ways of making contact with him—for instance, a certain letter drop in Athens or an old woman in Beirut. A second visit, however, was totally out of the question. GRU, KGB, CIA, even Mossad, every secret service in the world had its informers. Sooner or later word would get out that there was something or someone of interest in the U.S. Virgin Islands.

If the messenger returned, he would have to kill him . . . after he heard what the man had to say. In this business the messenger was always expendable. Everyone knew it, except for those picked as messengers.

"Donald, where are you?" Marie Deaquino asked. She was a West Indian mixture of black, French, Spanish, and English.

Moran turned from the window. Marie lay beside him in the big bed, one of her long, soft brown legs thrown over his waist. She had come over from Tortola a few days earlier. They had met at the Pusser's Café in Cruz Bay, and she had moved in with him. Just for the long weekend. She had gone to England for her education, and she wanted to go back. She was only twenty-five, but she had the West Indian combination of naiveté and world-liness that just now Moran found charming. And she was beautiful.

"I was thinking that I might have to go away," he said, a very slight English accent in his strong, clear voice.

Her full lips formed a pout. "Not soon, I hope. At least not until after breakfast."

Moran laughed. He touched her flanks and let the tips of his fingers trail upward to her firm breasts. The dark nipples instantly responded. She shivered.

"How do you know to do this to me?" she asked languidly, letting the words die in her throat as he bent over and kissed her slightly rounded belly, lingering with his tongue for a long moment around her navel.

"Donald," she said softly, her hips moving away from him so that he would have more room.

He looked up. Her eyes were bright, her mouth was open, and her hands were together over her head on the pillow as if her wrists were tied together. She was watching him the way a feral animal might watch its prey. Or vice versa.

"Perhaps you would like to come with me this time?" Moran said. He let his fingertips trace a gentle pattern from inside her knees up to the sensitive areas of her thighs and then very lightly across the lips of her vagina. She let out an involuntary gasp.

"When?" she asked.

"Soon," Moran answered. He knelt between her legs and continued with his fingertips to trace her nipples, her belly, her thighs, and finally her pubis. She was already very moist. She was barely in control, and it amused him. "Perhaps in the next day or so."

"Where are you going?"

"Does it matter?"

"Only if you plan on leaving me someplace bad."

"Perhaps the Riviera. The Île du Levant. There are a lot of nice young French boys there on the navy base," Moran said. He took her hands and lifted her up so that they were kneeling as they embraced.

Her body was starting to thrum, her hands on the mounts of his buttocks, pulling him tightly against her.

They parted again. She wore black lipstick, and it was shiny with moisture, high contrast with the perfect white of her teeth.

Her eyes were very dark, and as she studied his, he could see that her irises were surrounded by tiny diamond-shaped dots.

"Is there anyone in Road Town who would miss you?" Moran asked, but he kissed her deeply before he would allow her to answer. "Anyone who would raise a hue and cry if you just dropped off the face of the earth?"

"I'm related to half the island, Donald," she said, biting at his lower lip. "But no one would miss me. I come and . . . I go."

Moran smiled. He pushed her back on the bed and then rolled her over on her stomach, gently spreading her legs with his right hand while caressing her pubis from the rear with the fingers of his other."Oh, God," she cried, her ass rising to meet him as she got up on her hands and knees.

Marie went into the bathroom when they were finished. Moran poured himself some of the champagne from last night and lit a cigarette just as the telephone rang.

He reached over and picked it up. "Yes?" he said neutrally.

"Dis is Wesley, down d'bay. You got company, mista." Wesley was one of the taxi dispatchers off the ferry docks in St. John's only village, Cruz Bay. In the evenings he ran the most successful cockfighting bar and arena on the islands. Moran had backed him.

"Same as before?"

"Same fella. Be out your way 'bout five minutes."

"Get my boat ready, would you?" Moran said, glancing at the bathroom door. He could hear the shower running. "I'll pick it up later tonight. He and I are heading out. The girl, too." There weren't many secrets on the island. But they were well kept from outsiders if you were acceptable. Moran was.

"I hear you," Wesley said. "You watch yourself, mista. Dis one a bad fella, I think."

"He's a Russian spy."

Wesley guffawed and then hung up. The local rumor was that Moran was some sort of drug lord with connections from Miami to Bogotá. No one bothered him.

He got out of bed and padded silently out of the bedroom, down the breezeway, and across the living room to the front veranda, which looked past the pool facing the driveway. Nothing moved on the steep gravel road down to the highway. He unlocked the door and left it ajar before going back into the bedroom.

Marie was just coming out of the bathroom. She saw the change in his attitude. "What is it?"

"I have company coming," he said, pulling on a pair of shorts.

"That was quick," she said a little bitterly. "Shall I go?"

Moran smiled gently and shook his head. "Not that kind of company. This is a man. Business. Just stay out of sight. He might get nervous if he sees someone other than me."

Her nostrils flared, but she knew enough not to ask any more questions. "I'll get dressed and go for a walk on the beach."

"I'll call you when he's gone."

"Yeah, do that," Marie said, grabbing her brightly colored sarong and wrapping it around her.

"Marie," Moran said.

She stopped what she was doing and looked at him.

"I mean it," he said. "Don't run off on me now. Be there when I finish. I won't be long. You're important. Believe me."

She softened, and he could see that she did believe him. She nodded. "Sorry." She smiled. "Don't be long, Donald."

She slipped into her sandals because the path down to the beach was rocky, and before she went out, she brushed a kiss on Moran's cheek. She smelled of soap and shampoo, yet a sexual heat still radiated from her.

The moment she was gone, he went to the bed and from beneath it on his side pulled out his weapon, a Beretta .380 automatic with a Kevlar silencer. Heading back out to the living room, he levered a round into the firing chamber and switched the safety to the off position. He laid the weapon on the cushion of the crowned wicker chair that faced the couch across a coffee table.

Next he rolled up the small area rug between the couch and the front door and stuffed it into a closet, leaving the white tile floor bare.

He was just sitting down when he heard the taxi come up the driveway and stop in front. The gun was out of sight beneath his right leg. He felt for it, made sure he could put his hand on it with ease, then lit a Dunhill red.

He heard the car door closing a second or two later and then the sound of the cab's tires crunching on the gravel as it left.

Someone came up the walk, hesitated at the front door, and then came into the house. From where he was seated Moran could see that it was the Russian from the last time. He was a GRU captain. Dmitri Svetanko. He was sweating profusely, even though he was dressed in khaki shorts, a gaudily colored sport shirt, and a straw hat. His legs were very white.

"Ah, Mr. Moran," he said, coming the rest of the way in.

Moran motioned toward the couch, but the Russian stopped about fifteen feet away and shook his head. "I'm taking the noon ferry to St. Thomas. You can drive me back. We'll talk on the way.

"You shouldn't have come."

The Russian shrugged. "They are in a hurry. They wanted to make sure there were no mistakes." He glanced around the room and then up at the slowly revolving fans hanging from the tall ceilings. "Are we safe here?"

"Perfectly," Moran said. "Tell me, Dmitri, is it a go?"

Svetanko nodded. "Five million dollars in mixed Western currencies have been deposited into your Barclays Channel Islands account. The other half will be paid if you are successful."

"I will verify that before I make my first move."

Svetanko took out a manila envelope from beneath his shirt. It was wet with sweat. He dropped it on the hall table. "These are travel documents, itineraries, and travel routes where possible. We're still suggesting Geneva as a prime target area. The city is open; there will be ample opportunity. Plus you will have the assistance of our embassy at Bern."

"If it is to be Geneva or anywhere else, for that matter, I will require no assistance," Moran said.

"In the package there is a number for you to call in case there are any last-minute changes of plans. You may use it in case of an emergency."

"Does this person know about me or about what I have been hired to do?"

"No. He is merely a messenger. An answering service."

Moran nodded thoughtfully. "Do you have something else for me?"

The Russian seemed uncomfortable. Again he looked around the room and glanced up at the ceiling. "On the way into town."

"Now."

"I am authorized to give you one name, not the other—"

"Conspirators," Moran finished the statement for him. "I will be the judge if the one name is sufficient."

"Zuyev," the Russian whispered.

Moran grinned and nodded. "General Anatoli Vladimirovich

Zuyev, commander of the Moscow Military District. Possibly one of the most influential men in the Soviet Union. This is a big step even for a man of his stature."

"Will you do it?"

"Yes," Moran said. "Wait for me outside. I'll get the car and meet you out front."

The Russian stared at him for a long beat, then turned and started for the door. Moran picked up his pistol and fired two shots, catching Svetanko in the spine just at the base of his neck and in the back of his head, driving him forward. He stumbled to his knees and then fell facedown, his forehead bouncing on the tiles.

Moran ground out his cigarette in the ashtray beside his chair, then got up and went to the body. He knelt and felt for a pulse. There was none. He chuckled. The Russians were gullible.

After locking the front door, he went back into the bedroom, where he tossed his gun down on the bed, then went out onto the veranda. He was in high spirits.

The house was perched on the edge of a low hill, the beach about fifty feet below. He could see Marie sitting on the sand looking out to sea. There was no one else in sight except for a parasailer a mile or so to the west toward Fish Bay and a pair of sailboats on the horizon to the south.

It was too bad about her, he thought, heading down the path to the beach. But she had simply shown up at the wrong time. A couple of months ago or a couple of months from now would have been different. Yet it wasn't entirely her fault. It was he who had initiated the meeting the other day, knowing full well it would probably come to this. It was the bloodlust thing again. He needed the kill, like an addict needs the fix.

She heard him coming, and she turned around and got to her feet as he came across the beach, a big smile on his face. She lit up.

"Is he gone already?"

"Just us now. Let's go for a swim."

"I don't swim very well, Donald. I told you that yesterday."

"I guess you did," Moran said. "But that's all right, darling. I'm a very good swimmer. Trust me."

He took her hand, and she followed him into the water, hesitantly at first, but then with growing confidence. What could happen?

6

oran waited until four o'clock in the morning to move
the bodies out to his twenty-two-foot Boston Whaler,
which he had anchored just off the beach.

The water was chest-deep, and after he had brought his two
leather suitcases aboard, he'd first floated Svetanko's body out,
heaved it up and over the gunwale, then had gone back to the
beach, where he'd hidden Marie's body in the bushes below the
house.

In the bright starlight her face was pale, almost white. He
pushed a strand of damp hair off her sandy forehead and gently
kissed her lips. Her face was contorted into a mask of absolute
terror. She had cried out only once as he shoved her under, and
because of it, she had drowned very quickly, taking a deep breath

almost as soon as she was beneath the surface. Yet she had fought very hard for her life.

He smiled wanly. There was something wrong with him. There had always been something wrong with him. But he was a professional, and Marie had simply been a loose end.

As soon as he had her body aboard, he started the Whaler's two-hundred-horsepower Evinrude, pulled up the anchor, and headed southwest the twelve miles or so to Charlotte Amalie Harbor on St. Thomas.

There was no going back now. But then he had known for the last six months or so that his tenure in the Caribbean was coming to an end. Everyone here came to know everyone else's business sooner or later. Either his drug lord cover would be penetrated and questions would be raised, or he would be arrested *because* of his cover.

When he cleared Dittlif Point, he could see the lights on the larger island, houses and cars up in the hills, and the small powerboat rose to run with the three- to five-foot east-going swells. He locked the wheel down, then sat back with a cigarette as he contemplated his next persona. Before St. John he had lived for a time in South Africa, and before that the South Pacific. It was time, he thought, to return to Europe. Perhaps the Riviera after all, or Paris again, or Rome. The authorities would never expect him to remain on the Continent after the kill. There would be an international hue and cry, but their efforts would be concentrated outward.

He was leaving behind nothing that money couldn't replace, so there were no regrets whatsoever. It was just at times like these he was torn between a vaguely felt nostalgia for something he did not have, never had had—a real background, a genuine life, a place—and the mounting excitement for the job at hand. Moran was a sociopath in that he had absolutely no conscience, while at the same time he was addicted to the adrenaline brought on by danger. It was a deadly combination.

Turning around, he glanced back at the two bodies. They seemed to be embracing. Sooner or later Marie's people would come looking for her. Someone must have known that she'd come to St. John. Of course, they wouldn't find her, leastways not for a very long time, but they would come. The Russian's people, on the other hand, knew he was dead. They would not look for him.

He cleared Dog Rocks ten minutes later and turned a little

farther to the west. He could pick out the lighthouse on Buck Island, and he adjusted his course so that he would pass well south of it, in water that was nearly two hundred feet deep.

When the Whaler was settled on its new course, he made his way aft, where he separated the two bodies. Svetanko's was stiff with rigor mortis, but Marie's had retained its pliancy. It was different for everyone in death, he had learned from firsthand experience. In that, too, he had become something of a professional.

He opened one of the gunnysacks he had placed aboard and pulled out a fifty-foot section of half-inch chain. He started wrapping it around the Russian's body, beginning at the ankles and working upward. It was difficult and time-consuming because of the condition of the body, because of its weight and bulk, and because of the motion of the boat in the swells.

It took him nearly a half hour to finish. He stopped often to look up and check his course to make sure he would miss Buck Island. Twice he had to turn a little farther south as the current swept him toward the rocks.

He pulled the second length of chain from the other bag and wrapped it around Marie's body. Her sarong was plastered tightly against her body, and halfway through the job her right eyelid came open. He didn't bother closing it.

It was well after five o'clock by the time he was done with both of them, and already the sky to the east was beginning to get light. Sunrise occurred around six, and nautical twilight earlier. He had cut it close, but there was not another boat in sight.

Buck Island was now off to his northwest. He switched on the fish finder, which settled down to 187 feet over an uneven, rocky bottom. Two large fish were circling at about 60 feet. They were very likely barracudas.

Without stopping the boat, he heaved Svetanko's body up over the gunwale and rolled him into the water. He disappeared immediately.

When he turned to pick up Marie's body, she was looking at him, mocking him, her mouth curved into a smile.

He smiled back, then picked her up and rolled her into the water. Like the Russian, she disappeared immediately.

He undogged the wheel and turned hard to port so that he was running back along his own track. Within thirty yards he picked up one of the bodies on the fish finder, and he circled, watching it slowly twist end over end as it sank to the bottom. Already the two fish were circling in to investigate. He could not find the other body, but he figured it was the Russian's, and by now it was already on the bottom.

Turning north, he shoved the throttles forward, and the Whaler leaped up over the waves heading toward Charlotte Amalie. The morning flight to Miami left at eight-thirty, giving him plenty of time to make it into town, change into street clothes, have some breakfast, and get out to the airport. He would be in New York later this afternoon and Paris tomorrow morning.

There was nothing or no one on this earth to stop him now. He felt good, better than he had in months. He felt like God.

He began to sing "Nessun Dorma," the aria from *Turandot* in which Calaf sings of his love for the princess. But the words meant something entirely different to him.

Nessun dorma! Nessun dorma!

No man shall sleep! No man shall sleep!
You too, O Princess,
in your chaste room
are watching the stars which
tremble with love and hope!
But my secret lies hidden within me,
no one shall discover my name. . . .

Ganin got up before Antonia and dressed in his chief investigator's uniform, which was navy blue with four brass stars on the epaulets. He had a quick cup of tea at the militia officers' restaurant on Kuznetskiy Street around the corner from headquarters, then went up to his office.

No one had come in yet, though the restaurant had been full. He transferred the copy of the tape recording, a copy of the transcript that Sepelev had typed last night, and his own report from the envelope to a buff-colored file folder and walked across to the chief prosecutor's office.

Neither Yernin nor his staff had arrived, so Ganin laid the file on the chief prosecutor's desk. No one would touch it there. It would be safe.

Whatever happened now, the case was definitely in official

channels. The KGB would almost certainly take over despite the thin evidence. The Soviet rules of evidentiary procedure required a witness or a confession to a tape recording. Neither was likely now. Yet they simply could not ignore the threat. He had been a young man when Kennedy had been assassinated. Everyone in Russia had held his or her breath waiting for the Americans to fire their missiles.

In the meantime, it was still his case.

He retrieved his car from the parking lot and drove out Kalinina Prospekt, where he took the Boulevard Ring Road south to the Moscow Military Academy on Zubuvskaya Street. The imposing brick building was set back away from the street across from one of Moscow's many lovely small parks. He presented his credentials to the receptionist in the lobby, a broad-faced Great Russian in a lieutenant's uniform.

"I have come to see General Karpov this morning," Ganin said.

"Is he expecting you, Comrade Captain?"

"No, but he will see me."

"We shall see," the lieutenant said with a smirk. He picked up the telephone, said something softly into it, listened for a moment, then nodded and said something else. He hung up. "You are in luck. He has just arrived." He wrote out a pass, handed it up, and started to give directions.

"I know my way," Ganin said, and he hurried down the corridor and took the elevator into the basement.

Yevgenni Karpov had once told Ganin's father that a man had to make general by the time he was fifty or he would end up getting himself shot. Of course, a lot of men who made general were shot anyway, but generals had a better chance in the long run. Karpov was one of the men who had survived all the purges and all the differing philosophical points of view for the simple reason that he had set himself up as a keeper of history, specifically of Soviet military history. No one wanted to disturb that house of cards lest it fall down around him.

The basement of the military academy was a rabbit warren of low-ceilinged rooms and corridors with stone walls. Everywhere there were file cabinets bulging with documents, rusting metal shelves overflowing with books, racks loaded with newspapers, and map cases stuffed with campaigns that had been fought since the Revolution.

There was the odor of dampness (no basement in Moscow was ever completely dry because of the many underground rivers), mixed with the thick mustiness of decaying paper.

General Karpov was at his desk. He had been a big, handsome kulak who had come off the *kollektiv* to carve a career for himself in the Army. His frame had shrunk so that he had become a wizened little old man with wisps of white hair and long white eyebrows that went in every direction. But his eyes were still dark and clear. He was in his late seventies and was fond of telling anyone that he had lasted from Ilyich to Ilyich (Vladimir Ilyich Lenin to Leonid Ilyich Brezhnev) and beyond. As much as the cult of personality had begun to return he was an institution.

Ganin sat down across from him. The office was large and incredibly dingy. It was still a little early for the other archivists to come in, so they were alone.

"How is Tonia?" Karpov asked, a slight waver in his voice. It sounded like the rustling of dry parchment.

"Fine, General. She sends her love."

"It has been a long time since I have seen the family. And what about you, Nikolai Fedorovich? Are you a father yet? Has that little pecker of yours been up to some good?"

"Not yet. But I have come to ask for your help. I need some information."

Karpov hooted and sat back in his thickly padded chair. "I would have been able to help you with that once upon a time. But now you're on your own."

"There was a meeting last night at Orlovo. I need some names."

Karpov looked at him, a shrewd expression in his eyes. "This is something new for you, Nikki. What interest does the Militia have in Orlovo?"

"There was a murder yesterday here in Moscow. A young lieutenant. The Army is denying him."

"KGB?"

"They say no, although he almost certainly was from the Third Directorate. Colonel Valeri Markelov seemed interested."

"Watch that one. He is a dangerous bastard. He was at this meeting?"

"No. There were some generals there, at least three. I need their names. One was Riza Petrovich."

Karpov said nothing.

"The other was Viktor. A third they called the most important man in the room. Oh, and there was another one called Sergei, though I don't think he was one of them. He came in later."

"A little bird told you this, Nikki?"

Ganin shrugged.

Karpov shook his head. He would either tell the truth or say nothing. There had never been a middle ground for him. Keeping his mouth shut at the correct times had probably been one of the contributing factors to his longevity.

"I don't know Sergei. But Riza Petrovich would be General Truchin, commander of the Nuclear Forces. Viktor would be General Pavlenko, commander of the Missile Forces. And since the meeting was at Orlovo, and they called the third man the most important one there, he would be General Anatoli Zuyev, commander of the Moscow Military District. Were there others at this meeting?"

"Possibly."

"It would have included General Gennadi Matushin, commander of the Air Force." Karpov sighed. "A powerful bunch of bastards. What you would call old guard. Stalinists. Real *pizdas*. Dangerous men, Nikki."

"Matushin just lost the election," Ganin said, remembering the name now. The old guard had been losing ground to the younger officers in the Congress of People's Deputies for the past few years.

"That's the one," Karpov said. "None of them can be happy about it. But what are they planning out there? A putsch?"

"I don't know."

"Don't lie to me," Karpov said, sensing something. "You came for my help, now don't tell me lies in return."

"I won't, but you must stay out of this, Uncle. I'm investigating a murder. But it may soon be out of my hands."

"If you get yourself caught in the middle of a faction fight, you will be the one to lose. Even the KGB will have a hard time keeping those old bastards in place. If they mean to start something . . ."

"Thank you," Ganin said, rising.

Karpov started to say something else, then smiled wanly and nodded. "It was good of you to come by to see me, Nikki. Say hello to Tonia for me. And get busy with . . . You know we Great Russians are becoming a threatened minority?"

* * *

Memories of an earlier time, when they all were a happy family, rode on his shoulders like a burden all the way back to militia headquarters. It was a long time ago, yet sometimes even the good memories were painful.

Sepelev had finally arrived, and he was nursing a large cup of tea. It was clear he was suffering from a hangover after last night's drunk.

"The chief prosecutor's office has been calling for you," he said when Ganin came in.

"You look like shit."

"True, but I feel worse, believe me. Where the hell have you been all dressed up?"

"To see a friend. Get me some tea, would you?"

Ganin sat down at his desk, wound a piece of paper into his typewriter, and quickly wrote out an addition to his initial report, including the names of the four generals who had probably taken part in the Orlovo meeting. He left out his specific source, citing only "military records."

Sepelev came up behind him and read over his shoulder. He whistled. "Hot stuff," he said. He set the tea down. "Didn't I tell you that this was something for the KGB?"

"You were right, Yurochka," Ganin said, pulling the paper out of the typewriter and getting up. He grabbed a quick sip of the tea, then hurried out. He crossed the courtyard and went upstairs to the chief prosecutor's office.

Yernin was expecting him, and he was allowed straight in. He laid the amended report on Yernin's desk and came to attention.

The chief prosecutor looked up at him for a long moment, then carefully reached out and picked up the new report. He took his time reading it, and when he was done, he took off his wire-rimmed glasses and rubbed his eyes.

"So, four very important generals have planned to have someone assassinated, possibly in Geneva, in an operation they have code-named counterstrike."

"The evidence is so far unsubstantiated, but it is of some value."

Yernin put his glasses on. "What are your recommendations?"

"It should be given to the KGB."

"Give it what? As you say, this is unsubstantiated evidence.

We would be remiss in our jobs if we handed over something so flimsy as this."

"Excuse me, but President Gorbachev will be meeting with President Bush in a few days' time. I think that we must do everything within our power to prevent a tragedy."

"I agree. But with communism's new freedom of speech also comes responsibility. We do not have the right to shout fire in the crowded Bolshoi unless indeed there is a fire."

"Yes, but—"

Yernin pushed a thick manila envelope across his desk. "These are your travel documents. You and Detective Sepelev leave in the morning. You will be in Geneva for lunch."

After last night Ganin had expected anything but this.

"Try La Perle du Lac, on the Rue de Lausanne," Yernin said. "I think it's one of the best restaurants in the city."

The cabby dropped Moran at the corner of Library Place in downtown St. Helier on the British Channel Island of Jersey. The weather was pleasant. Palm trees lined many of the avenues and boulevards, their fronds rattling in the nearly constant breeze.

He paid the driver and, when the cab moved off, hefted his two leather bags, waited for a break in traffic, and went across the street.

There was money and arrogance here among the quaint narrow streets and behind the impassive facades of the dozens of banks. The Channel Islands had very nearly replaced Switzerland as a bastion of currency transactions free from the prying eyes of government. Any government. Moran had been doing business with Barclays Bank for a number of years now, and so far as he knew, it was not aware of his profession, nor was it in the least bit interested. He was a zero-eight account holder, which meant he had in excess of one million dollars American on account at any given time.

He angled across the sidewalk away from the public lobby and entered the commercial section. A small, tastefully decorated reception area was manned by a severely dressed older woman, who looked up as Moran set his bags on the polished marble floor.

"Good morning, sir," she said. "How may I be of service?"

Moran took out a gold ballpoint pen from his jacket pocket and jotted down his account number on a pad on the woman's desk. "I would like to speak to someone pertaining to my account."

The receptionist tore the top sheet off the pad and glanced at the number. "Yes, sir," she said. She picked up the telephone, spoke a few words softly into the mouthpiece, and then hung up. "Mr. Kenbraithe will see you. The second door on your right down the corridor."

"Will you see to my bags?"

"Of course," the woman said.

Moran went down the narrow corridor, knocked once on the second door, and let himself in. A tall, distinguished-looking Englishman, dressed in a three-piece blue serge suit, with gold pince-nez and longish white hair was just rising from behind his desk. He extended his hand.

"Good morning, sir. Welcome to St. Helier. I'm Thomas Kenbraithe."

Moran shook his hand. "I have some business to attend to."

"Of course. Please have a seat."

They both sat down, and the bank officer passed a pad of paper across to Moran. "If you will just give me your account number once again, and your name, we can proceed."

Moran wrote out his account number, and beneath it the name he used here. It was not Moran, nor was it his real name. He pushed it across.

The bank officer opened a desk drawer and typed something on a keyboard. A second later he compared Moran's number and signature with those on file. The glow of the computer screen was reflected in the man's glasses.

"How may I be of service?" he asked, looking up.

"Two things. First I would like to confirm the balance of my account."

Kenbraithe glanced again at the screen, then jotted something down on a pad of paper, which he passed across to Moran. His account balance currently stood at something in excess of eight million dollars. His previous balance had been a little over three million. The Russians had done what they'd promised to do.

He smiled. "And secondly, I need to make a withdrawal from one of my safety-deposit boxes."

"Which one?"

"Nine-three."

Kenbraithe entered the numbers and request on his computer and then sat back, assuming a pleasant, relaxed air. "It will be just a moment or two, sir," he said. "Are you enjoying your stay on Jersey?"

"Yes, very much. It is always pleasant here."

"Will you be staying long?"

"Unfortunately, no. Business must take me elsewhere."

The bank officer inclined his head slightly as if to say that Moran had just uttered something so self-evident that it could have gone without saying.

A minute and a half later the door opened, and a younger man carrying a large steel box came in. He set the box on a table beside the window, then turned without a word and left as quietly as he had come.

"Do you wish for privacy?" Kenbraithe asked.

"It is not necessary," Moran said, rising and crossing the office. He took out his key, unlocked the box, and took out the only item it contained, a large, fairly heavy attaché case.

He glanced out the window into a very pleasant courtyard garden nearly in full bloom. It was so filled with life, he thought. Happiness, joy, brightness, even peace.

He turned back to the bank officer. "Our business is concluded for the moment. Thank you."

"Have a pleasant journey," Kenbraithe said.

Moran smiled. "I will."

The French Cotentin Peninsula was pitch-dark. Cherbourg was far to the north, and St.-Malo well to the south. Along this stretch of coastline there were only a few widely spaced small towns—Portbail, St.-Germain-Plage, Pirou-Plage, Coutainville— and very little in between.

Moran had hired a thirty-five-foot sport fisherman with a

captain and mate, no questions asked. They'd made the twenty-five-mile run from St. Helier in a little less than one hour, and they stood a hundred yards offshore now, watching for traffic along the coast highway. It was three in the morning, and nothing was moving.

"George will take you ashore in the dinghy," the captain said. He was a big barrel-chested man, with a handsome face and dark wavy hair. "If you head inland toward Caen, you should be able to hitch a ride when it gets light."

The mate was releasing the rubber dinghy from its davits. A fairly good swell was running here.

"Thank you for your help," Moran said. He had changed into khaki slacks, a dark sweater, a watch cap, and battered deck shoes. His two leather bags and the attaché case were stuffed into an old olive drab duffel bag.

"For the money you have paid, the pope would have taken you across."

Moran stepped a little closer. "It would be most unfortunate if anything were to go wrong this morning."

The captain shrugged. "I have brought you this far. That is my only obligation. Once you step ashore, I will have forgotten about tonight. I assure you."

Moran nodded. It would be as the captain said. He could see it in the man's eyes.

When the dinghy was in the water, Moran handed down his duffel bag and climbed over the rail. They swung around the stern of the fishing boat and headed directly to the beach, the well-muffled small outboard motor not making much noise.

A minute or so later they bumped up on the rocky beach, and Moran scrambled ashore. The mate passed up his heavy duffel with a grunt, and Moran shoved the dinghy back out into the water.

Not a word had passed between them, and even before the mate had the tiny boat turned around, Moran was heading up through the tall grasses to the coastal highway. He wanted to be in Caen by early morning and in Paris later in the day.

There were still several things for him to accomplish before he could go to Geneva, and his time was growing very short.

Geneva, he'd decided at the beginning, was an opportunity too rich to ignore. Normally he spent up to six months planning a hit. This time he would accomplish his objective within a few days. It would be a record of sorts, a record he was looking forward to setting with pleasure.

The long black Chaika limousine pulled into the vastly empty parking lot of the Moscow Hippodrome southeast of Frunze Central Airfield and headed slowly around the big stadium.

It was very early in the morning. The sun had not yet come up, and the Chaika's headlights stabbed the darkness, flashing off the gray brick walls, the recessed entryways and the black iron grates over the performers' entrances.

The driver came to a halt at the entrance marked и and doused the headlights. "We are here," he said over his shoulder.

At first nothing happened, but then the stadium door opened and someone came out of the darkness, crossed in front of the car, and got in the back seat.

"Were you followed?" the passenger asked.

"No, Comrade General, but then I am not the one under suspicion," the newcomer said, a smile on his narrow, bloodless lips.

"It is unfortunate about that tape. But it has been contained, as you say."

"In that we were lucky, but the operation must be called off or at least postponed. You do understand that."

General Anatoli Zuyev nodded his leonine head. He looked out the window toward the lights of Moscow. The Germans had come across the southwestern plains. He remembered seeing their lights like the devil's pinpricks on the horizon. In the early days they had been arrogant enough not to hide their position. There had been no one to stop them.

He turned back to the other man. "You are correct, of course. I will have the message sent."

"Counterstrike down?"

"Yes."

"Are you certain he will get it, Comrade General?"

"I am sure."

"But will he heed it?"

"Why not? He isn't crazy, is he?"

9

The sign on the side of the bus was printed in Cyrillic letters and said: WELCOME COMRADES! MARCH ONWARD TO WORLD PEACE!

The bus was parked outside the Geneva Airport terminal, the twenty-five delegates from the Congress of People's Deputies streaming across the sidewalk to it. Several television crews were waiting for them, and with security people everywhere and the traffic running in and out of the passenger pickup and discharge areas, the scene was a madhouse.

Ganin led Sepelev toward the cab rank, away from the hubbub. They did not need any attention. Yernin had been very specific about that. There was no telling if the Swiss were somehow involved in this plot—if indeed, there was a plot. It was one of the reasons they had tagged along with the delegation. At least their baggage had been allowed through customs unchecked on diplomatic exemption.

A younger man dressed in a dark business suit had gotten out of a small Mercedes sedan, and he came across the sidewalk, intercepting them.

"Excuse me, Chief Investigator Ganin?" he asked in English.

Sepelev was surprised. His mouth dropped open. But Ganin wasn't. "Who are you?"

"Detective Mueller. Federal Police," the young man said. He carried a gun beneath his jacket on his left side. "We were told that you spoke English. I'm afraid that my Russian isn't very—"

"We have a meeting to attend this afternoon. What can I do for you?"

"Yes, sir, I know. There is someone in the car who wishes to have a few words with you. We can drive you into the city."

Ganin glanced over toward the Mercedes. He could see that someone was seated in the back. "I don't think so," he said. He started to step around the Swiss cop, but the younger man blocked his way.

"Fuck you, Ivan. You're in Switzerland now, and you'll do as you're told like a nice little boy."

Sepelev had half turned away. Now he turned back and grabbed the man's testicles, bringing him instantly to his tiptoes. "Cunt."

Ganin reached inside Mueller's jacket pocket and took out his wallet. Inside was the identification card of a Swiss Federal Police. So far as Ganin could tell it was legitimate. He put it back.

"Well?" Sepelev asked.

"He is who he says he is, Yurochka," Ganin said, stepping around Mueller. "Perhaps you should let him go."

Ganin walked over to the Mercedes. The back window was down. The man inside was square-jawed, his leaden gray hair cropped very short. Ganin figured he had to weigh at least one hundred kilos. A very formidable opponent if it came to that.

"May I offer you a ride into town, Chief Investigator Ganin?" the man said. "My name is Ernst Reisch. I'm a police officer."

"We have a meeting to attend. I have been instructed not to speak with anyone until afterward. You understand how it is. Higher-ups . . ."

Reisch nodded. "Then perhaps later this afternoon. But can you tell me if you are here to provide additional security for Mr.

Gorbachev? Or has something ... more specific brought you here?"

"As you say, we might have a few words later this afternoon," Ganin replied pleasantly. "Our hotel is the Moderne on—"

"Yes," Reisch said. "I know."

Ganin turned and beckoned for Sepelev, who had backed a couple of paces from Mueller. The men were looking at each other.

"See you," Ganin said, and he and Sepelev went over to the cab rank and got into the first taxi.

The summit meetings had been taking place at the Palais des Nations in the Ariana Park. Security was being directed from an annex building of the World Health Organization. Each afternoon at five the various security chiefs met to discuss the next day's itinerary and any problems they might encounter.

Ganin left Sepelev at their hotel and went out to the meeting alone.

"I'm told that you had some kind of incident at the airport this afternoon," Feliks Vilov told him in the hallway. Vilov, a smooth, very urbane man, was head of KGB operations in Switzerland. (Because of the large amount of banking the Komitet did here, he was an important, powerful man.)

"It wasn't much, believe me," Ganin said.

"The Swiss are very touchy; it wouldn't do to upset them. Everyone wants this summit to continue to run smoothly, if I make my point."

Vilov was a worried man; it was clear on his face. It had to do in part, Ganin supposed, because the Swiss government had been making noises lately about completely revamping its banking laws. There would be a lot of fallout from the cracks such a shake-up would produce.

"I'll try not to do anything upsetting," Ganin said.

"I don't care why you are here, but Kokorov will. A word to the wise, stay away from him, Chief Investigator. He is a powerful enemy to have, especially for a simple militia detective."

Colonel Vladimir Kokorov worked in the KGB's Ninth Directorate, which had a function similar to that of the American Secret Service. His people provided physical security for Soviet leaders. They were the most trusted men in the Soviet Union.

Only Ninth Directorate personnel were allowed to be armed in the presence of the government leadership.

Again Vilov gave him a hard stare. "I've been asked to co-operate with you, as a courtesy from one branch to another. But unless you have some information vital to the summit to impart to us, you will keep your mouth shut. You are simply an observer. Clear?"

It was not clear. There was a definite danger. But he had his orders. He nodded.

"And whatever you do, stay away from the Americans."

"They will be here at this meeting?" Ganin asked, genuinely surprised, though he couldn't really say why.

"Of course, and they'll have a few questions if they spot you. I don't have any of the answers. Do you?"

"No," Ganin said sheepishly. "I'm just here to keep an eye out."

"For what?"

Ganin shrugged. "Anything."

Inside, Ganin sat alone at the rear of the lecture hall. Only the first four rows of seats were occupied. The briefing was being conducted by two men, one of whom was Colonel Kokorov, a thick, brooding man who stood and walked with a hunch, and the other an American who was introduced as McKinnon, whom Ganin took to be John McKinnon, the head of the Secret Service contingent that had come here to Geneva to run security for President Bush. He was a tall, well-built man who, according to the information Yernin had provided, had been a New York City captain of detectives. He was bright and very streetwise.

Vilov said something to them, and they glanced up at Ganin. Vilov said something else and then sat down. A few others in the audience turned around for a look, but then McKinnon began the briefing by calling for reports from the various security details that were being manned jointly by the Americans and Russians with Swiss observers.

So far there had been no untoward incidents—a few instances of journalists who had barged into areas they had no business being in; a drunk who had gotten lost; two separate cases of Jewish extremist groups that had wanted to deliver a message to the Russian leaders—but nothing important.

President Bush would be arriving in Geneva in less than two

days, on Thursday at noon. Gorbachev would be coming in two hours afterward. Their first meeting would be held at a small dinner party that evening here on the palais grounds. They would meet again at ten in the morning. And at four in the afternoon the two leaders would sign the Geneva Accord in a ceremony, followed by speeches outside in the courtyard in front of the palais.

That evening the formal dinner would be held here at the palais, starting at eight. Gorbachev would be leaving that night for London and meetings with Margaret Thatcher. President Bush would be returning to the United States at eight the next morning.

Only five hundred diplomats and their wives would attend the dinner, but an expected crowd of more than ten thousand people would be at the speeches. Security would be extremely difficult to maintain, despite the fact that Bush and Gorbachev would be spending most of their time indoors or, while outside, behind a bulletproof Lexan screen at the speakers' platform.

"Gentlemen," McKinnon said, summing it up, "we all know perfectly well that under these conditions an intelligent, determined assassin is almost impossible to stop. It will be up to all of us to keep on our toes and pass that message down through the ranks."

Ganin sat back and touched the bulge of his gun beneath his jacket with his elbow. What good could he do if he simply followed his orders and kept his eyes open, but his mouth shut. What could two men do against a determined assassin that all these men could not?

Kokorov was at the lectern now, but Ganin listened with only half a mind. This evening he would write out his report, and in the morning he would fax it to Yernin. There was nothing here for him and Sepelev. Nothing that the Militia could do. He would recommend that despite the unsubstantiated nature of their information, it should be immediately turned over to the KGB. Short of that, President Gorbachev's plans should be changed.

He didn't know how far he would get, but he knew for certain now that there was nothing he and Sepelev could do here.

The Palais des Nations was headquarters for Woodrow Wilson's League of Nations from 1919 until 1936. Now it was the European headquarters for the United Nations.

Ganin had slipped out of the meeting early. There were no cabs and the evening was pleasant, so he started on foot toward the park exit at the Avenue de la Paix. There were a lot of trees here and well-manicured shrubs, walkways crisscrossing the entire area.

A hundred places for an assassin to hide. A thousand places where he would go unseen until the moment he struck. But if he was very good (as the generals said he was), then he would have a plan for escape, which of necessity limited his hiding places.

"You left early, Chief Investigator," someone said from behind him.

Ganin turned around as the Swiss cop Ernst Reisch came up from one of the side paths. His hands were in his pants pockets, his jacket flaps behind them, exposing his pistol. Ganin thought the pose was studied.

"Mr. Reisch," Ganin said politely.

"Ernst will do. And I would like to apologize for Joachim. He is young, and he gets himself excited sometimes. This is a very big business for him. The biggest."

Ganin nodded his understanding, and the Swiss cop fell in beside him. They continued toward the exit.

"How is it that you came to know my name?" Ganin asked.

"Ah, we Swiss are a very efficient lot," Reisch grinned. "At least our passport control officers are. But what intrigues me is why a pair of Moscow militia detectives have come to Geneva."

"Summit security."

"But I think it is more than that; otherwise I wouldn't bother with you. Quite frankly, Chief Investigator, you stand out like a sore thumb, if you know what I mean."

"It is an American expression."

"So it is. Have you ever been there?"

"No."

"Neither have I, but I hope to someday," Reisch said. "You and your partner are not registered with the security contingent here."

"Check again."

"You were not at the beginning. Why are you here?"

"As I have told you—"

Reisch pulled his hands out of his pockets and stopped to face Ganin. "You are carrying a weapon, yet you are not here on any business that is recognized as official by my government. For that I could have you deported from Switzerland. Immediately. Now, tonight."

"If I wanted to stay, I would be back by morning."

The Swiss cop's eyes narrowed. "What are you talking about?"

"We will most probably be leaving tomorrow."

"Then you have found what you came looking for?"

"There was nothing to find."

"Come on, Ganin, don't give me a line of horseshit. Someone went to a great deal of trouble to get you and your partner here. I want to know why."

"Is that another American expression? A line of horseshit?" Ganin asked. He shook his head. Imagine it, he thought. "Why aren't you back there with that group?"

Reisch glanced back toward the palais. "Not my department."

"What is?"

"Homicide. Which is what assassination is. How about you?"

Ganin looked a little closer at the Swiss cop. He did not look like a homicide detective or at least none of the ones he had come into contact with. That, of course, meant nothing. Yet there was something about him, some arrogance perhaps, that most homicide detectives did not have. Very probably Reisch worked for the Swiss Counterespionage Service, one of the best in the world.

"I, too, am a homicide detective."

"Then you are here chasing a murderer?"

"We thought it was possible that a suspect came here. But we may have been mistaken."

"Why here? Or let me put it another way. If your killer came to Geneva practically on the eve of the accord, then why haven't your Ninth Directorate people mentioned it? They should be getting nervous up there about now." Again Reisch shook his head. "Come on, Ganin, you tell me. What the hell is going on?"

"Nothing," Ganin said. He turned and started down the path.

"At least tell me what counterstrike down means," Reisch called after him.

Ganin turned back. "Where'd you hear that?" He could hardly believe the Swiss cop had said it.

"You tell me what it means and I'll tell you where it comes from."

Reisch was who he said he was, insofar as he worked for the

Swiss government. Vilov had confirmed at least that much. But did the generals' reach extend this far? He decided it was not likely.

Ganin walked back to him. "Counterstrike may have been the code word for a possible assassination attempt."

"Against whom?"

"I don't know."

Reisch started to object, but Ganin held him off.

"I don't know for certain, but I believe the target may have been our president."

Reisch was visibly shaken. "May have been?" he asked.

"You said counterstrike down. Negative. The assassination has apparently been called off. Where did you hear this?"

Reisch studied him for a long moment. "We intercepted a radio transmission last night."

"What was the origin of this transmission?"

"In the East somewhere. Moscow perhaps."

"Where was it beamed?"

"Here. To the West."

"What else was contained in the transmission?"

"So far as I know, nothing," Reisch said. "What about the identity of your assassin?"

"Unknown."

"Do you have a description, a name, anything?"

Ganin shook his head tiredly. What had happened to make the generals change their minds? What had spooked them? Better judgment, or the fact of Lieutenant Kobysh's death and the missing tape recording? He looked up. But that would mean that the generals or the GRU knew the details of his investigation. Knew what was contained in his reports to . . . Chief Prosecutor Yernin.

It had to be the GRU because the KGB had denied Kobysh. It knew nothing about the tape. In fact it would have no reason to suspect the existence of the recording. It would have reasoned, correctly, that the GRU had tumbled to Kobysh's true identity and had chased him to the Lubyanka's front door where the GRU killed him. Nothing more. It would explain why the KGB denied him. If it did not know he had discovered something, it would not want to tip its hand that he was indeed a KGB infiltrator into the military.

Reisch had been watching him closely. "What is it?"

Ganin blinked. "Nothing," he mumbled, turning away. "Nothing." If the assassin were still here in Switzerland, he would have him.

"Ganin," Reisch shouted after him, but Ganin ignored the Swiss cop. The answer was in the files they had brought with them.

He never saw Reisch raise the walkie-talkie to his lips, nor did he see the pair of headlights come on at the end of the block and the car pick up the Swiss cop.

By Swiss standards the Hôtel Moderne wasn't very nice; but compared with hotels in Moscow, it was fine, and Sepelev was enjoying himself.

He was halfway through the bottle of vodka and a plate of cheeses and pickled pigs' feet when Ganin returned.

"Fuck your mother, Nikki, but this isn't so bad."

"Pull out the file and tell me who the military attaché is at our embassy in Bern," Ganin said, pulling off his jacket and tossing it down on the bed. He went to the window and looked down at the street. Normal traffic, which meant nothing. Reisch and his people could be anywhere.

Sepelev had pulled out the thick manila folder Yernin had supplied them with. In it was a list of contacts here in Switzerland. "Major Oleg Lazarev."

"GRU," Ganin said.

"Naturally."

"Then he is our man, Yurii," Ganin said turning away from the window.

Sepelev's eyes were bright. "The assassin?"

"Next best. The assassin's contact."

10

The fire engine red Mercedes 500 SEL convertible pulled up the sweeping driveway of the Beau-Rivage, Geneva's finest luxury hotel, a few minutes after two in the afternoon. Two doormen, uniformed in cutaway coats and plumed hats, hurried to help the gentleman with his three pieces of obviously expensive luggage. He preferred to carry his own attaché case.

"I will be here several days, during which I will have no need of the car. If you would be so good as to find a secure parking place for it?"

"Yes, sir," the one doorman said, and Moran handed him a fifty Swiss franc note.

"Have you been to Geneva before, monsieur?" the doorman asked.

"Yes, many times. It is a lovely city."

"Just now very busy."

Moran was dressed in an English tweed jacket, gray slacks, and highly polished jodhpurs. He strode imperiously through the immense lobby and approached the front desk. His reservations had been telephoned ahead for him by the George V, his hotel in Paris. Only a suite was left. It suited him just fine.

"Good afternoon, Mr. Peyton," the clerk said. "I hope you had a pleasant drive from Paris."

"Very nice, thanks," Moran said. There had been no need to state his name; the clerk had accurately guessed it. He handed over his platinum American Express card, and the clerk slid a registration card across to him.

"If you will just sign this, sir. And fill in your passport number, please. Your suite is ready."

Moran did so. His passport was British, identifying him only by name. He signed the register as Major General N. Peyton, London.

"Ah, General, sorry, sir," the clerk said. "I was not informed of your rank."

"Mr. Peyton," Moran said. "I'm here in mufti, you understand." He handed the man a hundred-franc note.

"Of course," the clerk said, smiling. "I understand perfectly. If there is anything I can do to be of assistance, please don't hesitate to call either me or the concierge."

"There is one thing for now. I would like my presence here kept confidential."

"Naturally."

"No telephone calls or messages are to be accepted on my behalf."

"I understand," the clerk said. He returned Moran's credit card and gave the suite key to the bellman. "I trust your stay with us will be pleasant."

"Yes," Moran said. "And profitable."

"Ah, but then this is Geneva," the clerk said.

Riding up on the elevator, Moran allowed himself just a moment of smug satisfaction. All had gone exceedingly well to this point. He had gotten cleanly out of the Caribbean, despite the last-minute complications; he had conducted his business on Jersey, and he had made his way onto the Continent without being detected. From Paris onward, however, he had begun to lay down his track. The clerks and concierge staffs at the George V and here at the Beau-Rivage would not forget him: He was the good-looking *pale* Englishman who paid so well.

In a little more than twenty-four hours his work here would be completed, and he would melt into the background. Major General Newton Peyton would simply cease to exist. It would be as if the earth had swallowed him.

The first two digits of the telephone number the Russian messenger had supplied him with were three-zero, which placed his contact in the city of Bern.

It rang three times before a man answered. *"Da?"*

"It is me," Moran said in Russian. He stood at a public phone in the Cornavin Main Railroad Station half a dozen blocks off the lake. The concourse was filled with people, and the noise level was very high, echoing off the marble floors and vaulted ceilings.

For several long seconds there was only silence on the line. Moran thought that the connection might have been broken and he was about to hang up when the man finally spoke.

"Counterstrike down."

"What?" Moran asked sharply.

Again there was a hesitation, but this time, when the man was back, he spoke in English. "I said counterstrike down. Do you understand what I am telling you?"

Something was wrong. Why English? What did this bastard know? He stepped a little closer into the shadows and turned his face away from the main entrance.

"Do you know who I am?" he asked.

"Listen, it has been called off. I don't know what has gone wrong, but that message has come from a very high source. The highest. You must not go ahead."

The GRU messenger had been lying, or he himself had been lied to. Whoever this contact was, he knew about the plan, and it was even possible that he knew Moran's identity. Here in Switzerland. It was galling.

"We must meet," Moran said. "Tonight. Can you come to Geneva?"

"Impossible. You don't understand—"

"It is you who do not understand. I have some very important information that I cannot tell you on an open line. It is too dangerous. We must meet tonight. Can you come to Geneva?"

"Yes, it is very dangerous . . . but where will we meet?"

"The cathedral. Do you know it?"

"St. Peter's, yes. It is under reconstruction. What time?"

"Ten o'clock. How will I know you?"

"You won't, but I will know you. Besides, there will be no other people there at that time."

"Come alone," Moran said.

"Of course. What do you take me for?"

He dressed in dark clothing and left the hotel unseen through a back exit. The Beau-Rivage was on the Quai du Mont Blanc, facing the lake. At nine in the evening there were a lot of people strolling arm in arm. In a way it reminded him of the Riviera at Nice. Out on the lake the big fountain spewed water high into the air, beyond which during the day Mont Blanc could be seen. But this evening everything beyond the spume was in glittering darkness as Moran headed toward the river.

He kept off the main avenues and boulevards as much as possible, working his way up the slight hill that rose into the Old Town. This part of the city was mostly quiet in the evening, although there were a few small restaurants here and there. There was less traffic and fewer pedestrians than along the quays.

He had to duck back into the shadows of a shop doorway when a blue and white police car crossed the intersection at the Rue du Rhône. When it was gone, he turned up another side street and hurried the last couple of blocks to the big cathedral.

A plywood construction barrier surrounded the church. Along the north side there was a door, which Moran pushed open. He stepped inside. The cathedral's tower rose solidly two hundred feet into the sky. Yellow ribbons stretched across the courtyard, marking the path to the entrance.

He pulled out his Beretta automatic, checked to make sure a round was in the firing chamber, and then screwed the bulky Kevlar silencer onto the specially threaded barrel.

The front face of the cathedral was well illuminated by floodlights, but just within the fence the courtyard was in darkness, as were the upper reaches of the tower. He waited in the darkness for several long minutes, listening for sounds, any sounds from inside. There would almost certainly be a night watchman here. Except for the occasional traffic, however, the night was quiet.

Keeping the pistol hidden behind his right leg, he made his way down the path and entered the church through an ancient wooden door that swung silently on thick black hinges. It was dark in the outer corridor. But through the main doors into the nave he could see the scaffolding rising up to the vaulted ceilings. A thick odor of displaced brick and mortar dust along with oil-based paint hung in the air.

He turned and followed yellow marks taped on the stone floor toward the doorway into the north tower. He moved slowly on the balls of his feet, and as he walked, he flicked the Beretta's safety to the off position. He was suddenly smelling cigarette smoke.

The door to the north tower was open. A dim yellow light shown from within. Here the smell of cigarette smoke was much stronger, and Moran heard a man cough and shuffle his feet. He was very close.

Flattening himself against the stone wall, Moran eased around the edge so that he could just see into the stair hall. A old man in a guard's uniform sat at a small table next to the roped-off stairway. He was reading a magazine, a freshly lit cigarette dangling from the side of his mouth. He was alone.

Moran cocked the Beretta's hammer and stepped around the corner. The guard, hearing or sensing something, lowered his magazine and looked up.

"*Alors . . .*" he had started to say when Moran raised his pistol and calmly shot the man in the face. The bullet hit him just below the left eye, driving him backward, crashing off his chair to the floor.

Moran stepped back out into the corridor and waited a moment to make certain that no one had heard the noise and was coming. When he was satisfied that no one else was in the church, he went back and checked the guard's pulse. The man was definitely dead. He grinned.

He turned off the table light and in the darkness unhooked the rope from the stairway and hurried up to the bell chamber. He was barely winded at the top.

All Geneva was spread out below him, the city lights turning to darkness across the flat mass of the big lake, although in the distance to the north he thought he might be seeing the lights of Versoix.

Directly below he could see the street and the construction

fence through which he had entered church grounds. Two cars came up the Rue du Vieux Collège. One of them pulled over and parked, but the other continued, turned down the block at the next corner, and disappeared toward the lake.

Moran checked his watch. It was a few minutes before ten. A lone man got out of the parked car, hesitated for a moment, then, looking both ways up the street, crossed directly to the cathedral and entered the gate in the construction fence.

Moran turned and hurried back down the stairs to the stair hall, then across to the corridor doorway. He was in time to hear the outer door open and moments later close.

For a long time there were no sounds. Whoever had come in was remaining just within the doorway.

"In here," Moran called softly.

There was no answer.

"The north tower." Moran called out again.

He heard the footfalls starting down the corridor, and he rushed back to the stairs and started up, stopping on the third landing. It was pitch-black in the stairwell.

"Show yourself," someone said below. It was the same voice from the telephone.

"In the bell chamber. I want to make sure that you were not followed," Moran said, and he hurried the rest of the way up into the tower, stopping every few landings to make sure the other man was still behind him.

At the top he crossed to the diagonal corner and stood in the deep shadows between the open arches. He held the gun loosely in his right hand. He could hear the man coming up the last few stairs.

"In here," Moran said. "No one has followed you. We are safe." He glanced down at the street. Nothing moved.

The man stepped out of the stairwell and stopped. In the light from outside, Moran could see that he was of medium height and build but with very thick dark hair and a square face.

"Where are you? I cannot see you."

"Here," Moran said from the darkness, and the other man turned his way. It was obvious that he still could not see Moran.

"The assignment has been terminated. You may keep the money we have already given you, but it is over. Now, what is this important information you have for me?"

"Are you armed?"

The man hesitated but then shook his head. "No, I am not. I thought with a man such as—with you that it would be foolish. If you wanted to kill me, there would be nothing I could do to prevent it."

Moran stepped out of the darkness into the light spilling through the arches. "Come here," he said. "I want to show you something."

"Bring it here."

"You must see in the light."

The man hesitated again, but then he came across to Moran. He stopped short, his eyes growing wide, when he saw the gun. But Moran handed it to him, butt first.

"You must get rid of this for me."

The Russian looked at him. "I don't understand."

"I may have been traced into Switzerland with this weapon. It's become too dangerous for me. It's what I wanted to tell you. I'm going to need some help getting out of the country. You must have the connections. You're GRU, aren't you?"

The Russian said nothing, but he took the gun, an odd expression crossing his features. "It's warm," he said.

"Never mind. Now what about getting me out of here?"

The Russian unscrewed the silencer and stuffed it and the pistol into his jacket pocket. "There is nothing much I can do for you. At least not now. Not until the summit is over. Is there someplace you can hide until afterward? Maybe something could be worked out."

"All right," Moran said. "In the meantime, I want to know what has gone wrong. Does someone know about me?"

"I don't know, but I don't think so. I think the trouble is in Moscow. There was some KGB prick who may have found out something."

"Are we going to try again?"

"I don't know that either. But maybe."

"I just want to know what I should do."

"I don't know what you're worried about, Moran. You've been well paid."

Moran looked at him. This one knew. How many others were there? "Did you tell anyone you were meeting me tonight?"

"Of course not. What do you take me for?"

"You've already asked me that once," Moran said. He stepped back as if he were suddenly overcome with fear, and he glanced out of the arch. "It's over," he mumbled half under his breath.

The Russian stepped closer. "What?" he asked.

Moran turned back, grabbed a handful of the man's jacket, and in one easy movement pulled him around. The Russian's right hip just caught the steel safety rail, and his body flipped out over the edge through the arch.

"No," the man screamed, but then his head smashed on a stone ledge ten feet beneath the arch and his body was flung away from the tower and plummeted silently to the pavement.

11

Across from the cathedral the side street was in darkness. Ganin and Yurii Sepelev had parked their rental car and hurried back in time to see the Soviet military attaché disappear through the construction fence. A few minutes later they heard the shout.

"What the hell was that?" Sepelev asked.

Ganin stepped out of the shadows. "It came from the other side of the tower."

"He's in there. The assassin," Sepelev said. He was agitated.

They had been tailing Oleg Lazarev all day, knowing finally that they were on the right track when the man drove down here to Geneva. He hadn't had a clue that he was being followed; that made their job easier. Anytime but now Ganin figured he might wait it out, separate Lazarev from the assassin. But Gorbachev and Bush were already in the city. In less than twenty-four hours they would be signing the accord and would be making their speeches outside in front of thousands of people.

He could not take the risk.

Ganin took out his Makarov pistol and checked to make sure it was ready to fire. Sepelev was impressed. He pulled out his own pistol.

"We're not going to shoot anybody unless it becomes absolutely necessary, Yurochka," Ganin said softly.

Sepelev nodded. He was shivering. He had never been on anything this important, and more than once he confided to Ganin that he didn't want to fuck up. This was his chance.

"Watch yourself," Ganin said as they started across the street. "He'll be very good."

"An ambush artist. I'll bet the bastard never shot anyone face-to-face."

"Neither have you," Ganin said.

They went the rest of the way in silence, letting themselves into the church grounds through the gate in the construction fence. For a few seconds they stood in the relative darkness. Nothing moved.

Ganin looked toward the top of the tower, which disappeared above the upper reaches of the spotlights. Who had called out and why?

"Check the other side of the tower. I'll try inside."

Sepelev stepped over the yellow ribbon marking the walk to the church entrance and headed across to the north tower. When he was gone, Ganin followed the path and pushed the door open gently with the toe of his shoe. He flattened himself against the rough stone wall and listened for a long second or two before he stepped inside, keeping low, sweeping his pistol left to right.

No one was there. Only the darkness greeted him in the broad corridor, and the vague outlines of scaffolding in the nave. And yet something had happened here. Just moments ago. He tightened his grip on his pistol.

Someone outside came running along the cobblestones. Ganin swung around and dropped to one side as Sepelev appeared.

"Nikki?" he whispered urgently.

"Here," Ganin said, stepping out of the darkness.

"It's Lazarev. He's dead. Splattered all over the pavement around the other side of the tower."

"Are you sure it's him?"

Sepelev nodded. "Looks like he fell from the top. Or was pushed."

"Which means the assassin is still inside," Ganin said. "And he knows we're here."

He turned and went back into the church, motioning for Sepelev to take the opposite side of the corridor, and together they headed toward the tower, careful to make as little noise as possible. It was at least thirty meters away. As they got closer, Ganin thought he smelled cigarette smoke.

He raised his hand for Sepelev to hold up and then carefully approached the open door himself, just easing around the corner. The cigarette smell was much stronger here. The room was dimly lit only by what filtered through a small square leaded glass window.

He entered the tower stair hall and was moving toward the stairs when he spotted a figure lying on the floor. He pulled up short. He knew what it was. He had seen enough bodies in his career.

"What?" Sepelev asked.

Ganin went forward and bent down over the dead guard, whose face was puffed up from the tremendous force of the bullet. There wasn't much blood, which meant he had died instantly.

But there was cigarette smoke. Straightening up, Ganin spotted the still-lit cigarette in the corner across the room. It was barely ashes by now and nearly out, but it meant that the guard had been killed only minutes ago. Just before the shout.

"Who killed him?" Sepelev had started to ask when they heard the outside door softly close, the latch echoing sharply when it fell.

"Shit," Ganin swore, spinning around. "It's him." He shoved past Sepelev and headed in a dead run down the corridor. The assassin had evidently hidden in the darkness, probably in the nave, until they had passed and then had slipped outside.

He reached the door and tore it open just as the plywood door in the construction fence banged shut. A car passed outside on the street, and in the distance he thought he could hear a siren.

Sepelev was directly behind him as he raced down the cobblestoned path and yanked open the door.

The figure of a man dressed in dark clothing was walking down the street, angling toward the corner a half a block away.

Ganin ran out into the street and raised his pistol. "*Stoi! Stoi! Militia!*" he shouted, and he fired three shots in rapid succession as the dark figure sprinted for the corner and disappeared. He knew damned well he had missed. It was too far.

Car tires screeched behind him.

Ganin turned around as a police car slammed to a halt and two police officers, their pistols drawn, scrambled out.

"*Halt! Polizei!*" one of them shouted.

Sepelev was staring at them openmouthed. Ganin smiled bitterly and raised his hands over his head. "Do as they say, Yurochka."

Police headquarters was located around the corner from City Hall just a couple of blocks from the cathedral. Nobody had said much of anything to them although their Moscow Militia identification booklets had raised a few eyebrows.

They were being held in a small interrogation room furnished only with a steel table and four chairs. Ganin had earlier asked to speak to someone from the Soviet Embassy or short of that, with Colonel Kokorov, who, he explained, was chief of security for President Gorbachev. His request could have fallen on deaf ears, though they were not treated unkindly.

At quarter to three in the morning the door opened and Ernst Reisch came in. They caught a glimpse of Joachim Mueller in the corridor.

Reisch laid a thick file folder on the table and sat down. "I have been in contact with your embassy, which in turn assures me that Colonel Vilov will be around shortly to collect you." He looked earnestly at Ganin and then Sepelev before turning to his file folder and opening it. "We have worked with incredible speed this evening and morning. I hope you will appreciate our efforts to expedite this matter so that you will be allowed to leave. I hope you will also appreciate that we are doing this out of respect for the fact you are fellow police officers."

"Has the man I shot at been picked up?" Ganin asked.

"The police officers on the scene are quite certain they saw no one."

"The bastard must have crossed the street right in front of

them," Sepelev shouted. "Do you hire blind men to drive your radio cars?"

"The dead man at the base of the tower has been identified as Oleg Lazarev, the military attaché from your embassy."

"We know," Sepelev snapped, unable to keep silent.

Reisch turned to him. "Do you also know, Investigator, that the gun that killed the church guard was found on *Colonel* Lazarev's body?" He accented the rank.

"But there was a third man in the church," Ganin said calmly. "I saw him."

"Describe him for me."

"Medium height, medium build, wearing dark clothing."

Reisch looked at him, a faint smirk on his lips. "Large nose, wide eyes, perhaps blue, chief investigator? Distinguishing marks? A tattoo on his left forearm, perhaps? A scar on his forehead?"

"I don't know," Ganin admitted.

"No," Reisch said. "Now you will tell me, please, what you were doing at St. Peter's at ten o'clock in the evening?"

There was absolutely nothing to be heard in the small sound-proofed room except for the faraway hum of air conditioners. They could have been five thousand meters beneath the surface of the ocean.

"Was Lazarev your would-be assassin?" Reisch asked. "Did you kill him?"

"No. There was a third man there, as I have told you," Ganin said. "Were there any other marks of injury on Lazarev's body? Gunshot wounds?"

"None. No signs of a struggle so far as our pathologist can determine. He jumped, fell accidentally, or was pushed when he wasn't expecting it. Perhaps by someone he knew. Perhaps someone he was meeting there."

"It's how I see it," Ganin said.

Reisch was about to speak; but then something crossed his mind, and his expression changed. "Ah," he said. "It was the message we intercepted. Counterstrike down. It was directed to Lazarev, who we know worked for the GRU. It was he who was passing the message on to your assassin."

Ganin said nothing. Reisch was working it out for himself in big leaps of intuition.

"Either that or the GRU was on to the plot as well as the

Militia . . . but I don't think so. I think it's a military plot to kill
your president. Is that what you're trying to tell me, Chief Investigator? God in heaven."

"I don't know."

"But I think you do. You followed Lazarev from Bern, didn't
you? Right to St. Peter's. Who is he, your assassin? Have you any
idea?"

"No," Ganin said after a beat. "But he is here in Geneva, and
I suspect that he killed Lazarev despite the message. Which means
he intends going ahead with it."

"Is he Swiss?"

"I don't know."

"Russian?"

"We are not a nation that breeds assassins, though it is not
unknown."

"Neither are we," Reisch said. He closed his file folder and
got to his feet. "Your people will be here soon to pick you up."

"In the meantime, I would like to speak with your passport
control people. Perhaps there is something we can pick out—"

Reisch was shaking his head. "You do not understand. You
and your partner are leaving Switzerland in just a few hours.
There is a flight out at eight. There will only be enough time for
you to collect your bags from your hotel and get out to the airport."

"You mustn't," Ganin said, getting up.

"I have no choice. You fired a weapon, yet you were not here
on official business. If you had only come with me when I asked,
we might have been able to set up something at the church. Your
assassin would not have escaped. As it is, he is now alerted, but
contrary to your belief, I do not think he will be so foolish as to
go ahead with his plan. Even now he is probably escaping across
the border."

Ganin nodded. "And good riddance to him, correct?"

Reisch looked at him coldly.

"As long as he is off Swiss soil. As long as it was only a Russian
who was killed."

"The church guard—"

"Who you believe was murdered by Lazarev." Ganin smiled
sardonically. "Very neat, Herr Reisch. Very Swiss. Very efficient."

Reisch turned without a word and left the interrogation room.

"What do we do now, Nikki?" Sepelev asked.

"There isn't much we can do except get aboard the airplane

like good gentlemen and allow the Swiss Federal Police to handle this matter."

Something in the way Ganin said it struck Sepelev, and he glanced pointedly at the ceiling and then back at Ganin, who nodded. The message had been passed between them that the interrogation room was bugged. Russians were old hands at that sort of thing.

At six-thirty they were led upstairs, where Feliks Vilov was waiting for them. Their identification booklets and other personal effects were returned. But their weapons would have to remain in Switzerland for thirty days. It was the law.

Outside, they got into the back seat of a large Mercedes sedan, and the driver pulled out into traffic.

"Your suitcases are in the trunk," the KGB station chief said. "We are going directly to the airport."

"What about the assassin?" Ganin asked. "Has Colonel Kokorov been informed?"

"Yes, he has. As a matter of fact, he and Ernst Reisch along with John McKinnon are working together on this matter."

"It's a GRU plot—"

"Let me finish, Chief Investigator," Vilov said harshly. "We do not need the Militia to tell us our business. There is much here that you do not understand."

"Yes?"

"We happen to agree with the Swiss that the assassin has left the country. He knew that someone was on to him when you two showed up at the church, and by now he is out. He would be insane to do otherwise."

"If not?"

Vilov looked at him contemptuously. "Go home, Nikolai Fedorovich, and chase your wife beaters, drunks, and black marketeers. Moscow is crawling with them."

The morning sun streaming through the high arched windows illuminated the chandeliers, paintings, brocade chairs, and the long table in the Hall of Presidents.

For the past twenty-four hours the place had been a beehive of activity. Stewards had been busy setting up the huge room for the signing ceremony. Soviet, American, and Swiss security people had been crawling all over the place. And the electronic media people had been busy setting up their equipment here and outside at the podium where the speeches would take place.

Unable to sleep, Mary Frances had gotten up early and had left her hotel for the Palais des Nations. Technically her work here in Geneva was finished. And it had been hectic but satisfying. Jack Dillinger, the *World News This Week* Geneva bureau chief, was pleased. Her senior editor, Bob Liskey, back in New York was pleased as was the ME, Lawrence Weaver. But most of all, she was pleased with what she had done. She had handled herself very well in her private interviews with Bush and with Gorbachev. So well that a number of the other journalists had afterward come to her for advice about both men, about the continuing development of *perestroika* and *glasnost*, about the relations between the United States and the Soviet Union, and her thoughts on the accord.

It was heady stuff; but after this afternoon's ceremonies it would be over and done, and she would be on a plane back to New York. She wanted to savor the last hours.

"Self-congratulation is a particularly nasty habit," Dillinger said. He had come out with her to make sure everything was set up for the photographers. He was a tall, thin man, without a single hair on his head, not even eyebrows.

Mary Frances laughed. "A woman's prerogative."

"Don't let it go to your head, kid. It's ruined more than one good reporter."

"Not to worry."

Dillinger smiled wryly. "It's my job," he said, and spotting one of his photographers, he hurried across the long hall.

Mary Frances worked her way around to the back center of the long, highly polished table, where Bush and Gorbachev would actually sign the accord documents, which were bound in a tall red leather volume. She rested her hands on the back of one of the chairs and looked across the room. She could feel the power here. These were the fingers that pushed the buttons. They were more powerful than Adolf Hitler or even Joseph Stalin, but she had discovered that they were merely men. Charming at times, nervous at others.

Her father had told her a story about Winston Churchill. It was during the war, before she was born, when the British leader came to the air squadron at Blenley shortly after his "We shall fight on the beaches" speech, which had so inflamed the British spirit. He came over to shake the hand of each pilot who was helping keep the Germans at bay over the Channel, and when it was her father's turn, he told her that he was nearly bowled over. The old man was a heavy smoker and was known to drink a few, and at that moment he smelled like a Soho pub on the morning after. His breath had been absolutely horrible. He was just a man, after all, with his own set of faults.

"Miss," someone said at her elbow.

She turned as an American Secret Service agent, his security badge clipped to his lapel pocket, came up. He smiled.

"I'll ask you to step away from the table now. No one is allowed this close. Security." He smiled again. She had seen him around.

Mary Frances looked across the hall again from over the back of the chair. Power. Her father had never been able to listen to Winston Churchill again with the same awe. Nor would she be able to see Bush or Gorbachev in the same light as before this week.

"Sure," she said, turning back to the agent.

Ganin and Sepelev had spent an unpleasant couple of hours in the airport VIP lounge with Feliks Vilov, who had remained to make certain they took the flight.

Their plane was going first to Paris, where they would switch to the Aeroflot flight direct to Moscow, so Ganin had insisted they keep their overnight bags with them. Vilov had no real objections; he merely wanted to see them off and get back into the city.

When it was time to leave, they all stood and shook hands formally. "My report will be favorable," the KGB station chief said. He attempted to smile.

"Thank you, comrade," Ganin said pleasantly.

"It is too bad about Colonel Lazarev, but your job was to stop a possible assassination attempt. You have done just that."

"My report will be inclusive as well," Ganin said. "It will, of course, mention your contributions."

Vilov wasn't quite sure how to take that, but he nodded. "Have a good flight home."

"We will," Ganin said, and he and Sepelev turned, handed their boarding passes to the attendant, and entered the boarding tunnel.

"The *pizda*," Sepelev mumbled under his breath.

At the first turn Ganin pulled him aside and let the couple behind them pass. "Wait."

"What now?"

"Just a minute," Ganin said softly.

A half dozen other people came down the tunnel from the lounge, and then there was no one else. They could hear the murmurs of people talking in the aircraft hatchway and the high-pitched whine of the idling jet engines.

"Let's go," Ganin said.

"Where?"

"Geneva, of course. The Palais des Nations."

Sepelev grinned broadly.

The VIP lounge was empty except for the bartender, two stewards, and the boarding clerk. Vilov was gone.

The clerk looked up, a surprised, concerned expression on his face, when they reemerged from the boarding tunnel. "Sir. Is something wrong?"

"No," Ganin said. "There is something of importance that we must do first."

"I'm afraid that the flight cannot be held up, sir—"

"It's all right," Ganin said reassuringly. "We'll catch the next one. Thank you."

Donald Moran sat back in the cab as it turned left off the Avenue de France onto the Place des Nations, where they were stopped for the first security check. It was a few minutes past two. Security throughout the United Nations compound was tight despite the dense crowds.

He had been jumpy all morning after what had happened last night. For a time he had even considered calling the entire thing off. But he had dreamed again about the dark angel coming to him out of the pitch-black night; from the jungles of Nam, where he'd first seen him, out of the Negev desert, out of the sea, out of the highlands of Colombia. Each time it was the same; the apparition gave him the ultimate choice: Kill or be killed. Blood must be spilled, yours or theirs. Protect yourself. Insulate yourself carefully and completely because the VC are coming. The avengers. The stalkers. They are all around us. They must be stopped. It is your only salvation.

Blinking, he cranked down the window as two West German soldiers wearing United Nations helmets and blue and white armbands approached.

They came to attention and saluted when they saw his uniform. He was dressed as a U.S. Army major general.

He returned the salute and handed out his orders and identification.

"*Entschuldigen, Herr General*, but we were not told of your visit," the captain, whose name tag read "SCHILLER" said crisply. He quickly scanned the orders. The other man was a sergeant with a broad forehead and narrow pig eyes.

Already several cars had pulled up behind them. Other soldiers were watching them. Beyond the striped barrier Moran could see the crowds and the television remote trucks and satellite dishes.

"Of course not, this is an inspection tour," Moran said. His orders identified him as a special security investigator with the inspector general's office at SHAPE (Supreme Headquarters Allied Powers in Europe) in Heidelberg.

"You will need a pass, nevertheless, *Herr General*, and you will have to sign in."

"No pass," Moran snapped. "I was never here, do I make myself clear?"

The captain glanced down the entry road toward a pair of military vans. "I must report all entries."

"When your duty shift is over, not before," Moran said. He took a spare set of orders out of his briefcase and handed them over. "Keep these, Captain. I understand your position."

Still, the man seemed uncertain.

"Of course, you may send an escort to see that my driver leaves as soon as I am dropped off," Moran said. He stared up at the West German officer. The sergeant had backed up a pace and stood flat-footed, his right hand on the butt of his pistol in its holster. He looked very determined. Even more cars were backed up now. They were creating too much attention here.

"If need be, Captain Schiller, call your superior officer for instructions. But be quick about it," Moran said. His left hand went carefully into his still-open briefcase; his fingers curled around the substantial grip of the nine-millimeter Graz Buyra automatic.

The captain hesitated a moment longer, then nodded and handed Moran's ID back through the window. "Sorry for the delay, sir." He turned to his sergeant. "Follow them, make sure the driver returns as soon as he drops off the general."

"*Jawohl, Herr Kapitän*," the sergeant said.

The captain turned back, saluted, then walked around the front of the cab and raised the striped barrier. He stood aside as the cab moved slowly through, and the sergeant came up behind them in his jeep.

"Where do you wished to be dropped, *mein Herr*," the cabby asked.

"The International Red Cross," Moran said without hesitation.

Gorbachev and the American President would come outside at four-fifteen. Moran glanced at his watch. It would happen in less than two hours. He smiled.

Moran emerged from the International Red Cross head-quarters building twenty minutes later, a red-bordered all-sections security badge clipped to his uniform lapel, and strode purposefully across the rear mall toward the World Health Organization headquarters building adjacent to the palais itself.

The briefcase from Jersey was heavy, but he swung it as if it were light. It was part of his deception.

Be obvious in your coloration and tradecraft so that those who look upon you will see exactly what they expect to see.

He'd learned the CIA's drill. Those who did survived. Those who did not fell by the wayside, either gunned down by a security officer somewhere or, more rarely, convicted and left to rot in some third world prison cell.

Most of this afternoon's activity was out front, along the main mall and traffic circle, although many of the electronic vans and trucks that the various television networks had brought were set up in the rear parking areas, their thick cables snaking in some cases through open ground-floor windows and in others up to the roof. A few technicians watched from open doors as he walked past but then went back to their work. The UN compound was crawling with military officers; even two-star generals rated no special attention.

Under normal circumstances more than a thousand people were employed in the various offices throughout the compound. Over the period of the summit meetings that number had nearly doubled. Today, however, was a holiday. No regular business was being conducted. In fact, most of the offices were deserted. Those who had managed to get security badges had gone around front to watch the ceremonies. The others had wisely remained at home, where they could see everything on television.

Moran threaded his way through the television vans and

crossed the parking lot. He mounted the stairs to the main rear entrance of the WHO building.

The door was locked, as he expected it would be. He rang the buzzer. Moments later the door was opened by an Italian army lieutenant in battle fatigues, the blue and white armband above his left elbow identifying him as UN Security.

"Who else is on security detail with you on this floor?" Moran demanded.

The Italian officer came to attention. "I am alone here, *signore generale*."

"What about upstairs?"

"On the roof. But begging the general's pardon . . ."

Moran opened his briefcase and reached inside. "Yes?"

"I have not been told of your visit."

"No," Moran said, smiling gently. He cocked the Graz Buyra's hammer as he withdrew the weapon, and he fired one shot at point-blank range into the face of the Italian, whose head snapped back as he was driven to the floor.

The noise of the silenced shot echoed dully in the broad corridor. Fifty feet away it would not have been heard or recognized for what it was.

Moran waited for a second or two to make certain that no alarm would be sounded, and when the building remained silent, he turned and made certain that the rear door was locked. After setting his briefcase aside and jamming the pistol in his belt, he dragged the Italian's body into the women's rest room across the corridor. He propped it up on one of the toilets and closed and locked the stall door. He climbed over the top and on the other side grabbed a wad of paper towels from the dispenser.

Back in the corridor he wiped up the blood from the floor and then disposed of the paper towels in the women's room.

Time. It almost always came down to that. If the Italian officer was missed, it was unlikely that anyone would think to look in the toilet stalls in the women's room. At least not at first.

Of course, by then it might not matter. A room-by-room search of the building could be conducted. The ceremony outside could be canceled or delayed.

The fourth-floor corridor was empty like the others. There was the fifth floor above, then the attic, and finally the roof.

For a moment he considered the security people stationed

up there. He had expected them. They were a significant factor, but one which he had accounted for.

Slipping out of the stairwell, he moved silently to the end of the corridor and knocked at the last door. There was no sound from within. Taking a slender case-hardened steel needle from a leather case in his pocket, he had the old lock picked in under twenty seconds, and he let himself in. He closed and relocked the door. He propped a chair under the doorknob.

Putting his briefcase on the desk, he went to the window as he unbuttoned his uniform blouse. The traffic circle and broad lawn were filled with thousands of people, cordoned off from the inner mall by more than a hundred UN security forces. From this vantage point he was looking down over the dozens of snapping flags directly onto the podium, which was set on a raised platform and backed by the UN symbol.

Stepping away from the direct line of sight of anyone below, he unlatched the window lock and slowly raised the bottom half.

He watched the crowds for a full sixty seconds to make certain no one had spotted him. When he was satisfied that no one had, he backed away from the window and took off his blouse, hanging it on the back of another chair.

Opening his briefcase, he withdrew the four sections of his single-shot 50 mm sniper rifle and began assembling it.

"Ah, General, what a pleasant surprise."

Moscow Town Prosecutor Arkadi Yernin, wearing only a snow-white towel around his waist, crossed from the changing rooms to the bathing pool. Faintly sulfurous steam rose from the water.

General Anatoli Zuyev, nude, was seated alone at a low table ladened with spiced vodkas, mineral water, bread, caviar, salmon, and other delicacies. They were fifty meters below the Alexander Garden just across the avenue from the Kremlin. The bathhouse had been built over a fifteen-year period starting in 1885. The walls were lined with aromatic cedar, the floors were paved with Carrara marble, and crystal chandeliers hung from the tall ceilings. The membership was strictly limited.

"You look like shit, Arkadi Alekseyevich," the general said, looking up. He shook his head. "The first strong wind that comes along will blow you away like a straw man."

"Then it might be wise if I hid behind you. In the lee, so to speak."

"All of Moscow does."

"As goes Moscow, so goes the Union," Yernin said, repeating the oft-told formula used by conservatives and radicals alike.

The general poured him a vodka and heaped a pile of caviar on a thin slice of white bread. "It's Iranian. The best."

Yernin smiled as he ate it in one bite. "They would kill to have this in the States."

"Perhaps we could set up an export company. They won't buy direct from the ayatollahs, but maybe they would from you, with your connections."

"Ah," Yernin said, touching a fingertip to the side of his nose. "It is *glasnost* combined with democracy. Interesting new combinations for us to consider. Is socialism dead, or are we simply reaching for new heights? For new planes of existence?"

He drank his vodka and poured another for himself as well as another for Zuyev.

"Falling into the sewer," the general grumbled. He was a large barrel-chested man with thick dark hair and bushy eyebrows reminiscent of Brezhnev. His men called him the bastard both affectionately as well as disparagingly. Nearing eighty, he could and often did beat men twenty-five years younger in a whole host of endeavors, not the least of which were leg wrestling and vodka drinking.

"But that's right, you're a Shishkin man. You want the old days."

"Take care, Arkasha, you are merely a Moscow town prosecutor."

"And you are simply the Moscow Defense District commander. Neither of us is above the law."

The general's eyes narrowed. He looked very dangerous just then. "I will support my government to the death. My forces are committed. And as you say, as goes Moscow, so goes the Union. It is something to keep in mind."

"Yes, one would do well to keep such things in mind. And it is already after three in Geneva. Within the hour the accord will be signed."

"Yes."

"With no interference."

"None," the general said.

"Although you feel it is wrong."

General Zuyev shook his head in irritation. He sat forward, his meaty forearms on the black lacquered tabletop. "Look to the west, Arkasha, and study what you see."

"What might that be?"

"Europe is gone."

"We had no need of it."

"You have a very short memory. The Germans will rearm, and we will be in trouble again, with absolutely nothing on European soil to defend ourselves with. Is that what you want? But then you were just a snot-nosed little prick when the Germans drove through our front door."

"Not so young I didn't raise a rifle at the end."

"Even worse. Now you think you have the right to tell the rest of us not to worry."

"On the contrary, I think we all have very much to worry about. Much to repair, much to . . . change."

Zuyev looked at him for a long moment or two, the expression in his eyes unreadable. "So it is true what they say," he said finally.

Yernin shrugged.

"That you were corrupted by the West. Perhaps you should have stayed. You could have become a banker, an entrepreneur. I hear the opportunities are there for everyone."

"And here, too."

Sergeant Sergei Anastratov, the general's bodyguard, came from the changing rooms. He wore a towel around his neck. He was a very large man, and Yernin could not recall ever seeing him smile. He had been with Zuyev since before Afghanistan.

General Zuyev looked up.

"Pardon me, Comrade General, but you have a visitor who wishes to have a word with you."

Zuyev nodded and got ponderously to his feet.

"Ah, but then there is no reason for you to go out into the chilly corridor. Have your guest shown in. I think we can bend the club rules just a little."

"It's not necessary," Zuyev said.

"I insist."

"No," the general said with a faint smile, and he followed Anastratov around the pool and through the doors.

As soon as they were out of sight, Yernin got to his feet and, with a glass of vodka in hand, ambled around the pool to the changing alcoves adjacent to the entry hall. Pulling the curtain closed, he put down his vodka and climbed up on the wooden bench so that he could just see out of one of the tall windows.

Zuyev stood with his bodyguard and another man, dressed in street clothes. At first Yernin could not get a good look at the man's face, but then Anastratov moved to the left. It was Ivan Borisov, one of Zuyev's aides and also a GRU major. He looked clearly agitated.

Stepping down, Yernin put his ear to the wooden wall, but he could hear nothing.

He pushed back the curtain and walked around the corner to the entry hall, where he held up just beyond the last changing room. Now he could hear, but he was in a vulnerable spot. Everyone in the pool area could see what he was doing.

"There is no mistake then?" Zuyev was asking.

"It was Lazarev, General."

"Which means the bastard is there in Geneva. He got the message, and he killed the messenger."

"Both. There still is no word from Captain Svetanko. We can assume he is dead."

They fell silent for a second, and Yernin edged a little closer. He didn't want to miss anything. Yet the game he was playing was a dangerous one. Zuyev would not try anything here in front of witnesses. But if he knew that he had been eavesdropped on, he could arrange an accident.

"There is still time," the general said softly. "You are to make contact with the Americans. The CIA. Give them Moran's description. After all, he is one of theirs."

"But he has your name, Comrade General."

"Who will believe the word of an assassin—"

"Arkadi Alekseyevich," someone said behind Yernin, and he turned in time to see the first secretary of the Ministry of Internal Affairs (which was responsible for the Militia) approaching.

He stepped away from the doorway. "Valentin Valentinovich, nice to see you."

"Come and have a drink, a little something to eat if you can tear yourself away from your duties. There is someone who wants to meet you."

"Of course," Yernin said, and he moved off with the first secretary as Sergei Anastratov watched through narrow eyes from the doorway.

14

Ganin mounted the stairs of the World Health Organization building and tried the steel security door. It was locked. He rang the buzzer. Sepelev stood just below, looking across at the television vans.

No one had bothered them through the long morning and even longer afternoon. The security badges that Yernin had provided them with before they left Moscow helped, of course, as did the fact that they stayed out of everyone's way as much as possible and kept on the move.

But now, as it neared three-thirty, Sepelev was ready to give up and Ganin was becoming frightened. The assassin was here somewhere, he was convinced of it. He had killed Colonel Lazarev for some reason; that meant he was not accepting the COUNTERSTRIKE DOWN message. Presumably he was going ahead with the assassination attempt, which made him crazy, in addition to being invisible. It was a frightening combination.

They had watched the main entrance to the park for much of the morning until the West German security people began to get jumpy. Ganin had not gotten a decent look at the retreating figure, yet he felt as if he might instinctively recognize the man, much as he could sometimes pick out the killer in a lineup by the look in the man's eyes.

For a couple of hours they had circulated through the crowds that had continued to stream into the Ariana, and finally they had begun a building-by-building search.

"He's got two choices if he wants to make his hit and have any chance of getting away," Ganin said. "Both of them will be strikes from long distances. One somewhere from the fringes of the crowd and the other from the roof or an upper window of one of the adjacent buildings."

"The roofs are all manned," Sepelev said.

Ganin looked up and picked out the security people stationed on top of each building.

"And if he's going to fire from the crowd, there won't be much we can do about it," Sepelev continued.

"Then we check the upper floors of all the buildings along a direct sight line with the podium."

The fronts of all the buildings facing the courtyard were sealed off by now, so they had come around the back.

Ganin rang the buzzer again.

"Shit," Sepelev swore behind him. "Nikki."

Ganin turned as two bulky plainclothes security men came up the driveway. From the cut of their suits it was obvious they were Russian. He stepped away from the door.

"Get down from there," one of them said.

"We've got work to do, comrades. What do you want?"

"There is someone who wishes to speak with you. Now."

"There is no time—"

"We have been authorized to use whatever force is necessary, Chief Investigator," the other man said. Neither of them had made any move toward his weapon. Somehow Ganin didn't think they would need guns.

He shrugged and came down the stairs. In front the band started to play "Hail to the Chief." The American President had arrived.

They went a hundred meters around the corner, where they were admitted through a rear entrance into the palais. There were security people everywhere. Aides scurried back and forth, and every second person, it seemed, was in uniform. Television power cables snaked in big bundles down the corridor into the Hall of the Presidents, which was busy with technicians making last-minute checks on their equipment. Ganin recognized Grigori Slavin, Moscow Television One's most popular news reader. His was the second most known face in the Soviet Union behind Gorbachev's.

Ganin and Sepelev were ushered into a large room adjacent to the hall that was being used for operations. Activity here was at a feverish pitch. Telephones jangled, teletype machines clattered, portable computer screens flashed data, and fascimile machines spit out photographs and other documents. It was impressive.

Colonel Kokorov stood hunched over across the room deep in conversation with a group of men. He suddenly stepped aside and turned around as they approached, and Ganin nearly stumbled when he realized that one of the men was President Gorbachev himself. Sepelev blanched.

"We finally found them, sir," one of the security officers said.

"Where?" Kokorov asked, studying Ganin.

"Trying to get into the WHO building across the parking lot."

Kokorov nodded. "Why, Chief Investigator?" he asked.

"I believe that there may be an assassin here somewhere within the compound whose intention is to kill President Gorbachev."

A faint smile played at the corner of Gorbachev's mouth. "I have read your reports, Chief Investigator. Very enterprising."

Ganin didn't know if the Soviet president was referring to him or to the assassin. It didn't matter. "Comrade, he may have already positioned himself on one of the upper floors of a building facing the courtyard—"

"The buildings have all been sealed," Kokorov said. "Checked, double-checked, triple-checked." He shook his head. "You have become quite a nuisance."

"No, Colonel," President Gorbachev said. "Let us admire the chief investigator's zeal and dedication to duty." He turned to Ganin and Sepelev. "I would like you in the hall with me for the signing ceremonies, and afterward you may accompany me outside. You will see with your own eyes then."

It was the worst of possibilities, to be tied down like that, Ganin thought. But he had been backed into a corner. There was nothing else for it. He managed a smile, and he nodded. "We would be honored, Comrade President."

There were at least ten thousand people in the courtyard and spread out across the lawns. A few here and there had climbed up into the trees, but security people were bringing them down, checking them for weapons, and closely scrutinizing their papers. Beyond the fringes the entire area was cordoned by soldiers in UN uniforms, armored personnel carriers backing them up.

Directly below were bleachers fanning out from either side of the podium. Already they were mostly filled with diplomats in gray suits.

Security men, walkie-talkies in hand, were everywhere, some of them stationed in one position around the podium, others circulating through the crowds.

One section of the bleachers had been reserved for the news media. It had been mostly empty, but now a few reporters emerged from the palais and were hustled to their places by the security people.

Moran checked his watch. It was four. The signing ceremonies would be nearly finished inside. Gorbachev and Bush would be coming out at any moment.

He lifted his rifle and sighted through the powerful scope down into the courtyard. When he moved his aim slightly to the left, the podium, bristling with microphones, came into sharp focus. It was blocked off by a transparent screen of bulletproof Lexan plastic. But from his vantage point he was looking down over it. The screen had been designed to protect the speaker from someone in front and below or perhaps at the same level as the podium, not from someone above and to the right.

A ripple went through the crowd. Moran switched his aim lower, but from his position he could not see the doorway to the palais. The signing ceremony was completed, however, and the two leaders were about to emerge. He could tell from the reaction of the crowd, the tenseness, the expectation. Suddenly they all began to stand.

The band began to play the national anthem of the Soviet Union.

Moran opened the breech of his rifle and inserted a long, fat fifty-millimeter cartridge. The ammunition, like the weapon, was of his own design. The problem was noise. It did little good to silence a rifle if the bullet traveled through the air with such force that it broke the sound barrier, thus creating the whiplike crack of a sonic boom as it passed. Yet if it didn't travel at very high speeds, it lost accuracy and stopping power.

Moran had solved the first problem by being an outstanding shot and the second by virtue of the fact that the bullet was huge, larger than even the mass coming from the business end of an elephant gun. His weapon could reach, and had on three other occasions brought down, men at ranges of four and five hundred yards, even though it was subsonic.

He closed the breech and once again sighted on the podium the great seals of the United States and Soviet Union affixed side by side.

He stood well back within the office so that there was no chance anyone would spot him from below. The long silencer tube and rifle barrel were painted matte black so that there would be no stray reflections. Even the lenses of the powerful scope were made of nonreflective glass. Nothing had been left to chance.

The band had begun to play the national anthem of the United States, and many of the people in the bleachers and in the crowd raised their hands to their breasts as they stood at attention. The security people, however, did not.

Ganin and Sepelev stood just behind and to the left of President Gorbachev and Colonel Kokorov. President Bush was on the right with his security people, his hand on his heart.

They had stopped at the top of the broad stairs. Ganin scanned the upper-story windows of the adjacent buildings, but he could see nothing amiss. Security people were visible on the roofs, as well as around the podium and intermingled with the crowds. The assassin might be able to fire his shot, but he would never have a chance to get away. But this one was planning on escaping. He knew something they did not; otherwise he would not have come here. He knew that he could escape. How?

The last strains of the music died, and the presidential party moved down the stairs and across the courtyard to the podium behind the snapping flags.

The people were applauding, and all the diplomats on the

grandstand had stood and were clapping as well. Media photographers and cameramen were crowding in around the platform; the security people had trouble keeping them back.

Ganin and Sepelev stepped back out of the way as Bush and Gorbachev mounted the three stairs to the speakers' platform.

"He's here somewhere," Ganin said, scanning the crowd and the buildings on the opposite side of the courtyard.

If it was going to happen, it would be here and now, he was convinced of it. Later this afternoon the Soviet president would be at his hotel. And tonight's guest list for the ball was strictly limited. Security would be much tighter.

He almost missed the open fourth-floor window; his eyes slid past it and then up to the security troops on the roof. But then it struck him, and he looked back.

The window was definitely open. He couldn't see anything inside, but he could definitely tell that there was no glass in the lower half of the frame.

The crowd roared as Gorbachev and Bush shook hands.

"There, the fourth floor," Ganin shouted, and sprinted up the stairs onto the platform, Sepelev right behind him.

The people on the speakers' stand had no idea that anything was wrong at first. Gorbachev and Bush continued to shake hands as they looked into each other's eyes. This was a start, both men were thinking earnestly, yet there was so much remaining to be done that they had barely scratched the surface.

Three hundred yards away Moran held the cross hairs of the scope centered on Gorbachev's head, just behind the famous purple birthmark. He could see the Soviet president's lips moving as he said something to President Bush. Gently Moran squeezed the trigger.

The same instant that the rifle bucked stiffly against his shoulder, someone burst up onto the platform and bodily shoved Gorbachev aside. The shot missed.

Moran was suspended in time and space for several long beats, the rifle still at his shoulder, his eye still at the scope. He watched as the newcomer turned from where he was crouched half over Gorbachev and pointed up at him.

He stepped back. It was the same one from the cathedral. He was sure of it. A Russian by the look of him. Somehow he had found out about the meeting and now about this. Somehow he knew. He knew!

Laying the gun down, Moran calmly pulled on the uniform blouse and cap. He let himself out, relocked the door, and hurried down the corridor. It would take them a few precious minutes to get organized down there. That was all he needed.

He took the stairs two at a time, making as little noise as possible. He stopped at the second-floor landing when he heard a door in the stairwell slam open and the sound of several pairs of boots tramping on the stairs. But then he continued down when he decided they were above him. The security people on the roof had already gotten the word.

Cautiously he peered out into the ground-floor corridor. Nothing moved. But it would not last much longer.

He raced down the corridor past the women's room to the back door, which he opened a crack in time to see half a dozen soldiers and plainclothes officers rushing across the parking lot. He closed the door, turned, and raced back down the corridor. He let himself into one of the ground-floor offices whose windows looked out on a broad lawn on the opposite side of the building from the courtyard. No one was in the immediate vicinity. Everyone seemed to be heading toward the action in the courtyard.

Unlocking the window, Moran slid it open and slipped outside. He held himself up on the windowsill by one arm and reached up with the other to close the window.

Dropping down to the lawn, he turned and walked out to the front, where he mingled with the crowd, straightening his uniform as he went. No one had spotted him emerging from the building. He was seething inside for missing the easy shot, yet his concentration now was directed toward his escape. There would be another time and place. He had been betrayed. But there were ways around that.

The people were now converging on the WHO building, as more and more security troops and agents rushed from the courtyard.

In the distance he could hear sirens. Overhead three helicopters rushed in from the west at treetop level.

By now Gorbachev and Bush both would have been hustled out of here. Before long, if it hadn't already happened, the entire park would be sealed off. But they were looking for an assassin, not an American two-star general with orders.

He would not leave. Not just yet. But he would keep away from the center of activity until it was safe to slip away.

He turned as a young good-looking woman stumbled into him and nearly fell. He had to grab her arm. She seemed to be in a great hurry.

"Ah, shit, sorry, General," she said. Her accent was British, but the cut of her clothes was definitely American.

"What's going on?" he asked.

She looked sharply at him. "You don't know?"

He shook his head.

"Someone just tried to kill Gorbachev."

"Christ. You'd better get out of here."

She stepped around him and was immediately lost in the gathering mob.

Moran stared after her for a long time, then turned and headed in the opposite direction.

Ganin and Sepelev raced down the corridor to the open fourth-floor office door. Kokorov's people were already there.

"We missed him," a KGB officer said.

John McKinnon, the American Secret Service chief, looked up as Ganin came in. He had been the first off the speakers' platform. "What does he look like?"

"I don't know. I never saw his face."

McKinnon stared at him for a measure, but then he raised a walkie-talkie to his lips. "Are Able and Baker clear?"

"That's a roger."

"All right, we're sealing off the park. I don't care how long it takes; he's here, and we're going to find him."

Ganin shook his head. He walked over to the sniper rifle lying on the desk. It was a very large weapon. Obviously custom-built. The assassin knew what he was doing. He had missed, but not by very much. Ganin had practically felt the bullet passing his ear.

"Yes?" McKinnon said to him.

Ganin looked up and shook his head again. "You won't find him. Not here. He is already gone, or he will be disguised as someone whose credentials are beyond question."

"How do you know this?" the American asked sharply.

"Because he came here knowing that he would be able to escape. He was on no suicide mission."

"Bullshit," McKinnon said.

Ganin didn't hear him. He had the uncomfortable notion that the assassin was not going to give up. He didn't know why he thought that except for the fact that the man had made the attempt even though the COUNTERSTRIKE DOWN message had been passed on to him. He just thought it.

And he was going to have to catch him.

PART TWO

All day dark clouds had been building up from the west, and by nine o'clock a cold drizzle was falling over the city of Moscow. Two men had been waiting in a Moskvich sedan across from the U.S. Embassy for most of the afternoon. They were well-trained, patient men and were prepared to wait for days, if need be. But they had become increasingly puzzled by the sequence of events that had developed over the past couple of hours.

Normally the afternoon shift got off between five and six, and the embassy settled down for the long night. But this evening no one had come out; instead, people had been showing up in a steady stream. The entire compound was alive with lights.

"What the hell are they doing in there?" Anatoli Rozanov

asked through clenched teeth. He had become increasingly nervous with nightfall. "I don't like it."

"Neither do I." Viktor Malyshev answered him. He had been watching the militia sentry box in front of the embassy gate. The two militia officers had been huddled inside since the last person had shown up about twenty minutes ago. "If someone told me that it was an emergency, I would not be surprised."

"It's the coincidence that has me worried. We're past our five o'clock deadline."

"What do you suggest? He's not at home, so he's here. And if he refuses to come outside, what else can we do but wait?"

"I don't like it," Rozanov said again. Unlike most GRU legmen, he had an active imagination. In his spare time he wrote poetry. It was the national mania, and some of his work had been published by the Union of Poets. Other pieces had even been circulated in samizdat (self-publishing) circles. Just now he was imagining all sorts of possibilities, none of which included a happy ending for him.

"We can call in if you want."

Rozanov ignored him.

"It is a coincidence . . . our orders and whatever is going on inside."

"I don't know," Rozanov said. He peered through the drizzle at the sentry box.

"Anatoli?"

Razanov opened the door and got out.

Malyshev jumped out after him. "What are you doing?"

"Wait here," Rozanov said, and he went across the street to the sentry box.

The two militia officers were seated next to an electric heater. They jumped up.

"I need to get a message inside," Rozanov said. He took out his GRU identification booklet and flipped it open. The militiamen were impressed.

"No one has said what is going on tonight. Can you tell us?"

"No. But I want you to get hold of Richard Sweeney. Tell him there is a package for him out here." Rozanov motioned toward the car across the street. "I'll be waiting for him over there."

The militiamen were nodding dumbly. "What if he asks who brought the package? I don't think he'll come out here for you, comrade."

Rozanov smiled. "Tell him it has to do with Geneva. I think his curiosity will get the better of him."

In the third-floor safe room, where classified conferences were conducted, Richard Sweeney, assistant chief of station for CIA activities in Moscow, sat halfway down the long table, loading his pipe as he listened to his boss, Kelly Pool, outline the work ahead of them. Because of the assassination attempt in Geneva just three hours ago, they were on emergency footing. All twenty-seven agency duty officers were crowded into the room.

As the ambassador said, "A shot was fired, and President Bush was up on that speakers' platform along with Gorbachev. Who can tell me for certain which man was the intended target?"

No one could.

Sweeney was a very strongly built man, with a thick waist, massive shoulders, and a neck like a bull's. He was the complete opposite of Pool, who was tall, very thin, and almost effetely delicate. But both men got along very well; their physical and mental attributes were opposite but complementary. They'd worked together in Moscow for nearly two years.

"Our first duty is going to be to our networks, of course, but also to our contacts," Pool was saying. "We will not allow our daybooks to dry up like they did during the Kennedy assassination and to a lesser degree on the heels of the attempts on Ford and Reagan."

"What's the latest from Geneva, sir?" asked one of the operatives, who worked under the cover of a cultural affairs officer.

"They've got their hands full, as you can well imagine. The President is gone, of course, as are most of his security detail. But the Swiss are cooperating with our people."

"And with the Russians," Sweeney interjected.

Pool nodded. "I have Archives searching for any references to those two militia officers who showed up out of the clear blue sky. But they've come up with nothing yet."

"They're probably not militia," someone down the table commented.

"The word is they are," Pool replied.

The telephone next to Sweeney buzzed. He picked it up.

"Sorry to disturb you, sir," the night shift marine guard duty officer said. "But I've just been given a message for Mr. Sweeney."

"Speaking," Sweeney said. "From whom?"

"Someone is waiting outside for you. The militia guards called. Sir, they said it has something to do with Geneva."

"Any idea who it is?"

"There is a car parked across the street. Two men. Maybe KGB. The militiamen wouldn't say, of course."

"Right. I'm on my way. I want a couple of armed men standing by, just in case."

"Aye, aye, sir."

Sweeney hung up and got to his feet. "Seems the Russians want to make contact."

"Geneva?" Pool asked sharply.

Sweeney nodded.

"Anderson . . . Sims . . . Beagley . . . go with him."

"Let's not scare them," Sweeney said, waving back the three. He took his .38 snub-nosed revolver out of its holster and transfered it to a jacket pocket. "Besides, Smitty's people will be standing by."

"Watch yourself nonetheless."

"Right," Sweeney said.

He had been inside all day. He was surprised how cold and nasty it had gotten. But then, he thought, at the best of times Moscow was a dismal city.

He stood just at the gate, a pair of marine guards armed with M-16's backing him up. One of the militia officers walked over.

"Good evening, Mr. Sweeney. There is a gentleman across the street who has a package for you."

"KGB?"

The militia officer smiled. "I wouldn't know about that, sir." He glanced at the marines. "There will be no trouble here tonight?"

"Not unless you people start it," Sweeney said, and before the militia officer could reply, he stuffed his hands in his pockets and headed across the street.

Rozanov and Malyshev got out of the car. Sweeney stopped about ten feet away, the fingers of his right hand tightening on the pistol's grip.

Rozanov held out a manila envelope. "This is for you, please," he said in broken English.

Sweeney just smiled. "Sorry, but I don't except gifts from strangers."

Rozanov apparently wasn't sure of the English. "I am not selling this information. I am giving it to you for no money. Do you understand?"

"No, I don't," Sweeney said. "Who are you? Let's start with that."

Rozanov stared at him for a long time. Finally he shook his head. "Maybe you are filled with problems tonight. This is information you must have about . . . Geneva."

Still, Sweeney made no move to take the envelope.

The Russian shrugged after another moment, tossed the envelope down onto the wet pavement, and got back in his car. Malyshev got in on the passenger side. A second later they drove off.

Sweeney stood there for a couple of beats, then bent down, picked up the envelope, and started back across the street. He expected lights to come on at any moment and soldiers to come out of nowhere, guns drawn. It was an old Russian ploy, handing an American classified documents and then arresting him in the next breath. But nothing happened. The militia officers remained in their sentry box, and no one came out of the shadows.

At the gate Sweeney stopped to look the way the two Russians had gone. The street was deserted.

"You'd better let us take a look at that, sir," one of the marines said.

Sweeney handed it over. The embassy, so far as he knew, had never received a letter bomb, but there was always a first time.

Inside, the Marine ran the envelope through the fluoroscope. So far as he could tell, there was nothing but paper inside.

On the way back up to the conference room Sweeney opened the envelope and pulled out the contents, among them a photograph of a good-looking olive-complexioned man who was identified on the back as Donald Sullivan Moran, St. John, U.S. VI.

16

Moran had gone into hiding.

He stood within the lengthening shadows in the widely spaced woods across the long sward from the palais and the park access road. It was dusk. In another twenty minutes or so it would be fully dark. Already the jeeps and trucks ran with their headlights on, and it was hard to distinguish individual people in the distance; the slowly thinning crowds, which had gathered at the only egress point, were an amorphous mass.

He had thought that he would have been well away by now, but he had delayed too long. It was a mistake. He did not make many of them.

By the time he had approached the main gate on the Avenue de la Paix, the entire road was choked with people all scrambling to get out. There were at least a hundred soldiers, their automatic weapons at the ready, funneling the crowd through half a dozen checkpoints.

At first he thought he would be able to pass through with no problem on the strength of his orders, but wisely he had hung back at the fringes of the crowd for a full ten minutes while he studied what was actually happening.

Everyone had to present his or her papers, of course. There seemed to be no exceptions. In most instances people were then allowed to pass through. But after a short time he noticed that a pattern had emerged. For men of medium height and build, whether or not they were in uniform, the check was far more rigorous. In several instances the suspects were hustled over to a communications van, where presumably their credentials were checked much more thoroughly.

It was an examination he knew that he had no chance of passing. Once again it pointed back to betrayal, to the two Russians he had encountered at the cathedral and again on the speakers' platform.

The question was, did they know his face?

Once he got out of the park he would be all right. He didn't think that anyone would connect his present disguise with that of a British general traveling in mufti. Not for a while longer yet. In any event he would not remain long at his hotel. By midnight, or much sooner if he was lucky, he would be across the border into France, at which point he would have to begin making plans for his next move. Returning to St. John was out, of course. He had other places to go to ground, but he knew in his heart of hearts that he was not ready to give it up. Not yet.

The immediate problem, then, was getting out.

Moran turned and headed directly away from the palais, at right angles to the access road, working his way from tree to tree. He thought he was going in the general direction of the lake, though from within the trees he could not see the city to orient himself.

He had no certain knowledge how far the park stretched to the east, though he thought that the northbound rail line might cut between him and the lake. And there was the lakeshore drive. But he was putting distance between himself and most of the soldiers and security people where the search was being concentrated for now.

A helicopter passed low in the sky to the south. He could just make out its running lights for an instant, and then they were gone. But he thought he saw the flash of a very strong white light.

For a second or two he was puzzled by what it could mean until he realized that whoever was in charge of the search was smart. The helicopter was sweeping the woods with a powerful spotlight. Anyone moving out here at this hour would be automatically suspect.

Turning, he doubled his speed, moving low and fast from the shadows beneath one tree to the shadows cast by another. It was becoming increasingly difficult to see anything but vague shapes more than ten or fifteen yards out.

The helicopter swept much closer this time, but still to his south, its spotlight slowly cutting a swath through the dark woods.

He cut to the north for about twenty-five yards to put more distance between himself and the oncoming machine and then turned back directly toward the eastern boundary of the park.

Moran heard the traffic sounds of the highway before he saw the flash of headlights. He continued walking and reached a tall chain-link fence a couple of minutes later. He could see down onto the roadway, beyond which were railroad tracks and what appeared to be another park on the other side. He realized at this point that he was still more than half a mile from the lake, but once over the fence he would be able to hail a taxi for a ride back into the city.

With a feeling of relief, he turned to look for a climbable tree. . . .

Two West German soldiers wearing UN armbands came out of the darkness. They both were armed with .45 caliber Mac-10 submachine guns. *"Entschuldigen, Herr General. Wer sind Sie?"* one of them asked.

Moran forced himself not to react with surprise or alarm. They both were sergeants, very possibly professional soldiers. But they were searching for an assassin, not an American general.

"Ich bin ein General. Und Sie?"

"Sorry, sir," the one said politely, but neither of them came to attention. "You've entered our patrol sector. We have orders that no one is to pass."

"I should hope not. Has anyone passed?"

"No, sir. May I ask exactly who you are and what you are doing here?"

"General Horvak," Moran said. "Timothy Horvak, SHAPE

IG, Heidelberg." He reached inside his blouse for a copy of his orders.

Both soldiers instantly stepped back, bringing their weapons up.

"Easy," Moran said. "My orders." He pulled them out slowly and held them toward the nearest man, while stepping closer to the other. "If you'll just let me use your walkie-talkie, I'll let them know where I am."

The man on his left lowered his gun as he reached for the orders, while the other man reached to his hip to unclip his walkie-talkie. It was a mistake on both their parts.

Moran stepped inside the second man's guard, shoved the barrel of the gun aside with his left hand, and drove his right fist into the man's solar plexus, shoving him backward, all the air exploding out of his lungs.

The first soldier was off-balance, reaching for the orders. He stumbled. Moran swiveled on his left heel and kicked out with his right foot, catching the soldier on his lead leg. The shinbone broke with a loud pop.

The man screamed as he went down. Nevertheless, he tried to roll over so that he could bring his weapon to bear. In that moment, however, the side of his head was exposed, and Moran kicked him, the steel-reinforced toe cap of his uniform shoe catching the sergeant in the temple. The man went back like a felled ox.

Moran turned back as the second soldier managed to stagger to his feet, vomit down the front of his uniform. His gun lay on the ground behind him. His mouth was opening and closing in terror as he fumbled for the pistol at his hip.

Moran stepped forward and chopped the man's Adam's apple with the side of his hand, crushing his windpipe. The soldier reeled backward, clawing desperately at his throat, harsh gasping sounds coming from his mouth as he vainly tried to draw a breath.

He sank to his knees, his face starting to turn purple. Before he fell back, he looked up at Moran in wonderment and hurt. Then he keeled over.

Moran checked his pulse. It was weak and thready for a full two minutes until it fluttered a few times and finally stopped.

The helicopter was back, this time much closer, and Moran instinctively ducked down, averting his face until it was past.

When it was gone, he jumped up and hurried along the fence. He found a proper tree within twenty or thirty yards.

Looking back to make sure no one else was coming, he scrambled up the tree and out onto a branch, from which he jumped to the other side of the fence.

He remained where he had dropped until a big truck had passed below on the road and then, brushing himself off, headed down the hill.

17

Angry, Vladimir Kokorov slapped a file folder against the side of his leg. He had a broad, square peasant's face, dark eyes beneath thick eyebrows, and massive arms and hands that looked as if they could crush a man. Except for his hunched posture he could have passed for Joseph Stalin.

"You should not have come here in the first place. This was a mistake. The Militia has no business, no charter outside the Soviet Union. This was explained in detail to Major Vilov." He stopped to look past Ganin, toward the entrance to the auditorium. "You and your partner are leaving tonight, under armed guard if need be." He was keeping his voice low. Still, what he was saying and his attitude were amazing to Ganin.

The interrogations had been moved to the auditorium on the first floor of the WHO building. Besides the medium-built men (of whom there were a surprising number), they had detained anyone who had been anywhere near the speakers platform as well as anyone within a hundred yards of the WHO building just after the single shot had been fired. Kokorov and some of the other Russians were huddled on the stage. They'd been there since the beginning. By now the auditorium was quite full and very noisy.

"Had I boarded that flight, it is very possible that President Gorbachev would not be alive at this moment," Ganin said.

Kokorov's nostrils flared. He put the file folder down and leaned forward, his meaty knuckles planted firmly on the table between them.

"I understand that, Chief Investigator. And believe me the *Rodina* thanks you with all her heart. But not only are the Swiss now all over my ass, but they have Vilov and half of his staff spotted . . . staff assigned to watch you, I might add. Staff that could better have been used for security this afternoon."

"None of them knew about the assassin. And all I have been doing is following my orders. If the KGB had—"

Kokorov straightened up, shaking his head in amazement. "You must leave now."

Ganin turned to Sepelev. "We will begin by questioning everyone who was in front of the building just after the shot was fired. The back exits were covered. He could not have escaped that way."

One of Kokorov's people had started around the table, but the big KGB chief held him off. "There were a half dozen security men in front. They saw nothing."

Ganin smiled gently as a father might at a son who'd made an elementary mistake. "If they were in place, as you say, they saw the assassin. They know what he looks like."

"They just didn't recognize him, is that it?"

"That's correct."

"And where is he now?" Kokorov asked.

"Certainly not in the park. He's got a place in the city, or he's changed his disguise and is probably out of the country or on his way. The border should be closed."

"To whom?"

"Give me a couple of hours, and I'll have his description."

"If he's already out of the country, as you suggest, closing the border would be a waste of time . . . assuming, of course, the Swiss agreed to go along with us," Kokorov said.

Ganin smiled. "So it would be. But it would give the Swiss something to do while we accomplished the real work."

Kokorov stared at him for a long time. "Get them out of here," he said through clenched teeth. "If they resist, shoot them."

"What is it, Comrade Colonel?" Ganin asked, lowering his voice so that his words were only for Kokorov. "Are you a part of the plot, or is it simply that the KGB does not wish to be shown up by the Militia? I did not get a good look at this man, but I did manage to get off a shot at him after he killed our military attaché. He's a very intelligent, motivated man. Despite the fact he'd been called off, he went ahead with his attempt, and he very nearly succeeded. He will not stop."

"Then he will have to come to Moscow."

"Are you willing to bet that he won't?"

Kokorov stared intently at him again. Finally he shook his head as if he could not fathom what he was seeing or hearing. He turned away. "Make sure they're on the airplane this time."

One of Kokorov's people came around the table. The other one held off to one side. They were expecting trouble. "We have a car waiting outside, comrades," the guard said, smiling.

John McKinnon and some of the other American security people were gathered halfway up the aisle toward the auditorium's doors. They were interrogating mostly Americans and Europeans, leaving the Russian nationals to the KGB.

Ganin had an insane thought that he would ask McKinnon for help. Perhaps even asylum, at least long enough for him to accomplish his work here in Switzerland. The bullet had not been found, forensics had not had a chance to examine the rifle or the corpse of the Italian soldier they'd found in the women's room, and of course, they had not had a chance to interview everyone they had rounded up. But even these days leaving the *Rodina* was a one-way street. There weren't many doorways out, and once you managed to find one and squeeze through, you could never return, unless it was for your nine ounces—a Stalinist era euphemism for a nine-millimeter bullet in the back of the head.

"What about our bags?" he asked.

"Where you left them, at the gate," the guard said. "We'll pick them up on the way out."

Kokorov had his back to them. There were no more appeals. Ganin shook his head, went down the stairs to the auditorium floor, and headed up the aisle, Sepelev right behind him and the two KGB guards behind him.

McKinnon and a couple of other men were talking with a young good-looking woman, who wore a news media badge on the lapel of her charcoal gray jacket. She looked up as Ganin came abreast of her, and he could see that she was frightened and uncertain of what was going on. She had, he thought, the most startlingly green eyes he had ever seen. They were wild, exotic; he didn't know what, only that he was immediately drawn to her by them.

He stopped. "Hello."

She managed a thin smile. "I didn't see anything," she said.

"Go," the guard growled half under his breath. Ganin ignored him as well as McKinnon, who had tried to step in front of the woman.

"Where were you when the shot was fired, Miss . . . ?"

"Mary Frances Dean," she said. "But I didn't hear any shooting; that's what I'm trying to tell these people."

"Get him out of here," McKinnon snapped.

"Just a minute, if you please," Ganin said. "If you heard nothing, then what are you doing here?"

She shrugged. "So far as I can tell, they've rounded up everyone who was anywhere near this building or the speakers' stand."

McKinnon bodily shoved him aside, but Ganin sidestepped the two KGB guards and stepped inside the American's reach.

"Do you want to create an incident here, Mr. McKinnon?" he asked.

"What do you want?"

"The assassin."

"Not on my time . . ." McKinnon had started to say when Ganin shouldered him out of the way.

Mary Frances didn't know what was going on. She started to get up so that she could move out of the way, but Ganin smiled reassuringly at her. Sepelev had stepped in between him and McKinnon.

"Where were you at the time of the shot then?" Ganin asked.

"Just in front."

"Did you see anyone?"

She smiled uncertainly. "Of course. I mean, there were lots of people everywhere."

"All of them heading here, toward this building?" Ganin prompted.

Again she shrugged, but then her face started to light up as if she had suddenly remembered something.

"Yes?"

There were hands on Ganin's shoulders, and he was being pulled backward. Mary Frances started to reach for him, stepping forward, but then McKinnon was there again, taking her hands and sitting her down.

"Excuse me, miss, but I'm going to have to ask you not to say anything else to this man."

"What?" she sputtered.

The two KGB guards and a couple of McKinnon's people had surrounded Ganin and Sepelev and were hustling them up the aisle.

"No more trouble now, Chief Investigator," one of the KGB officers said in Russian. He was grinning ear to ear.

"Fucking squareheads." An American swore half under his breath.

The smile left the KGB officer's face; but he said nothing, and moments later they were out in the busy corridor and headed toward the doors.

"See, comrades, it appears that no one likes us," Ganin said.

"Keep your mouth shut," the KGB officer snarled.

"First an assassin tries to kill our president, and now they call us names," Ganin went on. "Perhaps it is time for us to return home after all, Yurochka." He looked over his shoulder and winked at Sepelev. The Americans had gone back inside. No one in the corridor was paying them any attention.

Outside, a brown Peugeot pulled up. One of the KGB guards went ahead and opened the rear door. "We've got a couple of hours before your flight leaves, comrades, but I will feel a little better when you're at the airport."

Ganin and Sepelev got in the backseat; one guard climbed in with them, and the other got in front with the driver. They all were husky men, and they were packed in the small car. The communications radio was blaring as the search continued. No one seemed to be paying any attention to it.

They immediately pulled away from the curb, and Ganin sat back. There had been something about the young woman, Mary Frances Dean, that he could not quite put his finger on. Some quality, something in her face or attitude, that was arresting. But then he smiled inwardly at his own foolishness. She was an American journalist, nothing more. And she had probably not seen a thing.

But there was more to be done here. Much more.

He glanced past Sepelev at the KGB officer, who was staring straight ahead. They were not expecting any trouble, but they were very well trained to deal with any eventuality. Once he made a move he would only have a split second to gain the upper hand.

Their ruse at the airport would not work a second time.

Suddenly he reached over Sepelev and grabbed inside the KGB officer's coat for his gun.

The agent reared away, but there was not enough room for him to move. He started to push Sepelev away, but Ganin had his pistol out and he shoved it in the man's face.

"Shit," the officer swore.

The KGB officer in the front looked around, his eyes growing wide when he realized what was going on. Sepelev reached over the seat and took his pistol.

"Turn the car around," Ganin said grimly. "We're going back."

"Tell the driver to do as he says," Sepelev warned.

"You stupid bastards, do you realize—" The KGB officer in the front started to protest.

"Do it, comrade." Sepelev cut him off.

"Fuck," the man said, shaking his head. "Do as they say, Gennadi. We'll let the colonel have their balls."

The driver slowed the car and turned around in the broad road a couple of hundred yards from the still-busy checkpoint. There were a lot of angry people down there, Ganin figured, and there were going to be some angry people back at the auditorium, too.

"Control, we've got . . . ah, what looks like two men down at the perimeter," the radio blared.

Ganin sat forward all of a sudden, but he kept his pistol on the KGB officer.

"State your unit and position."

"This is Helo Three, we're over the east perimeter fence . . .

ah . . . looks like sector one-seven-echo. Two men down, no movement."

The voice from the helicopter sounded American; the other, Swiss or perhaps German. They spoke in English.

"Roger, Helo Three, maintain your position, someone is on the way."

"I've changed my mind," Ganin said, turning back. "I want to go there."

"What are you talking about, Ganin? Where?"

"To where the helicopter is standing by. The eastern perimeter. Sector seventeen echo."

The officer looked at the radio and then back at Ganin, understanding beginning to dawn on his face. "I don't know where that is. We'd need a grid overlay and a map—"

"I know where it is, comrades," the driver said.

"Shit."

Two jeeps filled with UN security troops raced past them, their sirens blaring. They turned down a dirt maintenance road that led into the trees across from the WHO building.

"There," the driver said.

"Follow them," Ganin ordered.

"What is it, Nikki?" Sepelev asked.

"It's our boy, I think. And if he's killed these two men, we'll at least know what kind of weapon he's using."

Sepelev shrugged.

"It's something."

Within minutes the narrow clearing along the fence was filled with soldiers and a few civilian security people, and still more were coming.

Pocketing the pistol, Ganin had leaped out of the car and raced the rest of the way through the woods before the KGB officers could stop him. As he ran, he clipped his militia identification to his lapel pocket, pushing his way through a line of soldiers.

A military doctor was bent over the two bodies.

"Are they dead?" Ganin shouted over the noise of the chopper's rotors.

The doctor looked up and nodded, his face harsh white in the glare of the spotlight from above and from the headlights slanting through the trees.

Someone was running toward them through the woods. He thought he heard his name being called.

"How long have they been dead?"

"I don't know. Not very long. Maybe an hour, probably a lot less."

"Wounds?"

"None visible other than a crushed windpipe and an indented temple. Broken leg. They weren't shot to death, that's for sure." The doctor shook his head. "They were killed in hand-to-hand combat."

"But they were armed," one of the soldiers said.

"Yeah, but that'd be my guess."

18

After Geneva, Moscow seemed drab by comparison. A thin drizzle fell from an overcast sky. Almost all the cars and trucks seemed old and cheap, the buildings gray and run-down, and even the pedestrians scurrying to work seemed drab.

Ganin and Sepelev had taken an Air France flight to Paris, where they had picked up the late Aeroflot flight direct to Moscow. They touched down at Sheremetyevo Airport in the early-morning hours.

Ganin, lost in his thoughts about the assassin, had gotten no sleep on either flight. The man was right-handed; he had gotten that much from the doctor before he and Sepelev had been pulled out. But he also knew that the man was very good at unarmed combat. He was ruthless. And he was very dedicated.

On the way into the city in a taxi, he thought about Oleg

Lazarev, the COUNTERSTRIKE DOWN message the military attaché had apparently received from someone in Moscow, and his futile effort to stop the assassin.

He had lost his life for the try, as had the Italian soldier and the two West Germans. The assassin had a nasty habit of killing anyone who got in his way.

Coming down Leningradskoye Road into the city, Ganin turned his thoughts from what the man had done to what he had nearly accomplished and what he would probably still try. He was going to have to be stopped, of course, and Ganin knew that he could not trust the KGB to do the job. The GRU would do everything within its power to see that the Komitet failed. And without a doubt there were plenty of high-ranking officers at the Lubyanka who secretly agreed with General Zuyev and his old guard and wanted to see Gorbachev removed. But then, he wondered, what could a couple of militia officers do against the entire might of the secret services?

They would have to go through official channels. Every move they made would have to be meticulously documented so that they could not be ignored or sidestepped or ordered off because they were operating beyond their charter. The KGB people would have to cooperate if it was put to them, piece by piece, that way.

Ganin was going up against an establishment that was much older than Gorbachev and, in fact, much older than the Great Patriotic War fossils who had hired the assassin. It was a challenge, something he'd not had for . . . How long? he wondered. Or had there ever been any challenge in his job other than the politics of advancement and, of course, the party?

In the Soviet Union murder was almost always committed by a drunken husband, sometimes by thieves who had a falling-out, and occasionally by one man fighting another over a woman. Almost never were murders planned and then carried out with skill. They were done on the spur of the moment. Crimes of passion.

It was nearly seven o'clock when the cabby finally dropped them off at the side entrance of the Militia Headquarters downtown. Ganin paid him, and they got their overnight bags out of the trunk.

The overnight clerk was asleep behind his counter, and they had to ring for ten minutes before he finally opened up for them.

Upstairs they tossed their bags down, and Sepelev cleared his desk with one sweep of his arm and lay down on top of it, closing his eyes. Ganin wound a piece of paper into his typewriter and started on his report. He wanted it ready by the time Chief Prosecutor Yernin came in.

"I want to be well rested when they come to take me to the Lubyanka," Sepelev said.

Ganin smiled. "I don't think they're going to offer you tea and blinis."

"Fuck, no. A three-by-three, if I'm lucky."

"They don't even know you exist, Yurochka."

Sepelev sat up. "But you're going to change that, aren't you?"

Ganin glanced over at him. "Do you want out?"

Sepelev studied him for a long second or two before he finally shook his head. "Just let me know what's going on before it happens to me, okay?"

Ganin nodded. "But there's not going to be much of anything this morning. Why don't you go home and get some sleep?"

"The whole weekend with my wife?"

"You'll need the weekend to explain why you didn't bring her something from Switzerland."

"You're right," Sepelev said despondently.

After he was gone, Ganin turned back to his report, leaving nothing out concerning his conversations with the Swiss cop Reisch, the business with Lazarev, and his confrontations with Kokorov, Vilov, and the American Secret Service officer John McKinnon. He did not mention Mary Frances Dean, although he did speculate that the assassin might be an American.

There had been something about him, something that Ganin had sensed from the retreating figure in black in front of the cathedral. The man had run like an athlete, but not delicately like a soccer player. America was about the only country in the world where soccer was not the universal sport.

When he was finished, he went next door to Yernin's office, but the prosecutor was not in, though it was well past his usual arrival time. His secretary took the report.

"The general sends his compliments, Chief Investigator, and asks that you and your wife join him this weekend at his dacha."

"He won't be here today?" Ganin asked the smug young man. Moscow seemed filled with them this year. They were probably imitating a character in a western movie. A few years ago everyone played Clint Eastwood. Before that it was Dustin Hoffman.

"No, comrade."

"But you will be in contact with him?"

The secretary nodded. He wore glasses, and a strand of his hair kept drooping across his forehead.

"Then see that he gets this report."

"Naturally, and what about his kind invitation?"

"Of course, we'll be there," Ganin said. "You?"

Chief Prosecutor Yernin's dacha was thirty-five kilometers west of Moscow in a village of dachas called Zhukovka which catered almost exclusively to high-ranking politicians and bureaucrats as well as space scientists, nuclear physicists, and, for some reason, artists.

All the way out Antonia kept bubbling about what an honor it was. They had been here before, but it had been a long time since their last visit. She was conscious of the fact that her husband needed to be promoted soon or his career would stagnate. And promotions came only to those who got noticed.

Ganin parked their Volga station wagon down the gravel road from the house, and they hurried the rest of the way on foot past a dozen other cars, most of them Chaika or Zil limousines.

It was raining very hard out here in the country, and by the time they made it to the big, rambling house, they were soaked. But Antonia was laughing. She loved the adventure.

"In here out of the rain." Chief Prosecutor Yernin beckoned from the doorway as they mounted the steps. He was dressed in an old sweater, corduroy trousers, and felt boots.

A fire was going in the fireplace, and heaps of food and liquor and wine and beer were laid out on three big tables. Some American music was playing, and several couples were across the room dancing. A dozen others were gathered around a big-screen television set, watching CNN out of London via satellite. Most of the men were old. All of the women were young.

Yernin apologized. "You two are the only marrieds here. But it will do them good to see a successful Soviet couple."

Antonia had brought a couple of jars of her pickled mushrooms. She handed them to Yernin. He beamed and kissed her on the cheek.

"Have you seen my report?" Ganin asked half under his breath.

"Of course, of course," Yernin said, still smiling. "But I would not worry about the KGB. There will be no repercussions, I promise you that." He turned to the living room. "I would like you all to welcome my ablest chief investigator, Nikolai Ganin, who leaves for America tomorrow to arrest the man who was involved in that . . . incident in Geneva."

Everyone turned, and many of them applauded warmly. Ganin heard none of it, however. His attention was locked on General Zuyev, who was seated in front of the television set. The general had turned around and was staring at him, a faint smile on his cruel lips.

"Nikki, it's wonderful," Antonia was saying in his ear.

"I didn't know," Ganin mumbled, but she hadn't meant what he thought she had. She was pointing at Yernin's secretary across the room by the buffet.

"My God," she bubbled, "isn't that the American movie actor William Hurt?"

Mary Frances Dean was dreaming that she was trying to get into a tall office building, but she couldn't seem to make her hands work on the doorknob. In the distance she could hear a bird or some other animal chirping insistently. For some reason it annoyed her.

She woke up, the telephone beside her on the nightstand ringing. It was still dark outside, and she could hear rain gusting against the windows.

As she fumbled for the phone, she focused on the clock. It was barely five in the morning.

"Yes . . . hello," she mumbled.

"Ms. Dean?" a woman's voice asked. "Mary Frances Dean, *World News This Week*?"

"Yes, who is this?"

"Thank Christ," the woman said. "I'm Doris Reid, Twenty-four-Hour News Network. I produce the Sunday morning panel show *Face the People*, and I've got one hell of a crisis on my hands. I'm wondering if you could help me out. I'd appreciate it."

Mary Frances fumbled for a cigarette before she remembered that she had quit. She turned on the light and sat up, hugging her knees to her chest. "This is a joke, right?"

"I wish to hell it were," Doris Reid said. She was crude, her voice sharp. "The fact of the matter is, my airtime is three hours away, and Barbara Sutton called twenty minutes ago. She's got strep throat, which leaves me up shit creek. Can you help?"

"What are you talking about?"

"Do you know the show?" Doris Reid asked, obviously trying to hold her exasperation in check.

"Yes, I've seen it."

"Thank God for that much at least. This morning's show, which airs at eight, is supposed to feature four journalists who covered the accord meeting. We've got ABC, the AP, the *Times*, and we had *Newsweek*. We need a newsmagazine, and you were there. Will you bail us out? I'd be eternally grateful. I'd kiss your feet, your ass . . . anything."

Mary Frances started to laugh. "Hold on, just a second," she said. "I'll do it, or at least I think I will. But I'm going to have to clear it with my magazine first. When do you need me down there?"

"As soon as, sweetie."

"What's the topic?"

"*Glasnost* and assassination. We figured that with all the new democracies over there, the kooks will start coming out of the woodwork, you know what I mean?"

"I think so," Mary Frances said. "I'll get right back to you."

"Please do. Oh, God, please do."

Mary Frances hung up and dialed Bob Liskey's number. It rang a long time before he answered.

"This better be good," he growled. She could hear his wife in the background asking who it was.

"Robert, Mary Frances."

"Do you know what time it is?"

"Twenty-four-Hour News Network just called. They want me on their *Face the People* program this morning as a replacement for *Newsweek*."

"What's the topic?" Liskey asked, suddenly very much awake.

"*Glasnost* and assassination, if you can believe that."

"You're damned right I believe it, sweetheart." He paused. "Weaver's incommunicado for the weekend, and I'm not going to call Harley Everton at this hour. Hell, do it, kid. Can't hurt the magazine, and it looks as if your fifteen minutes, à la Andy Warhol, are here."

"Watch me. I want to know how I did."

"Wear something sexy."

"Shit," she said, and she broke the connection. She called a very relieved Doris Reid and told her she would be there.

"PTL, in caps. Do you know where the studio is?"

"I can find it."

"Twenty-fifth floor. Cindy at the front desk will be expecting you."

It was after seven by the time she made it to the network's headquarters. The rest of New York was asleep. It was a Sunday morning. But in the studio there was a buzz of activity with technicians, camera operators, makeup people, and assistant producers running and screaming everywhere, telephones ringing, and television monitors to one side of the set tuned to half a dozen other networks and the cable news services.

Doris Reid was a short, dumpy woman of indeterminate age, with flaming red hair and bottle-thick glasses. She wore tennis shoes with a long green wool dress and a print scarf of silk.

"My God, you're gorgeous," she said when she came into the waiting room. "Get out of magazines, kid; you belong on the tube. I swear to God, you're a cross between Connie Chung and Kathleen Sullivan."

"This early in the morning, that's a real compliment," Mary Frances said. "I take it you're Doris Reid?"

"Who else? Come on, I'll take you over to makeup, and afterward you can meet the director."

"Who else will be on this panel with me?" Mary Frances asked as they left the waiting room and walked a few doors down a narrow corridor into a three-chair makeup salon. A young man wearing a straw cowboy hat and a lot of gold chains around his neck was waiting for them.

"We've got Dick Lawson from AP. He's their lead political writer. Fred Drescher from the *Times*. He's a pompous ass, but he writes a damned good column and an occasionally insightful editorial. And Tom Ellison from ABC. He's a real sweetheart, and he's got brains besides."

Mary Frances was wearing patterned nylons with a dark A-line skirt and a white silk blouse with frills and a high collar. The makeup man carefully wrapped a towel around her shoulders, tucking it in the neckline.

"Who does your hair, darling?" he asked.

"I do."

"You need help."

"Fuck you, Barney," Doris Reid said good-naturedly. Despite herself, Mary Frances was beginning to like the woman.

"I'm sorry, but for the life of me I can't remember the moderator's name."

"Bob Bixby, but don't worry he won't be on this morning."

"Who then?"

Doris Reid had been standing by the door. She turned and looked down the corridor and smiled. "Here he comes now," she said. "You'll like him."

The makeup artist was just fixing her eyeliner when an extremely attractive older man with white hair and a face that was out of the past yet eminently recognizable came around the corner. Mary Frances lurched.

"Damn," the makeup artist swore.

"Hello Stewart," Doris Reid said, and the man kissed her on the cheek. "Come on and meet one of your panelists."

Stewart R. Kaltenbron looked at Mary Frances with a smile. "Hello," he said in the familiar voice.

"Hi," Mary Frances managed to answer. She could hardly move.

"Mary Frances Dean, Stewart—"

"I know," Mary Frances said.

Kaltenbron came in, took off his coat, and sat down in one of the salon chairs. Doris Reid took his jacket from him, hung it up, and then placed a towel around his neck.

"I read your dispatches on Gorbachev and Bush," Kaltenbron said. "I thought you did a damn fine job."

"Thank you, sir . . . I'm flattered."

Kaltenbron smiled again and shook his head. "Listen to me, kid, you're a first-rate journalist in a world of mediocrity. You don't have to call me sir."

Mary Frances didn't know what to say.

"I'm not going to give you a tough time out there this morning, but I'm not going to handle you with kid gloves either. We're talking about the real world in which real people . . . a lot of them . . . get killed."

"I know," Mary Frances said, finally finding her voice. "And I think the accord is a step in the right direction."

"Do you?"

"Yes, sir . . . Mr. Kaltenbron."

"Stewart."

"Stewart. I think it is a right step. We can't go on as we have forever. Sooner or later the unthinkable accident will happen."

"You believe Gorbachev is sincere?"

"Yes, I do," she said with much feeling. She had sat practically knee to knee with the man. She had looked into his eyes, had seen the set of his mouth, had heard the tone in his voice. "But it's an uphill battle for him. It's—"

"You don't think it's merely good PR? You think it's time to trust the Russians?"

"What other choice do we have?" she asked.

Kaltenbron smiled. Doris Reid was beaming. "I think we'll have a good show this morning," she said.

Tom Ellison appeared in the doorway, and he and Kaltenbron greeted each other like old friends. Mary Frances felt as if she were in a dream. This was heady stuff. Yet she told herself she was a world-class journalist. She belonged here, at least for the moment.

Donald Moran sat at the open window in his room at the Hôtel Negresco in Nice. The sea across the Promenade des Anglais was flat calm, the horizon lost in the haze.

Spread out on the bed behind him were newspapers from a half dozen world capitals. The television set, its sound turned low, was tuned to the 24-Hour News Network in English, relayed via satellite from New York out of London.

He'd gotten little or no sleep since Geneva, and brilliant flashes and daggers of light pierced his vision with increasing frequency. His head was pounding, he heard a nearly continuous ringing in his ears, and the palms of his hands were cold and sweaty. He felt disoriented. Alone. Paranoid. Afraid to go to sleep and afraid that he would suffer a complete breakdown if he did not.

But he had failed!

He was not afraid of the KGB's and GRU's retribution (though he was respectful of their power), and he knew that he could and should turn his back on the entire business and walk off with the five million dollars already deposited in his account.

But he had failed!

It was after two in the afternoon. He sipped his tea as he tried to calm down, as he tried to control his seething emotions. The early-morning news shows out of New York were starting to air about now. *Face the Nation. Meet the Press. Face the People.*

The assassination attempt had dominated the world news, though no one was reporting anything concrete. A shot had been fired from a fourth-floor office in the WHO building, where a UN security guard was found dead. No one had any clue to the assassin's motive, his identity, or even his nationality.

Moran turned and looked at the television set. Stewart R. Kaltenbron's face filled the screen. He could just make out the words.

"... *glasnost* and assassination. Perhaps one inevitably leads to the other."

The camera panned back to show three men and a woman seated behind a long table, and Moran sat forward so fast he spilled some of his tea.

The woman! He knew her!

Kaltenbron was introducing the panelists, their names and titles coming up on the screen one at a time. It was the woman's turn.

"Mary Frances Dean, *World News This Week* magazine, who was stationed in front of the WHO building at the time of the incident and may well have seen the assassin's face. . . ."

He stared at her image on the screen: her eyes, her sensuous mouth, the set of her chin. She had seen him! She knew his face!

"**H**ow reliable is your information?" the President asked.
"It hasn't been evaluated yet," CIA Director Robert Vaughan said. "But I think we should follow it up. Ed Wilder agrees."

"Then you'd both better come over here," the President said. "I can give you thirty minutes. Two o'clock." The President had become personally and actively interested in the case not only because of its international ramifications (already the word was that the would-be assassin was probably an American) but because he had been standing on the platform when the shot was fired.

"Yes, sir," Vaughan said. "Perhaps John McKinnon should be on deck as well."

"Very well."

Vaughan hung up the telephone and buzzed his secretary. "Get me Wilder again."

While he waited for the call to the FBI director to go through, he got up and went to the windows and looked out across the rolling Virginia countryside. He was a tall, round faced man with a bulbous nose, high, thin eyebrows, and no hair on his liver-spotted scalp. He had spent his life in government service; he never regretted one minute of it.

Wilder was on the line a minute later. He had been expecting the call.

"We see the Man at two. Anything yet from your people in St. John?"

"They got to St. Thomas an hour ago. Should be over on St. John by now. Gives them time for a quick sweep. Have you talked to McKinnon yet?" Wilder asked. He was a businessman and the fourth director of the bureau since Hoover. He ran the place like IBM.

"No, but he'll be at the meeting."

"We've come up with nothing in our files on Moran."

"How about the fingerprints?"

"Two sets on the rifle and one on the briefcase. Turned out to be from two Russian security agents. They contaminated the scene after all."

"Stupid bastards," Vaughan said. "We'll make sure McKinnon hears about that. It was his bailiwick."

"Nothing on the rifle, though it's a hell of a fine piece of workmanship. My experts tell me that the number of smiths in the world capable of that caliber work is not large, but we'd never be able to run them all down in ten years. And of course, there's no workman's mark. The briefcase is Louis Vuitton, but the serial number has been carefully filed off. Another dead end."

"We'll just have to go with what we got, unless your people get lucky in the Caribbean. This is number one priority."

"I understand, but something else has come up that you might not like."

Vaughan's jaw tightened. "Go ahead."

"Have you read McKinnon's initial report?"

"I saw it," Vaughan said.

"The Russians sent a pair of militia detectives to Geneva. Well, one of them, Chief Investigator Nikolai Ganin, is due here at four this afternoon."

"Whose brilliant idea was that?" Vaughan groaned.

"It came into the agency through routine channels. We always try to cooperate with a foreign police force, even with the Russians . . . or I should say *especially* with the Russians these days. Anyway, State gave the approval, and I just happened to see the request."

"What is he after?"

"That's why I saw the paper work. He's coming here to investigate a man suspected of a murder attempt. He gave only the last name, but he has a partial description which matches what we have from Geneva."

"Moran?" Vaughan asked.

"That's right."

Special Agent Vivian Hammer did not like to sweat. But from the moment he and Special Agent Tom Petit had stepped off the plane at St. Thomas's Cyril E. King Airport, it had been pouring off him.

"Goddamned tropics," he grumbled as the open-air cab slowly wound its way up into the hills outside Cruz Bay.

"People pay good money to come here on vacation," Petit said.

"Crazy son of a bitches," Hammer said, not caring who heard him.

A few tourists in the big taxi bus glanced over at him but then quickly averted their gazes. Hammer was a very large man, over six feet four and 240 pounds. Everything about him was huge: his hands, for which he had to have custom-made gloves, his feet, which were size 17 EEE, and his shirt collar, which was 20½ inches. No one, not even his friends, ever asked him about his first name.

He had been with the FBI since coming out of army intelligence as a captain in 1972, working his way up to chief investigative officer with the bureau's Special Investigative Division in the first eight years and refusing all further advancement. He was a man perfectly suited to his job, and he was doing exactly what he wanted to be doing.

He and Petit had been met with a certain amount of hostility when they'd shown up on the island. It was obvious they were not tourist or even land developers, so the only other real possibility was law enforcement. Hammer had seen the look before. Often.

The cabby dropped them off on the highway at the foot of Moran's driveway above Fish Bay on the south side of the island.

"That's private property up there, man," their driver told them. "Don' go messin' around."

Hammer and Petit ignored him as they started up the driveway, and the cab finally left. They could hear it grinding up the steep hill toward the other side of the island.

Hammer and Petit looked at each other, silently nodded, and took out their pistols, then went the rest of the way up the rutted gravel driveway.

The house was low and rambling, portions of it screened by thick foliage. A small swimming pool faced the front, behind which appeared to be a breezeway leading back to the main body of the house.

Hammer motioned Petit to go around back. He took the front, flattening himself against the cement-block wall beyond the pool and listening for any sign that someone was inside.

But the day was quiet except in the distance, perhaps down on the beach, someone was shouting as if he were playing a game.

The breezeway door was unlocked, but the main door into the house was secured with an ordinary tumbler lock, which Hammer had picked in under ten seconds.

Rolling through the doorway and sidestepping to the left, he swung his gun left to right. Nothing moved. The house was definitely deserted, and he slowly straightened up.

"Tom?" he called out.

"Nothing," Petit answered from the back of the house.

"No one's home."

Petit appeared at the doorway from the kitchen. He holstered his gun. "We'll have to get a team down here, might be able to pick up some prints, depending on how thorough he was."

"He's not coming back," Hammer said, sniffing the air.

Petit shook his head. "It doesn't look as if anyone ever lived here. Really lived here."

The agency limousine turned off a nearly deserted Pennsylvania Avenue a few minutes before two, was passed through security onto White House grounds, and pulled up at the West Portico.

The President's national security adviser, William Tyrell, was there to meet Vaughan, and together they headed up to the Oval Office.

"He wants to get to Camp David as soon as possible," Tyrell said. "So we're going to have to hold your briefing to a half hour." He was a Harvard cum laude graduate who had been close personal friends with the President since the congressional days. He was part of what was being called the New Establishment.

Vaughan resented his interference. Traditionally CIA chiefs

had the direct ear of the President. But he held his irritation in check.

"Is Ed Wilder here yet?"

"Just arrived along with John McKinnon. They're inside now."

They went in. The President was standing at his desk. He was a tall, lanky man, all angles, with a surprisingly soft voice in person. Wilder was just taking something out of his briefcase, and McKinnon was scowling. They were seated on the small couch along the north wall.

"Am I late, Mr. President?" Vaughan asked.

"No, just on time, Bob." The President came around his desk and directed him and Tyrell to chairs facing the couch. The President sat down in his rocking chair. "Any of you want coffee?"

Vaughan shook his head no, as did the others.

"Okay, what have you got for me this afternoon?"

Vaughan opened his briefcase, took out a file folder, and extracted the fascimile copies of the material that had been handed over in front of the embassy in Moscow. He handed a couple of photos to the President. "His name, so far as the Russians know it, is Donald Sullivan Moran. Five feet eleven, a hundred eighty pounds, dark complexion. Birth date: nine October 1952. Current place of residence, the U.S. Virgin Islands."

"I have two of my people down there now checking it out, Mr. President," Wilder said. "So far they've found nothing."

"This file was handed over to Dick Sweeney, our assistant chief of Moscow station, by two unidentified Russians, probably KGB, Friday evening. *After* the assassination attempt. Apparently it was a mixup on their part that caused the delay. But evidently they knew or suspected that Moran was in Geneva to assassinate Gorbachev, and they wanted our help to stop it."

The President was looking at the photographs. "Is he an American after all?"

"We think so," Wilder said. "But we've got nothing on him in our files."

"We do," Vaughan interjected. Wilder's eyes narrowed. "At least it looks as if we do."

"What do you mean?" Tyrell asked. He was polishing his thick glasses.

"There was nothing in our files on him under this name, and

when Ed told me that his people hadn't come up with anything either, I began to wonder how the Russians had found out so much about him. So I put myself in their shoes, or at least I made an assumption that someone over there had hired him to do the job."

"What?" the President demanded.

"Please bear with me for a moment, Mr. President. If people over there wanted to get rid of Gorbachev, for any number of reasons, they would naturally want to hire an assassin who was not Russian. They would want an outsider. Someone who was very good. The best."

"But these men don't advertise in the yellow pages or *Soldier of Fortune*," McKinnon said.

"No," Vaughan replied dryly. "I sent my people looking for a man of that caliber, someone who had demonstrated his abilities. We backtracked assassinations over the past ten years in which no arrests had been made, putting together what little scraps we could come up with from our files as well as from Interpol's International Computer Network."

"And came up with Moran's name?"

"No, but we did come up with three descriptions, one of which matches Moran's and leads back to the Caribbean. His name three years ago may have been Richard Parmenter, a liquor importer. Before that he might have been Anthony Thomas, a wealthy playboy in Paris and Nice."

"Why wasn't he arrested?" the President asked.

"Not enough evidence. What we found was buried deep."

"But what you're saying is that the information the Russians gave us is probably accurate," the President said.

"Yes, sir."

The President was very interested now. He leaned forward. "Gorbachev said nothing to me." He turned to his Secret Service chief. "John, did the Russians say anything to you?"

"First I knew that anything might be out of line was when the two Moscow militia detectives showed up. But we never dreamed they were trying to stop an assassin."

"Did they say how they came to have this information, that there was an assassin there in Geneva at that moment?"

"No, Mr. President," McKinnon answered.

"We can ask them in a couple of hours. Or at least one of them," Wilder said.

"Ganin?" McKinnon said. "He's coming here?"

"Yes. Looking for Moran."

"No—" McKinnon started to say, but the President waved him off.

"I'm going to have to overrule you on this one, John. We are going to cooperate with them. One hundred percent. Give him whatever he wants if it will lead to the arrest of this man, Moran, or whatever his name is."

"If it is Moran, Mr. President, he's an American," Vaughan said. "Surely you don't mean to let Ganin take him back to the Soviet Union for trial."

"No crime has been committed on U.S. soil."

"Yes, sir, but—"

"We'll turn him over to the Swiss authorities. After all, he killed five men there and attempted to kill a sixth."

Vaughan had to smile inwardly, and he saw that both Wilder and McKinnon had the same reaction. The assassin, if he turned out to be Moran, was an American. Trying him in the Soviet Union would be very bad for our public image. Trying him here would leave us wide open to criticism. But turning him over to the Swiss was a stroke of genius.

"All we need to do now, gentlemen, is catch the bastard," the President said.

Vivian Hammer stood on the white sand beach looking across the Caribbean toward St. Croix, the big island thirty-five miles to the south. It was barely visible in the mist.

Just now the trade winds breeze was pleasant. His jacket was back at the house, and he had unbuttoned his collar and loosened his tie.

He had to admit to himself that he might prefer this to Washington's heat and humidity during the summer and its penetrating cold in the winter. But then the action was in the nation's capital, which probably had more crooks (white-collar and otherwise) per acre than anywhere else in the world.

It would be several hours yet before the forensics team arrived from Miami, and in the meantime, they had been given strict instructions not to touch or disturb anything.

Well, almost strict instructions. Still, it was up to the first investigators to make their initial evaluations before the scene was torn apart.

They had learned at least one thing so far: Moran was a cold fish. There was nothing of any human personality in the house. Nothing that would indicate its occupant had any hopes or dreams or desires other than staying alive; no interests or loves or hates. The house was even more sterile than a hotel room.

Flipping his cigarette out into the water, Hammer turned and made his way back up to the house. Tom Petit, wearing surgical rubber gloves, was just hanging up the telephone.

"They've already left Miami, so it looks as if we're not going to have to wait much longer."

"Good," Hammer said. He started to turn away as Petit hunched down in front of the small telephone stand and reached for the drawer pull. "Don't touch that."

"Shit," Petit said, and he opened the drawer.

A huge explosion blew out the entire wall behind the telephone stand, flinging Petit backward twenty feet across the room. Hammer was knocked off his feet, something heavy falling on him from above.

"Tom?" he shouted, but he couldn't hear his own voice. He was seeing bright yellow and orange spots.

He crawled out from beneath a section of ceiling that had collapsed on him and scrambled to where Petit lay half over on his side. He eased the man over but then reeled back on his heels. Tom Petit's head and shoulders were gone. A whole cement block jutted from his thorax where his chest had been.

The airliner approached Dulles Airport from the north, giving its passengers a good look at the Potomac River and the city with all its monuments and important buildings.

For a lot of them this was their first good look at America, as it was for Ganin. Everyone was excited.

Leaving Moscow at eight in the morning (it was midnight there now), he had chased the sun over the Pole, and he was tired and cramped. Sepelev had driven him out to the airport with all sorts of instructions on how to behave once he got here.

Life in the Soviet Union was still highly organized despite the new openness. The government provided nearly everything, even under *perestroika*. The average Russian believed that because of the dazzling array of choices everyone in the West was faced with on a daily basis, the average person there was very susceptible to insanity.

It was a national article of faith, that belief, and Sepelev had given voice to it all the way out to Sheremetyevo.

"I won't be there that long, Yurochka," Ganin had assured him. "Maybe I'll only go a little crazy."

"Just keep your feet dry. Those bastards don't give a damn about you or about this investigation. It wasn't their president being shot at."

Ganin had smiled and patted Sepelev on the arm. "Anything you want me to bring you or Larissa?"

Sepelev's eyes lit up, and he pulled out a folded sheet of paper, which he pressed into Ganin's hand. "Just a few things, Nikki. I wouldn't have said a thing unless you brought it up first. And most of this . . . crap is for Larissa anyway."

Ganin hadn't looked at it until they were across the border and out over the North Atlantic. "Larissa's" list consisted of ballpoint pens (for which she had no use); Billy Joel and Paul Simon tapes (she hated rock and roll); Kentucky blended whiskey, which was all the rage this year in Moscow (she didn't drink); Marlboro cigarettes (she didn't smoke); and laser disks with any kind of music (which might have been for her, but he didn't think the Sepelevs owned a disk player).

The plane banked sharply for its final approach, and Ganin could see vast paved fields that contained only a few cars but could easily park thousands upon thousands. He didn't understand, because none of the highways they'd crossed over seemed particularly busy. In fact, he thought there was even less traffic than in Moscow.

Another highway slid by beneath them, and then there were rows of warehouses and other windowless buildings, another narrow parking lot, a grassy field, a drainage ditch, and the spindly instrument landing system markers, and they were over the end of the runway.

"The FBI will cooperate with you, Nikolai Fedorovich," Chief Prosecutor Yernin told him at the dacha. They'd gone for a walk along the river so that they could be alone. Antonia was content to stay behind and talk to Yernin's secretary even if he wasn't an American movie actor.

"Why not the KGB? I'm only a Moscow militia investigator," Ganin had asked.

"For the simple reason that the FBI would *not* cooperate with the KGB."

"But they'll believe that I'm a KGB officer."

"True, but they won't *know* it, Nikki."

Ganin shook his head. "What do you expect me to do over there?"

"What you do best. Investigate."

"I don't know the country. I don't even understand their customs—"

"But you understand the language, and it is time you learned the rest." Yernin stopped. "Listen to me. In this world a man cannot be complete without an understanding of the West."

"But will they cooperate with me? Really?"

"Of course. But it will be up to you to infuse in them your enthusiasm for the hunt. This is an American assassin, but his target was and possibly still is a Russian. Let us not forget that."

The plane touched down with a bark of tires. It had reached America.

It was twenty after four by the time the airliner got to the terminal and the passengers began to disembark. Ganin waited until most of them were gone before he got his single bag down from the overhead locker.

Signs in English and Spanish directed him to the baggage hall and customs. Yellow and red lines were painted on the floor, leading what few Americans were on the flight one way and non-Americans another.

He had stopped for a moment to figure out which way he was supposed to go when two men, wearing nicely cut lightweight business suits, came up to him.

"Chief Investigator Ganin?" one of them asked. He was tall and rawboned. There was something wrong with his face, and it took Ganin a moment to realize that he was sunburned. It was extraordinary.

Ganin nodded.

"Do you speak English?" the other, much shorter, broader man asked. There was no humor in either of them.

"Reasonably well. May I ask who you are? Are you here to meet me?"

"May I see your passport, sir?" the sunburned one said pleasantly enough. But there was something wrong.

Ganin nodded again and handed over his passport.

The sunburned one examined the passport closely, then handed it back. "I'm Special Agent Stewart McGowan," he said. He nodded toward the other man. "Special Agent Mark Hardy. FBI. We were sent to meet you and get you to your hotel." They showed their IDs.

"Thank you. Will I be working with you?"

Hardy snorted and looked away.

"If you'll just come with us, our car is out front," McGowan said.

"I have a sealed package which will be waiting for me at customs."

"Customs won't be necessary. And you won't be needing your piece here," McGowan said. "Come on."

Ganin followed them past the customs counters, none of the agents even bothering to look up, and then they went through the terminal and outside. The afternoon was very warm and humid compared with Moscow. The air smelled of a combination of burned jet fuel, car exhaust, and something else, perhaps freshly cut grass; something different from home.

They got in the car, Hardy behind the wheel, McGowan in the passenger seat, and Ganin in back, and took off at a high rate of speed, merging with light traffic on a broad divided highway running northeast. For the first few minutes they drove in silence. Ganin took out a cigarette, crushed the cardboard filter, twisted it ninety degrees, then put it in his mouth and lit it.

Hardy was watching him in the rearview mirror. "Christ, do you have to do that in here?"

Ganin ignored him. "Special Agent McGowan, if you are indeed a federal police officer and not CIA, then I would be delighted if you would share with me the fruits of your investigation."

"Jesus Christ, did you hear that shit?" Hardy said.

"Just McGowan will be fine." He also ignored Hardy. "But we're not part of the team, so I can't tell you much."

"But you know why I have been sent here."

"Yes, we were told that."

"Then can you tell me what has happened?"

McGowan shook his head. "I don't understand what you mean."

"Has there been a development in the case? In the search for Moran?"

"Jesus . . ." Hardy swore.

"Shut up, Mark," McGowan snapped. "Yes, there has been a development. One of our people was killed this afternoon. Just a few hours ago. But you have my assurance that the Bureau will cooperate with you, one hundred percent."

"This happened here in Washington?" Ganin asked sharply.

"The Virgin Islands."

Ganin shook his head. "What is this place?"

"What the hell are you talking about, you bastard?" Hardy shouted. "Your people sent us the bullshit about where Moran lived. His goddamned house was booby-trapped."

"My people?"

"Yeah, the KGB."

"I'm not KGB."

"About what we figured you'd say."

Ganin turned back to McGowan. "I'm sorry, but I don't know what is going on. You say the KGB gave you information about Moran? What information?"

"His name, photographs, where he lived. The Virgin Islands are in the Caribbean. Southeast. Below Cuba."

"When and where was this information handed over?"

"I don't know. Moscow, maybe."

Ganin sat back. "I would like to go there, to the Virgin Islands. I need to see this house with my own eyes."

"We're taking you to your fucking hotel," Hardy said. He was a little calmer now, but he kept glancing in the rearview mirror.

"I can't do my investigation . . . or help with yours if I am locked up in a hotel."

McGowan shrugged. "That one is out of my hands. But someone will be by to talk to you."

"When?"

"Tomorrow, I think."

They crossed the Roosevelt Bridge and got off the expressway on Constitution Avenue, the Washington Monument to their right and the White House to their left across the Ellipse. All the highways and streets were very broad, as if they could handle heavy traffic, yet there were very few cars out and about. It was a mystery until Ganin realized that today was Sunday. And in America everything closed on Sunday.

Five minutes later they pulled into the driveway of the Holiday Inn—Thomas Circle on Massachusetts Avenue. He had read about this motel chain. It looked very exotic. Like everything in America so far.

McGowan handed him a large plastic tab to which a key was attached. The number 2433 was painted in gold on the tab. "Second floor. Call room service if you want something to eat or drink. Don't leave the hotel."

Hardy had turned around and was grinning at him. "Go ahead and try it if you'd like."

Ganin looked at him for a long second or two; then he smiled. "We have people just like you in the Soviet Union."

"Yeah?"

"Their mothers usually spank them because it's a sign they aren't potty-trained."

23

Seeing Mary Frances Dean's face on the television forced Moran to make a decision he'd hoped wouldn't be necessary so soon.

One of the reasons for his success over the years was his ruthless preservation of his anonymity. Not once had he been concretely tied to the scene of a kill. No witnesses going in, and none coming out.

It was the reason he had killed the Soviet courier and one of the reasons he'd killed the woman in St. John, and it was the reason he had killed the Soviet military attaché. In all instances they could have provided damning evidence.

Mary Frances Dean would have to be killed, too, before he could continue with his primary assignment. It was annoying, and it would take time—thirty-six hours, perhaps forty-eight—but it had to be done.

He had finalized another lingering decision as well. When this was over, he would retire. That meant he was going to have to go deep enough so that he would never be found. After he killed Gorbachev, there would be a lot of heat for a long time by the KGB, which had its tendrils worldwide. In order to hide, he was going to have to pull the edges in around himself.

More risks, but necessary.

He parked the Mercedes in a ramp behind the Vieux Port of Marseilles and, shouldering his single black leather bag, walked away. He dropped the keys down a sewer grate a few blocks away.

It was nearly midnight, and the old port area, with its waterfront bistros, numerous sidewalk cafés, strip joints, and seamen's bars, was alive with activity. Three blocks off the Rue Canebière, Moran hesitated a moment at the corner to make sure that no one was watching him and then ducked down a narrow alley which he knew came to a dead end seventy-five yards back. It was dark and smelled of rotting garbage and open sewers. Much of Marseilles had been rebuilt after the war, but this section had remained essentially the same for the past seventy-five years.

The liquor warehouse at number 15 was dark, as was the apartment above it. Again Moran hesitated, all his senses alert for the slightest sign that he was walking into a trap. But no one knew his real name or at least the name he used when he came to this place. There was nothing to connect his Moran persona with Marseilles.

He let himself into the building with his own key and again stopped to listen. Nothing. By day the warehouse was busy, but at six in the evening all the workmen left. They did not come back until eight in the morning.

Upstairs he let himself into the apartment, softly closing and relocking the door. After putting his bag down, he made his way across the large main room and into the back bedroom. He could make out a form sleeping on the bed, and he could hear regular breathing. Silently he crossed to the bed and clamped his right hand over the man's mouth.

The Frenchman came instantly awake and tried desperately to get up, but Moran was too strong.

"It's me," Moran said. "Per Donastorg. Make no noise."

The Frenchman settled back. Moran removed his hand and stepped away from the bed. A light came on.

"Hello, Michel," Moran said, smiling.

The forger Michel Gavalet was sitting up in bed, a pistol in his right hand trained on Moran as he fumbled with his left for his glasses. When he had them on, he shook his head and lowered the gun.

"You are a surprise, monsieur. Are you in trouble?"

"Yes. I need some papers tonight. American."

Gavalet stuffed the pistol back under his pillow, threw back the bedcovers, and got up. "One of these days, my friend, you will get yourself shot coming to me in this fashion." He tapped his thin chest. "It's my heart. The walls are too thin, the plaque has built up too far, and my blood pressure is . . . you don't want to know. But it is horrible. I startle easy."

"The papers."

"Yes, yes." Gavalet waved him off. "You will have your papers and be gone before daybreak. You have always paid well in the past, and you will pay very well tonight." His eyes narrowed. "You were not followed here?"

"No," Moran said, smiling again. "No one knows I am here with you."

The sun was just beginning to tinge the hills east of Marseilles with red when Moran set his bag with the rest of the money he'd found in the hidden wall safe by the door, unsnapped the latch so that he could get out quickly, and then went back across the living room.

Gavalet, a big gash across the back of his head, was dead. He lay on his face beneath the heavy oak bookcase Moran had pulled down on his body. A short stepladder was overturned next to him, and an alcohol lamp, its fuel spilled in a big puddle, was beside it. Some of the alcohol had pooled beside the dead man's head. The smell in the apartment was cloying.

Moran had been smoking one of Gavalet's cigarettes. He carefully laid it down on the floor within half an inch of the puddle. A second later a thin blue flame began to rise and slowly crept across the floor toward the Frenchman's body and toward the bookcase and books and papers and photographs.

At the door Moran didn't bother looking back. Downstairs

he slipped outside after first making sure no one was out or about yet, and hurried up to the main street. He worked his way back to the Rue Canebière, where he caught a cab just coming on duty.

"Good morning, Father," the cabby said. "It will be a beautiful day."

"Yes, it will, my son," Moran said. "Could you please take me to the airport? I've an early flight to catch."

Maximilliano Torres grinned broadly when he realized who it was standing at his door. "Señor Tanner . . . or should I say Father Tanner? Come in, come in."

Mexico City stank; the air wasn't fit to breathe. Inside Torres's large, comfortably furnished home, however, the air conditioner made it tolerable.

"Father Daniel, if you'd like, Max," Moran said. Here his persona had been Bruce Tanner. His papers from France, however, identified him as Daniel Morgan, a Catholic priest.

Torres was one of the finest gunsmiths on this side of the Atlantic. It was he who had designed and built Moran's sniper rifle. "This is not merely a social call, I think," he said, leading Moran back to his study at the rear of the house.

"I need a weapon."

Torres looked sharply at him but said nothing until they were seated across his desk from each other. "Your beautiful rifle is lost . . . or out of your reach for the moment?"

"I don't need another rifle. A handgun with a silencer, I should think."

"A SigSauer, then? Nine-millimeter, fifteen rounds."

"Not quiet enough, even with the silencer. I'll need better."

"Twenty-two caliber? Perhaps you will go for a head shot?"

"Much better," Moran said. "And ammunition. Long rifle, hollow point."

Torres nodded. "Help yourself to a little brandy, my friend," he said, getting up. He left the room.

Moran remained where he was seated, listening to the sounds of the house. Large sliding glass doors led to a pleasant patio with a bubbling fountain. He'd always liked this house, though he despised Mexico City and Mexicans in general. Torres had been a lucky man, he thought. He was talented, he made sufficient money for his needs, and he was married to a beautiful, gracious woman.

Torres returned a couple of minutes later, carrying an olive drab metal box, which he placed on a cloth on his desk. He opened it, took out a .22-caliber automatic, and handed the weapon to Moran.

It felt good. "Light. Nice balance."

Torres handed across the long silencer tube, which Moran threaded on the end of the barrel.

"How is María?"

Torres smiled, handing a clip of ammunition to Moran. "Eighteen rounds. She is fine, and she wishes to say hello to you if you have the time. I haven't told her about your latest disguise, however. It will be fun to surprise her."

"Yes," Moran said, smiling warmly. He snapped the clip into the butt of the weapon, cycled the ejector slide, and, before Torres could move or say another word, raised the pistol and fired one round point-blank into the man's forehead.

Torres fell back in his chair and then slumped forward on his desk, dead.

Moran got up and, holding the pistol out of sight behind his right leg, went out into the corridor. "María?" he called out.

The room was dark except for the ghostly flickering light from the television set tuned to the CNN channel.

Ganin stood at the window, looking out on the quiet city. He could not sleep, and the hamburger he'd ordered from room service was too sweet (did they put sugar in their food in America?), the french fries were too greasy, and the beer was far too cold and watery.

No one had come for him, nor had anyone called. So far as he knew, he could have been simply dumped here and then deserted.

Around ten in the evening he had opened his room door and looked out into the corridor, but no one had been there. He had walked down to the stairwell and opened that door, but still no one had challenged him, no one had come running demanding

166

that he retreat to his room. He would have almost welcomed another confrontation with Mark Hardy. Being left alone like this was depressing.

He had discovered the telephone book and had spent more than an hour cross-legged on the bed looking through the yellow pages in one volume and the white pages in the other. In Moscow telephone directories were almost never seen, and when they were, they had to be treated with the same caution and respect with which the man on the street would treat a document marked "Top Secret."

Here everything was open. Unless the FBI, had placed the directory in his room simply to impress him. For some reason he didn't think it was that easy.

Turning away from the window, he started for his cigarettes on the bureau when he saw a familiar face on the television. It was the woman from Geneva, the woman McKinnon and the Americans had been speaking with.

He turned up the volume and stood in front of the set as an older man with silver hair who seemed to be the moderator was asking her a question.

". . . can't be sure?"

"Of course not," Mary Frances said with a half-smile. "I was asked about people in the crowd moments after the shot was fired. If I had noticed anything unusual. Anything or anyone out of place. And of course, I told them that I had bumped . . . literally bumped . . . into a two-star general who seemed to be heading *away* from the building, not toward it like everyone else."

She looked directly at the camera. Ganin was mesmerized again by her eyes, by the expression on her face, by her sheer presence. She was an exotic creature.

"What struck me at the time was that he hadn't seemed to be aware of what had just happened. I thought it very odd."

"Has he been identified?"

"I don't know, but I could provide a good description."

The picture flashed to a pair of news readers in what appeared to be a very large television studio or newsroom.

"There's been no word from the FBI or from the Secret Service, which is charged with security for the President, here and abroad, about Mary Frances Dean's speculations, Bob," the plain-faced woman told the man seated next to her.

"No, Sally, but from what I understand, the bureau will be releasing a statement sometime tomorrow morning."

"Then we'll just have to wait and see," the woman said. She glanced down at some papers in front of her and then looked up again. "In Moscow Ken Evans has a report on the Soviets' reactions to all of this."

It took him nearly an hour with the yellow pages and the telephone to find the correct number. He decided he didn't care if McGowan or Hardy was monitoring the telephone calls. He would be happy for a reaction from them or from anyone else for that matter. Any sort of reaction.

His last call was answered on the third ring. "Good evening, Trump Shuttle," a woman said in a singsong voice.

"Can you tell me when flights leave for New York City from Washington?"

"We have numerous flights daily, sir, several times per hour during peak times. Our first flight leaves Washington's National at seven A.M., our last at ten-thirty P.M. Do you wish to make a reservation at this time, sir?"

"No," Ganin said. "No. Thank you very much."

He hung up. Getting to New York, it seemed, would be no problem, provided the FBI left him alone. He was amazed at how easy it seemed.

The sun was rising, tingeing the eastern sky with red, as Ganin took a shower and got dressed. The street beneath his window, which had been clear of traffic yesterday afternoon and last night, was crammed with automobiles, taxis, and trucks. What amazed him mostly, though, was that there seemed to be more vehicular traffic than pedestrians.

He was just knotting his tie when someone knocked at his door. He slipped the chain and snapped the lock back.

"Yes?" he asked as he opened the door.

One of the largest men Ganin had ever seen pushed his way inside with one hand, while holding up his FBI identification with the other.

"Special Agent Vivian Hammer," he said.

Ganin just caught a glimpse of the ID as the man passed. No one else was out in the corridor. He closed the door.

Hammer checked the bathroom and then looked out the window before he turned around, his hands hanging at his sides as if he were a boxer ready either to strike a blow or to fend one off. He looked very mean.

"You and I are going to be working together," he growled.

Ganin stared at him for a long second or two. The man was huge, perhaps 130 kilos or more, yet he seemed to carry himself with the grace of an athlete.

"Have you spoken with McGowan or Hardy?" Ganin asked.

Hammer nodded. "They were the baby-sitters. They're gone now. It's just you and I, and I want to get something straight from the start."

Ganin nodded. It seemed reasonable, though he could not understand why everyone he had come into contact with so far seemed so angry. It wasn't their president who had been shot at.

"I don't like Russians, I wouldn't have cared if Gorbachev had bought the farm, I didn't ask for this assignment, and I've already lost one partner."

"You were in the Virgin Islands, at Moran's home?"

"Yes."

"I'm sorry about your partner—"

"The fucking place was booby-trapped." Hammer held up his big hands before Ganin could finish. "Our fault . . . my fault. We should have known better, I grant you that. But at least you sons a bitches could have warned us."

"About what, Mr. Hammer?" Ganin asked. He found that he felt sorry for the man. He could see his anguish over the loss. It didn't make him any less dangerous, however, perhaps even more so. "That Moran is a killer?"

Hammer started to reply but held back.

"If we are going to work together, then you must understand something as well," Ganin said. "I am not KGB. And I know nothing more about Moran than his last name, that he is right-handed, that he is an expert at hand-to-hand combat, that he is completely ruthless, that he is a master at disguise, and that it will be very difficult to catch him."

"They said you saw him."

"Only from the back. He was running away from me. I got a couple of shots off, but I don't think I hit him. He's athletic. He moved well."

"Five-eleven, one hundred ninety pounds," Hammer said, pulling a manila envelope out of his belt beneath his jacket.

"He's lost weight," Ganin said. "The man I saw was slightly built."

Hammer nodded. "No way of knowing how current this information is." He opened the envelope and laid out the photographs and documents on the bed.

Ganin picked up one of the black-and-white eight-by-ten pictures which showed a dark-haired dark-complected man coming away from a sidewalk café on what could have been a street in Paris. He was handsome in an almost aristocratically Spanish sort of way. But even at a distance you could see that there was something missing in the man, some furtiveness perhaps that made him wary of his surroundings. He seemed to be an animal making its way through the night jungle.

"Is this the information from Moscow?"

"That's what I've been told."

"How was it handed over?"

"I don't know all the details, except that someone showed up at our embassy a few hours after the assassination attempt. . . . KGB, GRU, we don't know. They asked for one of our people by name—"

"CIA?"

Hammer shot him a harsh look but then nodded. "From what I'm told. Anyway they handed this package over . . . or a package. This one is a fascimile copy. And that's it."

Ganin sat on the edge of the bed and quickly looked through all the material. Moran was evidently linked with a number of assassinations over the past eight or ten years, though the evidence seemed terribly circumstantial. The photographs had come from what may have been an Interpol surveillance, yet there were no charge sheets, nothing to indicate that Moran might be under investigation for any crime.

This information, he decided, was most likely the product of a KGB or GRU search of criminal organizations worldwide. Money would have been spent for such details; facts were a negotiable commodity just like wheat or bullets or lives.

"What did you find in the Virgin Islands?" Ganin asked, looking up.

"Nothing," Hammer said, and before Ganin could object, he went on. "I mean, Moran may have lived there at one time, perhaps even recently, but he's not coming back. The locals think he's a drug lord; nobody wants to talk to us. But he's not coming back."

"What happened?"

Hammer sighed deeply, and then he explained how the accident had happened. "Our team found half a dozen other traps. Reminded me of . . ." He trailed off.

"Yes?" Ganin prompted.

"Vietnam," Hammer said. "Reminded me of the welcome mats the VC used to lay out for us."

Ganin nodded. "He learned his combat and demolitions skills somewhere. Perhaps the Army or Marines in Vietnam. Has a records search been made?"

"We're working on it," Hammer said. "What were you and your partner doing in Geneva?"

"Looking for Moran."

"By name? You knew about this?"

"No." Ganin held him off. He stood up, looked at Hammer for a second, then got a cigarette off the bureau and lit it before he answered. The FBI agent had lost a partner, yet he seemed to want to deal straight. They would have to trust each other. At least for the moment.

Ganin turned back. "There was a hit-and-run in front of the Lubyanka—that's headquarters for the KGB—in which a young army lieutenant was killed."

Ganin quickly went over the details of his own investigation, including how he and Sepelev had found the tape recording, how they had passed it along to the Moscow town prosecutor, and how subsequently they had been sent to Geneva.

"It's a military plot against your government? A coup?"

Ganin shrugged "Not so much against our government as it is against the way it is going now under President Gorbachev."

"I thought he was called party general secretary or Chairman something."

"That, too." Ganin smiled. "So, it is an American assassin trying to kill a Russian. Now we are working together. Détente, I believe you call it."

"Who do you want to see in New York?" Hammer asked suddenly.

Ganin glanced at the telephone. "You do monitor telephones in American hotels."

"Not always, but this time, yes. New York."

"A woman journalist. Mary Frances Dean."

Hammer's eyes narrowed.

"She may have actually seen Moran in Geneva," Ganin said. "I'd like to take these photographs up there and perhaps take a sketch artist with us."

"I think we can dig one up, but if you're talking about this two-star general of hers, it's a dead end."

"It's already been checked?"

"As far as possible, yes. Everyone who came through the gates was legitimate. And her general was wearing a security badge."

"I'd like to talk to her anyway," Ganin said.

Hammer nodded. He pulled Ganin's pistol and ammunition wallet out of his pocket and tossed them on the bed without a word. Ganin nodded his thanks.

"There is another question. Vivian is a woman's name in English, is it not?"

Hammer's jaw tightened. He nodded curtly.

"Then I do not understand why it is your parents gave you such a name."

"It was to make me tough," Hammer said through clenched teeth.

"I see," Ganin said, shaking his head in amazement. There was much about Americans he was going to have to learn.

If Washington was a puzzle, New York was a grand mystery. Riding in the taxi from La Guardia Airport, Ganin was struck by the dirt and filth, by the junk cars, bottles, scrap paper, and other trash along the roadsides, by the graffiti on the walls, and by the drab sameness of the slum apartment blocks that in a small measure reminded him of sections of Moscow.

Washington had seemed like an imperial Roman city with its monuments, the capital of a vast empire. New York, on the other hand, seemed like the capital of the barbarian hordes.

He was confused, but all his thoughts melted to nothingness when he caught his first full look at the Manhattan skyline. He sat back in his seat.

"Oh," he said.

Hammer laughed. "What's the matter, Ganin, don't you have skyscrapers in Russia?"

Leon Siff, the sketch artist they'd brought along with them, grinned.

Ganin looked at them in open amazement. They did not understand. But then how could they? He looked again at the skyline. In the Soviet Union they said war was winnable. But seeing this now, he knew that wasn't true.

They were met in the thirtieth-floor reception room by Bob Liskey, the foreign reports editor. Hammer had telephoned ahead, but it had taken the magazine the better part of the morning to grant its permission for the bureau to speak with Mary Frances. A couple of years ago the First Amendment had received a serious challenge in the Supreme Court over the right to make public the names of crime victims. The news media were still skittish.

"We'll be meeting in the conference room, gentlemen," Liskey said, and he led them back to a large, airy room with big windows. The lights were on because it was still overcast and gloomy. In Moscow, Ganin thought, the fluorescents would have been turned on in any event to interfere with monitoring devices.

Two men were seated around a long, highly polished conference table with Mary Frances Dean. They rose, and Liskey introduced them as Lawrence Weaver, the magazine's managing editor, and Richard Knoepfel, its general counsel. But Ganin barely heard the names. His eyes were locked into the woman's. This close again, he could feel heat coming from her. He'd felt the same thing in Geneva, but he had forgotten it until just this moment.

She looked up at him, puzzled for just a moment until she recognized him. He could see it in her eyes.

"Hello again, Miss Dean," he said.

"Geneva," Mary Frances said. "You're Russian. A policeman."

Ganin smiled deprecatingly. The others were looking at them.

"They have sent me to America to look for the would-be assassin."

"You've not been here before?"

He shook his head.

"It must be very different from home."

Ganin glanced toward the windows. "Very different," he said. "I saw you on television. It was very nice."

There was an embarrassing little silence which Hammer filled by introducing himself, the sketch artist, and Ganin. "We have a few questions for Ms. Dean, and we want you to know that the bureau appreciates your cooperation."

They all sat down. Knoepfel was not smiling. "I have advised Ms. Dean and Mr. Weaver that we will take each question on its own merits as pertains to our answers or our silence. You can understand the delicacy of the situation, I trust."

"Yes—" Hammer said.

"Would you know the general if you saw him again?" Ganin asked Mary Frances across the table.

She nodded. "I think so. I got a good look at him, and I remember faces."

"See here," Knoepfel protested.

Ganin looked at him. "Forgive me, counselor. Was that a question that needed consideration?"

"I was under the impression that this interview would be conducted by the bureau. You are simply an observer here." Knoepfel turned to Hammer. "Am I correct in this?"

Mary Frances was seated next to her attorney. She placed a hand on his coat sleeve. "It's all right," she said. She looked across at Ganin. "You saw me on television talking about the general. You think he's significant?"

"Possibly."

"So do I."

Again Ganin turned to Knoepfel. The man was glaring.

Hammer sat forward. "Chief Investigator Ganin should be considered, at least for the scope of this investigation, to be an agent of the bureau, Mr. Knoepfel."

"I would first like to know where you intend taking this line of questioning."

"Agent Siff is a sketch artist. We would like Ms. Dean to describe the man she saw, and we will make a drawing. Later we'll ask her to look at some photographs so that we can compare the two."

Knoepfel seemed to think about it for a moment. "And then?" he asked.

"And then we would like to know everything she saw from a

few minutes before the shooting until a few minutes afterward. Anything at all, no matter how apparently insignificant."

Ganin thought that whatever Hammer's feelings were about Russians in general, he was cooperating nicely now. The man was definitely a professional.

Knoepfel looked to Weaver, who nodded, then he turned to Mary Frances. "It's up to you."

"They tried to kill Gorbachev. Of course, I'll help. I was only a small child when Kennedy was killed, but I still remember it."

Knoepfel nodded.

Siff pulled out his sketch pad, and Mary Frances got up and came around to him. She was standing just inches from Ganin, and he had the almost uncontrollable urge to reach out and touch her. Not in any sexual way, necessarily, but merely to make contact.

Feeling his eyes on her, she turned and looked down at him. For a moment she didn't move, but then she smiled and turned back to Siff.

"His face was full," she said.

"Round or square?"

"Round, I think, but that could have been his hair, the way it framed his forehead."

"He wasn't wearing a cap?" Siff asked, starting to sketch.

"Yes, but I could see his hair, his sideburns, the hair at the back of his head."

Ganin got up and stood behind her and watched as the sketch began to develop. Siff was very good, and Mary Frances knew exactly what she had seen because she directed him to make changes, correcting him when he took an item of description too far or not far enough.

The face that began to emerge was a fairly nondescript man perhaps in his mid to late forties. Definitely an American, and definitely not the man in the photographs Hammer had shown him.

"How big a man was he?" Ganin asked.

Mary Frances looked up at him. "Smaller than you—" she said, but then changed her mind. "Maybe the same."

"Height?"

"About your height. Maybe your weight. His shoulders might have been a bit more substantial."

It wasn't Moran's description, nor was it the description of the man he'd shot running away from the cathedral. But then Moran was the master at disguise. He could have been wearing padding beneath his clothing, lifts in his shoes. He could have worn makeup, of course, but Moran's face was oval, while the face Siff had sketched was round. Was it possible, Ganin wondered, for Moran to have worn some sort of dental padding inside his mouth, something that would have filled out his cheeks, giving his face a different shape?

"How about his voice?" Ganin asked. "Did you speak to him?"

"Just a few words. He said he hadn't known that a shot had been fired," Mary Frances said. She looked away in thought for a moment. "It's hard to tell. Maybe a trace of an English accent, though I don't think he was British."

"An affectation?" Hammer asked.

She shook her head. "Education, I'd guess. I'd say he was very well educated."

Hammer opened his attaché case and withdrew one of the eight-by-ten photographs of Moran. Knoepfel stood up and looked at it before he would allow Mary Frances to look.

"Is this him?" Hammer asked.

Mary Frances shook her head. "No . . ." She trailed off.

"Yes?" Ganin asked.

"The eyes . . ." she said, but again she trailed off. She shook her head, looking up. "Not the same man."

"You said something about the eyes," Ganin insisted.

"Not the same man I saw in Geneva."

"Too bad."

"If there are no further questions . . ." Knoepfel said.

"I'm curious about something," Ganin said. "The gunshot. What did it sound like from where you were standing?"

"I didn't hear a thing," Mary Frances said.

"But you said—"

"Something happened on the speakers' platform, and pretty soon everyone was shouting that someone had tried to shoot Gorbachev."

Leon Siff took a cab out to the airport to catch the next Washington shuttle. Ganin and Hammer went into a small coffee shop across the street from the magazine, where they got a table by the window.

Superficially New York and Moscow were the same. They both were large cities, lots of people, lots of traffic, pedestrians, shops, buildings. But it was different here. Vastly different in thousands of ways from the gross to the subtle. Even the look on people's faces was different.

He had heard it explained by Titorov, the historian, that Americans rooted for the underdog the same way Russians rooted for their government. Even if the underdog was bad, a Dillinger or a Willie Sutton, Americans loved him as Russians loved their government, Joseph Stalin notwithstanding.

And he had already seen signs of that here. The average person seemed to have little or no respect for authority, yet the perfect stranger was willing to lend a hand to an old babushka crossing the street.

He didn't think he would ever understand these people. But then he didn't intend staying long enough for it to matter.

"The bureau has been told to cooperate with you one hundred percent," Hammer said. "But that doesn't mean I have to go along with a wild-goose chase."

Ganin had to smile.

"It's not funny, goddammit."

"No, it isn't," Ganin said seriously. "You've already lost a partner. No telling what I might lose." For some reason he thought about his wife, Antonia, and his friend Yurii Sepelev back in Moscow. They were cut of the same cloth. It would have been better had they married each other. Yurochka would have genuinely appreciated what Tonia's family could have done for him, and she would have been grateful for his sensible understanding about the party and the system of life such as it was. They would have gotten along famously.

"There were a thousand generals there that afternoon. Doesn't mean the one this woman bumped into was Moran."

There was no answering that question.

"No way to run them all down."

There had been something incredibly smooth about the woman. Some electrical field that surrounded her or some footlights that illuminated her in the very best way. It reminded him slightly of the prima and assoluta ballerinas of the Kirov and Bolshoi ballet companies. Onstage they, too, had that magical, mystical aura about them. But up close many of them were drab little girls with furtive eyes and knobby shoulders. Not Mary Frances. Up close she'd been even better than from afar.

"It was the wrong face anyway."

Ganin glanced at him. "He disguised himself. We knew that before we started."

"Wrong height, wrong facial structure."

He'd never questioned his own values. It was something, his father told him, that he had been born with. Everyone else wondered sooner or later who the hell they were and where the hell they were going. Or if they were like the dissidents, they expanded their uncertainties to their own government. He'd never had to do that. He'd always known. "It's one of the many reasons I love you, Nikki," his wife said. "Standing next to you, holding your arm, sheltering in your lee, I know that nothing will ever hurt me. Nothing could possibly reach me, not as long as you are there beside me."

Well, it was becoming a burden, he thought. And he didn't know if he liked it much any longer.

Hammer was getting frustrated. "Wrong everything," he said.

"Except for his eyes," Ganin said. "She recognized them."

"She *thought* she recognized his eyes."

"From a photograph. Probably an old one at that. In person it will be different."

"You mean face-to-face?"

Ganin nodded.

"We have to catch the bastard first."

Ganin managed a slight smile. "Oh, we will because he's either here already or on his way here."

Hammer's eyes narrowed. "What the hell are you talking about?"

"You saw the clips of her television appearance. You heard what she said. Moran has seen it, too. She's a witness whom he cannot afford to let live. He must come here to kill her."

"Christ, he'd be nuts. . . ."

"That's already been established. But the thing is, he's also very good."

"He missed."

"He doesn't intend missing the second time, but first he must eliminate everyone who knows his face."

"Could be a lot of people. His gunsmith. His source of passports. Those people at least."

"That would be worth a look. It would be a start," Ganin said. "Because once he makes his big kill, he is going to have to retire. He'll have to go deep because believe me, if the KGB wishes to find you, anywhere in the world, it usually does a pretty good job of it."

"So I've heard," Hammer said dryly.

Ganin returned his gaze to the building across the busy street.

"Why don't they go after him?" Hammer asked softly. "Their Ninth Directorate is supposed to take care of your leaders just like our Secret Service takes care of our President and Vice President."

Ganin turned back to him.

"Why'd they send a cop? A militia investigator?"

"Maybe I am KGB," Ganin said. "Maybe I brought a hundred men with me. Even now they may be watching us, waiting for you to make the wrong move." Ganin raised his right hand, pointed his index finger at Hammer, and let his thumb fall. "Bang," he said.

"But you've already said it may have been some sort of plot. It's a first for you, isn't it?"

"Plots or assassination attempts? Russians love plots."

"Assassination attempts."

Ganin shrugged and looked again across the street. "Lenin was shot at in 1918, and Sergei Kirov was killed in 1934. . . . Of course, that was on party orders."

"Ancient history."

"In 1969 someone tried to kill Brezhnev outside the Kremlin, of all places."

"What happened?"

"The killer wasn't very good. He shot at the wrong man."

"Why'd they send you, Ganin? Why just you?"

"Because there may be a plot, as you say, Hammer. But it may be complicated by the possibility there could be a faction fight between the KGB and the GRU, as well as between what you would call the moderates and the conservatives."

"Same thing."

"No. The moderates want the increasing democratization of the Soviet Union. The conservatives want to keep the status quo. The 1930's status quo."

"Stalinists."

"See, you do understand after all."

Hammer followed his gaze out the window. "Then let's pick her up. Hide her someplace."

"Americans," Ganin said. "You monitor telephone calls from hotels, and now you pick up people without a bill of warrant? You are not so different from us perhaps."

"More different than you can possibly imagine, Ganin."

Ganin leaned forward over the table. "Not so different, you stupid bastard, that you can't understand something. If we hide her, Moran will never show himself."

It was Hammer's turn to grin. "Maybe we are getting somewhere," he said. "But we're going to need a lot of people to cover her."

"It must be one-on-one."

"What?"

"If Moran is as good as I think he is . . . and I think he may be better . . . then he'll spot your surveillance people. It would be too risky. If he could get past security in Geneva, he certainly would have no problems here."

"All right, then you and I will—"

"Just me," Ganin said. "You're going to start a wire check on recent murders of gunsmiths and passport forgers. We need to know when they were killed, where they were killed, and how they were killed."

"There's no way I'm going to let you run around New York City on your own."

"Didn't you say something about one hundred percent co-operation?" Ganin asked.

GRU Captain Boris Stepanovich Gordeyev and Lieutenant Vasili Pavlovich Vlasov watched the coffee shop from the lobby of an office building two doors north of the magazine.

They were assigned to the Soviet Union's UN legation, watching for FBI operations against their own diplomats, but last-minute orders had come direct from Moscow in a for-your-eyes-only dispatch.

It was big business, career-making or -breaking business, and both men, veterans of a lot of years of legwork here and in a half dozen other Western nations, were suitably impressed.

"They probably went up to interview the woman, so what the fuck are they waiting for now?" Vlasov asked his captain.

"Her, obviously."

"What?"

"It's simple, Vasili Pavlovich," Gordeyev said. "She was on national—international television, claiming to have seen the man who might have been the shooter. He will come for her."

"So they are going to watch her until he does show up."

"I think so."

"But they're alone. Only the two of them. They won't be able to do such a hot job."

Gordeyev smiled. "We're alone, too. We'll manage."

Vlasov nodded his agreement. There was a symmetry to every operation. When Moran showed up, they would kill him. That would be the final harmony.

"There," Gordeyev suddenly said.

Vlasov stepped closer to the glass door in time to see Nikolai Ganin and Vivian Hammer, the FBI special agent, coming out of the coffee shop. They stopped on the sidewalk and seemed to be arguing about something. They kept looking across the street, but they kept their gestures down as if they did not want to call attention to themselves.

It was the woman, Vlasov suddenly realized. She was on the move.

"*Yeb vas*," Gordeyev swore softly under his breath.

Seconds later Ganin and the FBI agent walked off in opposite directions.

"Now," Gordeyev said, and he and Vlasov stepped outside and merged with the crowds.

For a second or two Gordeyev couldn't quite make up his mind whom to follow, the FBI agent or his countryman. But then he spotted Mary Frances Dean crossing the street at the corner, Ganin right behind her, and his decision was made.

27

Mary Frances Dean entered a new apartment building on East thirty-sixth Street between Lexington and Park Avenue a few minutes before six.

Ganin stood across the street, rain dripping off his coat collar, looking into the window of a travel agency, watching the reflection of the apartment building in the glass. Twice he'd thought he might have spotted someone behind him, a pair of them, but each time he'd doubled back they were gone.

Either they were very good, or they were nothing more than figments of his imagination. But a nagging little suspicion that not only were they real but that they were Russians had begun to form at the back of his head.

It wasn't Moran; he was willing to bet on that because he was certain that Moran worked alone. But if they were Russians, who

184

were they, the KGB or the GRU? A lot could depend on which side they were on.

He waited in front of the travel agency for a full ten minutes to make sure they or no one else were going to show up before he crossed the street in the middle of the block and entered the apartment building. The concierge was seated behind a glass panel watching a couple of closed-circuit television screens. He looked up.

"Good afternoon, sir. May I help you?"

"I would like to visit with Miss Dean. She lives here?"

"Your name?"

"Nikolai Ganin."

The concierge gave him an odd look, but he picked up a telephone and called upstairs.

Ganin turned and looked out the door. From where he stood he could see out, but he didn't think anyone on the street could see him. There was still a lot of traffic and a lot of pedestrians but, so far as he could tell, not the two he had spotted earlier. If they were there, they were very good.

"Twenty-third floor, Mr. Ganin," the concierge said, hanging up the telephone. "Apartment C. To your left when you get off the elevator."

"Yes, thank you," Ganin said.

Mary Frances Dean, still dressed as she had been at the office in a blouse and skirt, but with her shoes off, was waiting for him at her open door when he stepped off the elevator.

"You're a surprise," she said pleasantly.

He crossed the corridor to her. "I hope I am not disturbing you or your . . . guests?"

"I'm alone, but I don't suppose I should talk to you without my attorney present."

She was smiling, and Ganin wondered for an instant if she found him amusing, his clothes or his accent odd. It was possible he was saying or doing something wrong.

"If you wish to call him, it will be all right with me."

She looked over his shoulder toward the elevator. "Where's your FBI friend?"

"Checking on something," Ganin said. "Miss Dean, the reason I've come here like this is to tell you—"

"Inside," she said, stepping aside so that he could pass. "It's impolite to conduct an interview in a corridor. Or is that how they do things in Russia?"

Ganin hesitated for just a moment but then went into her apartment. It was very large by Russian standards and beautifully decorated with very modern furniture. It reminded him of the things in the new Finnish store near Detsky Mir, except these things seemed to be of much better quality.

"Can I get you a drink, Chief Investigator Ganin?"

"No, thank you," Ganin said.

"What can I do for you?"

"There is something you must know, Miss Dean—"

"You've already said that."

He looked at her. He had never before met an American woman except for the few tourists who got into trouble in Moscow. They were few and far between, and none of them had been like this one. He was almost tongue-tied, and he felt foolish.

"I've come to warn you, actually, and ask for your help."

Her eyebrows knitted. "It was him, wasn't it?"

"I think so, but one can never be sure in situations like these."

She seemed to think for a moment or two, and then she looked up at him. "Don't mince words with me."

"I'm sorry, I don't understand."

"Tell it to me straight. Do you think he saw me shooting my mouth off on television, and now he's going to come here after me?"

"I think that is a possibility," Ganin said with a straight face.

She flinched. "Christ," she said softly. She managed a slight laugh. "Me and my big mouth. Andy Warhol might have been right, but he never warned us that it could be dangerous."

"You have two choices," Ganin said. "The first is that we hide you—the Federal Bureau of Investigation hides you. They have a program called Witness Protection. Agent Hammer explained it to me."

"I know all about it," Mary Frances said. "What's my other choice?"

"You remain here."

"Here in the city, in this apartment, what?"

"Yes, both, and your office. You would continue your normal daily routines."

"Waiting for him to take a shot at me."

"Yes," Ganin said. "But we would be near you at all times—"

"Sure, to protect me like you did Gorbachev?" she snapped, cutting him off.

"Yes, like that," Ganin said in innocence. "We saved his life; we can protect yours."

She looked at him, her eyes round. "You can't be serious," she said.

"But I am. I don't think we'll catch him any other way. And I think that sooner or later he will try again to assassinate President Gorbachev."

Mary Frances's professional curiosity was piqued. "Is Gorbachev planning another trip out of the Soviet Union in the near future?"

"Not that I know of. Moran means to come to Moscow to kill him."

She shook her head in disbelief. "Unless you stop him here."

"Yes, that's right."

"With me as bait."

It wasn't the word Ganin would have used, but it worked. He nodded. "Yes, with you as bait, and me and Agent Hammer as the bear trap."

She turned away and crossed the living room to the window.

"Please stay away from there."

It took her a moment to realize what he meant, and she stepped away from the window. "Is he here already?"

"He may be."

She turned back to him and after a long hesitation finally nodded. "I'll do it," she said. "I'll go along with you and the bureau on one condition."

"Yes?" Ganin asked.

"I get the exclusive."

"I'm sorry, I don't understand you."

"That's all right," Mary Frances said. "By the time we're done, if I'm still alive, that is, there'll be a lot of things you won't understand."

28

Moran was in New York.

It was just midnight when he got off the plane from San Antonio with the few others, trudged down the boarding tunnel, and followed the signs to the luggage retrieval on the ground floor.

He was tired, yet he was anxious to finish with his business this evening and be gone by morning before the New York City police or the FBI had a chance to react.

In many respects he knew that he was being foolish by coming here like this. He was indulging himself in a little game of fantasy in which he pitted himself against the entire law enforcement establishment: the local police, the FBI, CIA, and KGB, and even Interpol. Each time he was cornered he managed to extricate himself by dint of his superior intelligence. He'd never yet met a cop or intelligence officer who could find his ass with both hands. They were usually organization men, bureaucrats who spent more time protecting their positions than they did unraveling the data that streamed across their desks.

He had been on the go for more than forty-eight hours. This morning, after he'd left Torres's house in Mexico City, he'd taken an Air Mexico flight up to Monterrey, where he'd gotten on a bus for the 150-mile trip to Laredo. The border patrol had not even asked for his papers, merely asking him where he was born. He'd told them Omaha, Nebraska, and he'd been waved on, that despite his slight accent. He'd rented a car there and had driven up to San Antonio in time for the six-fifty flight to La Guardia, checking his single piece of luggage all the way through to New York with the redcap luggage service at the door.

A flight from Chicago had come in about ten minutes earlier, and the passengers were still waiting for their luggage. Moran lowered his eyes as he crossed the hall and positioned himself at the end of the carousel nearest the doors to wait.

An old woman looked over at him, nodded her head, and smiled.

Moran smiled back and mouthed the words, "God bless you," and her smile deepened.

The luggage came a few minutes later, and he went over to the Hertz counter, where he paid for a car with an American Express credit card under his Father Tanner identification. A shuttle took him out to the parking lot. The car was a maroon Chevrolet Cavalier.

Rain fell in a steady drizzle, headlights, streetlights, and the lights from billboards reflecting in multicolored streaks off the slick pavements. There wasn't much traffic at this hour of the night, though the roads were not completely empty. New York, like any large city in the West, was never completely still.

It was late, nearly one o'clock by the time he passed beneath the East River through the Midtown Tunnel. He had reservations on the 7:15 A.M. flight to Montreal, which gave him a little more than six hours to find the woman, kill her, and then get free. Unless he got lucky immediately, he figured he would have to take a few chances. But leaving her alive, he thought, entailed a much greater risk.

Manhattan was like a ghost town. Moran parked the car on an empty Forty-second Street just down from Grand Central Station and went across to the Howard Johnson's. The coffee shop was still open.

Inside, he got a booth and ordered a cup of coffee. When it came, he asked about a pay phone, and the tired waitress directed him to the back near the rest rooms. There were only a couple of other customers in the place. No one paid him the slightest attention. Priests were like cabbies and police; they were not out of place in the middle of the night.

There was no listing for a Mary Frances Dean in the telephone book, though there were several M. Deans, and one M. F. Dean in Brooklyn. He dialed the Brooklyn number, and after a half dozen rings a man with a gruff voice answered.

"Who the fuck is this?"

"Is Mary Frances there?"

"What the fuck you talkin' about? D'you know what time it is, you fuck?"

Moran hung up and called information. "I'd like the telephone number of Mary Frances Dean. I don't have her address."

"One moment please," the operator said. A recording came on almost immediately. "That is an unlisted, unpublished number."

"Operator?" Moran said. "It's the Mary Frances Dean in Manhattan, isn't it?"

"That is an unlisted, unpublished number." The recorded message repeated itself.

So much for luck, he thought, hanging up. But then he had established that she did live within the New York metro area. It was something, and given a little time, he would have no problem coming up with her address using legitimate or semilegitimate and therefore perfectly safe means. She worked at *World News This Week*. He could wait there until she showed up. Or in the morning he could check with the Social Security Administration in Washington and get her number. From it he could come up with her address. Or he could check with ConEd here in the city. Or the State Department of Taxation and Finance or the Credit Bureau. But all that would take time, and none of it could be done tonight.

Back at his booth he lit a cigarette and drank his coffee. He stared out the window until he had it. She was a magazine writer, which meant she was a reader. Simple.

He finished his coffee, stubbed out his cigarette, and paid his bill at the door.

The public library was only a couple of blocks away. Moran parked his car on Fifth Avenue and walked back. He ducked through the gate into the loading dock area at the rear of the big building.

He waited in the shadows for a few minutes to make certain that he had not been spotted by someone on the street or that a night watchman hadn't seen him, then scrambled up onto the loading platform as he took out his lock pick.

There were three doors, including the service door, all of them locked. Moran had the door that was in the deepest shadow open in under thirty seconds, and he slipped inside, where the musty smell of books was thick in the air.

Again he waited several minutes to make certain no alarm was being raised and then picked his way slowly across the receiving bay, through a door, and down a corridor that led into the main library itself.

Taking the stairs up to the second floor, he almost stumbled into the watchman, who had evidently just come down from the third floor and was starting his rounds on the second.

Moran pulled back into the stair hall and watched as the man slowly moved down the corridor, checking each door as he went.

Turning, Moran hurried silently up to the third floor and sprinted down the corridor. He picked the lock on one of the doors at random.

Inside, he went through a secretary's area into the inner office, but neither room contained what he was looking for.

Back out in the corridor he relocked the door and tried the office across the hall. Inside, he found what he wanted: a computer terminal at a secretary's desk.

After making sure the door was locked, Moran sat at the terminal, powered it up, and asked for a listing of files. A moment later the screen filled with a menu, "BORROWERS" listed under "F27." He punched the code and then "DEAN, MARY FRANCES." If she was a reader, he had reasoned, she had a library card.

A couple of seconds later her name came up on the screen, along with a history of her borrowing. She currently had a book about the Soviet Union—*Russia: Broken Idols, Solemn Dreams*: Shipler—overdue since April. Her address was a number on East Thirty-sixth Street. He memorized it and her phone number.

Moran smiled. "Thanks," he said softly, and he switched off the terminal.

Hammer didn't come up to Mary Frances's apartment until nearly 1:30 A.M., and the moment he let him in Ganin knew that something had happened.

"Where is she?" Hammer asked.

Ganin motioned toward the corridor back to the bedroom and bathroom. "She went to bed a couple of hours ago."

"She's agreed to cooperate?"

Ganin nodded. "On the condition we give her the exclusive, whatever that means."

Hammer chuckled despite himself. "She doesn't want either of us talking to the newspapers or television. She wants this story for her own magazine."

Ganin glanced toward the bedroom door, amazed again. Had

she actually thought he would talk to the news media people? In the middle of an investigation? While a would-be assassin was running around on the loose? He thought of an old Russian proverb: Once a word is out of your mouth, you can't swallow it. The peasants knew to keep their mouth shut. Perhaps even the furrows had ears. Who knew?

They went through a swinging door into the kitchen, where Ganin had made tea and they could talk without disturbing her.

"I had to bring a backup with me," Hammer said without preamble or excuses.

Ganin had figured as much. In many respects Hammer worked under the same kinds of handicaps that the Militia did.

"Orders from Washington." Hammer explained.

"Are they here now?"

"James and Howar. They're in a car parked up the street a little ways. They'll keep an eye on the front."

"How about the back door?"

"That's up to us. But there's no easy access according to the doorman. It's a sealed steel maintenance door that can be opened easily from the inside in an emergency but is impossible to get into from outside."

"An adjacent building?" Ganin asked. He was ashamed to admit that he really hadn't noticed.

Hammer shrugged. "He'd have to break through a concrete wall. There'd be a lot of noise."

"I meant the roofs."

"This building is eight stories higher than the building to the east and nine stories higher than the building to the west. He'd still have to access either building from the front. James and Howar are good."

"We were watching in Geneva, too," Ganin said thoughtfully. He didn't know what he was feeling now, other than jumpy. He had no instinct that Moran was here, yet it seemed logical—if you accepted a killer's logic.

"He's on his way. I'd be willing to bet anything on it," Hammer said.

Ganin focused on him. "You came up with something?"

Hammer nodded. "You're damned right I did. In the past thirty-six hours there have been only three deaths on the Interpol wire that might fit Moran's profile. The first was Sunday night or

Monday morning in Marseilles. Michel Gavalet, a suspected forger. He burned up in his apartment. It was listed as an accident under suspicious circumstances. A witness may have seen a priest leaving the apartment just before the fire began. Does that ring a bell?"

"A priest," Ganin said. "In Geneva he was a general. It enabled him to move freely throughout the palais grounds. Now as a priest he would be less likely to be thoroughly checked at a frontier crossing."

"From Geneva to Marseilles," Hammer said. "Next, Mexico City. Monday, the bodies were discovered by the maid at noon. Maximilliano Torres, a suspected gun dealer and smith. He was very rich, very influential, which was why he managed to keep a low profile."

"You said bodies?"

"His wife, María, was found shot to death as well. A twenty-two-caliber automatic. The same type, apparently, as our Army Delta Force people use."

"Very deadly at close range in the hands of an expert."

Hammer nodded. "He's on his way. Probably crossed the border into Texas later that day. We're checking now on the assumption he's still traveling as a priest."

"Which means he could be here in the city now."

"Easily."

The man was as arrogant as he was good. He was sending up red flags wherever he went. Catch me if you can, he seemed to be saying. But there was another message in his actions.

"He's going to retire," Ganin said. "As soon as he's finished here and in Moscow, he means to go into deep hiding."

"You've already said that."

Ganin nodded absently. "Yes, but I just realized something else. It was staring me in the face all this time. If he's going to retire for life, it means he is set up financially for life."

"Assassins are very often paid—"

"He's an American, with Western tastes. He would need a lot of money."

Hammer nodded his agreement.

"You said that he just walked away from his house on St. John."

"Booby-trapped."

"Yes, because he knew someone would be coming to check

up on him. He wasn't planning on returning. He'll have to start all over again. That kind of money—gold or Western currencies —is not such an easy thing to come by in the Soviet Union, and its transfer out of the country is even harder to hide."

"So you'll get your people when you go home," Hammer said. "Fine. In the meantime, he's coming here to kill the woman."

"Yes," Ganin said. "And he thinks he will succeed."

The kitchen door opened, and Mary Frances, dressed in a white terry-cloth bathrobe, was there. "Not very comforting," she said.

Ganin turned to her and managed a smile that he hoped would be reassuring. "But you'll get your exclusive."

Moran had donned a black raincoat and hat, the pistol in his left-hand pocket. It was his experience that even professionals never seemed to expect that someone would have a gun in a left pocket. It had once given him a half-second advantage.

He stood in the darkness just around the corner on Lexington Avenue, watching the front of Mary Frances's apartment building and the car parked across the street a little way up the block from it. He'd already been in place and about ready to move in when the three men showed up in the plain gray Ford, obviously a government car. One of them had gotten out and had entered the apartment building. That was twenty minutes ago, and still he had not come out.

At first he'd hardly been able to believe his eyes, but then it finally began to dawn on him that they knew he was coming here for the woman. Somehow they had figured out what he was going to do, and they meant to trap him here.

Well, he thought, in a way it was better. They were police officers, probably FBI. When all three of them were dead, along with the woman, the bureau would mount a nationwide manhunt which would keep it very busy.

Not one of them could possibly guess what his next move would be. No one could guess that.

Turning his coat collar up and his hat brim down, Moran stuffed his hands in his pockets, stepped around the corner, and started down the street toward the gray Ford.

A cab turned the corner behind him, its headlights throwing his shadow sparkling like diamonds down the street as it passed.

The door on the passenger side of the Ford opened, and a man dressed in a dark blue windbreaker leaned out.

Moran didn't alter his pace. He kept walking as if he meant to pass the car.

"Hold up there a minute, pal," the FBI agent said.

Moran stopped short as if he were startled, and he pulled his right hand out of his pocket and held it up. "Look, look, I don't want any trouble here, Mac. For Christ's sake, I don't have any money—"

The driver had leaned over in his seat, and he held out his open wallet with his shield. "Don't get shook up, we're FBI," he said.

Moran pulled out his pistol, thumbing the safety to the off position as the long silencer cleared his pocket. His first shot caught the driver in the mouth, and his second hit the nearest agent in the chest as the man reared back and clawed inside his jacket for his gun.

Moran stepped a pace to the left to get a better sight line on the driver, who was desperately reaching for the door handle, and fired another shot, this one catching the man in the throat.

The agent on the passenger side had propelled himself out of the car onto his right knee, and he was rolling to his left, his pistol coming out of his jacket.

Moran fired two more shots, one hitting the agent in the side of his face in front of his ear and the second entering his chest, piercing his heart.

"*Yeb vas*, it's him," Lieutenant Vlasov whispered urgently.

Captain Gordeyev rushed to the window and looked down at the unfolding situation on the street. They had positioned themselves in a second-floor office across the street from the woman's apartment. He realized at this moment that it had been a mistake.

A man in a dark raincoat and hat was lifting a man's body into the gray Ford that had pulled up twenty minutes ago.

It was Moran. It had to be.

"Come on," Gordeyev shouted as he spun on his heel and rushed to the door. He had his pistol out even before he was in the corridor.

Moran took the driver's wallet and shield, which identified him as FBI Special Agent Robert Howar, and stuffed it into his right pocket as he hurried across the street to Mary Frances's apartment building.

The concierge looked up when he entered.

Moran quickly appraised the situation. The man was safely ensconced behind what appeared to be a shield of either Lexan plastic or very heavy glass. Either would be impervious to a .22-caliber pistol shot. He had closed-circuit television and a communications board that not only connected him with the apartments but also probably connected him directly with the fire department, ambulance service, and police.

Moran yanked out the FBI identification and held it up to the glass.

"There's been a shooting in front. Call Ms. Dean's apartment and get my man down here. On the double."

The concierge was just staring at him, openmouthed. He wasn't moving.

"Christ, call him!" Moran shouted.

The concierge was shaking his head in fear.

Moran suddenly realized that his raincoat had opened and his clerical collar was visible. "I'm on a stakeout, you stupid bastard. A disguise. Now get him down here on the double. We don't have much time."

The concierge, finally spurred into action, picked up the telephone and called upstairs. Moran could not hear what the man was saying; but he seemed very agitated, and he talked for only a couple of seconds before he hung up.

"Now get the hell out of there," Moran shouted, glancing at the elevator indicator, which was on the twenty-third floor.

The concierge was shaking his head again. He pressed a button on his panel. "I'm supposed to stay in here no matter what happens."

"If they get this far, they'll fucking blow you out of there. If you value your life, you'd better get your ass down to the basement."

The concierge got up, opened the door at the back of the cubicle, and stepped out into the lobby. Moran had his pistol out, and he shot the man in the head.

The elevator started down. Moran pulled off the sodden raincoat and tossed it into the concierge's cubicle. Holding the pistol under his left arm, he dragged the dead man inside and pushed him beneath a desk so that he would be out of sight from anyone in the elevator or the lobby.

He studied the control board for a second or two and found the switches for the lobby lights. He shut them off, then stepped back out, the pistol held loosely in his right hand, a faint smile playing at the corners of his mouth.

Her voice and face were clear in his mind. She had seemed self-assured on the television screen, in her element with the other newspeople.

It was too bad that she would have to die so suddenly, without preamble. There were a number of things he would have liked to ... discuss with her. She had evidently met and spoken with Gorbachev. She had looked into his eyes, she'd told her panelists, and had seen sincerity. The Russian leader wanted European disarmament. He wanted to end the stupid, budget-defeating arms race. He truly wanted peace.

Well, Moran thought, soon he would get his wish. He would be at peace for all time.

The elevator was passing the tenth floor. It seemed to be taking forever. The FBI agent would be expecting trouble; it was the only way to get him down here. His service revolver would probably be drawn. But he wouldn't expect the enemy to be here in the darkened lobby waiting for him. He wouldn't know that because of it, he would be backlit in the elevator car. A duck in a midway shooting gallery.

Behind him the lobby door crashed open. Moran started to swivel on his right heel while bringing his pistol around when two shots were fired in rapid succession, and then a third. One of them slammed into his side just below his right armpit, bouncing him off the corner of the cubicle.

He got the impression of two men filling the doorway, one swinging right and the other charging straight at him. He managed to fire five shots as he fell off-balance to the floor.

The lead man went down, his head bouncing on the marble floor, his weapon skittering to the elevator door.

Moran noted that it was a Russian automatic. A Tula-Korovin, and in that instant he realized the error he had made coming here without further precautions. The Russians who had hired him had tried to stop him, for whatever reasons, in Geneva. When that hadn't worked, they'd sent the GRU or KGB legmen here to finish the job, evidently figuring, as the FBI had, that he would be coming for the woman. It was even possible, he thought, that the woman had been in on it from the beginning. She may have voluntarily offered herself as bait.

The second Russian fired two shots from the open stairwell door, the first hitting Moran in the right thigh and the second ricocheting off the marble floor, embedding several large chips of marble as well as bullet fragments into the right side of his face and forehead, peeling a big piece of skin and meat from his cheekbone and folding it over his nose in a spray of blood.

It felt as if a sledgehammer had been driven into his temple, yet he was still conscious. He pushed himself upright in time to see the Russian fumbling with his weapon which must have jammed.

Moran laughed out loud as he fired three times, hitting the Russian in the head with all three shots, driving him back against the stairs.

The elevator stopped on the second floor, and as the doors slid open, Ganin turned sideways to present less of himself as a target in case someone was waiting on this floor.

The corridor was empty.

He turned to Hammer. "He's down there, but so is someone else. Those shots came from a T-K automatic, I think. A Russian weapon, six-three-five. What do your officers carry?"

"Thirty-eights. KGB?"

"Or GRU," Ganin said. He stepped off the elevator as the doors started to close. "Nothing fancy, Vivian, he's very good."

"You too, Nikolai," Hammer replied.

As he sprinted down the corridor to the stairwell door, Ganin had a momentary pang of doubt about leaving Mary Frances alone upstairs. But there were only two ways up, the elevator and the stairs. They were covering them both.

Easing the door open, Ganin held his breath to listen for any indication that someone was in the stairwell, either above or below. But there was nothing, only silence, and he slipped inside, switched the safety catch of his Markarov automatic to the off position, and started softly down the first course of stairs.

Moran had managed to stand up, bearing almost all his weight on his left leg. He didn't think he was fatally wounded, but he was in a tough spot here. On the one hand, he knew he had only seconds to get clear, yet he was driven to finish what he had come here to do. Not only because the woman was a witness, but because of revenge now. He had been betrayed. He had a very powerful urge to even the score.

Propping himself against the cubicle, he had started to eject the nearly empty clip from his weapon when the elevator indicator dinged and the doors started to slide open.

He had just run out of time.

The lobby was in relative darkness, and the elevator lights were very bright. Hammer couldn't see a thing as he stumbled forward.

Moran fired two shots, the first hitting the FBI agent in the chest and the second hitting him in the collarbone, driving him backward as he bellowed in pain.

"Moran," someone shouted from the stairwell door.

Moran turned in time to see a man stepping over the body of the GRU agent, and there was a gunshot. A tremendous pain shoved him sideways onto his right leg, which collapsed beneath him.

He brought his pistol around and pulled the trigger. Nothing happened. It was empty.

Ganin fired again at the same instant. The shot hit Moran's jaw, the bullet knocking out several teeth before exiting from the opposite cheek. There was no pain as his forehead touched the cool marble floor.

Ganin swept his pistol left to right, then hurried across the lobby to where Moran was down and kicked the silenced .22 automatic away from his hand. The man was breathing in big blubbering gasps.

The elevator doors started to close, then rebounded off Hammer's legs.

Ganin turned and went to him. He was awake, blood staining his light-colored shirt in a very large still-spreading patch and dribbling out of his mouth and down his chin as he breathed.

"Is he . . . dead?" Hammer asked, coughing up blood. He was in a great deal of pain.

"He's down, but I don't think he's dead," Ganin said, laying his gun on the floor. He yanked off his jacket and then peeled off his shirt, which he roll into a big wad and pressed against Hammer's chest wound. He placed the FBI agent's hands over the wad. "Press down on this," he said. "I'll call the ambulance. What is the number here in New York? Is it zero-three like in Moscow?"

Hammer was pressing his left hand against the wadded shirt over his wound. He picked up his gun with his right and held it out to Ganin. "Finish it, Nikolai. For my . . . partner."

"What is the ambulance?" Ganin demanded, taking Hammer's gun and laying it aside. "You need medical assistance or you will die. Please help me."

"Nine-one-one," Hammer said, and he closed his eyes. "Christ . . . kill him."

Ganin straightened up and stepped off the elevator. Moran seemed to be barely breathing. He had not moved. Ganin stepped over him, pulled open the door to the cubicle, and went inside. He thought maybe the concierge had been lucky and had been able to hide himself, but he saw that he was wrong.

He dialed 911, and the call was answered on the first ring.

"Nine-one-one."

"This is an emergency," Ganin said, keeping his voice calm. "I need at least two ambulances here. There is an FBI officer down and several others with serious gunshot wounds." He gave the address.

"What is your name, please?" the woman asked.

"Special Agent Hammer," he lied. It would be easier this way. "Please hurry." He didn't want to explain he was Russian.

"Sir, the ambulances have already been dispatched. Can you be more specific about the nature of the injuries?"

"I said gunshot wounds . . ." Ganin started to say. He had turned around and looked out the window. Moran was gone, and the elevator doors were closing. For a split instant he simply could not believe his eyes. The man had been down, hard. Barely alive. He had taken at least one shot to the head and more to the body.

"Sir, we need this information—"

Dropping the telephone, Ganin slammed open the cubicle door and barged out into the lobby. But he was too late; the elevator was already on its way up.

Mary Frances. The thought crystallized in his head. The bastard was going after her despite his wounds and despite the fact that Hammer was in the elevator.

It was hardly believable.

Ganin spun on his heel, crossed the lobby in several quick steps, leaped over the GRU agent's body, and started up the stairs.

As he ran, he reached for his pistol in its holster, but it wasn't there. He had laid it down on the elevator floor when he helped Hammer, and he had not picked it up.

It was too late to go back and get a gun from one of the downed GRU agents. Too late to do anything except race up the stairs.

On the twenty-third floor Mary Frances was getting nervous. She had thrown on a pair of blue jeans and a sweat shirt and stood now in the middle of her living room.

Twice she had looked out the windows down onto the street, but there was nothing to be seen except for the gray Ford glistening in the rain. Nothing moved. Nothing normal or abnormal.

Ganin, before he had raced out with the FBI agent, had impressed on her the need to stay put. To hide herself, if need be, but not to move. Except she was feeling cornered now. Something had gone wrong downstairs. They were in trouble. She was sure of it.

Ganin had also impressed on her just how good Moran was.

"He's been in this business for a long time now without getting caught," he'd said. "This time around he's already killed at least eight people, possibly more. And now he's come for you because you're a witness."

"Shit . . ."

"Stay here."

She picked up the phone and dialed the concierge's desk in the lobby. The line was busy. She hung up and tried again, but it was still busy.

Something was wrong; only she didn't know what to do except that she no longer wanted to stay here in the apartment. Somehow Moran had found out where she lived, and he had come here for her, just as Ganin said he would. He had come here from Europe with the express purpose of killing her. She shuddered.

It wasn't real. Yet she knew it was.

In the kitchen she yanked open one of the drawers, pulled out a nine-inch butcher knife, and carefully stuffed it in the waistband of her jeans, pulling the sweat shirt over the handle.

She felt ridiculous but a hell of a lot better than she had before.

Back in the living room she put her ear to the door and listened for several long seconds, but so far as she could tell, nothing was moving in the corridor.

She slipped the chain, snapped the lock, and eased the door open a crack. At that moment a bloody hand violently shoved the door the rest of the way open, propelling her backward off her feet.

Ganin was slowing down. His legs were like rubber, and his lungs burned as if he had inhaled molten lead. It was the damned cigarettes and the lack of exercise. If he wanted to go someplace, he drove. If he could not drive, he usually didn't go.

It was different in the early days. In the Army he had been in perfect condition. And when he and Antonia had gotten married, they used to take great long walks along the Moskva River, and sometimes they would go cross-country skiing at her uncle's dacha on the Istra River. But that was years ago.

He passed the eighteenth floor, wheezing, and kept going. There was nothing else for it.

The thing standing in her doorway was an apparition from hell. If it was the man she'd seen in Geneva or the man in the photographs that Ganin and the FBI agent had shown her, she could not tell. His face now was almost completely destroyed. Blood drooled out of his mouth, and she could see that several of his teeth had been smashed, leaving ragged stumps. A big piece of meat and skin hung loose from his cheek and nose, exposing the bare bone and cartilage beneath. His right eye protruded as from a death's head. His jacket and right trousers leg were soaking wet with blood.

Moran laughed, the sound liquid, gurgling in his throat, and he raised his pistol.

The sound, more than the movement of his gun hand, galvanized Mary Frances into action. She scrambled backward past the edge of the long white couch and frantically threw herself in front of it as something sharp sliced her thigh and Moran fired, the noise of the gunshot deafening in the confines of the room.

Christ, had she been hit? She could feel blood welling up from her leg wound.

Moran was suddenly overhead, his grisly lips parted as if in a smile. Mary Frances backed up against the coffee table as Moran raised his gun again.

She reached behind her in one last desperation move, and her fingers curled around the heavy glass ashtray. For some insane reason she remembered that she'd bought it in Thailand two years ago and had carried it wrapped in tissue paper all the way home with her on the plane.

Moran seemed to be having trouble focusing. He reached out a hand to steady himself against the back of the couch at the same moment Mary Frances threw the ashtray.

He saw it coming, and he reared back; but he wasn't quick enough. The ashtray caught him full in the face where he had been wounded, and the gun discharged, the bullet smacking into the wall.

Mary Frances reached in her waistband for the butcher knife, realizing at that moment that she'd cut a deep gash in her leg on the blade when she'd fallen.

She pulled it out, leaped up, and scrambled over the back of the couch, feeling more like a primordial woman than a *Homo sapiens*, the cavewoman on the hunt. It was life or death now. Kill or be killed.

Moran had fallen back on one knee, blood gushing from his

nose and mouth and even his eye socket. He managed to raise
his head as she came at him, knife raised, but he could no longer
move.

"No," someone shouted from the doorway.

She was beyond recall. She only wanted to kill. She could feel
the bloodlust rising in her gorge. She wanted to tear out his throat,
hurt him worse than he was already hurt for his terrible invasion
of her home and her person. He had come here to kill. She would
defend herself.

Moran growled something unintelligible as she hit him, driving him backward. And she was on top of him, raising the knife
high over her head. She wanted leverage so that she could bury
it to the handle in his chest.

"You bastard," she screeched as she started to drive the knife
downward.

A hand grabbed her wrist and violently pulled her aside,
bodily yanking her away from the downed Moran.

For an instant she could see nothing but sparks and stars in
a red haze. She was screaming something, but her voice was very
far away even to her own ears.

Ganin was there, over her, holding her wrist, shielding her
body with his, saying something to her that she couldn't make out,
calming her down, bringing her back from the brink of madness.

Special Agent Mark Hardy came to the open door of the
hospital room. "All right, shake a leg, you've got a plane to catch,
Ivan."

Ganin ignored him. He smiled, and Mary Frances managed
a weak smile in return. He thought she looked very small and
defenseless in the hospital bed, the IV tube snaking to the needle
in the back of her hand.

"You'll be all right now," he said gently.

She nodded and tried to say something, but her lips barely
moved.

"You've been given a sedative; don't try to talk." Ganin patted
her arm. "We have him now, and he won't hurt anyone again. It's
over."

"Let's go," Hardy said. "Chop-chop."

She licked her lips. "Will I . . . see you . . . again?" she asked
weakly.

Ganin shook his head. "I don't think so. I'm leaving for Moscow in a couple of hours. But you can write to me if you wish. I'd like to hear from you."

She smiled again; but then her eyes fluttered, and she drifted off.

Ganin turned and brushed past Hardy into the corridor. There were police and FBI agents everywhere. The waiting room beyond the nurses' station was filled with newspeople. A hospital spokesman was briefing them.

Hardy's partner, Stewart McGowan, hurried down the corridor. "You about ready, Chief Investigator?"

"Not quite. How's Hammer?"

"He's sleeping now. The way it looks, Moran figured he was already dead in the elevator, so he left him alone."

Hardy tried to take Ganin's arm, but Ganin pulled away and then turned back so that he was just inches from the agent. He could smell mint of cloves on the man's breath. It was sickeningly sweet.

"Back away from me, Mr. Hardy, or I will break your fucking arm off and beat you to death with the bloody stump," Ganin said softly. "Is my English clear?"

Hardy's eyes widened, and his hand went into his jacket; but McGowan pulled him roughly aside.

"For Christ's sake, Mark, cut the man a little slack."

Ganin stepped around the two men and went down the corridor to a room guarded by a uniformed cop and an FBI agent. The cop started to block the door, but the agent held him off.

"It's all right."

"Thanks," Ganin said. He pushed open the door and went inside.

Moran, his face swathed in bandages, only his mouth, nose and left eye uncovered, was lying on his back in the hospital bed. His right leg, in a cast, was suspended on a wire attached to a frame above the foot of the bed.

He'd been on the operating table for nearly four hours, but for all the damage that had been done to him, he had come out of it in serious—not critical—condition.

"Quite a strong man," the doctor said. "Except for his wounds and the loss of blood, he is a perfect physical specimen."

A killing machine, Ganin thought, looking down at him.

Moran's eye opened.

It was like an electrical jolt to Ganin's heart. "Can you hear me?"

The fingers of Moran's left hand formed a fist and then relaxed.

Ganin moved a little closer. "You're done, Donald Sullivan Moran or whoever you really are. If I had my way, I'd shoot you dead here and now. But I don't, so you're safe."

Moran just stared at him.

"I hope you like cages," Ganin said, not knowing why he was taunting the man. "Because the Swiss are going to put you into one for a very long time."

"*Yeb vas,*" Moran croaked in Russian. Fuck you.

PART THREE

PART THREE

32

The guards in front of the Council of Ministers building snapped to attention when General Anatoli Zuyev got out of his Chaika limousine and mounted the steps, his bodyguard, Sergeant Sergei Anastratov, directly behind him.

Zuyev moved through the lower corridor like a battleship through calm seas, and took the elevator up to the third floor, where he was met by a ministerial aide.

"Good evening, Comrade General," the younger man said, helping Zuyev off with his coat. "Do you wish some tea?"

"Yes," Zuyev growled. "Stay here," he said to Anastratov, and he went the rest of the way down the corridor alone. He entered the big outer office of the first secretary of the Ministry of Internal Affairs, then crossed into the inner office. He knocked once and went in.

"Good evening, Anatoli Vasileyevich," First Secretary Valentin Valentinovich Sherstnev said, rising from behind his desk.

Zuyev crossed the Oriental rug to him, and they shook hands. "I have an officers' mess later tonight, which means I'll have to drive all the way back out to Orlovo, Comrade First Secretary."

"Always a man straight to the point. A decisive man. I like that."

Zuyev's eyes narrowed, but he didn't rise to the bait. Sherstnev was, among other things, the minister in charge of the Militia. It was he whom Anastratov had seen speaking with that prick Yernin at the baths last week. Circles within circles. Who knew what alliances had been made, what information passed, what promises tendered in return?

"Please sit down," Sherstnev said.

Another aide came in with the tea things, which he set on the edge of the big desk, then withdrew silently. Sherstnev poured.

"Were you at the Congress this afternoon?" the first secretary asked conversationally.

"I am no longer a deputy, so I don't waste my time anymore."

Sherstnev looked at him shrewdly over the rim of his tea glass. "Our president has their support. They actually stood and applauded him. They were cheering. It was quite a sight."

"I'm sure it was," Zuyev said dryly. "Petr Yesenin telephoned me. He said that we're going to wait for the American Congress to give its approval to the accord before we move on it." Yesenin was editor in chief of *Krasnaya Zvezda*, the armed forces' newspaper.

"That is my understanding."

"Why?" Zuyev barked sharply. "Or isn't he in such a hurry to finish giving away what little advantage we have left in Europe now? Are we going to let the Americans do it for us?"

"Don't be so certain that the situation is as simple as it may seem on the surface."

"Don't toy with me, First Secretary," Zuyev said. "We both are busy men. If you have something to say to me, then let us without delay get it out on the table where we can deal with it."

"The future is his who knows how to wait," the minister said, quoting a peasant proverb.

"I have never had the problem," Zuyev said, putting down his glass.

Sherstnev nodded. "An American, Donald Sullivan Moran, has been arrested in New York City."

A cold fist clutched Zuyev's heart, but he let nothing of his sudden fear show in his face.

"He was gravely wounded, but I am told that he will recover so that he can be extradited to Switzerland to stand trial."

Zuyev shrugged, and Sherstnev smiled.

"He is being charged with murder. It is expected he will mount a rigorous defense. I am told he is wealthy even by Western standards. He could afford a first-class defense with the finest international attorneys."

A message was beginning to come clear to Zuyev, and he was having just a little trouble believing his good fortune. "A man such as he could prove to be an embarrassment to somebody."

"My sentiments exactly. It would be most unfortunate if he were actually to stand trial."

"The Militia—" Zuyev started to speak, but Sherstnev held up a bony hand.

"The Militia is concerned *only* with what happens on Soviet soil."

Zuyev nodded his final understanding, though he could not fathom why Sherstnev was handing him this favor. The quid pro quo would come, however. It would not be cheap.

33

There were masses of flowers in her office when Mary Frances returned to work on Friday morning. She'd already missed the magazine's midnight Thursday deadline, so there'd been no real reason for her to come in until Monday, except that she'd wanted to get a running start on the next week.

As soon as she opened the door, the riot of colors and rich scents hit her, and she choked up, her eyes instantly becoming moist.

"Shit," she said.

"You're going to have to stop using that vulgar word sooner or later," Bob Liskey said behind her.

She turned, laughing. He and the other staffers stood out in the corridor with big grins on their faces. Three of them were holding up a big sign which read WELCOME HOME WAR HERO.

"It's been only three days," she protested.

One of the older office women laid a hand on her arm. "I've heard of giving your pint of blood at the office, kid, but do you suppose you got carried away?"

Everybody laughed.

"We've got cake and punch for afterward," one of the other women said.

"And the deli is sending up sandwiches and beans and potato salad for lunch," another of the staffers said.

Mary Frances was a little confused. "Afterward?" she asked Liskey. His grin broadened.

"Almost forgot. There's someone who has been waiting for you upstairs."

"Weaver? Has he got my assignment?"

"He's up there, too. Just come on," Liskey said. He took her by the arm and led her through the staff to the elevator. "I'll bring her right back. You can set everything up in the meantime."

"Aren't you going to tell me what's going on, Bob?" she asked on the way up in the elevator.

"Not this time. Strict orders."

She shook her head but said nothing.

They got off on the fortieth floor and went down the broad carpeted corridor into the publisher's office. His secretary, an older woman, got to her feet and rushed around the desk to take Mary Frances by the arm. "You poor dear," she cooed. "We've all been so dreadfully worried about you."

"Are they ready for us?" Liskey asked her.

"Yes, you can go right in," the woman said. She gave Mary Frances a pat, then opened the polished oak door to the inner office. "They're here," she announced.

Harley Everton, the grand old man of newsmagazines and the publisher of *World News This Week*, got up from behind his massive desk and came around as Mary Frances and Bob Liskey entered his office. He was very tall and gangly, all elbows and knees, with an Ichabod Crane Adam's apple, a Norman Rockwell profile, red suspenders, and a polka-dot bow tie ridiculously too large. His hair was thick, too long, and absolutely white. In winter he always wore hunting boots, and in summer high-top sneakers. The man was eccentric, but he was brilliant and one of the grandest old-world gentlemen in all of New York City. People on his staff loved him even though they were afraid of him, too.

"There she is," he said. They shook hands.

"Good morning, sir," she said.

"Sit down, please," Everton said, holding the chair for her.

Lawrence Weaver was sitting on the couch across the room. He smiled. "How do you feel?"

"A little stiff and still sore, but a lot better, sir."

"Would you care for some coffee?" Everton asked, going back behind his desk. He motioned for Liskey to have a seat with Weaver.

"Yes, please," Mary Frances said.

Everton keyed his intercom and was about to speak, but his secretary was first.

"I'll be in with it in a minute," she said.

Everton studied Mary Frances for several long seconds, making her just a little uncomfortable. But then his lips pursed, and he shook his head ruefully. "It must have been absolutely dreadful for you. Killing all around, and suddenly he's there with the intent to do you bodily harm."

"It wasn't one of my favorite moments, Mr. Everton."

"No," the publisher said. "Thank God for that Russian cop."

Her mind was drawn immediately back to those moments of rage. Her gut tightened, and the seven-inch gash in her leg began to throb. She would have killed him had it not been for Ganin. The Russian had saved a life, but it hadn't been hers. And now she found she was embarrassed by the entire thing, by what she had almost become.

She nodded. "Yes, sir."

Again Everton stared at her, as if he were trying to come to a decision, make up his mind about something concerning her.

"Can you walk all right? You don't need a cane or anything like that?"

"I'm not going to go dancing for a few weeks, but I can get around okay, sir."

"Are you on any medications?"

"I took the last of the antibiotics this morning, and I was given pain-killers; but I haven't used them."

"When do your stitches come out?"

"A couple of weeks."

"Will you need plastic surgery?"

She hesitated. She looked pretty good in a bikini, and the

doctor said the wound would leave a big scar, but she had hurt herself; it had been her fault. "I don't know," she said. "Maybe, but I'll take care of it, if and when."

"No," Everton said, and his tone was final. "When you're ready, say the word, we'll take care of it."

"Thank you."

Everton sat back in his chair at the same moment his secretary bustled in with a coffee service on a tea cart. Weaver got up and came across to her. "Thanks, Maggie, I've got it."

The secretary left, and Weaver poured them coffee. When he was finished, Everton picked up where he'd left off.

"Do you believe you're ready to come back to work?"

Mary Frances nodded. "Sure."

"You looked good on *Face the People*, and your dispatches from Geneva were first-class."

"Jack Dillinger gave her top marks," Weaver said. "In fact, he wanted to know if he might have her for a year or two."

"How would you like to work for him in Geneva?" Everton asked.

She was being tested; she could feel it. She didn't think they were going to send her back to Geneva and certainly not for as long as a year or two. Except for the summits and an occasional to-do in the United Nations European Headquarters, not much of any real interest happened there.

"Mr. Dillinger is a good man. I wouldn't mind working for him."

"But you have something else in mind?"

Mary Frances didn't move a muscle. She knew exactly what she wanted, and she didn't want to blow it now by doing something stupid.

"Well?" Everton said sharply after a second or two.

"Moscow," she blurted. "I'd like to be assigned to our Moscow bureau."

"What would you do there, Ms. Dean?" Everton asked. He smiled faintly. "Other than report the news, that is."

She sat up a little straighter. "Well, first of all, I would like to follow up with this assassination attempt. In Geneva I think I established a good rapport with Mr. Gorbachev, and I think he might be willing to talk to me again."

"In a week or two that will be old news."

"The accord is running into some opposition in the Kremlin, in the Congress, especially among the military deputies. I think Mr. Gorbachev may be under the gun, so to speak."

Everton was nodding. "*Glasnost* nearly got him the assassin's bullet in Geneva and now a congressional bullet back home."

"It would be worth a try, sir," Mary Frances said.

"All right," Everton said. "Moscow it is."

34

It was night, but there was increasing activity on the hospital's fifth-floor isolation ward. Telephones were ringing, nurses scurried back and forth, their thick-soled rubber shoes squeaking on the tiled floor, and the murmur of voices rose in the corridor.

Moran lay quietly in his hospital bed, listening to the sounds, letting them flow around him, letting their exact meaning slowly sink into his consciousness.

They were going to move him. He had known it now since this afternoon when a doctor came in with two armed guards and checked him thoroughly. They wanted to make certain that his condition was stable enough, as, of course, it was.

From the beginning he had not taken the pain pills he'd been given, merely hiding them beneath his tongue until the nurse left and then spitting them out. He wanted his brain to be sharp, and the pain, which had never been terribly bad, certainly not as bad as some of what he had endured in the North Vietnamese prison, had faded over the past few days.

His most serious physical problem, he had decided, was his loss of blood. But that had been taken care of within the first hours of his hospitalization, and each hour he could feel his strength coming back, though he hid it from the staff.

Beyond that, his main problem, once he got out of here, would be his physical appearance. Men dressed in hospital gowns, casts on their legs, their heads swathed in bandages could not get far without causing a stir. But lying alone in his room, feigning unconsciousness, he had figured a way around that problem as well.

He thought about his moves, step by step, as a complex ballet that would eventually lead him to Moscow, to Gorbachev's side, a gun pointed at the Russian leader's head.

And he could feel himself squeezing the trigger slowly, carefully, the gun bucking in his hand, the Russian's body flopping over on its side, dead.

Ironically it was the two Russians he had killed in the lobby of the woman's apartment building who would ensure his transfer from this hospital. The FBI's Counterintelligence Division would be asking questions about them. They would want to take charge of him; that meant they would move him either to a safe house or to another, more secure hospital.

He smiled beneath his bandages. But that would be a mistake on the part of the bureau agents because security could never be completely controlled during such a move. They would be armed men who would be very close to him, within touching distance. All he needed was an opening, just one, and he would do the rest.

He turned his head slightly so that he could look toward the window. It was still raining, but he could see the lights of another building or perhaps a wing of this hospital a short distance away. He had no idea where he had been taken because he had lapsed in and out of consciousness on the way here. In fact, he didn't even remember being taken out of the woman's apartment.

He turned that thought over in his mind as he listened to the rain beat on the windows, and his facial muscles twitched. When he had awoken in this room, he had been surprised to be alive.

He had seen the look in the woman's eyes when she had come over the couch at him, the long-bladed knife held over her head. She had the blood urge. She'd meant to kill him.

But he had seen much more. She had been waiting for him. It had been a trap, an elaborate setup to lure him to her apartment, where she was waiting to kill him. And she would have done it, except she had been stopped.

The FBI agent in the elevator had been dead, or near dead. That left only the Russian cop from the lobby. The one who had shot him, the one who had come here knowing his name. Probably the same one who had shot at him in Geneva. He must have run up twenty-three flights of stairs.

It meant this Russian was an innocent, a cop who had somehow stumbled on to the assassination plot. He was not a part of General Zuyev's group. In fact, he himself was probably in danger at this moment. The generals wanted to stop the assassination for whatever reason, and they were willing to go as far as killing their assassin. But they would also want to cover up any sort of investigation.

Moran turned back so that he could watch the corridor door, his gut churning. He would kill the cop and the woman for what they had done to him, and he would kill Gorbachev to show the world that he wasn't insane, that he knew what he was doing, that he was world-class.

The Russian was wrong. There wasn't a cage strong enough to hold him.

FBI Special Agents Ed Reid and Luis Vassilaros had been sent up from Washington yesterday to take charge of the Moran investigation or at least the physical handling of the man. But they had been thwarted in their desire to move him as quickly as possible by the attending physician, who said his patient wouldn't be ready to be moved for another twenty-four hours.

They had a lot of questions for Moran. They'd spent the last forty-eight hours studying the case notes in detail, and there were holes a mile wide that would have to be filled before he would be ready for extradition to Switzerland.

A safe house had been set up for them on Long Island. They had borrowed it from the bureau's Witness Protection Program and so far as they knew, it had not yet been fingered. The

Chicago Mafia informer whose house it was to have been was being transferred instead to a twenty-eight-acre ranchette outside Albuquerque.

They'd had a choice of keeping Moran under heavy guard at all times, thus announcing to the opposition exactly who and where he was, or of keeping the operation very low-key once they got him out of here.

"Either way we're going to be at risk, gentlemen," their supervisor had cautioned them. "We think there's a good chance that the Russians are going to want to silence him."

"They'd have to find him first," Reid said.

"They know he's at that hospital."

"If we can get him out of there without a fuss, they wouldn't have any idea where he'd disappeared."

"That's the bureau's thinking," the supervisor said.

"Why don't we just let them have the bastard?" Vassilaros said. "Save us all a lot of trouble."

"He knows something that the brass on the Hill would like to know. The CIA wants to send a couple of their people out to talk to him."

"Fuck it . . ." Vassilaros said half under his breath.

"At ease, mister. You guys are going to have all the time with him that you want. When you're ready, and only when you're ready, will we let the company have a crack at him."

Vassilaros turned away.

"What about security en route?" Reid asked.

"We'll keep it light. Two medical technicians will accompany you in the van, but from what I'm being told, Moran won't be any threat. He'll be able to talk to you, but that's about all. We'll provide chase cars for you away from the hospital. They'll drop off as soon as they determine you're clear." The supervisor shrugged. "The kind of surveillance operation they'd have to mount to keep up with you would stand out like a sore thumb."

Reid nodded his satisfaction. "How about the house?"

"In addition to the two techs coming up with you, there'll be a doctor, a nurse, six physical security officers, rotating three teams of two, as well as Sam Binks."

Binks was one of the interrogation psychologists who worked for the bureau. He was very good.

"Any deadlines?"

"That's up to you and Moran," the supervisor said. "I don't

want you to kill him, and I don't want you retiring up there on an old-age pension. Other than that, you're on your own."

"How far do we go?"

"He hurt Vivian badly, damned near bagged him," the supervisor said, and he didn't have to say anything more.

Dr. Benton Wood pushed the signed release form across the desk to Special Agent Reid and slowly laid his pen down. "As of this moment I am not responsible for the man's well-being."

"We understand, sir," Reid said. "We'll take good care of him."

The doctor smiled wanly. "I'll bet."

Vassilaros was waiting in the corridor. "Are we ready up here?" he asked.

Reid nodded. "How about downstairs?"

"The van is standing by in the garage, but I sent the chase cars ahead. We've got five of them, one-block intervals. They'll pick up and drop off on a three-two-one variation."

"I don't want them crowding us."

"No problem. In any event they're with us only until Nassau County. Everything looks good by then they'll head back to the barn."

"All right," Reid said. "Let's get him the fuck out of here. But I'm telling you straight, Luis. The son of a bitch gives us trouble, any kind of trouble, I'm going to waste him. Save us and the Swiss taxpayers some money."

Vassilaros grinned. "You're the boss."

Downstairs on the fifth floor the two medical technicians who had brought the van over were waiting at the nurses' station with a gurney.

"Give us a couple of minutes; then you can come in for him," Reid said as they passed. He'd not seen either of them before, but there were a lot of men in the New York office he didn't know, and they seemed to be competent. They were certainly big enough.

He stopped at Moran's door. The uniformed cop on duty got up from his chair and put down the newspaper he had been reading. Reid showed him his credentials and the transfer order.

"He's all yours," the cop said with obvious relief.

"Just hold on until we're out of here, if you would," Reid said. He had a lot of respect for Vivian Hammer. Everyone in the bureau did. Hammer would recover just fine, but he had been hurt badly. Any man who could do that deserved a lot of caution.

The cop shrugged.

Reid thought a moment, then pulled out his sixteen-shot SigSauer and handed it to Vassilaros. "I'm going in to have a word with him. Stay here."

Vassilaros looked into his eyes, then pursed his lips. He nodded.

Reid pushed open the door and entered the room, which was mostly in darkness except for what little light came in from outside. He remained well away from the bed for a full minute, studying the inert form. All the monitors and IV drips had been disconnected, as had the wires elevating his right leg.

"Moran," he called softly.

The figure on the bed did not move.

Reid came a little closer. He could see that the fingers of Moran's left hand were twitching as if the man were dreaming. He could also see that Moran's exposed eye was closed but that his eyeball beneath the lid was moving rapidly. It was REM sleep.

The man was definitely unconscious, and Reid allowed himself to relax a little. No threat here. At least not at the moment.

"Moran?" he said again.

Still the man did not move. Reid looked at him for a long time, trying to imagine him coming up against Vivian Hammer or that Russian cop who everyone was saying was so good, but he could not. The man lying in bed here was just an ordinary, slightly built man. It was hard to tell much more than that because of all the bandages covering his features. But Reid hoped that they would be together long enough for him to see Moran, actually see him face-to-face.

He opened the door and flipped on the light. "Let's get him out of here."

"Right," Vassilaros said. He handed Reid back his gun and then motioned for the two medical technicians to bring the gurney.

Reid holstered his gun and went back to the bed. Moran was still asleep. He pulled the sheet back. The man's legs were small, almost feminine, and Vassilaros snickered.

The uniformed cop had come in as well, and he looked down at the sleeping figure. "Doesn't look like much," he said. "Is he a nut case?"

"Probably," Reid said.

The technicians came in, and they all stood aside as the two white-coated men wheeled the gurney into place and gently slid Moran's body across to the cart. They placed a strap across his legs and another across his chest and left arm. His right arm, which was bandaged at the armpit, was folded high across his chest. A little blood had stained the bandages.

"Let's go," Reid said.

The technicians went first, wheeling the gurney down the hall to the elevator.

The on duty nurses all had gathered at their station to watch. Moran had been a celebrity patient.

The van was windowless. From the outside it looked like nothing. Even the license plates were ordinary New York State issue, not the special government tags the FBI normally used. Inside, it was laid out like an ambulance with a cot along the right side and a place for the gurney on the left. There was a heart monitor and oxygen equipment and a complete inventory of trauma equipment and supplies. The driver's compartment was separated from the back of the van by a thick curtain.

There was something wrong with the two technicians. Moran could feel it. Several times he had risked opening his good eye, once when they'd gotten off the elevator in the underground garage and again in the van after they'd pulled out.

They weren't Americans. The thought had come to him gradually. And watching them now and listening to them, he was convinced they were Russians here to kill him.

"How's he doing back there?" Vassilaros asked.

"Still unconscious," one of the techs answered. "Have we lost our tail yet?"

"Yeah, a half mile back . . ." Vassilaros started to say, but then there was a sudden movement beside Moran.

"Jesus H.—" Vassilaros shouted, and a silenced pistol was fired once.

The van lurched very hard to the right and then back to the left. "My God," Reid shouted desperately.

"Drive normally, Mr. Reid, or I will kill you now," the Russian gunman said.

Moran had relaxed his right arm and fist, and he managed to get it out from beneath the strap across his chest. The one Russian was holding his pistol on Reid, who was driving, while the other was intently studying the traffic behind them through a peephole in the back door. Moran undid the buckle on his strap and then the one across his legs.

"Keep driving. I'll tell you where to pull off," the gunman said.

Moran sat up. The Russian, sensing the motion beside him, started to turn at the same time Moran grabbed his gun hand in a powerful grip and pulled it and the man completely around so that the pistol was pointed toward the back of the van.

The second Russian turned around, his eyes growing wide when he realized what was happening.

Moran held the man's arm in an elbow lock with his left arm, his right hand covering the Russian's gun hand, and he squeezed while aiming the pistol.

"*Stoi*," the Russian in the back screamed as he clawed inside his white tunic for his own pistol, but the silenced pistol went off, the shot hitting him in the chest, driving him back against the door, where he collapsed in a heap.

The van braked hard and screeched to the right.

"You are the devil," the gunman screamed as he tried to struggle out of Moran's grasp.

"Yes, I am," Moran said, grinning beneath his bandages. He snapped the Russian's arm and yanked the pistol out of his slack grip.

The Russian howled in pain, his voice cut off in mid-scream as Moran fired twice, hitting him in the face and the windpipe.

The van had come to a complete stop, and Moran came off the gurney as Reid was trying to bring his own pistol to bear. But Moran was first, laying the barrel of the Russian weapon against the FBI agent's temple.

"If you do exactly as I say, I will not kill you. I only want to escape."

36

Now that Moran had finally been transferred, most of the cops had gone, and the hospital was starting to get back to normal. Several patients had already been moved out of their special rooms back to the isolation ward.

Dr. Wood had left his office and was in conference with the hospital's administrator. He wanted to lodge an official complaint with the bureau in Washington for its handling of the case, and the administrator was trying to talk him out of it.

In emergency, FBI Agents Tom Lazenby and Troy Miller had been talking with one of the nurses, who was clearly impressed by the fact they worked for the bureau. They were off duty as of now, and she would be getting off in another few hours.

Two city cops had come in with a shooting victim ten minutes ago. The kid had died, and the police were doing their paper work at an empty table in one of the examination stalls.

The stair hall door slammed open, and a young man in green surgical scrubs, a hospital security badge clipped to his left breast, came through in a run.

"My God . . . somebody help . . . help me . . . we've got a killer here . . ."

Lazenby dropped his coffee cup, pulled out his service pistol, and stepped to the side. Miller shoved the nurse away from him, yanked out his pistol, and dropped into a shooter's stance. They had the young man and the open doorway covered.

The surgical tech stopped in his tracks, his voice dying in his throat.

"No! No!" the nurse was screaming. "It's Dan . . . Daniel Tait . . . he's all right."

The two uniformed cops had been slower to react, but they, too, had drawn their pistols on the young man in the doorway.

"It's all right," the nurse kept repeating.

Slowly Lazenby and the others came down, and they unbent.

"There're two bodies," Tait said, swallowing his words.

"Where?" Lazenby shouted.

"In the garage. My car. The trunk. It's a white Taurus parked on the right. You can't miss it. God . . ."

"Who the hell are you?" one of the uniformed cops demanded.

Lazenby yanked out his ID and showed it to them. "We'll take it first. Call for backup and then come down, but goddamnit, let me know what you're doing."

"Yes, sir," the cop said.

Lazenby and Miller went to the stair hall door and carefully listened, but there were no sounds of movement from below. They looked at each other, and then Lazenby rolled through the doorway, sweeping his gun left to right.

"Clear," he grunted, and started down the stairs.

He stopped at the first landing long enough for Miller to come through the door and start down. He took the last course eased open the door to the garage level, peeked out, then rolled through the doorway and raced to a parked car ten feet away, where he held up.

Nothing moved in the garage. There were no sounds of cars moving or engines idling, no one running away, trying to escape.

He looked back. Miller was at the partially opened door. Lazenby nodded, and Miller came out fast, zigzagging to another
parked car.

A white Taurus was parked fifty feet to the right, just as the
kid said it would be. The trunk lid was open.

"We've got backup on the way," someone called softly from
the stair hall door.

Lazenby looked over his shoulder. The uniformed cops were
there. "Cover us from where you are."

"You got it," one of them said.

Lazenby motioned to Miller, and on his signal the two of
them popped up and rushed to the Taurus from two different
angles.

There were two bodies in the trunk, both of them males, both
of them stripped to their underwear. Lazenby holstered his pistol
and gingerly reached inside the trunk and turned one of the
bodies over. The face had been partially shot away, but he knew
this man. He had worked with him.

Miller was beside him. "That's Bill Mote," he said softly.

It all suddenly came together for Lazenby. "Oh, fuck," he
said. "He's a bureau medic. He and Van Hook were bringing the
van."

Miller didn't see it.

"The van—the one that took Moran out of here," Lazenby
said. "Let's go," he shouted, and he turned on his heel and raced
for their car.

Moran had transferred to the front seat, pushing Vassilaros's
body aside. He wanted to be able to see outside.

His jaw ached, and he was spitting a little blood from where
the dental surgeon had dug out the remnants of four of his molars
that had been partially destroyed when the bullet had passed
through his mouth.

Reid had done exactly as he was told without one word of
argument. It was clear that he was extremely nervous, but he
was letting no fear show, though Moran could practically smell it
on him.

They had doubled back and drove slowly now into a pleasant
neighborhood in Brooklyn Heights, the southern tip of Manhattan glowing just across the mouth of the East River. Most of the
apartment buildings and condos were along the river, while two

blocks inland were mostly single-family houses and some du-
plexes.

Moran finally found the number he was looking for. It was
a small two-story brick house with a big front porch. Lights were
on at the back of the house, and one window was lit upstairs; but
the front porch was in darkness.

"Pull over here," Moran said.

Reid did as he was told. "You have a friend here?"

"Her name is Ann Neil. She's a nurse, actually, from the
hospital. Poor girl, her mother died last week, and she lives all
alone now."

"Oh, Christ, Moran, why—"

"As I told you, nothing will happen to you or to the woman
if you just do as I say. You have my word on it."

Reid just looked at him.

"First I've got to change out of this hospital gown," Moran
said. He motioned with the gun. "Best we go in the back."

Reid shivered but did as he was told, easing out of the driver's
seat and crawling into the back. He never heard or felt the single
shot to the back of his head that killed him.

Moran grinned. "I lied," he said, crawling in back over Reid's
body and closing the curtains so that nobody could see inside.

Using a pair of shears, he cut the lightweight cast off his right
leg. The femur had been chipped by a bullet fragment, but the
bone had not been seriously damaged. He had gleaned that and
other information from the conferences at his bedside when he
feigned unconsciousness. If he favored the leg, he wouldn't cause
any further damage.

Vassilaros's clothing fitted him reasonably well, and when he
had finished dressing, he carefully cut the bandages from his face.
He found some gauze and a plastic tray of adhesive strips and
climbed back into the front, where he looked at himself in the
rearview mirror.

His face was a mess, swollen and black and blue, with stitches
in each of his cheeks and a jagged line of a dozen or more stitches
from his right jaw all the way up to his forehead where the surgeon
had put his face back together. None of his wounds was leaking,
however, so he didn't need the adhesive strips, but he knew he
wouldn't get very far looking like this.

In the back he rummaged through the medical equipment
and supplies, finally finding a long, slender, slightly curved stain-

less steel surgical probe. Pocketing it, he got out of the van, locked the doors, and limped up the walk to the nurse's home.

He mounted the steps to the porch and softly tried the front door. It was locked, as he expected it would be.

A car went by, and he averted his face until it was past. It turned at the next corner. Using the stainless steel probe, he had the door lock picked in under ten seconds and was inside a long, narrow hallway. Stairs led up to the second floor, and he could smell the odors of cooking food from the back of the house.

A dog barked once and came around the corner from the kitchen in a run. Moran took out the silenced Makarov automatic and shot the animal, its legs collapsing as it sprawled in a loose heap.

"Bo Jo?" the nurse called. She came around the corner, wiping her hands on a dish towel. For an instant she couldn't believe what she was seeing: the dog dead on the floor, the man in the front stair hall.

But then she opened her mouth to scream, and Moran shot her in the chest. The single bullet pierced her heart, killing her instantly.

37

Ed Wilder got out of his limousine and entered the White House, where once his briefcase had been passed through security, he was met by Dan Hardy, the assistant to Herb Goldman, who was the President's chief of staff.

"Thank you for being so prompt, Mr. Wilder," Hardy said. "Mr. Goldman asked that you be brought right in."

Following Hardy down the corridor, Wilder tried to clear the cobwebs from his brain. He had been called away from a dinner party last night and had been at his office ever since, directing the so far unsuccessful search.

As his associate director, Howard Fenton, had put it so succinctly around six this morning, when the eastern sky was getting light, "The son of a bitch has simply disappeared, and unless or until he makes a move, we're stuck."

And stuck they were, Wilder had to admit, but they knew a hell of a lot more about Moran, or whoever he really was, than they did yesterday or even last night. None of their new knowledge, however, was very comforting. In fact, it couldn't have been worse.

It was ten o'clock exactly when Hardy stuck his head in the office and announced Wilder.

The President's chief of staff was just pouring himself a cup of coffee. He looked up. "Good morning, Ed. Coffee?"

"Sure," Wilder said, crossing the room and putting his briefcase on a chair in front of the desk.

"Do you want me to stay?" Hardy asked.

"No," Goldman said, and his assistant left. Goldman poured a second cup of coffee and handed it to Wilder. "You don't look so good this morning. Burning the midnight oil?"

"You could say that."

"Any luck?"

"None. What was his reaction?" He nodded over his shoulder in the general direction of the Oval Office.

"He's been waiting for Gorbachev to call to congratulate us on capturing Moran."

"Christ."

"Yeah," Goldman said, going behind his desk and sitting down. He motioned for the bureau director to do the same.

"Bob Vaughan will be along soon, but I wanted you to bring me up-to-date first. I'll be briefing the President at noon, and he's going to want to have some answers."

"We believe that he's gone to ground, Herb, which is just as good as it's bad," Wilder said.

"Bad because you've no idea where he's gotten himself to?"

"He's close. He didn't have a chance to get very far. Every cop in the continental United States and Canada has been alerted for the van. It's disappeared, too, which means he's hidden it as well as himself."

"If that's the bad, what's the good?"

"In hiding he won't be killing anyone else. At least not for a while."

"But he will," Goldman said, "kill again?"

"Before he's captured? Almost certainly. He's as well trained as he is ruthless . . . we believe."

It was something new, and Goldman caught it. He sat up.

"You've found out who he is?" The chief of staff had a large, round face and dark, nearly black eyes. They were narrowed and penetrating now, his brow furrowed.

"Possibly, but it's part of the bad news, Herb. In fact, it's absolutely dreadful news."

"Fire away."

"We have it fairly well established that his name is not Donald Moran, nor do we believe the other aliases he might have used—Richard Parmenter and Anthony Thomas—were his real names either. But something the doctors who worked on him told us rang a bell with one of my forensics people. Moran has had plastic surgery before, possibly to repair massive damage that had been done to his face. Looked typical of the blast damage wounds the doctor had seen in Vietnam."

"Is he a veteran?"

"Looks like it."

"You traced him through his fingerprints?"

"Moran has no fingerprints. He apparently obliterated them with acid some years ago. But we did check men of his build and general looks with his approximate dental records, eye color, et cetera."

"And?"

Wilder girded himself. "We think his real name might be Peter Forsythe. If so, Moran is a highly qualified, dangerous individual. He was a commissioned officer, a first lieutenant at the time of his capture—"

"He was a POW?"

"For about six months before he escaped, bringing twenty-five other prisoners with him. He managed to kill thirty-seven North Vietnamese prison guards, totally destroy the compound, and then kill an estimated eighteen to twenty other North Vietnamese regulars on the way south."

"His face was . . . damaged?"

"Severely. He was given some plastic surgery, but he elected to have the majority of it done at his own expense after his discharge."

"What did he do over there?"

"G-two on Westmoreland's staff. He was rated as an expert at unarmed hand-to-hand combat, and he was a language expert specializing in Russian. But he was also fluent in all the Romance languages along with a few dialects of Chinese, Japanese, and Vietnamese."

"And?"

"He was considered to be a damned good combat helicopter pilot."

"And?"

Wilder hesitated long enough to open his briefcase and extract a document. He passed it to Goldman. "A copy of his citation for the prison escape."

"Don't tell me he was awarded a medal."

"President Nixon put it around his neck out back in the Rose Garden. The Medal of Honor."

"My God," Goldman said, deeply moved. "Why?"

"The psychologists at the time believed he may have been unbalanced by his experiences in the prison . . . and by his treatment afterward. His own unit commander wanted to have him court-martialed."

"Why?"

"He brought back only twenty-five prisoners. He left behind two hundred and fifty-six others."

"His obligation was to effect his own escape. Good Lord."

"The court-martial was dropped, of course, but it presumably left its mark on Moran . . . or Forsythe. And when he returned home, he was no hero, medal or no medal. No returning veteran was. And his face was disfigured. I have photographs here of before and after. He was a mess."

"What about afterward?" Goldman asked.

"We lose his trail. He simply disappeared for a number of years. It's possible he became a merc—a mercenary soldier somewhere, but we just don't know."

Goldman's phone rang. He picked it up. "Yes," he said. "Send him in." He hung up. "Bob is here. Have you told him any of this?"

"Not yet."

"Brief him. If by some chance Moran . . . or Forsythe does get out of the country, the agency will have to pick up the chase. They might as well be in on it now."

Wilder nodded.

Vaughan came in, glanced at Wilder, and took a chair. He handed across the routine intelligence briefing contained in a plain folder. It was clear he would have preferred to work directly with the President on this. There was a sour expression on his face.

"The bureau has come up with something on . . . Moran that you'd better listen to," Goldman said.

"Have we got him back?" Vaughan asked Wilder.

"Not yet. But we've come up with something that might be of interest."

Goldman got up and went to the windows that looked out on the West Court as Wilder quickly went over everything with the director of central intelligence. When he was finished, Goldman turned back.

"Well?"

"With all due respect to Ed and the job he is doing, I don't think the bureau will find him that easily, if at all."

"Not until he moves," Wilder said, a little warm under the collar.

"Forgive me, Ed, but the son of a bitch has a plan. He didn't just make a break, willy-nilly. He knows what he's doing. He knows what you're going to do as well, and he believes he has a way around you. I believe it, too."

"We're not just going to lie back and lick our wounds," Wilder snapped.

"I'm not suggesting that. What I'm saying is that we'd damned well better expect the unexpected with this one."

"Which is?"

"He's going to get out of the United States. He's going to heal himself, he's going to radically alter his appearance, and he's going to get into the Soviet Union, where he's going to make another try on Gorbachev." Vaughan shook his head. "You almost have to admire the tenacious bastard. But I think he's got a goddamned good chance of pulling it off."

"It'll take time," Wilder said.

Vaughan nodded.

"And time is on our side. Sooner or later he'll make a mistake and we'll nail him."

"He's already made at least one," the DCI said, "and your people got him because of it."

"What are you talking about?" Goldman asked.

"The woman. The reporter with *World News This Week.* He came back for her."

"Because she'd seen his face," Wilder said. "Now everyone knows what he looks like."

"She tried to kill him, Ed. He'll not be forgetting that. Nor will he be able to forget that it was because of her he was wounded and captured. He'll come back for her all right."

"Still," Wilder said, "we have time. He won't heal overnight, and the woman might keep him in the New York area."

"Thank God for that much at least," Goldman said.

Vivian Hammer took off his reading glasses and looked up at the man standing at the end of the hospital bed. It was three o'clock in the morning. The President had been briefed on this material fifteen hours ago.

"No word on him yet?" Hammer asked. He was beginning to mend. Though he still had a way to go, he was out of the woods. Already he was beginning to get ornery lying around doing nothing.

His friend had brought this report bootlegged out of the associate director's office at great risk to his own career. But Hammer had saved his life a few years back, and he owed him one.

"No."

"Nothing on Reid or Vassilaros either?"

"Not a thing. They could be anywhere."

Hammer thought for a long moment or two. The Forsythe connection made sense. Moran's St. John house had been set up like a VC-infiltrated village. Same use of explosives. Knowledge like that was not easily obtained. It pointed to someone who had been there.

He also agreed with the DCI's conclusions, which had been added to the report, that Moran would make a try for Gorbachev again.

"What are we doing out there?"

"Every available man is in on it," the special agent said. "It's like a crisis management situation at all levels."

"Anyone up in New York?"

"We've got four aircraft running shuttle back and forth, with comms links to the New York office as well as all field units."

"Are the city cops cooperating?"

"One hundred percent."

Hammer looked at the telephone. "We're not going to catch him. Not this time. Not this easy."

"If he gets out of the country, it's no longer our problem, Vivian."

"Bullshit," Hammer said absently. He picked up the phone, dialed for an outside line, and, when he had it, dialed the operator. "Give me the overseas operator, please," he said.

A moment later she was on. "What country are you calling?"

Hammer had taken a card out of his wallet. On the back of it he had written a number and a special priority code.

"I want to place a call to the Soviet Union," he said. "Person to person. Moscow City Militia Chief Investigator Nikolai Ganin. I have the number and the calling code."

"Go ahead, sir," the operator said.

Ann Neil had been a fairly large broad-shouldered woman. It was one of the reasons Moran had decided to use her.

He'd wrapped her dog in burlap and put him in the basement. Her car, a new Volkswagen Jetta, came out of the garage, and the van went in under the cover of darkness. And finally, he had taken her body upstairs and put it in bed.

She was off duty for the next two days, another of the reasons she'd been just right, so the chances that someone would miss her would be diminished, although there was the possibility that a friend or relative would call.

He'd checked the calendar on the kitchen wall beside the refrigerator, the note pad beside the telephone, and the contents of her purse but found nothing to suggest she had made any plans for these two days.

At the hospital she'd spoken fondly about her mother. She was going to miss her. Now that she was gone there was no one.

He slept well that night and rising late, made a huge breakfast of steak and eggs and watched television, especially the news reports. There was nothing about him. They were keeping it low-key. That made things easier. Sooner or later, however, all hell would break loose, but by then he expected to be long gone.

The mailman came around two in the afternoon, and at three the telephone rang five times, stopped, and a half minute later rang ten times. At six a woman dressed in red slacks and a pullover came up on the front porch and tried the door. She rang the doorbell and knocked on the door for a long time before going around to the back and looking through the kitchen door.

Moran watched from upstairs. She was obviously a friend, and she had seen the car parked in the driveway. He decided that if she persisted or if she looked inside the garage, he would have to kill her. But after a while she went away and the house fell silent.

Before it got dark, Moran, shirtless, sat down at the woman's dressing table and with a small pair of scissors snipped off the ends of the stitches, making them much less obvious. Next he put on a liquid skin-tone makeup that did a fair job of concealing the black and blue marks, redness, and even some of the stitch line, though nothing could do a completely satisfactory job. By morning he would have a definite six o'clock shadow, but by then he would be able to shave and renew the makeup.

He darkened his eyebrows and extended them, then put on some lipstick; it was surprisingly harder to do than he thought it would be. He applied a little blush to his cheeks and some mascara to his eyes.

The effect was ludicrous, but he was beginning to look less like the walking wounded fugitive that he was.

In the bathroom he took off his trousers and, sitting on the edge of the tub, soaped his legs and carefully shaved them. When he was finished with that task, he made certain that the bathroom was spotlessly clean before he went back into the bedroom and dressed in a pair of black nylons and a black long-sleeved dress. He packed a few of her clothes, along with Vassilaros's things he'd been wearing, in one of her suitcases, added some of her makeup, but not enough of any of her things that it looked as if something were obviously missing, and put the bag downstairs by the kitchen door.

Between what money he had found on the bodies in the van and the little cache he'd found in an upstairs drawer, he had a little more than fifteen hundred dollars in cash. It wasn't nearly enough, but there would be opportunities for more soon.

He did not want to use any lights in the house. Before it got too dark to see, he went through every room to make certain that there were no signs, except for the bodies, that he had been here or what he had done. Then, gathering Ann Neil's purse, one of the silenced Russian pistols, a black pillbox hat and veil, and a brunette wig, he took the suitcase out to the car, stuffed it in the trunk, and under cover of darkness eased out of the driveway and drove off.

It was nearly eight by the time he had crossed over into New Jersey, picking up Interstate 95 south. He pulled into a rest stop, where he used a pay phone to call TWA in Philadelphia, booking himself a round-trip economy-class seat to Los Angeles on the last flight out, which left at 10:00 P.M. He used the name Mrs. Hannah Pemberton.

Philadelphia was barely sixty miles away, but in traffic he made it to the TWA counter with less than a half hour to spare. He paid for his ticket with cash. The people in line, the ticket agents, the boarding gate attendants, and the flight attendants all were solicitous of him because of his limp and because of the black veil he kept over his face. They saw what they wanted to see.

He got a window seat alone and refused any service. After a while they left him alone. "The poor dear," one of the flight attendants clucked.

Soon, the lights of the eastern seaboard falling behind, he let himself sleep.

It was another of the old dreams, one that had not come to him in the night for a number of years, one that he had thought was past.

He was squatting chest-deep in mud and water in a pit that was covered with bamboo slats. The muck was too deep for him to sit, and the cage was too short for him to stand fully erect.

From time to time the North Vietnamese guards would dump

the slop buckets from the latrines down on him and a few of the other POWs who had been particularly troublesome. But always more slops were dumped on him, bucket after filthy bucket rising the level of the muck in his cage until it was up to his chin.

One more bucket and his cage would overflow. He would drown in a river of shit.

The Vietnamese soldiers were there, tipping the large bucket over. Always in slow motion the slops came pouring down into his cage, and he began to suffocate.

He awoke with a start when the pitch of the aircraft's engines changed and his ears began to fill. It was after midnight, and the plane was coming in for a landing. Los Angeles was a glow spreading in the distance to the west.

The Fasten Seat Belts sign came on, and the cabin lights came up. People were waking up, looking around, their eyes bloodshot.

One of the flight attendants came back. "Are you all right, ma'am? We're just coming in for a landing."

"Just fine, thank you," Moran mumbled, pitching his voice a little higher.

The young woman smiled.

He thought back to Vietnam, how different everything had been. Elemental. Life and death were not simply some abstraction that you thought about once in a while. They were constants; death was a very real and daily occurrence.

The plane touched down on time at exactly 12:37 A.M. and taxied to the terminal. Once the boarding tunnel was in place and the aircraft door opened, one of the attendants came back and helped Moran off the plane ahead of everyone else except for first class. The airport was not very busy at this time of night, and the baggage came up within ten minutes. He retrieved his single bag and limped outside to a taxi. The driver opened the rear door from inside, and Moran climbed in.

"Where to, lady?" the cabby asked. He was Hispanic, a cigarette dangling out of one corner of his mouth, a toothpick out of the other.

"Oh, I don't know," Moran mumbled, opening the suitcase and rummaging around inside. "North. Culver City or something like that. I have the address."

"Yeah, okay," the cabby said, and he pulled away from the curb.

Moran pulled out the pistol, pulled off his hat and veil once they were clear of the terminal driveway lights, and laid the barrel of the gun against the back of the cabby's neck.

"I remember now," he said in his own voice. "It's Century City."

"Jesus . . . motherfucker. What the fuck do you want?"

"You're going to take me to Twentieth Century-Fox Studios. A back gate."

"Listen, I don't want no trouble. You want my money? You got it. Fuck. I got a wife and a kid on the way. Come on."

Moran smiled. "Honest," he said. "Just do as I say and you can split. Nobody gets hurt, everybody is happy." He pulled a hundred-dollar bill from his purse and let it drop on the front seat. "No problems, man. I promise you."

It was a few minutes before six o'clock when the woman in the black dress, pillbox hat, and black veil presented herself at the Delta counter.

"Yes, ma'am?" the ticket agent asked respectfully.

"I would like a round-trip ticket to San Francisco on your six-fifteen flight this morning. Economy, please. I have one bag to check."

"Yes, ma'am," the agent said. People were watching the woman, who was obviously in mourning.

"The name, ma'am?"

"Pemberton," the woman said. "Mrs. Hannah Pemberton."

Moscow was a fairly low city. Lenin Heights, over which
Moscow State University sprawled, barely rose above the
level of the winding river. There were no real skyscrapers
like Manhattan's, no teeming metropolis, yet more than seven
million people lived here.

Ganin parked his car behind a Zil limousine on Karl Marx
Street a few blocks from the Lefortovo Prison and entered a small,
very exclusive French restaurant. A puffy little man dressed in a
tuxedo came out from behind a podium like a shot.

"Yes, Captain?" he said softly, eyeing Ganin's militia uniform.
"Were you expected?"

"Actually, no," Ganin said, looking into the man's eyes. "But
I promise that your name will not be mentioned, nor will the
restaurant's."

For a long second or two the maître d' had no idea how to react. But finally he nodded his understanding.

Ganin went into the dining room, where he spotted Chief Prosecutor Yernin seated with a young Mosfilm starlet. He went directly across to them, pulled a chair from another table, and sat down.

"You mean to spoil my lunch?" Yernin asked. "What do you want?"

"You weren't in your office," Ganin said. "Your secretary told me you were here."

"It could not have waited until this afternoon?"

"Pardon me, Chief Prosecutor, were you planning on returning to your office?"

Yernin shook his head irritably but then turned to the young woman, who was very beautiful, and smiled. "My dear, why don't you go powder your nose? Give us slaves to duty just a few minutes, won't you?"

"Of course, Arkasha," the girl said, her Russian rounded and very soft. She was probably Polish. She got up, Yernin rising with her, and she looked down at Ganin, who had remained seated. "You are no gentleman."

"Here I cannot afford it," he said.

She flashed him a coy smile and walked off. Every male head in the place turned to watch her go. Her walk was sinuous, and it was obvious she wore neither a bra nor panties.

"A pretty girl, isn't she?" Yernin said. "She's from Gdańsk. Says she knows Walesa. He's a real shit, according to her. What's called a media hound."

"He got their attention," Ganin said, though he didn't know why he was baiting the prosecutor.

"Yes, as you now have mine. Something has happened, some new information has come to light, and you wish a bill of arrest."

"I wish to have a private talk with President Gorbachev."

Yernin smiled indulgently. "Yes, and so would I. This Western invention of income taxes is taking things too far. I, for one, would like to see a change."

"I received a telephone call from the United States yesterday. From the FBI."

"The question is, why have you taken so long to come to me about it?" Yernin said. "I would assume your conversation had something to do with the arrest of Donald Moran?"

It did not surprise Ganin that Yernin knew about the telephone call. In fact, it would have surprised him if the chief prosecutor hadn't known.

"We were cut off before out conversation was finished. I've been trying to reestablish the call."

"Did you?"

"No."

"What now? Do you wish my help?" Yernin asked.

"No, Chief Prosecutor, not with that. As I said, I want to speak with President Gorbachev."

"Why?"

"His life is in danger."

Again Yernin smiled. "Which of us is not in danger, my dear Nikolai Fedorovich? I ask you."

"Moran has escaped."

Yernin blinked. He studied the wine in his glass and then looked toward the windows. Light came in around the edges of the thick drapes. "It was my understanding he was wounded. Near death. Incapacitated for a good long time. Your words, Chief Investigator."

"He is an extraordinary man."

"And your friend at the FBI called you with this startling news?"

"Yes."

"What else? What are his recommendations?"

"He thinks that Moran may be on his way here."

"To Moscow?"

Ganin nodded.

"To stalk Gorbachev?"

Again Ganin nodded.

Yernin, bemused, shook his head. "As you say, an extraordinary man."

"They think they may have identified him as Peter Forsythe, a Vietnam veteran and former prisoner of Hanoi."

"Ah, the American misadventure which we tried quite successfully to emulate in Afghanistan. He was highly trained, no doubt. An intelligence officer. Perhaps a combat veteran who came out of the experience a bitter man ready to strike back at society . . . his own for placing him there and ours for hindering his cause."

"It would seem he's a driven man."

Yernin thought about it for a second or two. "Which brought him to New York, to stalk the woman journalist. But he was unsuccessful. In fact, according to your report, it was you who saved his life. Had you not been there, she would have killed him. I would think that there is a powerful incentive to remain wherever she is, New York City, and try again . . . you see what I'm driving at. The FBI simply has to place a watch on her, and sooner or later this madman will show up to try again. Even so, you must admit that although he has apparently escaped from his hospital bed, he cannot get far, nor can he move very fast. He will have gone into a hole somewhere to heal himself. But that will take time. In the meanwhile, I have every confidence that the FBI will catch up with him. So there, you see, there is nothing for us to worry about. On the contrary, you have done a brilliant job. In Geneva you saved the life of the president. And in New York you arrested Moran. A successful conclusion, I would say."

He didn't understand, of course. Ganin didn't think anyone who had not come face-to-face with Moran could.

"Still, I would like to speak with Mr. Gorbachev."

"Impossible, so I suggest that you do not even try. He is safe, believe me. And he will be much safer if you vigorously pursue your investigation into who hired this assassin."

"We already know—"

"Ah, but, Nikki, it is not enough to know. We must have the proof. Bring that to me, and I will write your bills of arrest. Together we shall clean out this nest of plotters."

"What if Moran comes here?"

The girl was returning. Yernin looked up and spotted her. "If he does, you will know it and you will stop him. It is as simple as that." The chief prosecutor got to his feet. "I have every confidence in you."

Ganin returned to his office and poured himself a stiff shot of cognac from the office safe where the tape recorders were kept. One of the machines was missing. He laughed and raised his glass.

"To free enterprise," he said. "I hope the sorry son of a bitch gets something good for it on the black market, like a pair of good boots or perhaps a decent winter coat."

Without the active support of the prosecutor's office a militia investigator, even a chief investigator such as Ganin, who had connections through his wife's family and connections through friends of his father's, would be hamstrung. Or at least a sensible investigator would realize that the cards were stacked against him and that it was time to start the process of covering his own back in case it all blew up.

It was still raining along the eastern seaboard of the United States. He had seen it on television. There were floods in Maryland and New Jersey. Here the weather had turned nice, though a little cool for spring. Moscow and New York were more than a world apart in so many ways.

Sepelev came in carrying a cardboard carton, which he placed on Ganin's desk with a flourish. "You'll never guess what I've got here," he said, pulling off his jacket and dumping it in a ball on his desk.

Ganin poured him a drink. "He said no."

"Screw the bastard, we'll do our own investigation. Listen, Nikki, a friend of mine over at the Lubyanka has taken sympathy on us. He doesn't like that *pizda* Colonel Markelov any more than we do. So we've got our own private pipeline."

"Into what, Yurochka?" Ganin asked, opening the flaps of the box and looking inside. It was filled with what appeared to be computer printouts.

"Second Chief Directorate. Seventh Department, which, of course, watches tourists. First Section, which watches specifically American, British, and Canadian tourists."

Ganin shook his head.

"Don't you see, Nikki, if Moran is coming here, it'll be under one of those passports. Can he pass himself off as an Afrikaner?" Sepelev laughed heartily. A little too heartily. There was something else.

"Go on," Ganin said, putting down his drink. "You've already looked through all of this and you've come up with something?"

Sepelev's grin broadened. He nodded.

"Well?"

"You'll never guess who showed up at Sheremetyevo Airport last night," Sepelev said. "Not in a million years—"

"Mary Frances Dean."

Sepelev's face fell. "Fuck your mother, how did you know?"

Mary Frances Dean had a deluxe room on the eighteenth floor at the Rossiya Hotel just off Red Square.

At two in the afternoon Ganin called her from the lobby, but there was no answer. He went upstairs, showed his identification to the floor lady, and she let him in.

The room was quite nice by Russian standards, but after what he had seen in Geneva and again in New York, he looked at it through different eyes. The curtains were dirty, the Persian-style rug was practically threadbare, the bedspread was very thin, and the room smelled of cigar smoke and possibly, faintly, of urine. He didn't think she was going to be very happy here.

He was surprised by the amount of luggage she'd brought. Stacked in the closet were four large suitcases. Another, smaller suitcase was open on a stand next to the bureau, and in the bathroom were two large green nylon bags. One of them contained makeup, and the other was crammed with shoes.

He poked through the makeup and shoe bags in the bathroom, then transferred his search to the bags in the closet. But there was nothing of any real interest except for a lot of guidebooks about the Soviet Union, a dozen rolls of toilet paper, eight pump containers of toothpaste, ten boxes of deodorant super Tampax, two bottles of something called Woolite, and four boxes of something else called Summer's Eve disposable douche. Americans were amazing. American women were even more amazing.

He went around the bed to the window, and he found a Swiss-made portable typewriter in a leather case and another bag containing paper, carbon, ribbons, pencils, a stapler, paper clips, and other office supplies.

He sat down on the edge of the bed and stared at her things, trying to see beyond the mere fact of their physical presence, until he had it. It was so obvious, yet he could hardly believe it. Mary Frances Dean had *moved* to Moscow. She was no tourist here for a week or even two. She was here for a long time. Somewhere there would be a record of her application and its acceptance to practice journalism in the Soviet Union.

But it must have been hastily arranged. Moran would find out, of course. Sooner or later he would see a dispatch with her name, dateline Moscow. Sooner or later, then, he would have another incentive to come here. Somehow, incredibly, it was all happening.

The only thing missing, he decided, was a briefcase or an attaché case with dispatches or other material. The door opened, and Mary Frances came in, an attaché case in hand.

Ganin stood up. "Hello again," he said.

She looked at her typewriter and office bag, then at the open closet door, the bag on the stand, and the open bathroom door. "Is this the usual welcoming committee, or do I rate for some reason?" she said.

"I called from downstairs. But there was no answer."

She smiled sardonically. "So you just came up, let yourself in, and had a look around?"

"Yes," Ganin said. He held up his hand for her to keep silent, and he unplugged the telephone and the television set. She watched him through lidded eyes.

"Now I'm to believe that we can talk without being recorded?" she asked.

"Yes," he said, nodding. "You have come as a very large surprise."

"Unpleasant, I hope."

Ganin shook his head and shrugged. He didn't understand. Not completely, yet he suspected she was angry. "Have you heard that Moran has escaped?"

Her eyes widened, and her nostrils flared. "No."

"Special Agent Vivian Hammer telephoned me. Moran is gone. No one knows where he is."

She closed her eyes. "He's going to come after me again, isn't he?"

"I think so."

"What are you going to do about it?" she demanded, laying her attaché case on the bureau.

"If he shows up in Moscow, I will break into his room and look through his things. I promise you."

She turned to look at him, the faint traces of a smile at the corners of her mouth, except that she wasn't sure if he was kidding or not.

"Why have you come to Moscow?" he asked.

"None of your business."

"I am a police officer. Please answer my question."

She snorted. "Will you have me arrested if I don't?"

"Yes, if need be," Ganin said, amazed with the woman's massive contempt. He could not believe how changed she was from New York.

"Then plug the telephone back in. I want to call my embassy."

He shook his head. "I don't understand, Miss Dean."

"Are you going to plug in the telephone or shall I scream for help?"

He had never encountered a person such as she. "Would you have felt better about yourself in New York if you had actually committed murder?"

"I would have propably gotten a medal from your president."

"Thus admitting that the Moscow Militia was not doing its job properly? I don't think so."

This time she did smile, and she shook her head. "Are you for real? Is any of this for real? Shit, I can't believe it."

"You're here on assignment, aren't you?"

"If you know what I am doing in Moscow, then why did you come in here?"

"I didn't know until I saw all your suitcases." He smiled a little. "You know, Miss Dean, we have toilet paper and toothpaste here."

"I don't know anything about Russian toothpaste," she said defensively.

"No, I mean, you can get any American brand you want at a foreign exchange store. And there's always someone making a run down to Helsinki for supplies."

It was her turn to look at him with amazement. "You don't get it, do you?" she said. "There's something wrong with a country where its visitors have to cross the border to get some item of food they want."

"He's coming here, you know. Sooner or later he will recover from his wounds, and he will show up."

"Then it gives me some time."

"I'm telling you the truth."

"When he comes, you will arrest him, Chief Investigator. I have every confidence in you."

"That may not be possible . . . at least not in time to save your life. My primary responsibility is President Gorbachev."

"That's the KGB's responsibility. Ninth Directorate, if I'm not mistaken."

"You are not. But I do not have the manpower to assign someone to watch over you around the clock."

"Don't you people do that anyway?" she snapped. Her voice was becoming strident. She glanced at the telephone. "Microphones in my room, cops looking through my things. And how did you know I was here in the first place, except that your border patrol reported to you. KGB."

Ganin thought about his own experience in Washington when he had telephoned about the shuttle to New York. His call had been monitored. And Hammer had wanted to make an arrest without a warrant. Protective custody, he'd called it. Where were the differences, really?

"I'll limit my acquaintances to Americans I know and to Russians."

"He speaks Russian."

"Get out of here," she said. "Please, just get out of here, Ganin."

And then he had it. She had attended the usual welcome to the USSR briefing either at the embassy or at her office. Russia is different from the West. You are not free here. There is censorship of your dispatches. You can be sent home at any moment for a wide variety of infractions. You could be subject to arrest at any time. If they want you behind bars, they'll put you there. No writ of habeas corpus. (All that despite *glasnost* and *perestroika*.) Hell, in Moscow it is against the law to drive a dirty car. Once you have an apartment in the city, you cannot rent a hotel room. Do not attempt to purchase goods in a foreign exchange store with rubles. Do not attempt to purchase goods in a state or private store with Western currency. Do not deal with the black market. Travel, any travel outside the city must be approved by the Militia seventy-two hours in advance. . . .

She was frightened. It was plain.

Ganin took a card out of his pocket and laid it on the bed. "If you get into trouble or find a need just to talk, you can contact me day or night."

"Go."

"Welcome to Moscow," Ganin said softly, and he left.

World News This Week's offices were located in what had once been a warehouse building on Arbat Street. Mary Frances took a cab over from the hotel and went in. Ganin had not bothered to hide his presence behind her, but apparently she never noticed.

A few minutes before four she emerged with Benjamin Siegel, the bureau chief, and they went in his car over to the American Embassy on Tchaikovsky Street.

Ganin waited until after six, but they didn't come out, so he went back to his office, where he got quietly drunk. Alone.

Ganin was unable to sleep. He lay in the darkness in bed, smoking a cigarette. Antonia was silent beside him. She had gotten home a half hour after he had, but he'd not bothered to ask her where she had been, nor had she volunteered the information. The thought that she might be having an affair had crossed his mind, but he didn't think he really minded.

Besides, he was preoccupied with Moran. There was an answer somewhere, he supposed. He was just going to have to be bright enough to find it before Moran got here. But he was afraid he wasn't smart enough.

The telephone rang, and he got it before it could ring again. "Yes?" he said.

"I know it's late," Mary Frances said. "But I wanted to call to . . . apologize for my behavior this afternoon."

"I understand."

"No, you don't, but I'm sorry anyway. Good-bye." She hung up.

Ganin put the phone down.

"What did she want?" Antonia asked.

"She wanted to apologize."

"For what?"

"Nothing," Ganin said. "Go to sleep."

41

I t was a little before noon when Moran limped away from San Francisco's St. Francis Memorial Hospital, where the cabby had dropped him off. The neighborhood was pleasantly up-scale, and the morning was cool, the air fresh. It had been a couple of years since he had been here last, and then for only a couple of months after he had gone to ground over an incident in Atlanta. But a few telephone calls from the airport had told him that nothing much had changed in the interim.

The last time he was here, he had posed as a gay architect in town for some much needed R&R. Within an hour after he'd hit the first Fulton Street bar, he had matched up with Roger Schae-fer, a registered nurse at St. Francis and chief makeup artist for the San Francisco Amateur Repertory Theater. They'd had an interesting couple of months.

The house was a small but immaculately neat bungalow with a lovely flower garden in the front and an even lovelier Japanese garden in the back.

Moran let himself through the gate to the back and mounted the slatted veranda that overlooked the garden and fountains. Using the stainless steel probe he'd taken from the van in New York, he picked the lock on the back door and let himself in.

"Rog?" he called out. But there was no answer. As he suspected, Schaefer was probably still at work.

Closing and relocking the door, Moran went into the bedroom, where he laid down his bag and took off the pillbox hat, veil, and wig.

This would be just fine, he told himself, quickly searching the house to make certain he was alone. Just fine.

A few minutes after five the front door opened and someone came in. Moran was in the bathroom. He had run a bubble bath and had laid out a couple of fresh bath towels. He'd found a bottle of champagne in the pantry and had put it in an ice bucket and brought it and two glasses into the bathroom.

"Hello," Moran called.

There was a dead silence.

"Don't be a party poop. Don't you recognize my voice, Rog, or do I have to design you a house so that you'll remember?"

"Bob?" Schaefer called. "Bob Taich . . ." His voice was cut off in mid-sentence when he came around the corner to the bathroom door.

"Hi," Moran said, looking at Schaefer's reflection in the mirror over the sink. "I look like hell, sorry, but I was in this pretty bad accident."

"Jesus, I guess," Schaefer said.

Moran was nude. He turned around. He had an erection. Schaefer grinned uncertainly.

"Well, I'm happy to see that not everything got hurt," he said.

Moran smiled warmly, though he felt absolutely nothing. "Glad to see me?"

"You bet," Schaefer said. "I think I can get a couple of days off."

"Great," Moran said. "But listen, Rog, I'm going to need a big favor from you. You still doing your makeup over at the rep?"

Schaefer nodded.

"Well, good, 'cause I brought along some things . . . I want you to teach me how to use them. Help me hide . . . this." He waved his fingers lightly around his face.

"No sweat," Schaefer said. "When we get done, you'll be beautiful again."

"Just like you?"

Schaefer laughed. "Sure, Bob, just like me."

They had their bubble bath and made love. Afterward, while the steaks were on the grill and Schaefer was making them a salad, Moran laid out the things he had stolen from the Twentieth Century-Fox Studios in Los Angeles.

"You're serious about this," Schaefer said, glancing over his shoulder. He came over to take a closer look. "This is heavy-duty stuff. Professional. Where'd you get it?"

"I have my sources."

"I mean that the guy you got this from would be a hell of a lot more qualified to show you how to use this than me."

"But she's not nearly so much fun."

It was an answer Schaefer was hoping for. "We'll start right after supper. Who do you want to look like, Robert Redford?"

"You," Moran said. "Seriously. Here, let's use this. I found it in your bedroom." Moran laid out Schaefer's passport, open to his photograph.

"God, what a horrible picture," Schaefer said, without any suspicions. He was totally enamored. "It's your funeral."

No, it's yours, Moran thought, but said nothing.

It wasn't overly difficult to learn how to apply the quick-setting latex compound. When it was on and dry, and a little makeup applied, it was nearly impossible to tell it from real flesh. The difficult part was learning the art of application, to come up with the desired effect. It took most of the evening for Moran to reach the point of proficiency where he could do what was needed.

"You're a quick study," Schaefer said. "But with those healing cuts on your face I wouldn't leave this crap on for more than twenty-four hours at a time. I mean it'd be okay to fix yourself up so that you could go out for an evening, but beyond that I just don't know. What did happen to you?"

"I was shot."

"What?"

"A little territorial rights problem. It just got out of hand. They're still looking for the son of a bitch."

"Christ, Bob."

They'd set up a mirror on the kitchen table, and Moran was comparing his face with the one on the passport photograph. It was passable. He no longer was an old woman or a walking wounded. He'd just regained his freedom.

"Thanks, Bob," he said rising. He took the towel from around his neck, looped it over the back of Schaefer's neck, and drew him forward. "Now it's time for me to really thank you," he said softly.

Schaefer smiled, and as Moran brought him closer, he closed his eyes.

Moran suddenly crossed his grip on the towel and twisted it around the young man's neck. Schaefer reared back, his eyes wide, his mouth open, not understanding what was happening to him. He couldn't speak or breathe or even move effectively against Moran's superior strength, and slowly the light faded from his eyes, and he slipped into unconsciousness, collapsing in a heap on the floor.

It was after midnight by the time Moran had cleaned up. He went through the house, coming up with nearly three thousand in cash, along with several credit cards. The money was a bonanza he hadn't expected. Schaefer must have been planning something.

Using the credit cards would produce a paper trace, but no one would be looking for Schaefer for several days at least, and it would take more time to run down the credit card records to find out what happened.

He left Schaefer's Diners Club and MasterCard but took his American Express, Carte Blanche, and Visa cards. He also left a few hundred dollars in cash in the man's wallet to confuse the initial investigation a little further.

By the time the authorities understood what had happened here, it would be far too late.

Such crimes, he thought, standing in the bedroom doorway and looking at the body, were not unknown in San Francisco. In fact, such things happened quite frequently. The gay life-style, he thought, bred a lot more dangers than AIDS.

* * *

Moran packed a few of Schaefer's things in a couple of small suitcases. The clothing he had come with went into a paper bag. He caught a cable car across the street, and downtown, at the edge of Chinatown, he discarded the paper sack and, two blocks farther, caught a cab out to the airport.

He was forty-five minutes early for his 8:15 A.M. flight to Montreal under Schaefer's name, and after he had checked his suitcases through, he went into one of the small coffee shops, where he got a cup of tea and the morning newspapers.

There was nothing about him. Was it possible, he wondered, that the police still believed he was in the New York area? If that were the case, it would mean they hadn't discovered the body of Ann Neil or the van. Luck was with him.

His flight arrived in Montreal a few minutes early, giving him a full hour and fifteen minutes to clear Canadian customs and get over to the Finnair terminal, where he booked a first-class seat to Helsinki, still under the Schaefer name, using Schaefer's American Express card. When the ticket agent checked with Amex, she was told Mr. Schaefer's credit was triple A.

A chill wind blew off the Gulf of Finland as Moran put his bags down by the country gate and looked up the lane at the big whitewashed house with thatched roof.

It was noon, local, and he was dead tired and about ready to drop. His wounds ached, and he knew they were leaking a little. His face was on fire, and his jaw hurt. But he had come this far, and he would not stop now. He could not. The Soviet Union was only seventy-five miles to the east by land and barely fifty miles to the south across the gulf.

"Be so good as to keep your hands away from your body, and then turn around," someone said behind him in English.

Moran did as he was told. He smiled. "Hello, Alvar," he said in passable Finish.

Alvar Ehrenström, one of Finland's best armorers and forgers and Moran's last real resource anywhere, knitted his brows. It was clear he recognized the voice, but not the face. "Do I know you?" he asked, continuing in English.

"I should hope so," Moran said. "It's me, Ernst Leiter." He used his persona for here.

"Well, I'll be goddamned," Ehrenström said, lowering his shotgun. "So it is."

"I need some help."

"I should say. You look like a goddamned faggot."

"You don't know the half of it."

"Well, we'll have a drink, something to eat, and you'll tell me all about it. I suppose you're in a bloody great hurry again."

"Rather," Moran said. "I want to be over there by tonight. Moscow by morning, at the latest."

"Still leaves us time for a drink."

A very concerned doctor tried to keep Vivian Hammer from checking himself out of the hospital but spent a full five minutes for his trouble reeling under the most intense verbal lashing he'd ever been given in his life.

Incredibly, it had taken Ann Neil's friend Liz Horne three full days before she got up the nerve to call the police. A patrol car met her at the house, but the two officers were reluctant to make a forcible entry without probable cause that a crime had been committed. Besides, the friend told them that the nurse's car had been parked in the driveway as of three days ago but then had disappeared overnight.

So the woman wasn't home. Not everyone told friends everything.

The officers changed their minds, however, when they looked

in a window in the side of the garage and spotted the FBI's ambulance van. It was on their hot sheet.

They called it in, asking for backup to help secure the scene, and the request was relayed to the FBI's New York office, which told the NYPD, "Hands off," in no uncertain terms.

The message was flashed to Washington and came back to Hammer via his friend almost immediately. Hammer was on the scene barely one hour behind the FBI's first units. It was just nine in the morning.

"Jesus H. Christ, Vivian, I thought they'd planted you by now," the agent in charge, Sam Perlman, growled, taking the cigar out of his mouth when Hammer came in.

"I don't want any shit here, Sam. You know what's gone down with me. Was it our people in that van?"

Perlman and Hammer went back a ways together. They had a respect for each other. Perlman had a genuine concern for Hammer's well-being, but he knew it would be useless to fight him.

"Reid and Vassilaros. Both took hits, no telling for now what caliber, but I'd guess smaller than nine-millimeter. Two Russians with them . . . you heard about our medicos."

"Stuffed in a trunk of a car in the hospital's parking garage."

Perlman nodded. "I don't think these two are going to be tough to ID . . . KGB, maybe GRU. No word yet."

Hammer went to the foot of the stairs and looked up as Ann Neil's body was being brought down on the stretcher. "What the hell was he doing here?" he asked.

"Don't know yet. But he must have had a reason."

"Why here? She was a nurse at the hospital, but what was there about her, particularly, that brought him here?"

Liz Horne appeared at the head of the stairs with one of the FBI agents. She'd been crying, and it looked as if she were on the verge of collapse. The agent gently helped her down the stairs after Ann Neil's body was taken outside.

"Miss Horne?" Hammer said.

"Why?" she cried, looking up at him. "Why'd the son of a bitch do it, and then—"

"I don't know . . ." Hammer started to speak but then stopped. "And then what?" he asked.

The woman looked at him. "Why'd he kill her and then steal her clothes? Is the fucker a transvestite?"

Hammer and Perlman looked at each other.

"What clothes?" Hammer asked. "Can you tell us exactly?"

"I don't know," she said. "Her red dress and the white pumps she liked are gone. And her leather suitcase is missing."

"Anything else?"

"Yeah, the outfit she wore for her mother."

"Miss?" Hammer asked.

"Black dress, black veil, hat." She shook her head, her eyes filling. "Her mother died. What'd the son of a bitch want those things for?"

"I don't know," Hammer said. "But I promise you, we'll find him."

The agent took her away.

"Moran is on the small side for a man, and Ann Neil, as I remember now, was on the large size for a woman," Hammer said.

Perlman was shaking his head. "I still don't get it, Vivian. Why go through all that trouble? He's got her car, or had it. He switches for another, drives only at night—"

"No," Hammer said, picking up the hall phone. "His face is all fucked up, but he wanted to be a long way from here in a big hurry, which means the airlines. He needed something not only to disguise his identity but to hide his face."

"Jesus, the car will be at an airport."

"That's right."

Hammer got back to Washington in the early afternoon. His friend Don McKinstry, who had supplied him with the bootlegged reports on Moran, and the assistant director of the bureau's Special Investigative Division, William D. Seagraves, were waiting for him. "You should be in the hospital," Seagraves said.

"No time, sir. It's Moran, and he's on the loose."

McKinstry was excited. "We found Ann Neil's car at the Philadelphia airport. Long-term parking. It'd been there for three days."

"He's on his way to Moscow," Hammer said.

"If he is, he's taking the long way around," Seagraves said. They were seated in his office.

"Where is he?"

"Los Angeles," McKinstry said. "Or at least we think it was

him. A woman in a black dress and veil, who identified herself as Mrs. H. Pemberton, bought a round-trip ticket to L.A., out of Philly. She was due back on this morning's flight, but she didn't show up."

"Did she book herself on any other flight out of L.A.?" Hammer asked.

McKinstry was momentarily taken aback. "Sorry, I didn't think of that. But why'd he go to L.A.?"

"I don't know. He wanted away from the East Coast. Maybe that was the first flight out."

"We checked that. He could have gone almost anywhere that same night, if we assume he left the Neil house sometime shortly after dark to mask his movements."

Hammer didn't reply. He was trying to think it out. Trying to put himself in Moran's shoes.

"So why did he go to Los Angeles if he is supposedly on his way to the Soviet Union?" Seagraves asked.

Hammer looked up. "He has contacts, presumably all over the world. People who have helped him in one way or the other. The forger in Marseilles, the gunman in Mexico City. Why not someone in Los Angeles?"

"Then what?" the assistant director prompted.

"He is going to Moscow, Mr. Seagraves. One way or the other, that's where he's headed."

"To assassinate Gorbachev."

Hammer nodded.

"So he goes to Los Angeles, let's say, to come up with some papers," Seagraves said.

"He needs a new appearance first," Hammer said. A vague idea was forming at the back of his head. He didn't want to examine it too closely yet, lest it disappear. But it was something . . . about Los Angeles. Something about Moran's purpose or his methods.

"That'll take time," McKinstry reminded them. "I saw him before and after he went on the operating table. His face was messed up, never mind the other wounds in his leg and side. He's got to heal. Six months, maybe, before something could be done about the massive scaring."

"He won't wait months."

"He'll have to, unless he's a magician."

Hammer fell silent again, his thoughts running down a dozen

different paths, looking for answers, looking for possibilities that could be weighed against probabilities.

"Yes?" Seagraves asked.

"We need to check on flights out of L.A. under the H. Pemberton name, though I don't think he'll get that sloppy. But he's in a hurry and doesn't have too many options, so it's worth a try."

"I'll get on it immediately," McKinstry said, rising.

"Wait, Mac, I want you to check on two other things for me."

McKinstry waited.

"Have LAPD run down its offenders list for anyone who might be a makeup artist. Not an amateur, but someone who is good."

Understanding dawned in McKinstry's eyes.

"And I want you to check its incomings for the past seventy-two hours, from the moment that plane landed in L.A. until right now."

"For break-ins at makeup shops, supply stores, and warehouses, salons," McKinstry said.

"Little theaters . . . hell, it's Hollywood, better check with all the movie studios."

"Will do," McKinstry said, and he left.

"What do you think?" Seagraves asked.

"I don't know, sir. He's in bad shape; but so am I, and I'm moving."

Seagraves thought about it. "Do you want to call Ganin again?"

"I tried. They won't put me through."

"I'll see what I can do, but it might take a day or two."

"I hope we've got the time."

Hammer went home to get some rest around eight in the evening, but he couldn't stand the loneliness and inactivity and was back at the bureau by ten-thirty.

McKinstry called at midnight. "We came up with something, but then it dead-ends."

"Is it him?"

"A hundred percent. H. Pemberton arrived in Los Angeles a little after midnight, three days ago, and left six hours later for San Francisco. In the meantime, that night the makeup and special effects studios of Twentieth Century-Fox were broken into, and an undetermined amount of special effects supplies were taken."

"How about San Francisco?"

"Nothing. Totally blank."

"Keep trying. The son of a bitch has the means of changing his appearance now, and he'll use them. He'll be going to Moscow sooner than anybody thinks."

Mary Frances worked until six each evening and then walked to the corner where she caught a cab to her new apartment in the foreigners' compound near the Botanical Gardens.

It was a few minutes to six, and Ganin sat in his car across the street. The passenger side door opened suddenly, and Sepelev got in.

"I thought I'd find you here," he said. He pulled a bottle of spiced vodka from his coat pocket and offered it.

Ganin shook his head. "What do you want, Yurochka?"

"Just doing my job. She due soon?"

"Any minute."

"Then what?"

"Moran will show up here sooner or later. He'll come looking for her, and when he does, I'll be there."

Sepelev smiled indulgently. "Do you really believe that, Nikki?"

Ganin returned his smile. "Anyway, the FBI called and warned us."

"Ah, this Special Agent Hammer. You were turned by the skyscrapers and by this woman. Don't tell me you think this cop is better than me."

Mary Frances came out of the building and started toward the corner.

"Much better than you," Ganin said, opening his door and getting out. "He never nags."

He crossed the street and caught up with her before she got to the cab ranks. "They still haven't arrested him."

Mary Frances spun around at the sound of his voice, her eyes wide, her mouth open. "Are you following me?"

"Not really. I just wanted to warn you. Ask you to take care."

"Is he here already? In Moscow?"

"I don't know. It's possible."

Mary Frances glanced toward the cabs. "I'd ask you to give me a lift home, but I don't think it would be such a good idea."

"My car is just across the street."

Mary Frances smiled gently. "Yes, I know, and your wife is just across town." She looked deeply into his eyes. "You take care of yourself, Chief Investigator." She turned and left.

Ganin stood rooted to his spot, watching her walk away. He wanted to go after her. Stop her. Tell her . . . what?

He suddenly felt foolish. Tell her what? What words could he use to describe to her how he felt when he hadn't a clue to how he really felt . . . about her, about anything?

He turned and went back to his car. Sepelev was gone. Unaccountably he was very sad as he drove home, as if he had lost something dear to him.

Antonia wasn't home. Ganin waited for her until eight before he fixed himself a supper of herring, dark bread, cheese, pickles, and a bottle of beer.

She called a little after ten, when he was watching a replay of last week's soccer match between the Czech and All-German national teams in Prague.

"Hello, Nikki, I'm taking care of Uncle. Sasha called and asked for me."

Her uncle Vsevolod Yevgennevich had a huge old apartment on Gorkogo Street very near Chief Prosecutor Yernin's. He was nearly one hundred years old and actually was a great-uncle.

"How is he doing?"

"Fine," Antonia said after a slight hesitation. "Have you had your supper?"

"Around eight. Will you be staying the night?"

"I think so. Probably for the next few nights. Will you manage?"

"Yes, of course. I have a lot of work to do."

"Yes," Antonia said. "I know. Be careful, Nikki."

Before he could say anything, she hung up. Ganin slowly put the phone down. Had it been a warning? Be careful of what?

He picked up the phone again and dialed her uncle's number. It was answered on the fifth ring by Sasha Kupliakov, Uncle Vsevolod Yevgennevich's orderly.

"Yes?"

"Hello, Sasha, let me speak with Tonia, please."

"She's not here," the old man wheezed.

"I just talked to her—"

"Not here."

"I see," Ganin said, understanding. "How is Uncle?"

"Sleeping."

"Good. I'll come and visit soon."

Mary Frances had been in Moscow one week, and although she had already started work (gotten her feet wet, so to speak, at the Council of Ministers), she had not yet fully adjusted to the life.

Some journalists, she'd been warned, never did make it. That had been confirmed to her three days after her arrival, when Siegel sent one of the magazine's people home six months early. She'd met him only briefly at the office, but she could see he was burned out. He seemed extremely nervous, hardly able to sit still, his eyes constantly shifting, his hands shaking. She was told that when the bureau chief informed him that he was going home, he broke down and cried.

Here at the usual American Embassy Friday evening reception and cocktail party she could pick out a few others who were ready to get out. Not all of them were journalists.

"In one week you can already tell the difference, can't you?" someone said behind her.

She turned, drink in hand, to face an older distinguished-looking man, dressed in a three-piece blue pin-striped suit that was obviously not an off-the-rack product. She rapidly searched her memory, coming up with a name.

"Mr. Moore," she said, smiling and shaking his hand. Scott Moore was the deputy chief of the embassy's consular section. Before he'd come to work for the State Department, he'd been a district court judge in Maryland.

"My friends call me Judge. Anyway, welcome to our little Friday get-together. I sincerely hope you'll grace us with your lovely presence on a regular basis."

Mary Frances had to laugh. The man was old-world charming, even more so than her publisher, though he was about twenty years too old for her. She figured him to be in his mid to late sixties at least. But in good shape for it. Distinguished; the word came to her again.

"I hope that means yes," Judge Moore said, smiling.

"Resoundingly, Judge, if all your counterparts are half as charming and handsome as you."

"Now it's my turn to blush," Judge Moore said. "Actually it's my job not only to see that my little flock is in one piece and reasonably happy but to aid and abet their causes so far as they're in the best interests of the United States."

"I am in one piece, and I am happy . . . all of the above at the level of more or less. And yes, there is something you might be able to do for me. Two things actually."

"Name it, Ms. Dean."

"Mary Frances," she said. "I've made application to interview President Gorbachev. An aftermath piece from Geneva, as well as a status update on the accord. I'm told that he's running into the same sort of opposition with his Congress that President Bush is having with our Congress."

"You and several hundred other journalists would like the same thing. But seriously, I think you might have a better than even chance. From what I hear, you made a favorable impression on him."

"I think he's sincere."

Judge Moore looked at her seriously. "Be careful, Mary Frances, not to be taken in by the glitter that surrounds power. This is big business we're talking about. The biggest."

"I know that."

"I didn't mean to criticize, my dear, but the stakes are very high here. Not everything . . . or everyone is as it seems on the surface."

"But you'll see what you can do for me?"

"I'll see what I can do for you," Judge Moore said. "And what is your second request?"

Mary Frances turned her head. "See that man by the windows? Tweed jacket, pipe, talking with . . . Mrs. Franck, I think."

"She's the deputy ambassador's wife, but I don't think I know the man," Judge Moore said, then changed his mind. "Wait, I think he just arrived within the last few days or so. A fellow journalist, I think, but for the life of me, I don't remember which newspaper or magazine."

"American?"

"Australian, I think. Would you like me to find out for you, make the introductions?"

She'd seen him come in a half hour ago. He hadn't noticed her yet, but she had watched how he was working the room. He was obviously a professional on the prowl for information. From what she could tell, he was good at it. And he was good-looking, in a very vaguely familiar sort of way.

"No," she said, turning back to the judge. "I think I can handle this one on my own. But I would like to see President Gorbachev as soon as possible."

"I'll see what I can do, but no promises, of course."

"Of course," Mary Frances said, and she turned and headed across the crowded room to where the Australian journalist was still talking with the deputy ambassador's wife.

From what she could see he had a great ass and nice ears, though his hair was a little short for her liking.

"Hello," she said.

The deputy ambassador's wife looked up and smiled; but the Australian took his time turning around, and when he did, his eyes widened a little, as if he were surprised.

"Why, hello," he said, smiling warmly.

Again Mary Frances was struck by the vague notion that

she knew him. He wasn't as handsome close up; there was something wrong with his complexion. But then, she decided after a second thought, it made him look rugged, outdoorsy. She liked it.

"I'm Mary Frances Dean, *World News This Week*," she said, sticking out her hand.

His grip was warm and gentle and, she decided, sensual. "Roger Brett, free-lance for a consortium of Sydney papers."

"You don't sound Australian," she said.

"You don't sound like a Yank."

"I was born in Britain. You?"

"I'm the genuine article, I'm afraid. I was born on a station in the outback—that's a sheep ranch in the interior of the country—and went to school in Darwin."

"Aren't you supposed to say, gud-day and all that?"

"You saw *Crocodile Dundee*," he said, grinning. He had nice teeth, but he didn't show enough of them. His smile wasn't open-mouthed. But his eyes were the most gorgeous blue she had ever seen and comfortingly familiar.

"One and two," she said. "Do you know all about the aborigines and all that stuff?"

"I know Paul Hogan. A good guy, but believe me he doesn't know any more about the bush than I do."

"Well, do you?"

"Know about the bush?"

"Yes."

"Of course, I do. I was born there."

Mary Frances laughed. "Anyway, what are you doing here at the American Embassy?"

"We always gate-crash. The receptions at our place are horribly dull. I'll take you over one of these these days, you'll see."

"I'll take you up on that."

"Oh, dear." He turned. "I'm afraid we frightened the lady off."

Mary Frances realized they had. The deputy ambassador's wife was already halfway across the room. She giggled. "Was it worth the effort?"

"Come on now, I was just about to get the true gen on Gorby. Rumor has it he's about to leave the country again."

"All that in just a couple of days?" Mary Frances asked. She was impressed.

The Australian's eyes clouded for just an instant. "What'd you mean, luv?" he asked.

"Didn't you just arrive in Moscow?"

"I should say not. I've been in and out of this bloody place for nearly nine months. I'll tell you what, it's starting to get on my nerves."

"It happens," she said, and she related the story about her co-worker who'd been sent home early.

"You haven't seen anything yet. Wait until winter sets in. Another few months, and you'll be pulling on your fur-lined panties."

She laughed again. It was easy to do with him. "What about this rumor now?" she asked.

"Oh, Christ, don't quote me, but the word is floating around that the head Red is about to go someplace and pull another of his stunners. Hadn't you heard?"

"No, but maybe I can find out."

"Yes?" the Australian asked, interested.

"I've applied for an interview with him. Might go through. If it does, I'll ask him."

"You and bloody well a thousand others—" the Australian said, but then stopped in mid-sentence. "Holy Mother of God. Where's my manners? Mary Frances Dean, *World News This Week*. You were in Geneva when someone tried to pop the son of a bitch."

She didn't quite know if she liked his irreverence, but she nodded.

"He'll see you. Why not? He's a ladies' man. Didn't you hear what he said to Barbara Bush?"

"No," Mary Frances said, laughing despite herself.

"Shit, I was hoping you had, because I haven't either. How about dinner tonight?"

She was taken off guard. "I . . . can't," she said.

"Tomorrow then. I'll pick you up at your place, if you'll give me your address. There's a nice little spot called the Lastochka. It's a restaurant in a riverboat. Nice. Cheap. Even Aussie journalists can afford it."

She looked at his expectant smile. His lips were nice. "All right," she said. "Sevenish?"

"Sure, but have a late lunch. We'll go dancing first. In this town everyone has dinner late. It's almost as bad as Rio."

Moran could hardly believe his good fortune as he handed Mary Frances into the cab in front of the American Embassy. She would lead him to Gorbachev and he would kill them both.

"See you tomorrow, then," he said to her.

She looked up, smiling. "Gud-day."

He laughed. "Gud-day to you, luv."

From the moment Mary Frances Dean and her escort came out of the embassy, until they left in separate taxis, the two KGB surveillance officers in the third-floor window of the building across the street had taken seventeen photographs and had recorded their voices, using the hand-held parabolic antenna.

The woman was red-flagged, and anyone around her was of interest as well. Only the woman's cab was followed, however. There simply wasn't enough manpower to follow everyone.

The cameras were Hasselblads; the film was 3000 speed high-definition color created by the KGB's unnumbered Technical Operations Directorate.

Since Mary Frances's file was red-flagged, the film and audio-tape of her entry to and exit from the American Embassy were rushed to the Surveillance Directorate's Seventh Department laboratories for development and preliminary analysis.

Within seventy-five minutes of the time Mary Frances and her escort had left, the developed photographs and rerecorded tapes had gone upstairs to the directorate's deputy, General Konstantin Petrovich Yekuchov, in his third-floor office in the Lubyanka.

It was nearly nine in the evening, the building was quiet, and

General Yekuchov was alone; even his secretary had finally gone for the day.

He stared at the photographs for a long time. The woman was attractive, in a Western sort of way. She was too skinny for the general's tastes, but he could see where a young man might fall for her. He'd been told that the militia investigator Ganin had fallen under her spell; that was too bad because despite everything else that had happened, he was a good man. The kind that the *Rodina* needed during this difficult transition period.

Whatever happened in the aftermath of the fall of *glasnost* and *perestroika*, the country would need all the good and loyal men it could get.

He turned his attention to the man who had escorted her out of the embassy, but not in. He was being tentatively identified as a free-lance Australian journalist. He too had been attracted to the woman. New meat, the men of the journalists' corps called the women new to Moscow. A disgusting term in all its connotations, but somewhat accurate for all of it, from a limited male viewpoint.

This man was almost certainly of no consequence, but his background would have to be checked nevertheless. Tomorrow. And the militia detective would have to be shown these photographs.

The girl was the key. She would focus them on Ganin, who in turn would capture the plotters, the wreckers. But it would have to be done with extreme care. Gorbachev would fail; there was very little doubt in his mind about that. When he fell, the plotters would look to see who had most strongly opposed them, and they would mete out their retribution. On the other hand, if the plotters were uncovered and arrested before Gorbachev fell, the KGB would come under very close scrutiny for its action or, more pointedly, for its lack of action.

General Yekuchov picked up his private telephone that was swept for monitors on a daily basis and direct-dialed a number here in the building. It was answered on the second ring.

"Yes?"

"I thought you might still be here, Valeri Petrovich. I have something interesting up here that you should see."

"Thank you, Comrade General. I'll be right up."

General Yekuchov hung up his telephone and picked up one

of the photographs. Send the hounds after the quarry. Surround them. Tear them down. But with care.

Colonel Valeri Petrovich Markelov was the head hound master.

Antonia was still gone, and Ganin could not face going home to an empty apartment until it was time for sleep. He had a late supper of meat dumplings and tea in the commissary across the street. A few of the swing shift patrol were leaning against the counters, drinking or eating, and they eyed him nervously, afraid he was going to put them on report. He hardly noticed them.

He got his car and headed north across the river, not really conscious of where he was going, his driving purely automatic. There wasn't much traffic at this hour of the evening. On the weekend the streets would be full, but on nights like this people got drunk at home so they didn't have far to go when they started to fall down. Morning came soon enough as it was.

He parked half a block from the Botanical Gardens and sat in his car for five minutes before he got out and walked back to the block of apartment buildings where foreigners were housed. A lot of journalists lived here. Mary Frances's apartment was on the twelfth floor of the building that fronted on Andrianovskiy Street. She would have a good view of the gardens.

He stopped in the shadows across from her building and spotted a lone figure apparently arguing with the militiaman in his box at the front door.

The man turned as Ganin stepped out of the shadows and started across the street. He said something else to the militiaman, then headed away.

Ganin angled across the street in an effort to intercept him, but the man sped up.

"Wait a minute, I want to talk to you," Ganin shouted.

The man suddenly sprinted.

"*Stoi*, Militia," Ganin shouted, breaking into a run.

The figure ran past where Ganin had parked his car, passed under a streetlamp, and then headed diagonally across the intersection toward the main entrance to the Botanical Gardens. They were closed at this time of night, but Ganin couldn't remember what kind of gate was out front.

At that moment he wished Yurii were with him. Despite his friend's heavy drinking, he was several years younger and in much better shape. He often worked out at the gym to sweat the alcohol out of his system. It didn't work, of course, but it did increase his strength and stamina.

The front gate to the Botanical Gardens was nothing more than three turnstiles beyond the ticket huts. The lights were on in front, but inside, the gardens were in darkness.

Ganin stopped at the gate. He had not seen the man enter the park, but there was no other place he could have gone. Still, he would have to know that once inside, he would not be able to escape very easily.

From the turnstiles paved paths led in all directions into the park, winding their way through trees, shrubs, flowers, and other plantings from all over the world. It was a dark maze.

Someone ran down one of the paths to the left.

Ganin jumped over a turnstile and followed. Immediately he was plunged into darkness. Suddenly he knew the man was trying for the Prospekt Mira metro station, which was within the park. He had forgotten all about it until this instant.

"*Stoi! Stoi!* Militia!" he shouted, pulling out his pistol as he ran headlong down the path.

The lights of the metro station were ahead when someone came out of the trees to his right, slammed into him, knocking the breath out of him, and sent him sprawling on all fours. He was seeing stars.

"Stop," he said weakly, looking up. He had lost his gun.

A man stood over him, his face red, his neck thick and round, his hands large and beefy. He wasn't Moran.

"No," Ganin said.

"Fuck your mother," the man said, his Russian flat, and then Ganin watched dumbly as a thick-soled shoe came up from the ground in a short, vicious arc. The heel caught him squarely in the side of the head.

Mary Frances knew from the start what she was going to do and why she was going to do it.

Roger Brett was exactly the kind of man she had been looking for, she supposed, for a long time. Perhaps all her life. She didn't think at this point about marriage, only about taking him to bed . . . or, rather, maneuvering him into the position where he would take her to bed.

Her feelings and desires were totally shameless; women weren't supposed to act this way. Yet she didn't give a damn. She was in a profession that wasn't for women (except for a few pretty faces on television), and she had always done what she damned well pleased—ladylike, as her grandmother, the old Victorian darling, called proper behavior, or not.

It was late, well past eleven, yet there were still a few lights twinkling on the river. The evening was unpleasantly cool, but Roger had bought her a lovely shawl at a Beryozka shop (which accepted only foreign currency), and she sat at their table, waiting for him to come back, hugging it closely around her neck. Stupidly she had worn a low-cut cocktail dress, and she was freezing. Yet she had been pleased that he had noticed. In fact, he had not taken his eyes off her neck and breasts all evening. It gave her a warm feeling. And, secretly, a feeling of power.

"Miss me?" Moran said, returning to their table.

She looked up and smiled. "Terribly."

He stood there looking down at her and then, naturally and lightly, reached down and kissed her. An electric shock ran through her body, rebounding in the pit of her stomach.

He sat down across from her and poured them both another glass of wine. "Cold?"

"A little," she said, her blood still reverberating.

He motioned for their waiter.

"Where'd you go?" she asked. "You were gone for ages."

He started to laugh.

"What?" she asked, bridling.

"If we were in the bush, it'd be one thing, luv. But, Christ, didn't your mum teach you manners?"

She was at a loss, and she shook her head.

"I went to the WC, what'd you think?" He was laughing at her. "I took a pee. A piss, you know."

And then they both were laughing, uproariously, loudly, without control. The other diners in the riverboat restaurant were looking at them. The waiter came over.

"Please, sir, madame," he said.

Moran turned, almost languidly, and looked up at the man. He said something soft and low, in Russian, Mary Frances thought, and the waiter visibly blanched. He stepped back a pace.

"Our bill, please," Moran said in English. He turned back to Mary Frances. "And then what? We can take off our clothes and dive into the river for a midnight swim. We can go to Gor'kiy Park and ride on the Ferris wheel. We can go to—"

"My apartment for a nightcap," Mary Frances said.

Moran was going to say something . . . facetious, she thought, but then he smiled gently. "A lovely idea, Mary Frances."

* * *

Her apartment was dark; only what light filtered in from outside illuminated the living room. Green numbers on a clock radio illuminated the bedroom and short corridor. She made no move to turn on the lights.

"Would you like a drink?" she asked, locking the door and letting the shawl slip off her shoulders.

"I don't think so," he said softly.

He went to the window and looked down at the street, as if he were stalling for time, trying to make up his mind.

"You were right, you know," Mary Frances said.

Moran turned back to her. "About what?"

"Gorbachev. He's leaving the country."

"Where's he going?"

"London."

"When?"

"In a couple of days," Mary Frances said. "Anyway, he's invited me to come along on his jet. Russia One, I suppose you'd call it."

"Ah, hell, girl," he said with emotion, and he turned away again.

She crossed the room to him, her heart filling, reached for his shoulders, hesitated a moment, then turned him around. "You goddamned chauvinist," she said softly.

He smiled.

"There's nothing wrong accepting help from another journalist, even if she is a woman."

Moran nodded. "I know. I'm . . . sorry."

She leaned forward, and he took her into his arms, enfolding her in his masculine odors and safety. She was reminded for just an instant of her father, who had died when she was only sixteen. He'd been tall and strong, and when he'd taken his little M.F. in his arms, she'd known that nothing could harm her, nothing could ever be strong enough to break through that barrier. She felt the same now.

Moran kissed her gently on the lips, but when she tried to kiss his face, he moved away.

"What is it, Roger?" she asked.

"It's nothing," he said, apparently in some embarrassment. "I'll explain later."

"I thought you wanted . . . this."

Moran smiled. "I don't want you to think that I'm taking advantage of you, being new in Moscow and all that."

She shook her head.

"Or with your in to Gorby. It's big news, his schedule. Why is he going?"

"Margaret Thatcher is giving the accord some tough criticism. He wants to smooth the way."

"How do you know all this?"

"My press credentials and boarding pass were sent over to the office this morning, along with his itinerary and a brief press release. We leave Tuesday morning at two. Gets us into London at nine the same morning."

"When do you come back?"

"He'll be there two days. Thursday about four in the afternoon."

"I think I'm going to miss you," Moran said, meaning something completely different from what she thought.

She smiled warmly.

He turned her around, brushed his lips against the back of her neck, and slowly began to unzip her dress. "Now, what were you saying?"

47

G anin had spent Saturday at home in bed, nursing a boom-
ing headache that threatened to take off the back of his
skull. For most of the morning he was seeing double, and
he was nauseated. It frightened him that he had a concussion and
he didn't know how bad he was. But he could not go to a hospital.
The moment he checked in, a telephone call would be made and
he would be taken off the case. The investigation then would
switch from assassins to hooligans in the park. He preferred to
take his chances with aspirin and tea.

Antonia called late in the afternoon, and he was so groggy
that she thought he was drunk. He didn't ask her where she was
because, he'd decided earlier, it no longer really mattered to him.
Their marriage had been over for a long time now, despite their

best efforts to work at it. She hung up in disgust, and he found that he felt a little sorry for her; that, in the last analysis, was better than feeling sorry for himself.

In the evening he tried to watch television for a while, but the picture made his headache even worse. He tried getting drunk on vodka; but after an hour of steady drinking he was merely sick to his stomach again, and he threw it all up in the toilet.

From the living-room windows he had a pretty good view toward the center of the city, and he had watched how Moscow resisted going to sleep. It was a weekend night, and by midnight there was still a lot of traffic.

His telephone rang. At first he wasn't going to answer it. But it continued to ring, the strident jangling getting on his nerves, and he finally picked it up.

"Yes."

"Chief Investigator Ganin?" an officious voice asked.

"Yes, who is calling?"

"Sergeant Panchevsky, Chief Investigator. Pardon me, sir, but a package marked 'Most urgent' had just arrived for you from Chief Prosecutor General Yernin's office. Shall I have someone bring it out?"

"No," Ganin said. "I was coming in. I'll be there in a few minutes."

"Yes, sir. I'll put it on your desk."

Ganin took a long, hot shower, shaved, and got dressed. He felt better, but the simple act of walking down the stairs and getting into his car tired him out so that he had to wait for a few minutes to catch his breath.

In the squad room a couple of detectives were questioning four women, who, by the clothes they were wearing and their garish makeup, were probably prostitutes. Everyone was tired, and no one seemed to have much enthusiasm for his work.

Inside his office Ganin leaned against the door to catch his breath again before he turned on the lights and sat down at his desk. Yernin had sent him a thick manila envelope marked "Most urgent." It had been hand-delivered. The carbon of the delivery slip with Sergeant Panchevsky's signature was still attached to the back. The chief prosecutor had a flare for the dramatic, Ganin thought, opening the envelope.

His thoughts stopped in midstream as he saw the top photograph. Mary Frances Dean was coming out of the American Embassy on the arm of a slightly built man in a tweed sports jacket, a pipe in his mouth.

It was Moran. There was absolutely no doubt in Ganin's mind. The build, the look, the attitude, everything.

The shear audacity of the man! The brilliance! He was here in Moscow! He had found Mary Frances! He was stalking Gorbachev! The magnificent son of a bitch!

The other photographs were much the same. They were obviously the work of a KGB surveillance team. On the back were marked the date and time. Again he was hardly able to believe his eyes. These pictures had been taken around eight o'clock in the evening. Friday evening. More than twenty-four hours ago.

He jumped up, tore open his door, and raced through the squad room into communications. "Call Detective Sepelev," he shouted at one of the sergeants. "Tell him Moran is here in Moscow. Have him meet me at Mary Frances Dean's apartment in Dzerzhinsky. Immediately."

In the garage he jumped into his car and squealed tires all the way out. His heart was thumping in his chest. Thirty hours was plenty of time for a madman such as Moran to kill her and set up something with Gorbachev. He realized too late that he should have warned Colonel Kokorov at the KGB. It had identified the man in the photographs as an Australian journalist. The KGB didn't know.

Traffic was light enough so that he did not have to take the long way around on one of the ring roads. Instead he went directly through town, crossing the river on the Kamenny Bridge, racing across Red Square and up past the stone facade of the Lubyanka.

Another nagging doubt began to pluck at the back of his mind. He should have talked to Yurii himself. He should have warned him. Sepelev's apartment was very near Mary Frances's. If he hustled, Sepelev would reach her first. At least by five minutes.

But Moran wouldn't be there now. Mary Frances might already be dead, but there was no reason to suspect that Moran would be at her apartment at this particular moment.

Nothing seemed out of the ordinary when he pulled up in front of her building and got out of his car. A few lights were on in some of the windows, but for the most part the building was in darkness.

Still, there was something that didn't feel right to Ganin, and as he headed up the walk, he pulled out his pistol.

The militia box was dark. Ganin approached it with caution. "Hello," he called out, but there was no answer. He looked inside. The militiaman was sitting back on his stool, his arms at his sides, his head leaning back against the wall. He had been shot at close range in the middle of the forehead. Blood had run down between his eyes, dripped off the end of his nose, and collected on the front of his white shirt.

Ganin sprinted the rest of the way up the walk, flattened himself against the wall beside the door, and peered in through the glass.

Sepelev lay facedown in front of the elevator, his right hand outstretched as if he had been reaching for the call button, a pool of blood beneath his head.

The elevator indicator was still at the ground floor. There were no other signs of disturbance.

Ganin's gut was churning. He was heartsick as he went inside and approached his old friend's body. A rage threatened to rise and engulf his reason and sanity. This was Moscow, not some barrio in Los Angeles or slum in New York City. This wasn't supposed to happen here. Not to a man like Yurochka.

Sepelev was dead. He had taken a single shot to the back of the head. There were no powder burns or other marks evident on his skull. It meant Moran had probably come through the door right after Sepelev, spotted the detective, and shot him. Not knowing if others were on the way, he had turned around and got out, killing the militiaman in his box on the way.

It meant Mary Frances was probably all right.

Ganin took the elevator up to the twelfth floor, coming out into the corridor in a rush in case he was wrong, his gun sweeping left to right. But nothing moved; there were no sounds.

He knocked at Mary Frances's door and a half minute later knocked again.

"Yes, who is it?" Her muffled voice came from within.

"Chief Investigator Ganin. May I see you?"

There was a silence.

"Miss Dean?" Ganin called softly.

The door opened. Mary Frances, dressed in a bathrobe, her feet bare, squinted out at him. "What time is it?"

"Your friend the Australian journalist. Is he here now?" Ganin asked, barely in control.

"What?" she asked.

"The Australian, the one you came out of the embassy with Friday night . . . is he here, Miss Dean? It's a matter of life and death."

"No," she said. "He left about an hour ago. What the hell do you want?" She suddenly noticed the gun in his hand. She stepped back, her hand going to her mouth. "Oh, my God."

"He's Moran. He's just killed my partner downstairs and the militiaman in front. You are sure he is gone?"

"It's him," she cried in real anguish. "Oh, my God, he was here . . . we made—" Mary Frances was shaking her head. "Oh, my God," she said again.

Ganin brushed past her into the apartment and went to the telephone. "He didn't hurt you or threaten you?" he asked. A part of him was detached. He was going through the motions. He dialed the emergency militia number.

"No. I didn't know, I swear to God . . ."

The emergency duty operator answered on the eighth ring. "Moscow Militia."

"This is Chief Investigator Ganin. I have two officers down and a killer at large. I need assistance." He gave the address.

"He knows," Mary Frances was saying.

"What is this, some kind of joke?" the emergency operator demanded.

"You son of a bitch, if you do not dispatch units immediately, fucking immediately, you will be counting birch trees in Yakutsk. Have you got that?"

"Yes, Comrade Chief Investigator," a very impressed duty operator said.

Ganin slammed down the telephone and dialed Chief Prosecutor Yernin's number. He turned to look at Mary Frances. "He knows what?"

"Gorbachev's schedule."

48

Dawn was just lightening the eastern horizon when Chief
Prosecutor Yernin showed up, got out of his Zil limousine,
strode imperiously up the walk, past the militia box, and
entered the building.

Ganin stepped away from the windows in Mary Frances's
apartment. "He's on the way up."

"Again, Chief Investigator, I must protest, and will do so
officially as soon as I leave here with Ms. Dean," Scott Moore said.
Ganin had allowed Mary Frances to call her embassy, and the
deputy consular chief had shown up within a half hour.

"I understand, sir. But again I must remind you that Ms.
Dean is a material witness in a murder investigation."

She sat in the corner of the couch, still in her bathrobe, sipping a cup of tea Moore had made her. She hadn't said much since he'd arrived.

"Also nearly a victim in New York and again here."

"Yes, and believe me, her safety is foremost in my mind," Ganin said. He felt completely numb over Sepelev's death. It still wasn't real for him. "It looks very bad for our public image when we lose a Western journalist like that."

Moore wanted to respond in kind, but Ganin could see the man holding himself in check. "Nevertheless, Chief Investigator, I will take this up with your superior."

"Then you won't have long to wait. As I said, the Moscow chief prosecutor is on his way up in the elevator."

He had cleared all the militia people out of Mary Frances's apartment, giving her a little peace and quiet. But there were at least a dozen men still milling around in the corridor.

"Chief Prosecutor Yernin is on his way up," Ganin told them.

One of them held up his walkie-talkie. "Yes, sir," he said. "I've been told to tell you that Detective Sepelev's body has finally been removed."

"What was the delay?" Ganin asked dully.

"The coroner was not immediately available."

Ganin nodded. Yurii wouldn't have cared.

The elevator opened, and Yernin, alone, stepped off, spotted Ganin, and came down the hall. "The man is actually here. In Moscow. It's almost impossible to believe, Nikki. He must be a genius. But you predicted he would come here."

"The woman is waiting for you. I allowed her to telephone her embassy. One of her people is with her now."

"Who?"

"Mr. Scott Moore; he is the deputy consular officer."

Yernin smiled and nodded. "I'll speak to them, and then what do you recommend?" He looked at the bruise on the side of Ganin's head but said nothing.

"Send her to her embassy and ask that she remain there until . . ."

"Until what, Nikki? Until we catch this monster? Corner him and shoot him down like the dog he is?"

"Keep her out of harm's way."

Yernin thought for a moment. "I agree with you. But pressures are being brought to bear—"

"What sorts of pressures?" Ganin demanded, his hackles rising.

"Hear me out, Nikolai Fedorovich. Please, just hear me out. Certain pressures are being brought to bear by powers far beyond my own. Ms. Dean is what the Americans call a media star. She is to be treated well. Very well."

Ganin looked into the prosecutor's eyes. "I will tell you this, Chief Prosecutor: If she is allowed the run free, I cannot guarantee her safety, nor will I be responsible for her. Already I have lost a very good man."

"Yes, I know," Yernin said, patting Ganin's arm. "And a close personal friend. But this is out of my hands." He looked toward the open apartment door. The militiamen were watching them. He turned back to Ganin. "I will talk to her. Give them your recommendation. In the meantime, there is someone in my car who wishes to speak with you. Don't keep him waiting."

Ganin nodded.

Yernin went the rest of the way down the corridor and stepped into Mary Frances's apartment. "Judge Moore, good morning," he said.

Two old grandmothers with buckets and mops were cleaning the lobby, and another one was cleaning the inside of the militia box. Yernin's uniformed driver was waiting at the limo. He opened the rear door on the passenger side.

Colonel Vladimir Kokorov, the head of the KGB's Ninth Chief Directorate's detail that watched over President Gorbachev, looked up, grim-faced, and motioned for Ganin to get in.

"I require only a minute of your time, Chief Investigator."

Ganin slid in beside the much bigger, bulkier man, and the driver closed the door.

"You've been up all night; would you care to join me in a drink?"

"No, but I'm glad you're here, Comrade Colonel; it saves me the trouble of coming to your office," Ganin said.

Kokorov said nothing. He eyes were deep and broad. All of Russia was in them.

"Moran is here in Moscow. He knows that President Gorbachev plans to fly out of Moscow at two in the morning Tuesday, and he means to assassinate him."

"This information came from the American journalist, Miss Dean?"

"Yes," Ganin said. It was too late *not* to implicate her, and with any luck Kokorov would rescind her boarding credentials. That way no matter what happened she would be safe.

Kokorov nodded.

"The KGB is following her, isn't that so?"

"The Surveillance Directorate is handling it."

"They spotted Moran—"

"From what I understand, it was believed that he was an accredited Australian journalist. Very ingenious."

"He has contacts all over the world, a network of people whom he has hired to help him with his identities."

Kokorov nodded. "He's a real professional. Not uncommon."

"Your people saw him arriving here at her apartment. They must have seen him kill my partner and the militia officer at his post."

Kokorov's lips compressed. "It would seem possible, but I haven't seen their reports yet. Perhaps they were in no position to do anything."

Ganin turned away in disgust.

"Whatever you may think of me, Chief Investigator, I was sorry to hear that you had lost a partner this way. But I do not have all the details."

"The GRU is involved as well," Ganin said, turning back.

"Yes, that I do know. You had a confrontation with one of them the other night. Not too far from here."

"You knew."

"Yes."

"You also know about . . . General—"

"Yes." Kokorov cut him off. He seemed angry now. He was a very big man, but he was puffed up even more. "What do you think you know about patriotism, Chief Investigator?"

The question was totally unexpected. Ganin didn't know what to say.

After a moment Kokorov reached across Ganin and opened the door. "Until you can answer that question to my satisfaction . . . to your own satisfaction . . . don't tell me how to do my job. Not ever."

Ganin got out of the car, still not knowing exactly what had happened, as Yernin came down the walk, his expression heavy, but his step light.

"She is going to the embassy for now," the chief prosecutor said. "Beyond that I do not know."

"Yes, sir," Ganin said.

"Catch him for us, Nikki," Yernin said urgently. "Kill him if need be, but stop him. You have my backing, one hundred percent, no matter what you must do."

Yernin climbed into the car, the driver got in behind the wheel, and they left. Ganin, watching the car turn the corner, decided that he didn't understand anything.

49

Moran lay awake in his bed at the Solnechny Hotel, just beyond the ring road near the Warsaw Highway, watching the morning come to his window. He had to consider his next moves very carefully.

They had nearly killed him in New York, and it had been uncomfortably close last night. Had he returned a minute later, it would have been the Russian cop getting the drop on him instead of the other way around.

But our lives were forever dominated by chance. His colonel had told them that in Nam. "When it's time for the Man to come get your ass, son, there won't be a thing you can do about it."

Many times on the long trek from the north through enemy lines he had wanted to lie down, give up, pull the floor of the forest over his head, and die.

But he wasn't built that way. It was one of the reasons, he supposed, that his nightmares were beginning to come to him during the day when he was awake. He wanted to face his enemies head-on. But he could see the explosions lighting up the night sky; he could feel his embarrassment when he came home, how he'd hidden his medal. The President who had given it to him had even resigned in disgrace.

He'd also begun to see the faces of all the people he'd killed since Vietnam. The generals, the politicians, the writers, even the women . . . perhaps especially the women.

Mary Frances was a lot like them all. Self-sufficient women. Strong women. Purposeful women. Like his . . . mother in many respects.

He sat up and hung his head in his hands in an effort to blot out the worst of the memories.

Gorbachev was leaving aboard his private Ilyushin 86 from Sheremetyevo Airport at two in the morning Tuesday. The odd departure hour was necessary so that he would arrive in London at a reasonable time for diplomacy.

There were two problems Moran would have to overcome. The first was what to do with himself in the interim forty hours or so. At this hotel he was known as Eugene Stevenson, a student at the State University of New York working on his doctorate thesis. His area of specialty was Russian religious art from the third century until the end of the reign of the czars.

Sooner or later his name would come to the attention of someone at the museum or at Moscow State University. Questions would be asked. Russians were inordinately proud of their past achievements (provided they did not seriously involve politics before the Revolution). Someone would take notice even though the makeup materials he had brought with him from California and the identity papers that the Finn Ehrenström had provided him with were the very best.

And of course, they would be looking for Roger Brett, the Australian journalist. They had his description, possibly even a photograph if there had been KGB surveillance outside the embassy. Being close to her in a place such as that had been a mistake on his part.

The second was security at the airport. Mary Frances would have told the authorities by now that she had discussed Gorbachev's itinerary with him. The airport would be closed tightly. No one without the proper credentials would be able to get anywhere near the place.

Coming here to Moscow, he'd had only the vaguest of plans for getting to the Russian leader, using the name of a local supplier of Polish military plastique that Ehrenström had provided him with. It was possible, he'd thought, to get to Gorbachev's limousine, plant the explosives, and then watch from a distance. When the Soviet President was actually in the back seat of the limo, Moran would hit the detonator button.

But they would be watching for that now. Security, until he got aboard the aircraft and took off, would be impossible to penetrate.

He straightened up suddenly and got to his feet. He had it. The solution to both his problems at once: He would not kill Gorbachev here in Moscow, nor would he kill him on the ground. There was no need for either.

Today was Sunday. He figured he had at least twenty-four hours of relative safety here. Time enough, he thought, to get some rest and to do what had to be done.

He had brought three suitcases with him from Finland: one for his Roger Brett persona and two, including an aluminum case, for his Eugene Stevenson identity.

Opening the aluminum case, he took the 35 mm camera out of its cushioned slot, two of the telephoto lenses, and two of the canisters of film, which he took over to the table by the window.

Next, he pulled out the *Guidebook to Soviet History* he'd used as part of his Stevenson ID and opened it to the maps of Europe and West Russia.

When he traced it on a curved line (which was the shortest distance on a flat map between two points) from Moscow in the general direction of Great Britain, Gorbachev's flight would cross the coast into the Baltic Sea just north of the Latvian capital of Riga. Barely one hundred miles offshore was the island of Gotland, which was owned by Sweden. Safety. More important, even now there would be a Soviet coastal watch installation at Riga. Near every major border city there was such a KGB base.

Working quickly but carefully—he had the entire day—he disassembled the camera, lenses, and film canisters, which contained blank Intourist documents, stamps, ink, and a special marking pen used only by Soviet officials.

Within two hours he had completed the necessary travel permits, hotel and meal vouchers, and rail passes for a trip to visit the castle and three museums located in Riga.

Next, he cleaned and oiled the Makarov automatic pistol Ehrenström had supplied him. The silencer was the old-fashioned machined metal type, not the newer and quieter Kevlar model. He'd crossed the border at Vyborg by car with the gun hidden inside the body frame and had driven up to Leningrad, where he'd taken an internal Aeroflot flight to Moscow on which security was much laxer than on incoming international flights. One of Ehrenström's people had picked up the car by now and returned it across the border. It was a common occurrence, and the Finn had built in a lot of safeguards, including recording his movements and contacts in case anything should happen to him. They had saved his life.

About two Moran got dressed and took the metro up to the Riga station on the north side of Moscow, a couple of kilometers from Mary Frances's apartment. The situation still rankled him. One way or the other she had caused him trouble from the beginning. If there was time, he would go back and kill her. It would give him even more pleasure than making love to her, which had been considerable.

But then she was going to be on the plane with Gorbachev. He would forgo the pleasure now and kill two birds with one stone Tuesday morning.

Inside the station he had a late lunch of blinis, whitefish, pickles, and beer. Afterward he checked the schedule posted on the wall above the ticket windows. The first train of the day left at 7:00 A.M. sharp (all trains in the Soviet Union either ran on time or were simply canceled) and arrived in Riga at 5:00 P.M. It would give him only nine hours until Gorbachev's plane took off from Sheremetyevo and perhaps another hour or hour and fifteen minutes before it passed north of the Latvian capital on its outbound journey.

Time enough? It would have to be, Moran thought. He would make it do. This time he would not fail because nobody would be expecting him, not Gorbachev, not the woman, not Ganin, the Russian cop.

Ganin had just walked to his car from the security office at Sheremetyevo Airport when one of the clerks came running after him. It was a few minutes after eight in the morning, the weather crisp and clear.

"Chief Investigator, there is a telephone call for you," the clerk said, out of breath.

Ganin turned back. "Tell whoever it is that I have already returned to my office."

"It is General Yernin with a telephone call for you from the United States," the clerk said, very impressed.

It was Vivian Hammer. The connection, transferred through the chief prosecutor's office downtown, was surprisingly clear.

"You're a goddamned hard man to get in touch with, Chief Investigator," Hammer said.

"But I am happy to hear from you again, Special Agent Hammer. Have you any further information for me?"

"Is he there?"

"Yes," Ganin said. "And now the score is even between you and me."

"What? What do you mean?"

"We have each lost a partner," Ganin said, and he quickly recounted everything that had happened over the past thirty-six hours or so since the KGB surveillance team had spotted the Australian journalist coming out of the American Embassy with Mary Frances.

"Christ, how did you know it was him, Ganin? How?"

"I just did. The way he walked, the way he held himself, like an athlete. I just knew."

"Jesus," Hammer said. "You know by now he has the means to change his appearance. And he probably has the means to change his identity papers from this Australian to someone else."

"Apparently," Ganin said. He'd had the same thought. Everyone who had checked into a Moscow hotel over the past few days was being investigated. But that would take a couple of days at least.

"He's there to kill Gorbachev, and he won't stop until he succeeds or you kill him."

"Yes."

"But time is on your side, Ganin. Just keep your president in one place long enough and you should be able to dig him out of his hole."

"It's impossible. President Gorbachev is leaving for London tomorrow morning."

"What?" Hammer shouted. "How? Stop him."

"I don't think I can. And he is going by airplane, of course."

"Jesus," Hammer said softly. "Jesus Christ. There's something I didn't get to tell you before we were cut off the last time."

"What?"

"It's Moran . . . Forsythe . . . he was a combat helicopter pilot in Vietnam."

"I don't see—"

"Don't be fucking stupid. All he has to do is steal one of your military choppers, wait until Gorbachev's plane comes by, and bang, scratch an airliner."

"A helicopter, even a combat helicopter, can't climb to thirty-five thousand feet, nor can it travel at five hundred knots."

"You're right, Ganin, but the rockets they carry can."

Ganin got back to his office around nine. Yernin had come over and was waiting for him. It was an unusual enough occurrence for operations nearly to grind to a halt.

"I know what you're going to say, Nikki," the chief prosecutor said. "But my hands are tied."

"You spoke with Colonel Kokorov?"

"Yes. They're adamant over there. The Air Force will provide its protection. Government cannot stop because of a lone terrorist." Yernin was clearly shaken. It didn't do much for Ganin's confidence.

"So it's up to me again."

"Us," Yernin said. "There will be no cult of personality here."

Ganin said nothing. The silence stretched.

"What can I do for you, Nikki?" Yernin said at last. "Anything. Just name it."

"I don't know yet," Ganin said, standing by the window and staring outside. He lit a cigarette, the harsh smoke making him a little light-headed.

Moran had a plan. The man did not work in a vacuum. He knew what he was doing. He knew Gorbachev's schedule, and he certainly knew that Mary Frances had told anyone who would listen that he knew the schedule. That meant he would understand that Sheremetyevo Airport would be unapproachable.

Where did that leave him? The limo ride from Gorbachev's apartment to the airport? But that route was unknown to Mary Frances and, in fact, was unknown even to Gorbachev himself.

Which left what?

Ganin turned suddenly and went back out into the big operations room, Yernin right on his heels. He went to the big map of European SSR . . . from Moscow to the west.

"Who knows the route a jetliner would take from Moscow to London?" he asked in general.

None of the officers in the room moved. After a long second or two Yernin stepped forward, took a grease pencil, and drew a rough arc from Moscow northwest, crossing the coast north of Riga.

"About like that," he said.

Ganin looked at the track. Moran was not a martyr. He wanted to kill Gorbachev, and then he wanted to escape so that he could enjoy his life. He would make his attempt as near an escape route as possible. As near a border as possible.

"Riga," Ganin said, turning back to the chief prosecutor. "Do we have a military base there?"

"KGB border guards."

"Helicopters?"

Yernin nodded, understanding. "And rockets."

Ganin turned to the OD. "From Sunday morning around one or two until now, when was the first train to Riga?"

The man snatched up a telephone and dialed an outside number. Everyone was watching him. He had a brief conversation with someone. "Seven this morning," he said, looking up.

"When does it arrive in Riga?"

"Five this evening."

Again the OD relayed the question.

"Then, if he is headed to Riga, he's still on the train."

"Yes, comrade," the OD agreed.

"Get me a helicopter," Ganin said, turning back to Yernin. "I want to catch up with that train."

Moran traveled soft class, which was one step below deluxe. He shared his four-berth compartment with three women who were going to a Baltic resort for their annual vacation.

At first, when they thought he was an American, they were excited. But when he explained that he was an East German, they calmed down. One of them had had a poor experience with an East German engineer, and none of them wanted anything to do with him.

The train had departed on time, and after he'd had a cup of tea, he laid his head back and went to sleep. He was storing up rest. He had a feeling that once he reached Riga, there would be no time for sleep. If need be, he could go and had gone continuously for seventy-two hours at a time. His wounds were healing, although his face was on fire again. He realized that he should have changed the latex this morning, but there was no time for it now.

Lunch, which was ample and good, wasn't served until well after one o'clock, and when it was over, Moran decided to walk the length of the train for the exercise as well as the wish to know its exact configuration in case the need for such knowledge might arise.

They were passing through low farmlands on the right side of the tracks and wooded marshlands on the left. The sun was bright and warm under a cloudless sky, and the train was making good progress.

The train began to slow down suddenly. Moran was two cars from his compartment. Something was wrong. They were nowhere near a town or a scheduled stop. There was no reason to be slowing down here. He hurried to the end of the car and in the connecting compartment between cars opened the top half of the door on the right side and looked out.

In the distance he could see the red signal light, which was why the train was stopping, and fifty yards across the field was a Moscow Militia helicopter, its rotors revolving slowly. A group of men stood at the signal.

Moran ducked back inside and closed the door. There was only one reason they were here. Only one reason they were stopping the train. Only one reason they would send a militia helicopter here. They were coming after him. Somehow they had found out he was on this train. But how?

On the opposite side of the car Moran hauled open the top half of the door and without hesitation climbed outside. Clinging to the side, he managed to close the door, and then he pushed off backward, jumping as far away from the still-moving train as possible.

He landed badly on his left leg, nearly breaking it, before he tumbled down into a water-filled ditch.

Before he had completely recovered his senses, he scrambled up and away from the ditch into the birch forests and underbrush.

51

Ganin stood on the tracks a few meters in front of the locomotive, staring out across the marshy woodland that stretched to the south for as far as the eye could see.

They had missed him. He'd figured out what was happening the moment the train began to slow and had jumped. He would be invisible from the air, and by the time they could organize a search party with dogs he would be long gone.

Someone came running up the side of the tracks from the train, and Ganin turned around. It was a young militia sergeant who'd flown out with him.

"He's not on the train, comrade," the young man said. "But it was him. We found his two suitcases in a compartment with three women. He told them that he was East German, but they thought he was American."

"What was in the suitcases?"

"Clothes in the one, comrade," the young man said, grinning. "But the other contained photographic equipment. We took the camera and lenses apart. There are blank Intourist documents, stamps, inks, everything. It's him all right."

"He's not hiding on the train somewhere? You're sure of that?"

"Yes, comrade. The train has been thoroughly searched. And I took the liberty of calling for additional men. They should be here within two hours. I figure he jumped from the train as soon as it began to slow down and is out there in the forest somewhere. We will find him."

"Yes, we will," Ganin said. "But not out here."

"Comrade?"

"Riga. He's going to the KGB border guards base. We'll go there and wait for him."

Captain General Zuyev was a guest of a Politburo member in his dacha at Usova, twenty miles west of Moscow. They'd had a pleasant, diverting weekend, which had spilled over into Monday, but as night approached, nearly everyone had returned to the city.

Zuyev stood by the fireplace, nursing a glass of sweet champagne, feeling the warmth from the fire. The afternoon had turned a little chilly. By night it would be cold. Not like the winter nights when the Nazis had been stopped, of course, but cold for spring nevertheless.

He had gotten word a couple of hours ago that Moran had escaped from Moscow and was on his way now to Riga. Apparently to the KGB base there. The militia investigator believed it was the man's intention to steal a missile-equipped helicopter and use it to shoot down Gorbachev's plane as it crossed the coast.

An ambitious plan, he thought. But essentially a foolish one. They were waiting for him. He would not get very far. And even if he did manage to penetrate base security and actually steal a combat helicopter, radar would immediately pick him up, and fighter-interceptors would be dispatched from the nearby air force base at Tallinn.

But he had come so close. He was a resourceful, tenacious bastard. Zuyev smiled inwardly. They could have used a squadron of men like him at Leningrad that winter.

He turned and looked at the telephone. The risks were enormous, but the *Rodina* was suffering. The motherland was being diluted by modernists whose ultimate goal was to produce a capitalistic democracy at home. They'd already given away their hard-won advantages in Eastern Europe. It was an outrage that made his blood boil.

It took him forty minutes to get General Gennadi Matushin, commander of the Air Force, on the telephone at his home in Moscow.

"Gennadi Feodorovich, there is one last thing you must do for me. It concerns our boys at Tallinn."

"What is it?" Matushin asked, his voice guarded.

"They think he is on his way to the KGB base at Riga." There was no need to mention whom he meant. "But he knows that the odds there will be stacked against him."

"You believe he will make a try for the air base?"

"I think it's possible. And I think it is time to help him. He has come this far on his own. I think with help he may succeed."

There was a silence on the line for a long time. When Matushin came back, his voice seemed firm. He had made his decision. "I agree. I'll take care of it."

Mary Frances rode out to the airport with Scott Moore in an embassy limousine. It was one in the morning. There had been some trepidation about allowing her to go. In the past twenty-four hours she had talked with a lot of people at the embassy, including Kelly Pool and Richard Sweeney, whom her boss, Ben Siegel, identified as probable CIA.

She had listened to them with a new respect, tinged with a little fear after that. But their message was essentially the same as Judge Moore's.

"We can't stop you if you want to go with the presidential party to London. In fact, it would be a feather in your journalistic cap. But Moran is here to kill Gorbachev. If you happen to be standing next to him, he'll get a two-for-one opportunity."

"Can't I persuade you to come back to the embassy with me?"

Moore said as they were passed through a second security gate
and drove over to the VIP parking area. There were uniformed
and plainclothes KGB officers everywhere.

"No," Mary Frances said. She was frightened, but she struggled not to let it show. "If you were a newshound, you'd understand."

"I suppose," Moore said.

A KGB officer, green piping on his uniform, came over to
them. Moore cranked down his window. The officer looked in at
Mary Frances.

"Miss Dean, if you will come with me, there will be a security
briefing inside."

"What about my bags?" she asked.

"They will have to be inspected. I will send someone to take
care of them."

Mary Frances looked at Moore and smiled. "Thanks, Judge,
I appreciate your help." She leaned over and kissed him on the
cheek.

Moore returned her smile but shook his head ruefully. "Take
care of yourself."

"Will do," she said. She got out of the car and followed the
officer inside.

Ganin slammed the telephone down and looked into the eyes
of Riga's base commander, Lieutenant Colonel Anatoli Yashchenko. "President Gorbachev just boarded his aircraft."

"We are doing everything humanly possible, Chief Investigator," the colonel replied, not bothering to mask his dislike. Militiamen did not give orders to KGB officers.

"He's here, or he's on his way. And he knows how he will get
onto the base and steal one of your helicopters."

"Then let him. It won't do him any good."

Ganin went to the windows and looked out across the base.
The alert hangars were lit up inside and out and were completely
surrounded by guards with dogs.

The perimeter fence, which was normally heavily guarded,
was being patrolled inside and out by one hundred extra troops
pulled from other duties.

Low-light high-resolution closed-circuit television cameras
covered nearly every square meter of the base. There was no
possible way Moran could get onto the base, let alone steal a

helicopter. And even if he did, each machine had been rendered unflyable by the removal of an electrical wire from its fuel pump.

Yet Ganin was becoming extremely apprehensive. Moran was somewhere near.

"You said yourself that he jumped the train because he knew you were on to him," Lieutenant Colonel Yashchenko said. He was trying to be reasonable. "No man in his right mind would come here knowing that. He'd have to realize that we would tighten security—"

"You don't know him," Ganin said.

"It seems, Chief Investigator, that you don't either."

Moran's left knee had swollen to nearly twice its size, and it took everything within his power to operate the stiff clutch in the old Lada farm truck. It felt as if he had ripped the cartilage holding the knee joint together. Once, when he stopped to relieve himself at the side of the road, his leg collapsed beneath him and he had to crawl back to the truck.

His hands were filthy and bloody, one of his fingernails pulled completely off, and some of the latex makeup covering his face had been clawed away, giving him a ghoulish appearance.

He had not counted on the farmer being so strong and so willing to defend the truck with his life. When he had come out of the woods a full eight miles from the railroad tracks, the dog had immediately attacked him, and he'd had to shoot it.

The man had come after him with a double-bladed ax. He'd managed to wound the man before he was on him, and it became a fight for life—his.

When it was over, he had hidden the body in the pigsty, pulled on a pair of old work coveralls and rubber boots, gassed the stake-body truck from jerry cans he found in the toolshed, and driven off.

The moment he had spotted the truck a new plan had formed in his mind. They'd come down from Moscow to stop the train because they not only knew he was on it but had evidently also figured out why he was going to Riga. Otherwise they might have waited until it got there and arrested him at the station. But the stakes were too high with Gorbachev about ready to leave for London.

The KGB border guards base would be locked tight now. The helicopters would be watched very closely. There would be no way in for him. At least none that wouldn't entail an unacceptable risk.

Even if he could get a chopper from the base, Gorbachev's jet would be diverted. Changing the flight path a hundred miles farther south or north would completely wreck any chances Moran might have had.

It gave him a small measure of pleasure to think of how they would be waiting at Riga. Ganin would almost certainly be there, satisfied that he had outthought the enemy.

Too bad, Moran thought, that Ganin wouldn't be aboard the jet airliner with Gorbachev and Mary Frances.

It was 1:30 A.M. when he topped the last rise and was looking down at Tallinn, the capital of the Estonian SSR, and at the lights of the Soviet air force base a few miles southwest along the coast. He breathed a sigh of relief. He had seriously doubted that the old truck could make the two-hundred-mile journey.

Fifteen minutes later he found a dirt track that led in the direction of the air base. A mile off the main highway he cut the truck's lights and went on in the darkness. Clouds had formed over the sea and had drifted in over the land, obscuring the stars.

The land was hilly here, gradually tumbling down toward the gulf, and wild, gnarled trees and windblown grasses hung stubbornly to the thin, sandy soil. At times he was not able to see the lights of the base at all, though from the crest of one rise he could pick out the white runway lights and blue taxi lights, running east to west.

He came to the tall barbed-wire-topped fence a few minutes before two, and he pulled the truck off the dirt road into the brush. Gorbachev's plane would be taking off from Moscow's Sheremetyevo Airport now, and if it was on schedule, it would be passing overhead to the south in a bit more than an hour. There wasn't much time left.

There were no warning signs such as those posted around American military installations; in the Soviet Union a fence such as this meant: "Government; keep out." Nor was it electrified; there was no need of it.

After pulling off the coveralls and tossing them up over the barbed wire, Moran managed to scramble up and over the fence, using his arm and shoulder muscles.

On the inside, he headed as fast as he could go toward the flashing beacon, somewhere near which would be the alert hangars and an aircraft he could use.

53

Moran was very good, but he wasn't a wizard. He could not do the impossible. Ganin kept telling himself that.

Gorbachev's plane had taken off a half hour ago; there was no turning it back now. But so far there had been no penetration of the Riga perimeter fence, nor had any word come from the alert hangars that there was trouble.

Yet Ganin's stomach was hollow, and when he raised the match to his cigarette, his hand was shaking. He was missing something.

"And now, if you please, Comrade Chief Investigator, may we stand down?" Lieutenant Colonel Yashchenko said.

They were in his jeep, returning from a final check on the perimeter guard posts. Yashchenko had become very irritable in the past hour since he'd telephoned his superiors at the Lubyanka in Moscow and asked for a clarification of the situation with Ganin. He'd gotten it, and it hadn't been to his liking. He'd been told to cooperate. Period.

"Not until the president's aircraft has passed safely by us," Ganin said. Something was gnawing at him. Something important.

Moran was no god, but he was intelligent and highly motivated. He had a plan. He knew what he was doing. He knew how he was going to shoot down the president's plane and get away.

How?

Ganin turned and looked at the base commander, a glimmering of an idea coming to him.

"How good is your radar here?"

Yashchenko glanced at him. "We can monitor air operations as far away as Helsinki's international airport."

"How about to the east?"

"The same distance." The base commander shrugged. "Maybe out to four hundred kilometers."

"We will be able to see the president's flight long before it reaches the coast."

"Yes, of course, but certainly our equipment isn't as good as that up in Tallinn."

Someone had jammed a brick into Ganin's gut. "What?"

"Tallinn. The air force base—" Yashchenko said, but he saw the look in Ganin's eyes, and he stopped short. He put it together almost immediately. "You didn't know. *Yeb vas*," he swore, and he hauled the jeep left and raced off toward the operations building.

There should have been sentries. Mobile patrols. Guards on foot. Dogs. Something, anything. But Moran had encountered no one.

The base was not deserted. There were lights shining, and he could hear generators and other machinery running. Across the runway the search and identify radars were rotating, and in one of the barracks a light had been switched off.

Where was security? This was an operational air force base with valuable warplanes and nuclear weapons.

But he was running out of time for such speculations. Gorbachev's plane would already be halfway from Moscow.

He'd come three miles from the fence, circling the eastern edge of the main runway and coming up behind the four alert hangars with their curved blast doors that bulged outward. On the hangar nearest to him an orange light was flashing. He had no idea what it meant, except that it had to signify something.

Keeping to the shadows as much as possible and moving with extreme caution, every one of his senses alert for some sign that they were waiting for him, that this was a trap, he approached the service door and quickly checked it for alarm wires. There were none.

Opening the door a crack, he looked inside the cavernous building. Four jet fighters were parked side by side, nose cones facing outward, their canopies opened, mounting ladders rolled up to the cockpits, and a dozen yellow arming safety ribbons dangling from various parts of the aircraft as well as from the deadly-looking missiles hanging from their mounts beneath the wings.

The jets were Sukhoi Su-24 all-weather attack-reconnaissance planes with side-by-side seating for a pilot and navigator-weapons officer, capable of speeds well above Mach 2 with a service ceiling of nearly sixty thousand feet.

Knowing such things was one of Moran's areas of expertise. Necessary for the kind of work he did. He could not fly this plane or any other modern jet fighter, but he knew what it was capable of and generally how its systems worked.

At the rear of the hangar light spilled from a partially open door. Moran froze in the darkness for several seconds as someone laughed, the door came all the way open, and a man in a flight suit stepped out, glanced at the aircraft, then turned and went back inside.

Angling over to the jet nearest the main doors, Moran quietly crept up the mounting ladder and looked inside the cockpit. He pulled the five safety ribbons out of the ejection seats and the avionics destruct device, then climbed back down. Working quickly but noiselessly, he removed the other safety ribbons from the jet and its weapons, starting forward of the wing on the port side and working his way completely around the aircraft.

When he was finished, he pulled over the starting cart and plugged in the umbilical cord. Finally he took the chocks away from the wheels.

Now it would take only a couple of minutes to start the jet, open the main doors, and get out. Just a couple of minutes. It was all the time he wanted.

He checked his watch. It was 2:40 A.M. Gorbachev's jet would be passing to the south within the next twenty to thirty-five minutes. He ejected the clip from the Makarov and counted the bullets. There were only three, plus the one in the firing chamber. If there were more than three or four men inside, or if his shooting was bad, he could be in trouble. He had no other weapon for now.

He stopped to listen at the partially open door. There were at least two, perhaps three men, talking in low voices. One of them laughed and did something. Cards? They were playing cards.

Cocking the pistol's hammer, he pushed open the door and stepped inside. Five men were seated around a table, playing cards, another two were playing chess at a smaller table, and an eighth was lounging on a couch, reading a book.

Four two-place aircraft . . . eight men. Of course. It was logical, but he had missed it.

They all looked up. One of them at the table jumped to his feet, his chair crashing backward, a look of horror on his face. "Fuck your mother," he swore.

"Be quiet," Moran snapped.

"Who are you?" the man was shouting when Moran shot him in the chest, driving him backward over the chair.

He pointed his pistol in the general direction of the others as he reached behind him and closed the door. "Which of you is the senior pilot?"

The men were staring at him, incredulous expressions on their faces. It was his makeup. Some of the latex had pulled away. He had to look like a monster. Or was it something else? Something about the lack of security on base was trying to make its way to the surface of his consciousness. But he wasn't making the connection. Not yet.

"If I have to kill you all, I will," he warned.

The man seated on the couch got to his feet. He was older than the others, his hair thining. "I am the senior pilot. Captain Dmitri Andreyevich Seregin."

"Are you armed?"

"Yes," Seregin answered after a beat.

Moran breathed an inward sigh of relief, though he allowed nothing of that emotion to show on his ravaged face. "I want you and your men to place your weapons on the table and then step away."

Again Seregin hesitated, but finally he nodded, carefully pulling an automatic pistol from a pocket in the chest of his flight suit. "The others are not armed," he said, laying his gun on the table.

But this was too easy. Why weren't they fighting back? There were seven of them. They could rush him; he couldn't take them all. Something wasn't right.

One of the men bent down to check on the man who'd been shot.

"Leave him," Moran said. "He's dead."

"Why?" the young man asked, straightening up. "You *pizda*, you weren't supposed to come here."

Moran's blood ran cold. "What did you say?"

The young man was shaking his head. Seregin took his arm and pulled him away.

"He didn't mean anything. They were friends. Besides, we're unarmed now. What do you want from us?"

"A jeep to get me the hell out of here," Moran said, his brain racing down a dozen different possibilities. But there was no time for anything fancy now. He needed to get airborne within the next few minutes if he was going to have any chance whatsoever of intercepting Gorbachev's plane.

"We will offer you no resistance," the senior pilot said.

"Turn around."

Seregin nodded, and he and the others turned. Moran stepped quickly to the table, snatched up the pistol, cocked it, flipped the safety to the off position, and began firing.

The first three died before any of them knew what was happening. The fourth and fifth managed to turn and sidestep the line of fire, but Moran was in his element now. One of them took a hit in the heart; the other, in his throat just below his Adam's apple. The sixth made a rush for the table, and Moran shot him at point-blank range in the middle of the forehead, driving him to his knees.

Seregin was shaking with rage. Moran held both guns on him.

"Why?" the pilot asked, barely in control. "They did exactly as you asked of them. They would have done more."

"There's no time for that."

"They were only boys."

"They were officers in the Soviet Air Force. They signed an oath to give their lives for their country."

"Defending him."

"They were," Moran said. "Let's go." He motioned toward the door.

"Where?"

"Flying."

Seregin nodded. "What if I refuse?"

"You will die immediately."

"Then you would have a difficult, if not impossible, time getting out of the Soviet Union."

"It would not matter to you, Comrade Pilot. Believe me, it is not worth your life."

"What about afterward? Where do you want me to take you? The West?"

"That depends entirely on you, Captain. Cooperate with me, and you will live to tell this story to your grandchildren. I promise you."

Seregin looked at the dead or dying men. He was still shaking. "At what terrible cost?" he whispered, but he had received his orders.

54

"Ten more minutes," Ganin said half to himself. They had tracked Gorbachev's Ilyushin 86 from the northeast, identifying it by its transponder code, which showed up on the radar screen as a four-digit number. It was just passing south of Tallinn, less than a hundred miles from the coast.

Lieutenant Colonel Yashchenko was perched on the edge of one of the consoles, a sour look on his face as he put down the telephone.

Ganin stood just behind the radar operator. He looked up. "They have had no trouble up there?"

"None," Yashchenko said. He had telephoned the operations officer at Tallinn Air Force Base. "Operations are normal."

Ganin turned back to the screen. A blip was just moving away from the air base. He reached over the shoulder of the operator and pointed at it. "What's that?"

The young *michman* flipped a couple of switches. "A fighter-interceptor. A Sukhoi. He is climbing very fast, past Mach one and still accelerating."

Yashchenko had gotten to his feet. He was shaking his head in disbelief. "They said they had no aircraft in the air."

"Call them again," Ganin said, a chill rising inside him. "Hurry, Colonel."

The Sukhoi's search radar was effective out to four hundred miles. Before they had passed through ten thousand feet, it had picked up an aircraft to the southeast. There was no other traffic coming from that direction. It was flying at about thirty-five thousand feet and was moving at slightly more than five hundred knots. Everything fitted.

"It is an airliner, I think," Seregin said from the left seat. The cockpit was noisy enough so that they had to communicate over the headsets.

"We're going to shoot it down," Moran said. The helmet and oxygen mask were causing him nearly intolerable pain. At times his vision went blurry, but he kept the pistol aimed at the pilot at all times. At this range he couldn't miss even if he was blind.

"Are you crazy?" Seregin shouted. "I will not shoot an unarmed civilian airliner with maybe two hundred or more civilians aboard."

"What about the Korean airliner?"

"That was different."

"Yes," Moran said. "This is a military target."

"I don't believe you." Seregin's voice boomed in Moran's ear.

But something was wrong now. It was hard for him to think. He knew that he should be aware of something. He looked at the pilot, then raised the pistol to the man's face and cocked the hammer.

"You will shoot that airplane out of the sky, Comrade Captain, as soon as we come in range of one of your missiles, or I will kill you. I believe I can fly this airplane well enough to get me into Finnish airspace, where I will eject."

A single thought was hammering insistently at the back of Moran's head. What was it? something about the radio. Something that had to do with the kid's reaction to him in the hangar. *You* pizda, *you weren't supposed to come here*. And now the radio. It was silent. They had not been challenged. Why?

Yashchenko was on the telephone, trying to raise the Tallinn Air Force Base operations officer again, but there was no answer this time.

They had tried three times to make contact with Gorbachev's aircraft, but there had been absolutely no response. Now Ganin watched while the much faster Sukhoi continued to climb and accelerate as it turned south toward the Ilyushin.

"It is definitely on an intercept course, sir," the radar *michman* said. The Riga operations center was very small. Only half a dozen men worked here. All of them were watching the unfolding situation.

"Can we call him?" Ganin asked.

The *michman* looked up. "We can try the standard military frequency, but there are no guarantees he'll answer us. The Air Force . . . doesn't like us."

"Try," Ganin said.

The radar operator flipped a couple of switches on his console and adjusted his headset. "Unidentified Sukhoi in Tallinn sector one-eight-seven alpha, please answer and identify. This is Riga border control."

The *michman* had switched the comms channel to a loudspeaker. There was no response.

"Unidentified aircraft in Tallinn sector one-eight-seven alpha, please answer and identify."

Still there was no answer.

Ganin grabbed the headset from the operator. "Moran, this is Ganin. I'm here, Moran. I know what you're up to. It won't work. Forsythe! I know about you. . . ."

"It's too late for you, Forsythe." The voice came over Moran's headset. It was definitely Ganin; he recognized the son of a bitch's voice. But how had he known? How could any of them have known? It didn't make sense.

He was back in the hooch, the bamboo slats above his head slippery with human shit, dripping down on him. The guards were saying something to him, and from some of the other pits he could hear men crying or screaming.

Outside the canopy the stars shone as hard points. They had

rocketed through a thick layer of clouds, which were well below them now. It was like being on another planet. Moran felt as if he were drifting.

The pilot was looking at him.

"Give it up, Forsythe, whoever you are, while you still have a chance." Ganin's voice was droning in his ear. "Head west, Forsythe. Go to Helsinki. Or better yet, fly to Stockholm. They'll accept you and the jet. You'll be a hero."

Moran switched the radio off. Seregin flinched.

"Bring it up on your targeting radar, pilot, and ready your missile."

"We don't have the proper weapon—"

Moran jammed the barrel of the pistol into Seregin's face just below his right eye. "There are two Aphid AA-8 Advanced Snap Shot missiles on this aircraft's pylons. I removed the safety ribbons myself. Believe me, you will shoot that aircraft out of the sky within the next one hundred twenty seconds or you will die."

Seregin seemed to be holding his breath. His entire body was rigid; his eyes were wide; his nostrils flared.

After several beats he turned back to the control panel and began flipping switches, activating the targeting radar systems. He had to reach past Moran to activate the Aphids for firing. The fear smell was strong on him.

Moran smiled, even though the slight movement, any movement, caused him excruciating pain.

Lieutenant Stepan Mikhailovich Kirsanov was the first into the alert pilots' lounge. Not knowing what to expect, he had run across from the barracks when the Sukhoi thundered down the runway.

The lights were off. He flipped them on and stood completely dumbfounded for the space of half a dozen heartbeats. He simply could not believe what he was seeing. The blood. The bodies. It was impossible.

Others crowded in behind him.

"Fuck your mother," one of the ground crewmen swore.

Kirsanov spun on his heel and rushed back out into the alert hangar. The door was open. One of the Sukhois was missing. Only one.

The bastard or bastards had killed all the duty pilots and weapons officers and had stolen one of their aircraft.

He grabbed one of the ground crewmen. "I'm taking two-four-three-one. Help me get out of here."

Seregin fired the Aphid while they were twelve miles out from their target. They could just make out the airliner's navigational and anticollision lights, but they could not tell its type from this distance.

The rocket left the Sukhoi on a long, fiery tail that wavered left, then right in a tight little spiral before it homed in directly on the target aircraft. Its speed was incredible, more than Mach 4 above their own.

Seregin started a long, arcing turn, and seconds later the missile struck. A huge fireball lighted up the distant sky, flaming pieces of wreckage and burning fuel spewing earthward, illuminating the tops of the clouds.

"God help them," Seregin said. Moran thought that was amusing, coming from a Russian.

"Head west and get us down into the clouds."

"No good," Seregin said, doing something with his rearward-looking radar. "We have company, and if my guess is right, it's one of the boys from Tallinn coming up to take care of us."

"Do it now," Moran shouted, pulling his feet closer to the seat and hooking his heels into the ejection seat platform.

"His radar will pick us up—"

"Now," Moran shouted. "Cut your afterburner! Slow us down!"

The other fighter had turned north, directly over the gulf and had dropped down into the clouds as his speed suddenly went subsonic.

Lieutenant Kirsanov pulled up sharply, cutting off his afterburners. At the top he rolled over and dived, his speed now only a couple of hundred knots above the other's.

His air traffic controller had begun giving him vectors just after the destruction of the aircraft to the southeast, and Kirsanov was too busy to wonder where he'd been earlier.

The cloud cover was at least a thousand meters thick. Kirsanov was just skimming the cloud tops above and behind his target when the firing solution came up on his Heads-Up Display. There were no ECMs emanating from the target, no jamming, not even any evasive maneuvers.

Kirsanov hesitated for just a moment, before he hit the launch button on his control stick, and the Aphid missile streaked away. A moment later he launched the second missile.

None of this made any sense to him. But he had seen the blood and the bodies. And his air controller had given his immediate authorization to pursue and destroy.

Seven seconds after launch both Aphids struck, one after the other. The clouds flashed for a brief instant, and the target disappeared from Kirsanov's scope.

Ganin stood with the others, watching the unfolding drama. When it was over, he turned away, an incredible sense of sadness and futility coming over him. Why? he asked himself. What had been solved?

"Now get the hell out of here, Chief Investigator," Lieutenant Colonel Yashchenko said. "Your job is finished." He was afraid of the taint by association.

Ganin looked at him and nodded. "You're right," he said. "Thank you for your kind assistance."

PART FOUR

55

Ed Wilder climbed tiredly out of his limousine and entered the west hall of the White House. Herb Goldman came down for him, and they headed up to the Oval Office.

"He wanted you included in the briefing," the President's chief of staff said.

"Bob Vaughan called a couple of hours ago, but he was damned cryptic. What the hell is going on, Herb?"

"You'll find out in just a minute."

It was eight in the morning, and although he'd spent a peaceful evening at home with his family in Chevy Chase, he was bone weary. He had not been sleeping very well these past ten days or so, ever since the Moran thing had broken open. The man was a monster, a crazed but efficient killing machine. No matter what happened, he would probably turn out to be a national disgrace because of his Medal of Honor.

"Is it about Moran?" Wilder had asked when Vaughan called, the sleep instantly leaving him.

"Yes," the DCI had replied tersely.

Now, entering the President's study, Wilder was apprehensive and not prepared for the expressions on everyone's face, especially Vaughan's and the President's. They seemed happy, even relieved.

"It's over," Vaughan said. "He's dead."

Goldman shut the door behind the FBI director. "Are we sure?" Wilder asked, coming across the room.

"Yes."

"Where?"

"Estonia," Vaughan said. "Actually the Gulf of Finland."

"How about Gorbachev?"

"Unhurt," the President said. "But Bob was just getting to that. What happened?"

Wilder took a seat, and Tyrell handed him a cup of coffee. Vaughan had apparently just arrived. He opened his briefcase and took out a folder stamped "Top Secret" top and bottom. It was marked "Operation Dogwood. National Security Agency."

"Tom Hart brought this over to my house last night around ten. He knew that I was personally interested, and he thought the material was too significant to wait for the morning reports. But I wanted to hold until I got confirmation from Kelly Pool at our Moscow station. That came at six this morning."

He handed the folder to the President, who opened it and scanned the first few pages before looking up.

"Operation Dogwood has been NSA's most successful program of monitoring Soviet military frequency transmissions to date," Vaughan explained. "It's only been since they were able to put a Cray supercomputer on-line that they were able to make some sense of the hundreds of thousands of transmissions every single day. Well, it's beginning to pay off."

The President handed the folder to Wilder, who leafed through some of its fifty or sixty pages.

"Give us the short version, Bob," the President said.

"They knew that Moran was coming to Moscow, and they set him up. They granted Mary Frances Dean, the *World News This Week* reporter, an early visa to come to Moscow. Gorbachev granted her an exclusive interview within the first days of her arrival, and once they were certain Moran was not only in the Soviet Union but in contact with the woman, they invited her to ride with Gorbachev on his plane to London."

The President sat forward. "I heard nothing about such a trip."

"That's because no such trip was ever planned, Mr. President. One of the KGB's bright stars, Colonel Valeri Markelov, worked up the scheme. Moran made contact with Ms. Dean, who obligingly told him about the supposed trip. Moran went to the Soviet air base at Tallinn, hijacked a jet fighter, and forced the pilot to shoot down what he believed was Gorbachev's aircraft, but what was in reality an unmanned drone controlled from a much higher-flying chase plane back fifty miles or so."

"This Russian pilot actually shot what he believed was his president's plane out of the sky?" the U.S. President asked.

"Yes, sir. We're working on the assumption that General Gennadi Matushin is one of the conspirators who hired Moran in the first place. He could have made certain that base security was lax and that the right men were available in the alert hangar."

"What happened next?"

"Moran and his pilot were shot down by another interceptor from the base, but not until after the bogus presidential aircraft had been destroyed. NSA monitored no ground traffic until *after* that event. As soon as the airliner was down, Tallinn Air Traffic Control began vectoring the new pilot toward his target."

"I assume he was successful."

"Yes, sir. At three twenty-eight A.M., GMT plus three, that would be local time at Tallinn, Moran's plane was shot down and completely destroyed over the Gulf of Finland."

The President sat back. He shook his head tiredly. "Thank God it's over. I'm sure that we can talk their people into cooperating with us on Moran's . . . or Forsythe's . . . true identity. There is no good reason to expose the fact that he was a Medal of Honor winner."

"No, sir," Vaughan said.

Vivian Hammer sat with his boss, William Seagraves, across the desk from Wilder, who had just returned from the White House and had briefed them on what he'd learned.

"No possibility of survivors, Mr. Director?" Hammer asked.

He didn't like what he'd heard. It wasn't neat. He wished Ganin were here to tell him the entire story.

"So far as is known to this point, no," Wilder said.

"No bodies either?"

Wilder shook his head, and Hammer glanced at Seagraves.

"I'm sorry, sir, but I am skeptical," Hammer said. "Until I see Moran's body with my own two eyes, until there is a pathology and forensics report nailing his identification cold, I think there's still a possibility, however remote, that he somehow survived."

"What do you suggest?" Wilder asked, studying Hammer through narrowed eyes. It was clear he wasn't happy.

"I'd like to go to Moscow."

"Even if he is alive, by some miracle, he certainly wouldn't be able to get back there," Seagraves said.

"I suppose," Hammer mumbled. "But I'd still like to go over there."

"It's over," Wilder said, rising.

"Yes, sir," Hammer said, he and Seagraves getting to their feet. "I'd at least like authorization to call Chief Investigator Ganin and speak with him."

"No," Wilder said without hesitation. "It is over."

anin rode with Chief Prosecutor Yernin to the Kremlin, where they were admitted through the Spassky Gate and directed to a parking place across from the Presidium of the Supreme Soviet.

The uniformed KGB guards at the door came to attention as they mounted the steps and entered the building. Inside, a pair of security officers checked Yernin's briefcase and relieved Ganin of his pistol, before another security officer, this one in civilian clothes, took them upstairs to a large anteroom bare of anything except a picture of Lenin on one wall, a huge Oriental rug on the parquet floor, and a long mahogany table covered with dozens of military and civilian hats.

"Wait," the officer said, and he left them.

"What is this all about?" Ganin asked.

Yernin smiled faintly and shrugged as he eyed the collection of hats. "I would say that we have been invited to a party, Nikki."

"Here?" Ganin asked. He'd been home fewer than eighteen hours, and he was dead on his feet. Antonia had promised to come home this evening if he would be there. She wanted to talk to him. It was already six o'clock.

"I don't know what it means, but it certainly won't harm your career, or mine for that matter, to be here like this," the chief prosecutor said sternly. They both were dressed in their uniforms, Yernin's was very impressive with all its ribbons and medals.

The double doors opened five minutes later, and President Gorbachev came in with Colonel Kokorov and a half dozen other civilians and officers.

"Ah, Chief Investigator Ganin, practically my guardian angel," Gorbachev said in his Western way, coming across the room. He took Ganin in a tremendous bear hug, then kissed him on the lips.

"It seems that my services were not needed after all, Comrade President," Ganin said when Gorbachev released him and stepped back.

Gorbachev smiled. "There you are wrong. Without your expert work the ruse would not have succeeded. Who knows? He might still be on the loose, killing people."

"I'm sorry I could not have done more."

Gorbachev looked at him shrewdly, a rueful set to his mouth. "I would like to award you the Order of Lenin," he said gently. "But though you deserve such a thing, it would, I am told, have the unfortunate effect of eroding the people's faith in the ability of the KGB to safeguard not only my person but its security as well."

Ganin said nothing. There was nothing to say.

"So in the end you will have nothing for your efforts but my thanks and my warmest personal affection."

"It is enough, Comrade President."

Gorbachev nodded, his eyes never leaving Ganin's. "Perhaps someday we will be able to tell your story, Chief Investigator."

Again Ganin held his silence until finally Gorbachev turned around and he and his party left the room.

"Well," Yernin said, beaming. "Well."

"Let's go," Ganin said tiredly.

"I will drive you home, Nikki. And I promise I will call you the moment Moran's body is found."

"How long will they search?"

"I don't know. They have found parts of the aircraft, and they have found pieces of the pilot's body. They will continue until they are successful."

Moran was terribly cold. It was the first sensation that he became aware of as he came slowly out of a deep sleep.

There had been dreams. Odd shapes and impressions. Bright yellow fireballs. Flaming wreckage falling from the sky. Something slamming at his body from above and ahead, sending him tumbling end over end in free fall and then in long, swinging glides. Finally there was water. He remembered that very clearly. Waves were breaking over his head, and he was afraid of drowning. And at last the hands, the voices.

He opened his eyes. At first he couldn't see much of anything; his vision was blurred. Was he in prison? Had he been captured by the Russians after all?

Gradually he came to realize that he was in a small bedroom, thick curtains covering the window, a tall pine chest in the corner, and a badly done painting on the other wall of Jesus Christ, his heart exposed and glowing.

He was in considerable pain. His entire body felt battered, and his face felt as if he'd been hit by a truck. It was bandaged, as were his knee, his left arm, and his upper torso. When he breathed deeply, he felt a sharp pain in his left side. He supposed he'd broken a rib or two. The important part was that nothing felt critical.

His mind was seething with dozens of thoughts and conjectures, but mostly he felt that there was peace for him just around the corner. It was very close now. He had seen the fireball and flaming wreckage that were Gorbachev's plane. He had watched it fall out of the sky. His work was done. It gave him a deep sense of satisfaction.

The door opened, and an older, kindly-looking woman with a beet red face and white hair pinned up in a bun looked in. She smiled.

"Where am I, Grandmother?" Moran asked in Russian.

The woman said something that sounded to his ear like Finnish.

"Where?" he asked, switching languages.

The woman's careworn face lit up. "Porkkala," she said. "Porkkala." She turned and called to someone. "Toivo, come. Your Russian defector is awake."

G anin was waiting for Mary Frances when she came out of the magazine with three other reporters and one of the editors. They were laughing nervously about something. It was a few minutes before six, and traffic was heavy along Arbat Street. He got out of the car and caught up with them.

"Ms. Dean?" he called out diffidently.

They stopped and turned back. She smiled. "You've finally got it right, Chief Investigator," she said warmly. The others were looking at him as if he were about to arrest them.

"What?"

"That we use Ms. instead of Miss, these days," she said.

Yernin had mentioned it. He smiled again. "May I drive you home?"

"I'm back at the Rossiya for a few days. They're doing something to my building."

"Yes, I know."

"Mary?" one of the reporters said.

She turned back to him. "It's all right, Eddie. You guys go on ahead. I'll see you later."

The reporter gave Ganin a long, hard stare and then reluctantly turned, and he and the others walked off.

"He seems very protective of you," Ganin said, taking her arm and leading her back to his car. He opened the door for her as he had seen Moran do it in a KGB surveillance photograph and then got in behind the wheel.

"I think he has a crush on me," she said. "It happens."

"Yes, I'm sure it does," Ganin said, pulling out into traffic.

They drove in silence for a little while, passing the Lenin Library and then following the broad river boulevard down toward the Kremlin. Her purse was on her lap, and she kept fiddling with the strap.

"We were told that he was dead, but the press agency officer wouldn't give us any details," she blurted.

"The aircraft he was aboard was shot down over the Gulf of Finland," Ganin replied carefully.

She looked at him. "He was after President Gorbachev's plane, wasn't he?" she said. "That's why we never took off. But they never told us anything. They just held us there until morning and then drove us back to our homes."

"It was a trick," Ganin said. "The KGB worked it out."

"I see."

"What about you?" he asked after a long minute. "Will you be going home now?"

"No. I'm on a three-year assignment here." She smiled. "For some reason your president has taken a liking to me. My magazine wouldn't pull me out of here for all the tea in China."

"You were a part of the plan—"

"An unwitting part," she corrected.

He conceded the point. "But a part of the plan, nevertheless, that saved his life. You're a genuine hero of the Soviet people."

"They want me to appear on one of your television shows."

"You will be treated kindly and with respect."

They passed the Beklemishev Tower on the southeast corner

of the Kremlin's ramparts, and Ganin shot through a break in traffic to the main curved driveway to the massive hotel.

He parked in front but made no move to get out. He felt awkward around her, as if he were a peasant who'd just gotten his first glimpse of a Moscow girl and didn't know that he should be wiping the mud off his boots. Next to her he was an onion in a patch of violets.

"What about you?" she asked.

"I don't understand."

"Now that this is finished, do you have any other interesting cases?"

"No."

"Will you be going on vacation? It's nearly summer. I thought—"

Ganin shook his head. "Nothing like that either. I guess I'll have to begin looking for a new partner. Yurochka . . . Detective Sepelev was a good friend."

"I'm sorry. It must be painful."

Ganin looked at her. Truly she was an exotic creature beyond anything in his wildest imaginings. In some respects she was as alien to him as the Venus de Milo, separated from his world by thousands of miles and eons of time.

"Good-bye, Ms. Dean," he said.

She, too, was studying his face. "Thank you," she said.

"For what?"

"For saving my life at least. And . . . for saving my sanity when I was about to kill him. It's something I could not have lived with."

"I know."

The silence seemed to grow exponentially between them. Ganin had to smile. He reached across and opened the door for her. "If ever you need any assistance, call for me. Day or night. I will be there."

"I know," she said. She kissed him gently on the cheek, then slipped out of the car and hurried into the hotel.

Ganin stayed for a minute or two, amazed that she had not questioned him more closely about Moran's destruction. He'd been careful not to tell her that Moran was dead, simply because no one knew that for a fact. They'd found most of the jet fighter and 90 percent of the pilot's body, including his helmet, which had still been filled with his head.

But so far there'd been no sign of Moran's body, or his ejection seat, or the canopy. The conclusion was obvious, or at least it was to him: Moran had managed to get out of the airplane just before the missile struck it.

If he'd been near enough to the explosion, it would have killed him. But even if he had survived all the way down to the frigid gulf, he would not have survived in those waters for more than fifty minutes.

But then, he told himself, he'd already had a career under-estimating the man.

Larissa Sepelev was wearing a gray warm-up suit about five sizes too big for her. "CCCP" was stenciled on the back of the jacket.

"Ah, and now it's the kind and patient friend come to pay his respects to the grieving widow," she said unsteadily. She'd been drinking; her face was flushed.

She turned and went to the couch, where she sat down and curled her legs up beneath her. Ganin came in and closed the door. The apartment smelled closed up, musty. Several half-empty vodka bottles, glasses, and a couple of platters of snacks filled the coffee table. She could have been having a party, but she was alone.

"I came to see how you were getting along, Larissa," Ganin said. "See if there is anything I can do for you."

"Send me to America," she said, reaching for her glass.

"What?"

"You heard me, Comrade Chief Investigator."

"Maybe you will go someday."

She laughed. "Sure."

"You're young, good-looking. There will be someone else in your life."

She looked up at him through bleary eyes, her lips half parted. Languidly she undid the zipper of her jacket, exposing her large breasts. The nipples were long and flaccid. He could see blue veins like spider webs just below the pale white skin.

"Would you like to make love to me, Nikki?" she asked. "I wouldn't tell Antonia, I promise." She giggled. "Besides, she wouldn't care anyway. She's a cow."

"No, I don't think so," Ganin said.

"No?"

He tried to take the glass from her, but she pulled it away, spilling half of the vodka down her front.

"You're no gentleman," she screeched. "You're as bad as the others. They didn't care about Yurochka either."

It was the first time he'd ever heard her refer to Yurii by that diminutive form. But it was the other thing that she'd said that really caught his attention.

"I'm sorry, Larissa," he said. He poured her some more spiced vodka, and she was slightly mollified.

"I meant it, you know," she said. "Every word."

He didn't know what she was talking about. "You said others, Larissa. What others? Was someone else here paying his respects? Maybe General Yernin?"

"That bastard?" She laughed derisively. "No, that prick was not here. But he did send me some flowers. It's the fucking I get for the fucking he got. Just like that other prick in his office, the one fucking Antonia."

Ganin looked at her in amazement.

"It's Yernin's secretary. They've been screwing for a couple of months now, so you see, Nikki, I think it's only right that you and I get together."

He found that he wasn't really surprised, though the thought that he was a cuckold hurt his pride a little.

"Nikki?"

"You said someone else was here to see you. Who was it?"

She hunched her shoulders and looked away. She had made an error opening her mouth, and now she obviously didn't want to say anything else. But she was afraid of him.

Ganin put down the vodka bottle and suddenly slapped the drink out of her hand, sending the glass shattering against the wall.

"Don't hit me, Nikki," she cried, cowering. "Please."

"Then tell me who was here."

She looked up at him fearfully, her eyes wide, her breasts still exposed. Ganin had never thought she was more than fairly attractive; Yurii had had stars in his eyes. Apparently so did Yernin.

"If I have to send you to the hospital, I will," Ganin said, his voice soft and menacing. He had never hit a woman in anger in his life. Despite everything, he didn't think he could start now.

"They said they were from the GRU," she whispered.

Ganin could hardly believe it, yet he knew that she was telling the truth. "What did they want?"

"They wanted to know what Yurii told me about the case you and he were working on."

"What did you tell them?"

"Nothing, Nikki. I swear it. I told them nothing because Yurochka never told me what he was doing . . . never. You must believe me."

She reached up for him, and Ganin's stomach flopped. He left the apartment in a hurry, but out in the corridor, waiting for the elevator, he had to hold on to the wall for support. The bastards had nearly succeeded twice in killing Gorbachev, and now they were trying to cover their tracks.

The United States Embassy was just a dozen blocks from the offices of *World News This Week*. Mary Frances rode over with Ben Siegel first thing in the morning.

The message that the ambassador had wanted to see her had come in overnight, in itself odd enough. But even stranger to Siegel's way of thinking was that they were to see him at the embassy itself, not at the ambassador's residence just around the corner from the magazine.

"He wants to meet you in a formal setting," the bureau chief said. "Or at least it would appear to be the case."

"Why?" Mary Frances asked. The word that Ganin had picked her up yesterday after work had gotten to him. He had asked her a lot of questions, most of which she had been able to fend off

341

with vague generalities. This, however, coming so soon on the heels of her meeting with Ganin, was making him nervous.

"It beats hell out of me," Siegel said. "I talked with Weaver early this morning. Frankly he wanted to know if you had gotten in over your head here."

Mary Frances eyed him speculatively. "What'd you tell him?"

Siegel shook his head. She thought he looked like a hound dog with his long, drooping face and sad eyes. "I told him that I didn't know but that I thought it was a real possibility. Are you?"

She shrugged. "The man has tried to kill me twice . . . three times if you consider the fact he believed I was aboard that aircraft he thought he destroyed, and you ask me if I'm in over my head." It was not a direct answer. She was having a hard time with those lately, nor did it include the fact that she had made love with the man.

She looked out the window as they crossed busy Kalinina Prospekt, Moscow's most modern street. Brett, or Moran, or whoever he really was, had been the kind of man she had been looking for. Gentle, understanding, funny at the right times, serious when it was called for. And he had been a wonderfully adept lover. It had seemed to her that they had been immediately comfortable in bed together. It was as if they had been making love with each other for years. He knew all the right buttons to push, the correct pressures, the correct places to touch, the perfect timing.

She sighed deeply, and Siegel looked over at her.

"It's all right, kid; we won't let them run you out of town. If a world-class assassin can't do you in or a top Moscow cop can't intimidate you, then the ambassador won't be able to do much either."

They were met in the lobby by Scott Moore, the consular officer, dressed impeccably as usual. But there was something about him this time that was off, slightly bothersome to Mary Frances. He seemed . . . almost brittle. His smile seemed a little fake.

"Thank you for responding so promptly," he said, shaking Siegel's hand.

"I didn't think there would be any objections to my tagging along with Mary," Siegel said.

"Oh, heavens, absolutely none," Moore said. "Believe me."

He smiled again at Mary Frances and then took them upstairs to the third floor.

Down the corridor from the elevator he showed them into a sparsely furnished conference room. The window that looked down into a courtyard at the rear of the building was covered with wire mesh. Besides the table and half a dozen chairs around it, the only other furnishings were a tiny roll-about cart and a secretarial chair in one corner. It reminded Mary Frances of the setup court reporters used.

"Just have a seat and someone will be with you," Moore said, and he was gone before they could ask him what was happening.

"What do you want to bet that it's not the ambassador who comes through that door next?" Mary Frances said, laying her purse on the table. The fluorescent lights made a buzzing sound that was slightly irritating.

"I don't think I'd put any money on it," Siegel said.

The door opened, and Richard Sweeney walked in. He'd brought several fat file folders with him. He laid them on the table.

"Ms. Dean," he said pleasantly, motioning her toward a chair across from him. "Mr. Siegel."

"We were told we were to meet with the ambassador," Siegel said irritably.

"I lied."

"Why?" Mary Frances shot back.

Sweeney smiled pleasantly. "Would you have come if I had left the message that the Central Intelligence Agency wanted to speak with you?"

"Perhaps," Mary Frances said, maintaining her cool. Siegel had suspected that Sweeney was a spook, but of course, there'd been no way of determining such a thing.

"Now, if you please," Sweeney said. "We have reason to believe that the man you've known as Donald Moran and Roger Brett may still be alive, and we'd like your help to capture him."

Mary Frances closed her eyes for several long seconds. She could feel herself swaying, but she didn't care. She'd known. Somehow she'd known that Moran wasn't dead. It was the answer Ganin had given her. The aircraft he was aboard was shot down over the Gulf of Finland. No mention of a body.

She sat down, Siegel beside her. Sweeney took a couple of photographs out of one of his file folders and passed them across.

"Just to establish without a doubt that we're talking about the same person," the assistant CIA chief of station said.

They were photographs of Roger Brett. Mary Frances looked up and nodded.

"The KGB supplied these to us." Sweeney was a large man. His expression got stern, and the effect was suddenly impressive. "What we are about to discuss is classified secret, do you understand?" He passed across an official Secrets Act declaration form which outlined the penalties for divulging classified information. There was a place for their signatures.

"I won't sign this," Siegel said. "I would be done as a newsman. Anytime you wanted to shut me up, you'd wave this in front of my nose."

"Only to the extent of the information we would be discussing here today, I promise you."

"I won't sign it either," Mary Frances said.

"Then you are refusing to help us catch this man?"

"I didn't say that," she replied. "What I am saying is I don't know if I'm going to keep your secrets to myself until I hear what they are."

Sweeney closed the file folder and got to his feet. "Thank you for coming, Ms. Dean, Mr. Siegel. Someone will be along in a minute or so to take you downstairs." He started to leave.

"Wait," Mary Frances said.

Sweeney turned back. "Yes?"

"Where is he? Still on Soviet soil, or did he make it across the gulf to the Finnish coast?"

Sweeney just stared at her for a moment. "What makes you think he might be in Finland?"

Without hesitation Mary Frances explained to him what Ganin had told her and what she had figured out on her own.

Sweeney held his silence for a long time, as if he were debating something with himself, but then he shook his head. "I'm sorry, but unless you promise not to publish or discuss anything that is discussed in this room, I cannot go on."

Mary Frances looked at Siegel, who shrugged. She turned back to Sweeney, hesitated a moment, then pulled a pen from her purse, and signed the paper. Siegel did the same a moment later.

Sweeney collected the signed statement and sat down. "The National Security Agency has developed the means to effectively monitor and keep track of Soviet military communications channels."

Siegel whistled softly.

"Exactly," Sweeney said, glancing at him. "From what we've monitored out of the bases at Tallinn and Riga, both on the gulf, we believe that there is a very good chance that Forsythe survived."

"Hold on a second," Mary Frances said. "Who is Forsythe?"

"Moran. Brett. We believe his real name is Peter Forsythe. A Vietnam vet. A Medal of Honor winner."

This time Siegel groaned.

"It doesn't get any better, believe me," Sweeney said, leaning forward. "Look, we think he may be in Finland somewhere at this moment. The Finnish Federal Police and Helsinki Interpol are searching, but there are a lot of places to hide in that country. So we're asking for your help."

"What do you want me to do?" Mary Frances asked.

"We'd like you to get on a Finnish television interview program and tell the world what a lousy lover he was."

Mary Frances's heart thumped. "A girl doesn't have any secrets these days."

"Sorry," Sweeney said. "Believe me, I am sorry. It's the business." He smiled. "Besides, I was only guessing."

"Shit," she said softly. "When?"

"In a few days. We think he might be hurt pretty badly. He's probably holed up somewhere, catching his breath."

"What good will it do? He's not stupid."

"Not stupid, just insane. Paranoid. Schizophrenic. We're hoping that when he learns he failed to kill Gorbachev and then sees you on television, mocking him in front of the entire world, it will unbalance him further."

"Enough so that he will come after me again?"

"The psychologists think so. You'll become the focus of his hate, his insane rage."

"Not very comforting."

"No."

She turned to Siegel, who was watching her with what she took to be sympathy. "I just might be in the wrong business."

"What do you want to do, kid?" he asked. "Whatever it is, I'll back you . . . the magazine will back you one hundred percent."

"I'll do it," she said in a small voice. "But first I'm going to be on Soviet television. I don't want to blow my chances here."

"It can't hurt," Sweeney agreed. "The Finns watch Moscow One. Mention, if you can, that you'll be going to Helsinki next."

"Sure," Mary Frances said, the deepest, coldest feeling of dread she'd ever experienced in her worst nightmares rising from her stomach.

59

The police had come early in the evening, pounding on the door of the cottage. The head of the household, Toivo Kauppi, and his strapping eighteen-year-old son, Erling, had hidden Moran in the salting cellar, where fish was curing, until the authorities were gone.

"Toivo, they have left. It is clear now," the old woman called down.

In the forty-eight hours he'd been here, Moran had learned that the Kauppis were a fishing family. They had been out on the gulf when they'd seen him plunge into the sea, his parachute making their rescue efforts nearly impossible. He had almost drowned before they'd gotten him aboard their boat.

They had taken him home and tended to his wounds because

they suspected he was a defector and they had absolutely no love for the Soviet Union.

If they'd thought the remnants of his latex makeup, or his previous wounds which were stitched, were odd, they'd said nothing so far other than "Eat, rest, get your strength back."

He felt detached now, as if he were floating a couple of inches off the floor, as if he were looking at his own body through the wrong end of a telescope. But he felt good about himself. He had succeeded, and when he was fit to travel, he would go deep.

"We can go up now," Toivo Kauppi said. He was a huge barrel-chested man with the weather-beaten face of a fisherman. "Have some supper."

Moran glanced up toward the open trapdoor. "Aren't you risking trouble with the authorities, hiding me here?"

Toivo laughed. "Those bastards piss in their pants every time the great bear rumbles a little."

His son smiled nervously. He sent him upstairs and then took a bottle of Finnish vodka and a couple of glasses out of the ice chest. When he poured the liquor, it was almost as thick as syrup because of the cold.

"You are a very important man, it would seem." Toivo said, knocking back his drink.

Moran did the same. The cold burned his throat. The Finn poured him another. "What makes you say that, the police?"

"The television," Toivo said. "Moscow One."

Moran started to say something, but Toivo's next words knocked the air out of him.

"It was Gorbachev himself. He is saying that someone has tried to kill him. Twice now. Once in Geneva and the second time two nights ago, near the gulf."

The man's words were washing over and around Moran, seeping into his body, inflating his brain so that he was afraid his skull would explode. It could not be possible. It was a lie.

". . . quite a looker. She is an American, but somehow she got mixed up in it." Toivo laughed and downed his second drink. "Those KGB shits got something right for a change. They're usually stumbling all over themselves."

"Gorbachev was on the television today?"

"Last night," Toivo corrected. "Drink," he said.

"The American woman. Was she on the television, too?"

"Just her photograph," Toivo said, his eyes narrowing a little. "But she will be on the television Saturday."

Moran put his drink aside and turned around. He grabbed the edge of the marble filleting table to keep from falling. All of it had been for nothing. The incredible bitch had betrayed him once again. From the beginning, even while he was making love to her, she had known, she had planned his death. It all had been a ruse. A trick. A sham. She had probably known all about him as early as New York, perhaps as early as Geneva. It was the only explanation of how she had come to be in Moscow so soon. Usually visa applications took weeks, if not months.

Toivo was chuckling. "You didn't know," he was saying. "You thought he was dead."

Moran reached out and picked up one of the slender bladed filleting knives. The edge was razor-sharp.

Toivo was laughing louder now. "All this time you thought you were a hero of the West. You didn't know. And this American woman—"

Moran spun on his heel and was across the narrow space in a split second. He clamped his left hand over the much larger man's mouth and drove the filleting knife to the hilt into his belly.

The Finn reared back, batting Moran's hand away from his mouth, and he started to scream as Moran sharply twisted the knife, pulled it upward, then to the right and finally downward in a large triangle. The man's intestines spilled out in a thick rush of blood and terrible odors, the scream dying on his lips before it emerged.

Toivo staggered back a pace, his eyes switching dumbly from Moran to the great pile of his insides trailing on the floor in front of him.

Moran shoved him backward up against a brine vat, a rage rising up and blotting out any sanity he'd had left, and he plunged the filleting knife into the fisherman's chest, yanking it left and right, destroying his lungs and his heart. He fell back with him, half into the vat, as he continued to stab and hack at the dead body.

"Toivo, what are you doing down there?" his wife called. "Grandmother has supper on the table. Remember our guest now. He must be hungry."

Moran stood, covered in blood, in a feral crouch, looking up at the open trapdoor.

"Toivo?" the woman called uncertainly now.

Despite his own injuries, Moran easily lifted the fisherman's body up, and silently levered it into the brine tank, then stepped into the shadows behind the ladder. She would see the body in the tank when she came down, but not until she was most of the way down the ladder.

He looked up as her legs came through the opening. "Toivo, I am not in the mood for silly games," she said crossly, coming down the ladder.

Moran was right behind her. Sensing something, she turned. Before the apparition she was seeing could really register in her brain, Moran stepped forward. He reached behind her, almost as if he were her lover, and drew her to him at the same moment he brought up the filleting knife and slit her throat ear to ear in a huge gush of blood.

She struggled for a full minute and a half before the light went out of her eyes, and her body went limp in Moran's arms. He looked into her lifeless face, drew her up, and kissed her sensually on the lips, his tongue darting into her mouth. "Good night," he said softly in Finnish. "It is time for my supper."

He picked her up and brought her over to another of the brine vats and slipped her in with the curing fish and salt and water. The blood washed away from the gaping wound in her neck, making it look black against her white flesh. He had never noticed the contrast before. It was nice, he thought.

"One, two, button your shoe," he said, turning and scrambling up the ladder into the back loading room. A maniacal glint had come into his eyes.

At the kitchen door he could hear the old grandmother talking with the son. Everything was normal. Everything was fine. Nothing to be worried about here.

"Three four, open the door," Moran mumbled as he yanked open the door and burst into the kitchen. "Surprise," he shouted.

The old woman screamed, and the young man jumped up, knocking his chair backward.

Moran came over the kitchen table at him, dishes and plates and food scattering everywhere, the knife making a big slice in the kid's arm and side.

Erling's mistake came at that moment when Moran was off-balance, his knife hand extended to the left, open and vulnerable. Instead of turning back and breaking Moran's arm, the frightened young man turned and tried to get away. It was all the space Moran needed. He scrambled off the table and caught up with Erling as the kid reached the living room. He grabbed a handful of his thick blond hair, yanked his head back, and cut his throat, just as he had the woman's in the basement.

Erling swung around like a wounded farm animal, shoving Moran backward, causing him to lose his grip on the bloody knife. But the kid was no threat. He thrashed around, spreading blood all over the tiny living room as he clawed at the terrible wound. Finally he sank to his knees and fell facedown on the scrubbed floorboards.

Moran turned and went into the kitchen. The old grandmother was cowering against the kitchen cupboard, a twelve-inch butcher knife in her shaking hand.

He crossed the room to her and grabbed the knife from her hand.

"You are the devil," she cried, crossing herself.

"Yes," Moran said. "Yes, Grandmother, I'm the devil." He laughed, and he began to stab and hack at her frail chest, her throat, her arms and shoulders, her face, blood and tissue and even pieces of bone flying, mingling with his sweat.

60

Despite Ben Siegel's assurances to the contrary, Mary Frances had come to believe that her very brief tenure in Moscow was coming to an end. Nothing was the same for her. In the few short days she'd been here, she felt as if she had come as a stranger, had rapidly learned something about the people and their customs, and suddenly it had all slipped away from her. She was a stranger again.

Tomorrow night she was scheduled to be on television. The next day she was flying to Helsinki. She didn't think she would be coming back.

Her apartment still wasn't ready. She supposed that the KGB wanted to keep her at the Rossiya in plain sight. Maybe it was better set up here for her protection.

Five times in the past thirty-six hours she had gone to the

telephone with every intention of calling Ganin, but each time
something stayed her hand. Some inner voice or pride or whatever
stopped her from calling a Russian, any Russian, even Ganin, for
help. What did he know of her problems? What could a man like
him possibly know of the complexities of life in the West? Especially life for a career woman.

And there was Richard Sweeney, her signature on the Secrets
Act form, and the entire might of the U.S. government to consider. In no uncertain terms the CIA agent had told her that she
would go to jail if she discussed what she knew with anyone. The
implication was, of course, that she could not discuss this with a
Russian. Especially not with the establishment. Especially not with
Ganin.

She didn't know if she completely understood Sweeney's explanation of the NSA's monitoring of Soviet military communications channels, but she knew it was extremely important. We
had the advantage. If the Russians were to learn of it, we would
presumably lose that advantage.

Yet she was terribly frightened. If Moran was alive and she
was to be used for bait in Finland, Ganin should know.

The room was dark. She sat on the edge of the bed, her hands
tightly clasped in her lap. She had taken a shower and gotten
ready for bed an hour ago, but she hadn't been able to bring
herself actually to go to sleep.

Lying next to her on the bed was the shawl Moran had bought
for her at the Beryozka foreign currency shop. He could have
been so good. Even perfect.

She looked away. She was so frightened it was hard to think
straight. So lonely. So uncertain.

Slowly she reached for the telephone, and when she had an
outside line, she dialed Ganin's number. He answered on the first
ring.

"Yes?"

"Can you come here?" she asked in a small voice. "Now?"

"Is something wrong?"

"Everything," she said. "Please hurry."

Antonia had come back to the apartment yesterday while he
was out. He knew because a few more of her things were missing.
But she had not telephoned, nor had he tried to contact her. A
word to General Yernin, and Antonia would be home directly.

She wouldn't dare go against him, especially if it was true that she was having an affair with Yernin's secretary, the one she'd so openly admired that weekend at the dacha. But he could not bring himself to make the call—either because he was afraid or because he didn't care; he no longer knew which.

There was a lot of activity in the Rossiya's mammoth lobby. A tour group of East Germans were drunk and arguing loudly about something, while the Intourist guides were standing by nervously.

Upstairs he showed his militia identification to the floor lady, who went back into her alcove. The KGB was watching all the exits from the hotel, of course, and he was certain that it would be electronically monitoring her room.

He knocked, and she answered the door immediately. For several long moments Ganin made no move to enter the room. The only light came from the window behind her. It made her head glow as if she were an icon painted on ebony. The effect was marvelous.

"Was he here?" he asked finally.

She shook her head.

"Are you all right?"

"I don't know . . . I just wanted to talk. You said that . . ."

Her eyes were wide. Even the irises were fully dilated from being in the dark so long. She stepped aside.

The room was very nice. Very large and extremely clean for a Russian hotel. He found the one microphone in the bathroom light fixture and the second in the telephone. He disconnected them both and unplugged the television set.

She watched him, her lips parted, her skin glowing like fine porcelain, her body tiny and delicate beneath her bathrobe.

"They think he's still alive. Somewhere in Finland," she said.

"Who does?"

"The CIA."

"They told you this?"

She nodded.

"How do they know?"

"I don't . . ." She shook her head. "They didn't tell me. But after my interview on Moscow One, I'm going to Helsinki to be on television. They want to use me as . . . bait."

She wasn't telling him everything. He could see that in her

eyes. But it didn't matter. The KGB would want to get it out of her, but he was no spy; he was simply a police detective.

"You don't have to go."

"No, but I don't know what else to do."

"If the CIA is interested, you will be all right. They'll take care of you."

"What if they don't catch him this time?"

"They will."

"What if he keeps coming after me?"

"I'll stay with you until he's caught," Ganin said, amazed with himself even as the words left his lips.

She flinched almost as if she had been slapped, but she said nothing. The way she was standing he could make out an artery throbbing in the side of her neck. He could see her breasts rising and falling beneath her robe as she breathed.

Her hands were shaking as she pulled off the robe. She was naked. "Please hold me," she said.

"You don't have to do this."

"You want it," she replied softly. "I want it."

He came to her, and she tilted her face up to his as he took her in his arms and kissed her deeply, her entire body thrumming like an electric motor.

He picked her up and laid her on the bed. She watched him through lidded eyes as he got undressed. When he got into bed with her, she parted her legs and pulled him on top. She was already wet, and he entered her, reveling in her feel, in the smoothness of her skin, the narrowness of her waist, the longness of her legs, and her scent, which was just as foreign as everything else about her.

"You're not in love with me, and I'm not with you," she said afterward.

"No."

"You will not leave your wife or Russia. Not for me, not for anything. Ever."

He was stroking her flanks. She took his hand and kissed the fingertips, then placed it on her breast.

"For now, though, let's pretend," she said. "Make love to me again."

61

It was five o'clock in the morning and the sun was just coming up as Interpol Lieutenant Hemming Kucharyski followed the dirt track southwest toward the end of the peninsula. He had been assured that the fishing village of Porkkala was somewhere near.

Kucharyski was in a foul mood. He had been working too hard lately and had partied with friends last night until nearly three in the morning—barely more than two hours ago. He'd gotten less than an hour's sleep when he'd been summoned.

"This had better be good, you miserable shit," he'd growled into the telephone.

"It is, Hemming," Helsinki Homicide Detective Sergeant Jainno Hakala said. "Believe me."

A uniformed police officer jumped out of his car parked at

356

the edge of the tiny village, and Kucharyski stopped and cranked down his window.

"It's to the left, Lieutenant," the cop said. "About three kilometers."

"All right," Kucharyski said, and he drove on. He came a couple of minutes later to a cottage a couple of hundred meters up from a sheltered little fjord. There were uniformed police everywhere, even down on the dock. The black forensics van was parked in front. A cop was holding on to the side of the van for support while he puked.

Kucharyski got out of the car and approached the house as Sergeant Hakala came out. The man's hair was pushed back, and his face was pasty white.

"Prepare yourself," he said.

"What is it?"

"An entire family wiped out. The son in the living room, the grandmother in the kitchen, and the father and mother downstairs in the fish cellar."

The cottage door was open, and suddenly Kucharyski thought he could smell something. He tested the air. It was an odd odor, unpleasant, like—He clamped the thought off. "Why did you call me out here?"

"This," Hakala said, holding up a clear plastic bag. There was something inside it that looked like skin or like rubber.

"Latex?"

"Just like on the wire from the States. I thought you'd better have a look."

William Seagraves personally made the calls about three in the morning, but it was Don McKinstry who met Hammer downtown in the J. Edgar Hoover Building.

"Apparently it came in over the Interpol wire about two hours ago," McKinstry said as they hurried down the corridor from the elevator to Seagraves's office.

"Who had the balls to call him at that hour?"

"There was a flag on the wire. Thank God the Finns were on the ball."

"Have you seen it?"

"No, and now you know about as much as I do, except that the Air Force took an SR-71 out of mothballs for you. It's standing by at Andrews."

Seagraves, in his shirt sleeves, was waiting for them in his office. He had put on the coffee, and when they came in, he raised his eyes from the papers on his desk. He looked owlish at this hour.

"You're taking off for Ramstein Air Force Base, Germany, in about an hour," he said. "It's not going to give you any time to pack, I'm afraid."

"I have a toothbrush in my desk," Hammer said. "Is Moran on the move?"

Seagraves nodded. He looked all in, as if he had not been sleeping well lately. "You'll connect with a Finnair flight out of Frankfurt am Main to Helsinki," he said. He glanced at a slip of paper on his desk. "You'll be met there by Interpol Lieutenant Kucharyski."

"What happened?"

"He survived."

"Who'd he kill this time?"

"An entire family. Fishing people on the coast in a tiny village. They were probably responsible for his rescue from the gulf." Seagraves seemed on the verge of losing it. "They fed him, most likely tended to his injuries, gave him a place to sleep, and even hid him from the authorities. And in the end he killed them and stole their boat."

"He's back in Russia."

"He'd never make it across the gulf. It's only forty miles wide at that point, from what I'm told, but the waters are heavily patrolled by the KGB. He's hiding somewhere down the coast. Most likely south."

"He's made it this far, sir," Hammer said. He sat forward. "With all due respects, Mr. Seagraves, get me a visa for Moscow. That's where he's going. Have our people talk with Chief Investigator Ganin's people. They should be able to pull some strings."

"We have no charter in the Soviet Union—"

"We don't in Finland either," Hammer snapped. "Goddamnit, Seagraves, are you going to wait until the son of a bitch succeeds? Sooner or later he will get to Gorbachev. An American. A Medal of Honor winner. Killing the president of the Soviet Union. Jesus Christ, what do you want here, World War Three?"

Seagraves said nothing.

Hammer jumped up and turned to McKinstry. "See to it,

would you, Don? And call Ganin personally, tell him I'm on my way."

"What else?" McKinstry asked.

"Call Langley. Have them put a twenty-four-hour watch on Mary Frances Dean. Her life is in danger, too."

The ancient truck with Kalinin plates wheezed to a halt in a cloud of blue smoke at the entrance to the Voldokolam-skoye Sŏsse main Moscow highway. Two militia highway patrol officers got out of their car and approached. It was nearly six in the evening.

Moran sat behind the wheel, his face, his hands, and his coveralls crusted black with blood and dirt. Flies were thick in the cab, and the stench was almost unbearable. But he no longer noticed it.

He had been on the go for what seemed like days. He was numb, yet his adrenaline was still pumping. It was revenge, a powerful engine driving him forward. Nothing would stop him. No force on earth was capable of interfering with his plans because he no longer cared about his retirement; he no longer cared about the money or even about Gorbachev. Only the woman, Mary Frances Dean, had any meaning for him now. He had been intimate with her once. His intention was to be even more intimate with her this time. Intimate in an entirely different way. He would sit next to her, hold her in his arms, and caress her face as he watched life leave her body. There was no higher form of love.

Moran turned and looked out his open window. He grinned, and the militiaman pulled up short, his face screwing up in an expression of disgust.

"Shit, what happened to you?" he demanded.

The second militiaman had stopped on the other side of the truck. He didn't want to get any closer.

"I'm doing my job," Moran growled. "What do you mean, comrade?"

"The blood, the stink. Have you been wallowing in your own shit?"

"It's honest labor, comrade," Moran growled louder. He shoved open the door and climbed down. The militiaman backed up a pace, his hand on the rifle slung over his shoulder.

"Let's see your papers," the officer said.

Moran pulled the papers he had taken from the dead driver's pocket and held them out with a bloody hand. The militiaman stepped a little closer and squinted at the documents, but he made no move to take them.

Moran was laughing inwardly. "You want to see in the back, comrade?"

"What are you carrying?"

"Cowhides, horsehides, pighides for the Gork'iy Tannery. Come, I will show you."

The militiaman hesitated.

"It's honest labor, comrades. Not everyone can drive around in a fine automobile." Moran turned and shuffled to the rear of the truck. He did not limp, and the effort left him light-headed.

He untied the canvas flap and lifted it open. A wave of flies came out, and the stench was so bad it was almost beyond belief.

The militiaman who had walked back with Moran gagged and nearly threw up. He quickly backed up and motioned for Moran to retie the flap.

"Get out of here, you bastard," the officer said. "Just take your stinking mess and get it away from here."

"Honest labor," Moran muttered, shuffling back to the front

and climbing back up into the cab. He nearly fainted before he had the truck started, and he took off with a lurch, grinding up the curve onto the highway. A little longer, he told himself. He had come so incredibly far he could not give up now.

There was almost no traffic on the highway, which went straight south through the birch forests toward Moscow, ninety miles away. Two hours, he thought. Only two hours.

They didn't leave the hotel all day, nor did they answer the telephone, which during the morning rang ten different times.

When the floor lady came to clean the room around two in the afternoon, Ganin sent her away. She seemed very frightened. She was the same one from before, and she knew that he was a militia chief investigator and that the woman was an American. She didn't understand.

At three Ganin went upstairs to one of the restaurants and brought them back a late lunch of *aládyi*, which were crumpets filled with various things—fish, caviar, sour cream—some pickles, a bottle of expensive French wine, and a bottle of even more expensive cognac. The server had given him an odd look but had said nothing. This was the Rossiya. Westerners and the Russians who dealt with them on a regular basis were odd.

"We don't love each other," Mary Frances said.

"Don't say that anymore," Ganin replied. They were sitting cross-legged on the bed across from each other.

"I don't love you," she said.

"I know. It's impossible."

"You called Tonia in your sleep."

"My wife."

"I see."

Ganin looked at her. She was naked. Her breasts were small, the nipples pointed. Her stomach was very nearly flat, even when she was sitting, and he could almost see her ribs. The hair at her pubis was only a narrow pale brown strip. She said she shaved the rest because she wore bikinis. She still wore a bandage around her leg where she'd cut herself with the knife, but she said it didn't hurt. Her legs were long and straight and ended in delicate ankles. But her feet were blunt, almost square, and she had no arches.

"When I was a child, my mother forced me to take ballet lessons," she explained. "Ruined my feet."

He was learning about her in leaps and bounds, and the experience was intoxicating.

"Tomorrow I'm going to Helsinki. I will not be coming back."

"I didn't think so."

"You won't come to America?"

"No."

"You wouldn't fit," she agreed. "You'd either end up in trouble or go into hiding like Solzhenitsyn, afraid that the life you wanted for yourself would end up contaminating you."

"It's supposed to drive us insane."

She smiled. "That happens plenty. My editor tells me that everyone in New York is in analysis or should be. I think it might be true."

Somehow that made him afraid.

The lecture hall was filled with important-looking people. The special eight o'clock news analysis program was being broadcast from the University of Moscow, which had much larger facilities than Television One's studios downtown. Everyone wanted to see the young American woman who had saved Gorbachev's life. The Soviet Union had learned from the West the value of media stars who could pass along its viewpoint.

"It is the cult of personality all over again," a general said to a minister.

"But then Stalin is dead."

"Yes."

It seemed almost odd to be wearing clothes again and to be among people. Ganin felt very much out of place here with Mary Frances. A lot of important people were watching every move he made.

"He couldn't have made it this far," she said.

"I don't think so," Ganin agreed. "But most likely he will see you on television, unless the CIA is wrong and he is dead."

"He's not dead."

Ganin shook his head. "I don't think so." He glanced down at the cameras and lights and interview set that had been arranged on the lecture platform. "You don't have to do this."

She smiled and squeezed his hand. "Just be here for me in the audience. Afterward we'll go back to the hotel, if you want."

"We cannot hide forever."

"No," she said. "I told you that I'm leaving tomorrow."

"I forgot," Ganin said.

She went down to where Grigori Slavin, the interviewer, was talking with the director. Ganin turned as someone took his arm.

"I thought you would be here, Nikki," Chief Prosecutor Yernin said. He was smiling, but it was clear he wasn't happy. "Let's have a word before the program begins."

"I have no explanations," Ganin said, looking him in the eye. "Or apologies."

"My dear boy, I didn't think you had."

They went out into the corridor and moved away from the doors. Big plate glass windows looked out across the campus down toward Moscow across the river. This was a modern building, but it was pretty.

"There have been messages for you last night and today," the chief prosecutor began.

"I know," Ganin said.

"Antonia called at least six times. She is angry with you. But . . ." Yernin shrugged. "And you had another call from Washington."

"Hammer?"

"One of his assistants. Hammer is on his way here."

"To Moscow?"

Yernin nodded and glanced down the corridor to make certain they were well outside the earshot of anyone. "There has been a killing in Finland. South of Helsinki in a little fishing village. Certain evidence points to Moran."

"Do the Finns know where he is?"

"A boat is missing. It has shown up east of Tallinn. Moran is back."

"Hammer knows of this?"

"Most of it. Apparently he has guessed the rest. In fact, he will be here within the hour. I have a car waiting for him at Sheremetyevo."

"You're bringing him up here?"

Yernin nodded, looking closely now at Ganin. He stepped in a little closer. "Tell me, Nikki, do you mean to defect for her?"

"Would it make any difference?"

Moran stood unsteadily on his feet in the middle of Mary Frances's living room. No one was here. It was obvious that she had gone. Some of her things were still here, but most of her clothes and almost all her things from the bathroom were missing. There was nothing left in the refrigerator except for a couple of bottles of white wine and some pickled herring, and the cabinets were mostly bare.

He lowered his pistol in frustration. He had come this far . . . for what?

The stupid bastards had not mounted any sort of a special guard downstairs. Only the one militiaman in his box, whose body now lay hidden in one of the big trash receptacles. It should have told him something. They would be watching her very closely now.

And something else was trying to push its way to the front of his head. Something he knew. Something he'd been told. But he could not focus on it yet.

After laying the gun down, he unbuttoned the filthy coveralls and peeled them off. Beneath, he wore his own clothing, which had been cleaned and pressed by Toivo Kauppi's wife.

He took those off as well and, taking the gun, went into the bathroom, where he took a hot shower, washing off all the blood and filth he'd spread on himself to fool the militia highway patrol or anyone else who might have stopped him.

By the time he was dressed again he had it. Toivo had told him that Mary Frances's photograph had been broadcast on Moscow's Television One, with the announcement that she would appear on television Saturday evening.

Today was Saturday. She was at the television studio. But it did not tell him where she had moved to. If she had gone to the embassy, it would be next to impossible for him to dig her out. Wherever she went someone would be with her, someone would be following her: CIA, KGB, Ganin. She had a lot of friends these days.

He turned on the television to Moscow One. A program about Chekhov was playing. He turned the sound low and began searching the apartment for some clue to where the woman had gone.

At one point in the bedroom he realized that *something* was missing, and he went looking specifically for it. A few minutes later he was satisfied that it wasn't here. She had taken the shawl he'd bought her. It meant something to her. He grinned, his skin pulling tight across his cheeks, his eyes intense, his mouth set, all of it making his face look like a death's-head.

He found the telephone number in a wastepaper basket in the kitchen. It was scribbled on a slip of notebook paper. But she'd written nothing else. No note. No hint whose number it was.

Back in the living room he picked up the telephone and started to dial the number when Mary Frances's face appeared on the television screen. He put down the phone and turned up the sound.

". . . journalist's job is not to interfere with the newsmaking process. But there are circumstances in which that becomes impossible."

She spoke in English. The translator repeated her comments

in Russian. "Morally journalists are forbidden to interfere with the news they should be reporting. But often this is not the case in the West."

Moran picked up the telephone, his eyes narrowed, his hate burning brightly in his gut. He dialed the number she had jotted down, and it was answered on the seventh ring.

"Rossiya Hotel."

He smiled again. "I would like to speak with Ms. Mary Frances Dean. I believe she is in room eighteen-thirteen."

"One moment, comrade," the operator said. He was back five minutes later. "Her room is thirteen-oh-five, but there still is no answer. Would you care to leave a message?"

"No," Moran said. He hung up the telephone, his smile broadening. He stared at her image on the television screen. She was speaking with a good-looking interviewer, whose English was quite good.

Stuffing the gun into his belt at the small of his back, he switched off the television and left the apartment, his step light, all his injuries and pains forgotten.

Yernin's driver came down the aisle, whispered something in the chief prosecutor's ear, and then went away. Yernin leaned over to Ganin.

"Your American friend is here," he whispered.

Mary Frances was answering another of Grigori Slavin's questions. She faltered slightly when she spotted Yernin and Ganin getting to their feet and hurrying up the aisle, but she recovered quickly.

Hammer was waiting for them in the corridor. His face was pasty, and a thin sheen of greasy sweat covered his forehead. He did not look good. He and Ganin shook hands.

"You come as a surprise, Vivian," Ganin said.

"He's an American; we sort of thought we should be in on his capture."

Ganin introduced Yernin. "The chief prosecutor is much like one of your assistant attorneys general."

"I studied law in your country, Agent Hammer."

"I see," Hammer said, slightly bemused. He turned back to Ganin. "Any word yet?"

"Not yet, but we're fairly certain he's on Soviet soil." He quickly explained what Yernin had told him earlier.

Hammer nodded. "It figures. He's coming here for her, you know."

"She's leaving for Helsinki tomorrow."

"We'll have to stop her."

Ganin had to smile. "You may try if you wish. But I suspect you won't be successful. Not with her."

Hammer looked at him sharply. "She's on the air now?"

"Yes."

"What about afterward?"

"She's staying at the Rossiya Hotel. We will take her there."

"Are there guards?"

"I've been watching her."

Again Hammer looked at him oddly. But before he could say anything, Yernin interjected.

"I will leave you two very capable investigators to work out the details of Ms. Dean's protection so long as she is on Soviet soil." He and Hammer shook hands again. "If there is anything that you require while you are here in Moscow, Agent Hammer, please don't hesitate to call on me." His expressions just then were very American.

"Thank you, sir," Hammer said.

Yernin smiled. "Actually we're all comrades here. 'Sir' is not necessary."

When Yernin was gone, Hammer went to the door of the lecture hall and looked inside. He shook his head. "That woman ought to have her head examined."

Maybe everyone in America was crazy, Ganin thought. "She is a very strong woman."

"She's a typical shark."

"What?"

"Some career women are like that." Hammer started to explain but then cut it off. "All right, so we stash her in the Rossiya, assuming that even if Moran makes it this far, he won't know where she's staying. What then?"

"He knows her apartment. He may go there. I'll have a watch put on the place. In the meantime, we'll go to my office and check the wire. If Moran is coming here from the Estonian SSR, he'll make ripples."

"Waves." Hammer automatically corrected him. "What about Helsinki?"

"I don't know. It's beyond my province."

"Mine, too," Hammer said. "Have you discussed with her the danger she's in?"

"She understands."

Hammer looked at him. "I hope so."

There was a reception afterward in the university's great hall. Scott Moore and a number of others were there from the embassy.

"I'm happy to see you here, Agent Hammer," he said.

"Thank you, sir, though I don't know if I'm very glad to be here. So far as I've seen, Chief Investigator Ganin is doing a hell of a job. Certainly as good as or better a job than the bureau could have done under similar circumstances."

Moore shook his head and left.

"Thanks," Ganin said. He looked at his watch. It was approaching midnight. "I think it is time to get her back to the hotel so that you and I can check the wire."

They were standing near the door. Mary Frances was across the room talking with two old men in civilian clothes. Ben Siegel and Scott Moore were hovering around her. Hammer leaned a little closer to Ganin.

"I know it's none of my business, Nikolai, but is there something going on between you and her?"

Ganin looked at him. "What something?"

"You know what I mean."

Ganin shook his head. He looked across at her. "No," he said. "It would not be possible. A Russian investigator and an American journalist." He turned back to Hammer. "No."

"Let's get her back."

Ganin crossed the room to her and touched her arm. She turned to him expectantly, her face lighting up.

"It's time to return, Ms. Dean," he said.

Moore and Siegel were glaring at him.

She nodded and turned back to the others. "It's all right," she said.

"Give me a call if something comes up," Siegel said.

"The embassy is open to you anytime," Moore said.

"Thanks," she said, and she went with Ganin outside, where Hammer was waiting. They got into Ganin's car and headed back down the hill and across the river. They didn't say much on the way into town. Mary Frances kept looking over at Ganin, making it obvious what she was feeling.

Hammer came up on the elevator with them, and together they made a quick but thorough check of her room.

"It's late, Ms. Dean," Hammer said. "I suggest you get some rest. You're leaving Moscow tomorrow?"

Mary Frances was looking at Ganin. She nodded. "At noon."

"Stay here," Ganin said. "Call no one, don't leave your room, and let no one in until we come back."

"When?"

"I don't know," Ganin said. "As soon as possible." He smiled softly. "You will be all right."

She said nothing.

Ganin went into the bathroom, where he reconnected the microphone, and he did the same with the one in the telephone. He plugged the television set in. This time he wanted the KGB to monitor what went on in here.

Mary Frances took off her charcoal gray jacket and laid it on the bed as she kicked off her shoes. The interview tonight had gone well, as had the reception afterward. Ben Siegel had kept telling her what a wonderful job she was doing for the magazine, and Judge Moore kept trying to convince her to come back to the embassy at least until her flight left tomorrow.

None of them understood that it was Helsinki that frightened her most. She was convinced that Moran would be waiting for her there. Nor had she told Siegel that she wasn't coming back, though she supposed he'd guessed by some of the things he'd said tonight.

At the windows she looked down across Red Square into the Kremlin. It seemed cold and unreal. She had no business being here. Not as a woman, especially not as a Westerner. What had surprised her most about these people was their Oriental cast. Most of them were not too far removed from the Siberian ethnic. It was where the future of the country lay, seven time zones to the east. There were the chemicals and ores, the raw materials, the timber, the water, and the space for a nation to develop.

But she didn't understand Orientals. God help her, she didn't know what to do.

She turned and looked at the door. She didn't know if she was going to see him again. Now, with the FBI agent here, he would probably be too busy.

Opening the door, she stepped out into the corridor. The elevator had just started down. Another elevator was stopped two floors above.

"Nikki?" she said, half under her breath, and she started down the corridor when Moran stepped out of the floor lady's alcove.

Outside, Ganin stopped and looked at the hotel, at the upper windows, which looked across Red Square. Was she up there watching them? The night and day he had spent with her seemed like an eternity, a block of experience that belonged to another universe. There were no bridges left between his world now and that one, if ever any had existed in the first place. Again he had an incredible sense of sadness for something he'd lost, though in his heart he knew he'd never really had it.

"Are you all right?" Hammer asked gently.

Ganin looked at him and nodded. "I think so, but you look ill."

"Tired mostly," the FBI agent said. "It's been a long couple of weeks."

"That it has," Ganin said, and they got in the car. "Will you go with her to Helsinki?"

"I suppose," Hammer said. "You?"

"I don't know yet. It will depend on my chief prosecutor. He carries some influence."

They pulled away from the hotel and crossed the river on the Kamenny Bridge. Ganin switched on the communications radio and picked up the handset.

"It might be better if you stayed here," Hammer said. "In case he gets this far, unless your people know what they're up against."

"They don't," Ganin said. He keyed the handset. "Headquarters, this is Ganin."

"Headquarters here."

"I want a unit sent out to Dzerzhinsky, to the apartment of the American journalist Miss Dean."

"Chief Investigator, we have four units out there now. The coroner has been dispatched as well."

Ganin's breath caught in his throat. "What is it?"

"One of our men has been found shot to death. His body was dumped in a trash bin."

"How long ago?"

"We don't know, Chief Investigator. Units are out there now questioning the building's residents."

"He's here already," Ganin said to Hammer as he hauled the car around in a tight U-turn in the middle of the street and headed back to the Rossiya.

"Are you en route—"

"Negative. I want every available man to converge on the Rossiya Hotel. Donald Moran is possibly there or on his way. I want the building and every street leading to it sealed off for a two-block radius. Call the KGB for help if need be, but do it now."

"Yes, comrade," the dispatcher snapped.

Ganin tossed down the headset so that he could concentrate on his driving.

"But he has no way of knowing where she's staying," Hammer shouted.

Ganin was shaking his head. "Would you be willing to bet your life on it?"

Hammer started to say something, but then he, too, shook his head. "Faster."

* * *

Mary Frances waited in the stairwell on the fourteenth-floor landing, listening for him. He would expect her to go down, try for the lobby, so she had gone up instead. There was a restaurant on the twenty-first floor where there would be a lot of people.

Something was wrong with his left leg, and he had not been able to move quickly enough to reach her before she had turned and sprinted down the corridor.

She had expected to be shot in the back at any moment, but she had made it to the end of the corridor, where she had torn open the steel fire door and had decided to go up.

Her heart was pounding so hard it was almost painful, and her breath came in ragged gasps. She had never been so frightened in all her life. This time she thought he was going to win; she didn't think she was going to make it.

The door one floor below opened and then closed. She held her breath.

He was down there, but he wasn't moving. He was listening for her.

"Mary Frances?" he called softly, his voice intimate, almost sensuous.

She shivered but didn't move.

"I know that you can hear me," he said. "I just want to tell you that I need your help. I'm hurt, and I want to give up."

She closed her eyes to hold back her tears. His accent had become almost Australian.

"I'm afraid that if I try to turn myself over to the police, they'll kill me. I want you to go with me."

She wanted to call out. She wanted to believe the Roger Brett personality she had known briefly, yet she could not blot out of her mind the Donald Moran she had nearly killed in New York.

She opened her eyes, and he was there, a few steps below her, grinning insanely. He had crept soundlessly up the stairs.

"No," she cried, stepping back against the door. He no longer looked like Roger. He was Moran, the wounds in his face red and angry-looking. A little blood had leaked down the side of his face, and saliva drooled from the corners of his mouth. She realized that he was completely mad.

He came up the last few steps and reached for her, as if he were going to gather her in his arms, and she suddenly came to her senses. She had been mesmerized.

"No," she shrieked again, and she shoved him in the chest with both hands.

He stumbled backward, caught off guard by her sudden move, and tripped on the top step. His arms waved as he tried to regain his balance, and then he fell backward, cartwheeling down the stairs to the mid-floor landing.

Blood immediately began to pool up beneath his head. She stepped forward and looked down at him, certain that she had killed him. But then he rolled over and sat up.

"Oh, God," she breathed.

He looked up at her and smiled sadly. "That hurt," he said. Almost languidly he pulled out a pistol.

Again she realized that she had been mesmerized by his eyes. She jumped left as he fired, the shot slammed into the steel door behind her with a tremendous bang, and then she was racing up the stairs as fast as she could make her legs work.

"Mary Frances," he called after her.

Her chest began to burn almost immediately.

"Mary Frances, you can't run away from me." His voice drifted faintly up to her as she passed the sixteenth-floor landing. "Come back, Mary Frances. Let's not hurt each other."

The first militia units had already shown up by the time Ganin and Hammer raced up the driveway and burst into the big lobby.

"Get everybody out of here," Ganin shouted, holding his identification booklet aloft. "Evacuate the lobby."

He and Hammer got one of the elevators and punched the button for the thirteenth floor. On the way up they said nothing to each other, but they both took out their pistols. Ganin looked at Hammer's. It was some exotic-looking weapon; he thought it might be a SigSauer or perhaps a Glock-17, which held seventeen or eighteen rounds. It was a formidable weapon.

After what seemed an eternity the elevator opened on Mary Frances's floor, and they emerged, splitting left and right, moving fast, keeping low, presenting the most difficult of targets.

Ganin reached her room first. The door was still partially open. He shoved it the rest of the way open, looked at Hammer, who nodded and then rolled inside.

The room was empty.

"No sign of a struggle," Hammer said behind him.

Mary Frances's shoes were lying on the floor next to the bed.

Ganin stared at them for several beats, knowing that he should be making a connection. He turned and looked at the open door.

"He's here," he said. "In the hotel, and he lured her out of the room somehow."

He and Hammer went out into the corridor.

"The stairs?" Hammer asked.

"She might have run," Ganin said, and they hurried down to the stairwell door. Inside they hesitated on the landing for a moment. Was there a noise somewhere above? Someone running? Ganin cocked an ear, but he could not be sure.

"I'll go up, you go down," he said to Hammer.

"Watch yourself."

Ganin started up and immediately found the blood on the between-floors landing. "Vivian," he called. "Up here."

Hammer was at his side in seconds. He studied the blood a second, and then they both looked up.

"It might not be hers," he said.

"There's a restaurant on the twenty-first floor," Ganin said. "She might be trying to make it that far. There'll be people there."

"Won't stop him."

"I know," Ganin replied tightly, and they started up.

Mary Frances burst out of the stairwell onto the twenty-first floor. For a moment or two she was confused. She was standing in a long, narrow space between an unpainted concrete wall and what looked like a garden latticework for climbing ivy. But she could hear the sounds of music and conversation just on the other side of the latticework. This was the restaurant.

Turning left, she followed the wall twenty feet, finally coming to a curtained opening into the restaurant's main dining room. She looked back in time to see Moran coming through the stairwell door, blood streaming down the side of his head.

He raised his pistol and fired a shot as she leaped through the opening and into the dining room.

The music stopped, and everyone looked up.

"Get down," she screamed as she raced across the big room. "Get down, there is a man with a gun."

But she was speaking English, and not many in the room understood her, although they realized something was drastically wrong.

The maître d' rushed up and grabbed her, spinning her around.

"No, you stupid fool," she screamed.

Moran fired another shot, this one catching the maître d' in the back.

Keeping low, Mary Frances dodged around another screen and pushed her way into the huge, steamy kitchen, diners behind her in the main room finally realizing that they were in mortal danger, screaming as they tried desperately to get out of the line of fire.

The cooks and kitchen staff all looked up as Mary Frances rushed through.

"How do I get out of here?" she yelled.

No one understood her.

The kitchen was a huge maze. There seemed to be no other way out. But there had to be.

"Mary Frances," Moran called to her.

She ran headlong into the arms of one of the cooks, sending him sprawling and her crashing into one of the big ranges on which half a dozen big pots were simmering. If this had been in the States, the stray thought hit her, the kitchen would be closed. But here everyone ate dinner late.

"Mary Frances," Moran called again.

He fired two shots, one of them hitting a waiter and the second spinning the cook she had bumped into around, sending him slamming into a rack of pots and pans.

Suddenly there was no place to run. He was there, a few feet behind her, his grin even wider than before, his expression totally devoid of any humanness. He had been reduced to an animal now. A creature of the jungle. Dangerous, feral, without remorse or pity.

"I love you," he said softly.

She was shaking her head in disbelief. "No," she whimpered. "Please, go away."

"Oh, no, Mary Frances," he said. "It's time for us to die now. Didn't you know?" He laughed, the sound high-pitched, unreal. "Time to die."

"Not like this, you son of a bitch," she growled from the bottom of her gut, and as Moran started to raise his pistol, she grabbed one of the big stockpots filled with bubbling sauce from the stove and, mindless of the flesh burning and blistering on her hands, threw the boiling liquid into his face.

He reared back with an inhuman scream, his pistol discharging; the bullet hit her left arm and knocked her off her feet.

Spinning around, he crashed into the pot rack and, firing his gun, blindly charged off in the opposite direction.

"Mary Frances," Ganin shouted from the kitchen doorway.

"Ganin," Moran screeched, and he fired toward the sound.

Ganin stepped aside and fired twice; both shots hit Moran in the chest, driving him backward, flat on his back.

Hammer was right behind Ganin.

Moran started to sit up, trying to bring his pistol up, when Hammer fired, the bullet hitting him in the forehead, taking off the back of his head.

Suddenly unable to sit up, Mary Frances pitched over onto her side, and the tile of the kitchen floor seemed wonderfully cool, and Ganin's hands holding her, helping her, felt wonderfully safe and protective. It was over now. Finally and at long last it was over.

65

Ganin sat with Chief Prosecutor Yernin in the Chaika limousine, watching the Sheremetyevo Airport VIP gate a half kilometer across the tarmac.

"You've made a wise decision, Nikki," Yernin said. "And you yourself might not even know the real reason for it."

Ganin turned to him. "The *Rodina* needs all the help she can get now."

Yernin smiled indulgently. "The *Rodina* has always needed all the help she can get. I, for one, am grateful that you will stay."

"Maybe I wouldn't be allowed to leave."

"I think you would, and I think you know it. That's not the issue. It's her."

Ganin looked away again. A dark American car had just pulled up at the gate. The guards were talking with the driver.

"A woman like her is best left free," Yernin continued.

Ganin had to smile. "You make her sound as if she were a wild animal who should be left in the jungle."

"To a man such as yourself, she is a wild and exotic animal. Her jungle is America. You would have no more chance of surviving there than she would here."

He was right, of course. Ganin had come to the same conclusion himself almost from the moment he had stepped off the airplane in Washington. Nothing that had happened since had done anything to change his mind. He was a Russian and would never be anything different, never could be anything different. He loved his country more than he loved the notion of what it would be like with her.

The American car was passed through the gate and started across the tarmac.

"You have family here. Aunts and uncles, friends, associates." He did not mention Antonia.

"Obligations," Ganin said.

"Yes, Nikki, obligations. Is that so bad after all? Isn't that what you have struggled for all your life?"

The car was much closer. Ganin could see Scott Moore in front with the driver and Mary Frances in back with Hammer.

Yernin smiled wistfully. "You are a good man. The best of investigators because you believe not only that the guilty should be caught and punished but also that the innocent should be allowed to live beyond suspicion."

Ganin opened the door and got out. Yernin leaned across the seat.

"That is a unique notion. Revolutionary."

The car pulled up, and Ganin walked across to it as the rear door opened and Hammer climbed out. Ganin always forgot how big the American was. Each time he saw him it came as a surprise. They shook hands.

"I think your parents played a cruel trick on you," Ganin said.

"How's that?"

"Naming you Vivian to make you tough. I think you have always been big enough to take care of yourself."

Hammer laughed. "You've got it wrong, my friend. You should have looked a little closer at my identification card. My parents named me Thomas Vivian Hammer. Thomas after my father. Vivian after my grandfather's middle name. He was supposed to have been a girl."

"So it was tradition," Ganin said. "But why call yourself Vivian now? Why not Thomas?"

"I loved my grandfather," Hammer said. "Besides, I've never thought I was tough enough."

Mary Frances got out of the car. Her hands were heavily bandaged, and her left arm was in a sling. She smiled uncertainly.

"Good-bye, my friend," Hammer said and he took Ganin in his arms and hugged him. "The next time you're in the States, give me a call. Last time I never had a chance to take you to dinner."

"Sure," Ganin said. "Good luck."

"You, too," Hammer said, and he walked off toward the departure lounge.

For a long time Ganin simply stood facing Mary Frances without saying a word. She looked a little pale, and he could see that she was in some pain. But she had been lucky. They'd all been lucky.

"I hate long good-byes," she said, breaking the silence between them.

He smiled. "In Russia it is just the opposite because when someone we love leaves us, there is no telling how long he or she will be gone."

"Maybe forever."

Ganin nodded.

"I'm not coming back."

"I didn't think so. You don't belong here."

"This is a very exciting place for a journalist."

"But not for you."

"No," she said. "Not for me."

Hammer came to the departure lounge door. "It's time," he called.

Ganin and Mary Frances glanced over at him. "I'm going to miss you," she said.

"And I will miss you."

She turned back to him and came into his arms. He was careful not to hurt her. Her smell was exotic, he decided again. Like nothing in all Russia. When they parted, he looked into her eyes.

"With care," he said softly.

"With care," she said, and she brushed a kiss on his cheek, turned, and hurried to where Hammer waited. She never looked back.

It was late, nearly midnight when Ganin finally went back to his apartment. The rest of Antonia's things were gone now, and he was glad.

He went directly into the bathroom, where he ran water in the tub and stripped. The water was very hot. Steam filled the tiny room. He stepped into the tub and lay back, letting the heat soak into his bones.

He would miss Yurochka most of all. Friends were not easy to come by. And now he had no one else. But Lenin had said it best when he told his countrymen to look to the future . . . always look to the future, never to the past.

In August Ganin was summoned to Lefortovo Prison and, along with Chief Prosecutor Yernin and a half dozen high-ranking military officers, was ushered into a small unfurnished room.

On signal, one of the officers stepped forward and drew back the heavy black curtains from a large plate-glass window that looked out into a courtyard.

Seven men were lined up against a heavily pockmarked concrete wall. They wore military uniforms from which all the ribbons, buttons, and insignia of rank had been removed.

Ganin recognized three of them. One was Captain General Anatoli Zuyev, commander of the Moscow Military District. Another was General Gennadi Matushin, commander of the Soviet Air Force. And the third was Aleksandr Borisenko, the American movie star look-alike who had worked as Yernin's secretary and with whom Antonia had been having an affair.

"The conspirators," Yernin whispered to Ganin.

"What about Borisenko?" Ganin asked.

Yernin smiled sadly. "It is too bad about him, but he was a traitor to us, Nikki. It was he who supplied the GRU with information about you and your investigation."

"Antonia . . ."

"Had stars in her eyes, and she was burned. I am sorry."

Ganin turned back to the window. "What about the others? Do I need to know their names?"

"No," Yernin said.

The men were strapped to metal poles, and black hoods were drawn over their heads.

"They were traitors, Nikki. But they failed. You stopped them."

They could not hear the shots. But suddenly all seven men reared back under the impact of the bullets smashing into their bodies, and in seconds it was over.